I0760311

AZIA

KINGDOM OF FAIRYTALES
SEASON ONE

You all know the story of your favorite fairytale, but did you ever wonder what happened after the fairytale ending? Well we know. Not all afters end up happily, sometimes the real adventure starts much later...

Following famous fairytale characters, eighteen years after their happily ever after, the Kingdom of Fairytales offers an edge of the seat thrill ride in an all new and sensational way to read.

Lighting-fast reads you won't be able to put down

Fantasy has never been so epic!

URBIS PRISON
SHIPLEY
BADALAH
THE VALE
AZREN
DESERT
DRACONIS
KISBU
ZHORE
MOSA
ELDER
ABORIA
AZURE
ENCHANTIA
AIRE
URBIS
EMERALD CITY
SKYLA
OZ
FLORIS
TULIS
THE FORGE
ARCADIA
RENAIS
MELFALL
ATLANTICE
ANTLA
KINGDOM OF FAIRYTALES

ISBN: 978-1-989997-23-9
Enchanted Quill Press

Contaact the author at www.enchantedquillpress.com
Cover by Enchanted Quilll Press
Interior Formatting by Enchanted Quill Press
Editing by Rose Lipscomb

QUEEN OF DRAGONS

PROLOGUE

No one understands what it's like when your mother is famous for her beauty, and you are, at best, average. Actually, I'm wrong. She wasn't famous just for her beauty, but that's how people tell the story, how people have always told the story. That was even her name for a while. No one remembered her real name. She was just the sleeping princess or Sleeping Beauty. Even all these years later, when the royals appear in the paper, my father, the king, barely gets a mention, and I'm only a footnote in my own life, destined to always be Sleeping Beauty's daughter

My name's Princess Azia Rose of Draconis, and here is my story...

1ST JANUARY

The sword glinted in the sun, golden flecks of light, turning to orange as the sun began its trek to the other side of the world. His colossal height dwarfed me, giving him the advantage in every way. He stood at nearly six feet five, towering over me, and his strength was unsurpassed in all the kingdom. I dodged him as he ruthlessly attacked, thrusting his sword at me mercilessly and without care. The complexities of sword fighting did not interest him. His aim was only to kill, his one desire to see his blade thrust deep into my belly. I danced around him as time after time he attacked, and I put into practice all the defense strategies I'd learned from watching my younger brothers' training. Training that, as a girl, I'd never received, and yet, here I was, embroiled in a fight to the death with a giant of a man. I knew how to handle a sword. Even without official training, I rivaled most men in the art of combat, but as my attacker wasn't schooled in good sportsmanship and his technique involved him waving his sword around haphazardly, there was very little I could do to anticipate where his next attack would come from. I thought that I'd be able to see it in his eyes, the little tells that would give away where he would next thrust his sword, but he was focused on the kill, and there was no telling where the sword would go next.

He murmured as he fought, a strange language known only to himself. A pep talk? Who knew?

I swerved to the side as he rushed at me full force, his blade missing me by inches. A momentary thrill of celebration ran through me, but it was short-lived. I'd barely turned back toward him when the full length of his sword was thrust into my side, right up to the hilt.

Tumbling to the ground, I clutched my belly, wailing in agony and then became still. My eyes closed, and my screams were silenced. I was dead.

Beside me, he giggled and rubbed his hands in gleeful euphoria. His enormous size made the ground beneath me shake with his quivering body as he too fell to the ground beside me.

With one of my eyes open, just a slit, I watched as my brother, Remy wailed in rapturous joy. I suppressed a grin. The dead don't smile, but it was difficult not to when his laughter was so infectious. He must have looked strange to an outsider, giggling like a young child, because that's essentially what he was. With the body of a man and the mind of a toddler, outsiders rarely understood him. Picking his trick sword up, I handed it back to him with a smile. He stabbed me a few more times in the belly for good measure, the fake blade retracting up into the hilt every time, and with every thrust, another giggle erupted from his mouth.

"Okay now," I said, ruffling his overly shaggy dark brown hair. "Time for dinner."

"Ta Aza." He pulled himself up into a standing position, the grin of victory still plastered on his gorgeous face. He pulled me into a bear hug, which was much more dangerous than the sword fight as he didn't know his own strength. As a young child, he'd broken my arm similarly, and since then, I'd had to use a safe word with him to make him let go for fear of being crushed to death in his muscular arms.

"Unsquash," I gasped, and he let go of me immediately.

"Uhsqua Aza," he repeated back to me in the best way he knew how. He pronounced my name as Aza although it was Azia. I loved hearing it because, of all my other siblings, mine was the only one he even attempted.

I felt rather than saw someone's eyes on us. Turning my attention away from Remy, I scanned the surrounding field. In the distance, the royal castle rose majestically against a backdrop of the Fire Mountains. The base of the mountain range was covered with thick purple heather, which gave the grey stone of the castle a pinkish hue in the evening light. As they rose into the clouds, they assumed a deep brilliant hue of red - one of the reasons the Fire Mountains got their name, the other being the dragons that lived up in the peaks.

The stone bridge leading from the main entrance away from the open portcullis was quiet as was usual this time of day, and the surrounding fields showed no sign of life except the castle horses sharing the field with us and the occasional fire butterfly that fluttered around our heads. Glancing back at Remy, I saw that he was engrossed in a flower—one of his many obsessions.

I couldn't see anyone else in the field with us, but the hairs on the back of my neck prickled, and the quietness set my teeth on edge. Scanning the perimeter of the field again, I finally saw him. Tall and blond, he stood against one of the Manzanita trees that dotted around the field. That's why I'd not seen him before. The reddish-brown of his clothes blended with the bark he leaned against. His hair was long and, at closer inspection, was not blond at all, but almost silver. The wind toyed with it, sweeping the ass-length locks out behind him in a wave of free hair and braids. He was too far away for me to see his features properly, but I didn't need to see the points of his ears to know he was a faery. I felt his magical energy even from here.

My stomach churned at the sight of him, and I shivered as his cold energy passed through my body.

"Come on, Remy, It's time to go to dinner." I stood and held my hand out for my brother to take.

"No, Aza." He pointed to the flower. He didn't want to pick it. He only wanted to sit with it, looking at it and occasionally stroking the delicate petals. That's why our castle garden was full of weeds and dandelions; he refused to let the gardeners pull the weeds up, not that much grew around here anyway in the deep-red Draconis soil.

"We can come back and look at the flower tomorrow," I urged restlessly. The faery watched us, making me nervous. Fae were not natural in Draconis, so he had to be from one of the other kingdoms where magic was more prolific. Enchantia, maybe, where they all knew magic. That made him a stranger, and I didn't like strangers. Especially ones that were unbidden.

“It needs to sleep,” I added. Sometimes I had to be a little economical with the truth when it came to Remy; otherwise, I’d have to drag him, and as he was twice my size, that just wasn’t happening.

I took his hand, leading him back to the castle, brushing the dirt from my leather clothing as I went. I was a princess, and I didn’t do dirt. At least, I wasn’t supposed to.

We crossed the field to the gate, which would lead us to the castle bridge. It meant we would pass the faery. He kept his eyes fixed on me as we got closer, putting me more on edge. His windswept hair was only the crowning glory to the beauty that sat below it. Tight muscular arms told me he was a fighter; some kind of warrior from another kingdom. My nerves clenched as we walked the path toward him. He held a sword in one hand—a work of art with amethyst stones in the hilt, and the other arm was casually draped on the tree next to him. As I got closer, I saw his eyes were the same color as the stones in his sword, giving an impression of otherworldliness. A pale purple that was no less dazzling for their lightness in color. I sucked in a breath at how beautiful he was. Utter perfection in faery form. No one in Draconis looked the way he did, and yet, the expression on his face was one of disgust. He wrinkled his nose and sneered at us as we got close to him.

I’d hoped to ignore him as we passed by, but he opened his mouth to speak. I readied myself with a hello on my lips. As a princess, my parents schooled me to be courteous to the people, even the awful ones, but it seemed he didn’t have the same schooling as I.

“Is he some kind of idiot?” He nodded to Remy, who gave him a smile. Remy didn’t understand what this man was saying, and even if he did, he would have loved him anyway. Remy loved everyone. Unfortunately, I understood perfectly, and his words sickened me to my stomach.

Clenching my teeth, I remembered what my mother had told me about politeness. Then I promptly forgot it. "With a remark like that, there's only one idiot around here, and Prince Remy isn't it."

I shot him a look that was certainly not fit for a princess and stalked past him, Remy's hand in mine, my breath held. I'd never insulted anyone before, but then again, I'd never heard anyone dare insult Remy in my presence before. The faery was lucky I didn't have my real sword on me, and that killing him would probably annoy my mother, not to mention getting blood on my tunic.

The energy the faery possessed coursed through my body as I walked by him, but I refused to look his way again, even though I could barely breathe with the force of it. Picking up my pace, I practically ran Remy over the bridge, and once through to the castle courtyard, I ordered the guards to close the portcullis. It was a little early—usually, it closed at sundown and reopened at dawn; but, although surprised by my command, the guards did as I asked. Being the heir to the throne did have its perks sometimes.

I was still fuming about the stranger when Remy and I traipsed into the castle dining hall. It was one of two. The grand hall we used for formal occasions and this one—the family dining room, which was just for us and our special guests should we have them. This evening, it was just the five of us. Mother, Remy, my younger brothers, Ash and Hollis, and lastly, me. My father often skipped dinners due to work commitments, and as he wasn't at the table, he would probably be at his desk in his study.

"Azia," My mother admonished, twirling her eyes skyward as she always did when I came indoors covered in mud. "Couldn't you, at least, wash up before coming to dinner? You are a princess, not a swineherd."

As if I was ever allowed to forget. She mentioned it at least five times a day!

"Sorry Ma," I said, kissing her cheek and sitting in my place at the giant oval dinner table. The second I sat down, one of the castle servants brought a bowl of soup, placing it on the table in front of me.

"Ooee Ma," Remy parroted, kissing her cheek and following my lead.

My mother's mouth quirked to the side as her eldest son kissed her, and all at once, I knew she would be mad no longer. Remy was my secret weapon. It didn't matter how awful a daughter I was or how unkempt I came in for dinner. Remy would always back me up.

My mother's face beamed and the beauty she was famous for shone out. Her gorgeous golden hair settled in waves down her back before curling under the bottom edges, and her makeup-free skin was flawless. She was the famous Sleeping Beauty, after all.

"You'll have to get ready for tonight after dinner," she said, turning her gaze back to me, now that Remy was happily tucking into his dinner. "I can't have my only daughter looking like an urchin. I've left a dress out on your bed and instructed your maid to turn that's rat's tail you call hair into something fit for a princess."

All around me, the scrape of forks against plates sounded out as my three brothers ate like we had no more food coming, despite eating a fine dinner every night. If anyone looked like street urchins, it was them, but that was ok because they were boys and boys were allowed to do what they pleased and look how they pleased. It was only I, as the daughter of the famous Sleeping Beauty that had expectations to live up to. Even though my father was the highest in all the land, his fame was eclipsed by the woman he married. And because of my mother's fame throughout all the kingdoms as the most beautiful woman to have ever lived, people expected me to be the same...except I wasn't. I wasn't even close, a fact that the press liked to point out at any given opportunity much to my chagrin.

Like her, I was blonde, but dark blonde that almost bordered on brown. My hair didn't have the same gold that ran through my mother's hair, catching the light, giving her the look of an angel. It was also, as my mother was keen to point out, usually a mess. Not that I could be completely blamed for it. Her hair had beautiful waves. Mine had unruly curls. Add that to the fact that I was adopted. There was no way in Draconis. I could look like my mother, and yet, everyone seemed to expect it. Expect it and then point out how disappointed they were that I didn't.

I sighed and caught my reflection in the back of a spoon. I still had mud on my nose. "What's happening tonight?" I asked casually, putting the spoon down and splashing tomato soup all over the clean white tablecloth while trying to remember what particular royal occasion I'd forgotten now.

"Your father wants you to meet someone, that's all," she replied airily, as though she'd not just dropped a bomb on me. Her words even caused two of my three brothers stopping eating and looking up from their plates.

"Who wants to meet Azia?" Ash, my middle brother

asked, soup dripping down his chin, reminding me of a vampire after a kill. He ran his fingers through his long brown hair to pull it back from his face. At sixteen, he was turning into quite the looker. In fact, all of my brothers shared some of the beauty of my mother. All of them had her long eyelashes and high cheekbones, but they all got their square chins, dark brown hair, and height from my father. As the only adopted member of the family, I was always painfully aware that I stood out amongst them.

"Never you mind. That's between Azia and your father," she said, sipping tea from the daintiest little cup, her little finger raised in perfect etiquette. Rosebud lips sipped at the tea, and I knew for a fact, that she wouldn't leave a lipstick stain on the teacup. Those cherry lips were all her.

Ash and Hollis' eyes swiveled towards me, and I knew what they wanted. They wanted me to ask who I was going to be meeting. Normally, I would let them suffer and carry on eating as though I didn't care, but curiosity burned through me. No one ever asked to speak to just me. I was only one member of the royal family and not a particularly interesting one to boot.

"Who is it, mother?"

She placed her teacup back on the saucer and gave me a warm smile, her eyes crinkling up at the edges. "You shall see after you've gotten yourself cleaned up. Now, eat your dinner before it gets cold."

A picture of the man I'd seen earlier flittered through my mind. I could still feel the energy he possessed even though he was no longer near. He had nothing to do with whatever it was my father wanted me for, but the coincidence of there being a stranger near the castle didn't sit well in my stomach, and after finishing my soup, I couldn't eat any more.

"Where are you going?" Mother asked as I took my leave from the table.

I took the napkin from around my neck and threw it on the table. "I'm not hungry. I'm going to do as you asked and get ready for Father." The quicker I found out what was going on, the sooner I could relax.

This brought a smile to her face. I left the room, my stomach in knots. Yes, I was the heir to the throne of Draconis, but up until now, my main responsibility had been to wear pretty dresses and be an accessory to my mother's beauty like a designer bag from Urbis or The Forge.

My maid Dahlia took one look at me and ordered me into the bath right away. She was a plump woman of about forty with permanently ruddy cheeks and a friendly smile. Not that her smile fooled me. She'd been my maid and governess since I was born, and I knew, behind that mild exterior, she was smart as a whip and took no-nonsense. As she worked on lathering up my hair, chattering away about her son who was failing in school, my mind drifted back to the stranger I'd seen earlier, making my stomach churn even more.

Once my bath was over, Dahlia worked on my hair, brushing the knots out and doing the best she could with my unruly curls. Next, she moved onto my face, expertly applying makeup. She really was an all-rounder, and that's why she'd spent so many years looking after me. She could turn her hand to anything. She was the only person in the whole kingdom my mother trusted to do my makeup for me. She certainly didn't trust me with it. Apparently the "just drawn on by a four-year-old with a crayon" look was not what my mother wanted, so Dahlia did it all. I happily let her.

Taking a deep breath, I tried to rid myself of the energy buzzing around my body. My heart was beating much quicker than normal, and the bath had failed to put me at ease. No matter what I did, the image of the man with the long silver hair kept coming back to me. The way he'd looked at me with such disdain. It hadn't been directed at Remy, despite the fact it was Remy he'd mentioned. He'd been looking at me; his piercing pale purple eyes had drawn me in. Now that I'd had time to think about it, I wondered if he'd used some kind of magic on me. It would explain the pounding in my chest and the electricity buzzing through my veins.

"There! All finished. You look beautiful."

I opened my eyes and checked out my appearance. I had to admit that when I wasn't covered in an inch of dirt, I did manage to look half-decent. Dahlia had shaded my eyes with a pale pink to match my dress and painted my lips a nude pink. I looked at my face, and two golden-ringed irises looked back at me, reminding me that although I was the heir to the throne of Draconis, I was just as much an outsider as the fae man I'd seen earlier.

In all my travels, and I had traveled a lot, I was yet to come upon anyone who had eyes quite as unique as mine. Not even the amethyst-eyed faery I'd seen before was as unusual as I was in the eye department. I'd met a few fae in my time, and they often had jewel-colored eyes. Yes, they were rare and in the kingdom of Draconis, even rarer, but my eyes were the rarest of them all.

After pulling the dress over my head and having the bows at the back fastened by Dahlia, my mother appeared at the door. She had also changed for the occasion...whatever it was.

As usual, she looked stunning, her beautiful golden hair tied back in a simple bow and a dress that was far less poufy than mine.

"Do I get to know who it is I'm meeting yet?" I asked, keenly aware that Dahlia was pressed up against me, almost as eager as I was to know what this was all about.

"Come with me," Mother said, taking my hand and ignoring my question entirely.

I followed her through the castle, the clack-clack-clack of her shoes echoing off the walls. She took me to the drawing room, the most comfortable room in the castle with pink upholstered chairs and beautiful tapestries hand-stitched by my mother hanging on the walls.

It was unusual to receive guests here. This was a room set aside for family only. My father stood to greet us as we walked in. He was still a handsome man, his dark hair showing the faintest signs of grey at the temples. The way his eyes lit up as my mother walked in the room made me slightly jealous. No one had ever looked at me as intently as my father did my mother every time he saw her. They'd been married eighteen years, and they were still like newlyweds.

I wished that one day, someone would look at me that way. No one usually noticed me at all if mother was around.

But someone did look at you that way only today!

A voice sounded in my head, but it was wrong. The faery had looked at me with intense eyes, but there had been no pleasure in them.

"Sit down Azia," my father asked gently, sneaking a quick reassuring glance at my mother.

Uh oh, this didn't bode well.

"This is important. You turned eighteen a while back, and we both think that it's time for you to be more active in royal life."

Uh, huh. "I am active Father," I replied, finding a seat on the elegant couch next to my mother and trying to figure out a way to sit comfortably with all the layers of skirt beneath my ass. "I attend all the royal parties and come with you on all the royal travels."

My father nodded his head, his expression turning serious. "I understand that Azia, but being a queen is a whole lot more than trips and parties, and one day you will be queen. We are only one of twelve other kingdoms, thirteen if you include Urbis itself. Being the ruler of the kingdom requires a delicate balance of strength and diplomacy. As you know, I've been very fortunate during my reign; there has been peace in the kingdoms, but it wasn't always that way. Before I saved your mother, Draconis was in the grip of a terrible curse."

"But you saved her and the kingdom by kissing her." I knew the story by heart. It was famous. Even I, with not an ounce of romance in my bones, loved the story. The story of Sleeping Beauty and her brave prince.

"Yes," my father nodded his head, thoughtfully. "But the truth is, something else happened at that time. Something that, to this day, no one understands. I'm not so arrogant to believe that I saved your mother. I'm glad it was me, but the truth was, anyone could have gotten through the brambles to kiss her."

My mother put her hand on his arm in a gesture of love. "Don't be so modest, darling. It was true love's kiss that awoke me. No one but you could have done that."

He gave her a smile that made my heart melt, and my stomach heave in equal measures. It really should be illegal how mushy these two were for each other.

"Maybe," he agreed. "I know a lot of people had tried before me, but why did I get through? Something happened at that time. It didn't just affect our kingdom. There had been widespread disquiet and war for years, and in the week I saved your mother, it was like all the bad in the world was vanquished. Anyway, I digress. Things have been very easy for me. It is always easy to reign when the people in the kingdom are happy, but things might not always be this way, and I need to prepare you for any eventuality."

"You want me to learn about ruling the kingdom?"

My heart took an unexpected leap in my chest. I'd been thinking about so many horrible things that could happen that I'd not prepared myself for something good. I wanted to learn more. I could never equal the level of beauty my mother possessed, but hopefully, I'd measure up in the strength and capability of my father. Before now, leading the kingdom had been something in the distant future, something I'd never been interested in, but now the possibilities seemed endless. One day, I would be queen of Draconis, and my parents were going to teach me how.

"Indeed I do,"

"Thank you, father!" I stood and kissed him on the cheek, but he brought me into a hug. As his warm arms wrapped around me, all my fears from earlier dissipated.

"So who was it you both wanted me to meet? A tutor of some kind?"

I saw a look pass between my mother and father as he let me go.

"Something like that."

Something like that? Uh, oh. What did that mean?

"I should go and see where he is," My father stood

up, his finger and thumb rubbing together. "I don't believe he's arrived yet. Darling, could you go and organize tea?"

My mother couldn't have gotten up faster if she had tried. She hurried out of the door, pursued by my father, leaving me alone with my anxiety. This was no tutor I was meeting, so who was it, and why had my mother practically bolted for the door at the earliest opportunity?

I waited for ten whole minutes, nerves frayed. The lack of information on who I was to meet was crippling. Why the secrecy? When my father eventually came back through the door, my heart did a lap around my rib cage, but he was alone, his face set in a look of confusion. "I'm afraid there has been a mix-up. The gentleman I was going to introduce to you has not arrived. I'm sorry for getting you all dressed up for nothing, Azia. I know how much you hate all the pomp that goes with these things."

These things? What things? He'd still not told me what exactly we were doing. My mother chose this moment to come through the door, a loaded silver tray with a teapot and three cups on it.

When she saw my father, she adopted the same look of confusion. She placed the silver tray upon the table, then turned her attention to my father.

"Where is he?"

"I've just had word from a servant boy from the town that he is late and will see us tomorrow."

"That's very rude of him," my mother said. If there was anything she hated (apart from me being constantly covered in dirt), it was tardiness.

My father shrugged. "Can't be helped. You head off to bed now, Azia. I'll take a trip into town and see what happened."

I trudged back to my room, unsure of what to think. Both my parents were acting strangely, and neither was particularly forthcoming as to why. The room was dark, which was unusual. Dahlia usually left the candles burning for me. I walked to the window and opened the curtains to let a little moonlight in. A shiver ran down my spine as I caught the sound of someone else breathing and the feeling of being watched gripped me as intensely as it had out in the field earlier. Holding my own breath, I strained my ears to hear it, but there was only the sound of one of the guards coughing outside. I felt for the matches, gazing out into the courtyard as I did. It looked as it always did, lit only by a sliver of light from the crescent moon. Two guards stood by the portcullis, and as I watched them, one of them coughed again making me relax a little. Apart from the guards, the courtyard was empty.

"You won't find anyone of interest out there."

My heart lurched in my chest at the voice coming from behind me. Turning quickly, I let go of the window that slammed closed behind me. It was him! The faery I'd seen earlier was now sitting on my bed as if he owned the place. His devastating beauty captivated me, leaving me breathless despite the fact he held his sword aloft, aimed directly at my throat. This was no social call. He was here to slit my throat.

2ND JANUARY

"How did you get in here?" I whispered, my voice tense, my breathing ragged. Having a sword held to my throat was not something I usually enjoyed. Hell, I wasn't enjoying it now.

In the moonlight, he was more beautiful than ever, but that didn't stop the adrenaline rushing through me. My mind whirled as my fight or flight impulse stalled. I could run, but to do that I would have to run past him. Fighting was my only option. Unfortunately, he still had that beautiful sword in his hand, and I had no doubt he knew how to use it. My own sword was old, stolen months ago from the armory in the basement of the castle. My mother would have pitched a fit if she knew I had it, so I kept it under my bed. The bed that he was currently sitting on. The only other swords I owned were the trick swords I'd had made for Remy who wanted to learn to fight almost as much as I did. Fat lot of good they would be against the thing of beauty the faery held in his hand.

Talking of things of beauty, the fae's eyes danced in the little light there was, eyes that pierced me, pulling me in. He was utterly devastatingly gorgeous only spoiled slightly by the fact that it seemed he was here to kill me. That kinda thing could really put a dampener on any relationship.

Scanning the room quickly, I picked up the only thing currently in reach. The candlestick by my side. Pulling the unlit candles from the top of their holder, I held it out toward him as I would if I was holding a sword. Except it wasn't a sword. It had three holders on one end that held the candles and a stand at the bottom to stop it from toppling over. It was far from ideal, but it was long, and with luck, I could inch my way around him.

He watched me intently as I walked around the bed to the door, but he didn't move except to follow me with his sword. Instead, he studied my movements, watching me intently like a feline about to pounce, the line of his sword never wavering. My hand grasped the door handle at exactly the same time that his hand tightened on the hilt of his sword. He moved so quickly that I almost missed what was happening. The door handle turned, then stilled as a flash of light came down between the faery and me. My breathing increased as he moved his face to mine.

"This isn't quite the welcome I expected," he said, pinning my back to the door and holding his sword to my neck once again. His breath warmed my cheek; he was that close. I sucked in a breath of my own, trying not to lose it. He smelled faintly of wood and leather. He let his gaze fall down my body, and, all at once, I became aware that only the thin, gauzy fabric of my gown separated us. His tongue licked his lips as he took me in, holding me defenselessly to the door. Not that I could move if I'd have wanted to. There was something holding me back. Even if he didn't have his sword to my throat, my muscles had completely forgotten how to work, and the energy I'd felt earlier coursed through me. Not any energy. Fae magic.

My muscles tensed as he pulled my gown tightly enough to see the shape of my body, the curves of my breasts and hips. I followed his gaze to the floor, where the candleholder was lying uselessly in two pieces. His sword had cut through the metal like butter.

His energy was overwhelming, but I had to try to fight. I didn't know why he was here, and I wasn't prepared to find out. Pulling my leg back as far as I could, I put all the strength I had left into it, kicking forward until my knee connected with his leg. Not quite where I was aiming for, but it took him by surprise. He pulled back, and as his sword left my throat, I dove down to the floor and slithered to the bed where my own sword was hidden. Now, my sword was no match for his, but it was forged from the metal mined by the dwarves under the Fire Mountains, which meant it was strong and held a magic of its own, not that I knew how to embrace that magic. I'd never trained as a warrior the way Ash and Hollis had, but I'd watched them intently, copying their moves, practicing where no one could see me.

The intruder seemed surprised by the turn of events, but there was no fear in his eyes. If anything, he seemed to relish the challenge.

I lashed out at him, trying to quell my own fear. A shaking hand had no place in a sword fight, but play fights with Remy aside, this was my first. He swiped my sword away with mild irritation, the way one might swat a fly. He wasn't even trying, and yet, I was giving him everything I had. It was woefully obvious that I was no match for him. While I was trying every move I knew, he'd not even broken a sweat. At one point, I swear, the fae bastard yawned.

"Are we done yet?" he asked lazily. Before he'd uttered the last syllable, my sword vanished into thin air with a flick of his hand, leaving me with nothing to defend myself but the scream upon my lips.

I don't know why I hadn't thought of it earlier. Maybe I wasn't the swordswoman I thought I was, but there were two guards on the end of every corridor who did know how to sword fight. Two guards who would be here in a moment at the sound of my screams.

As he realized what I was about to do, the lazy attitude he'd shown moments before left him, and he rushed at me, knocking me over onto the bed, his hand clasped firmly over my mouth.

I breathed deeply through my nose, trying to fend off the rising panic at this crazy faery, lying directly on top of me. His eyes softened a bit, but he didn't take his hand from my mouth.

"Have you had your fun now?"

I glared at him, my stomach tightening as he pressed in closer, the weight of him crushing me. Up close, I saw that his eyes were framed by lashes so dark and thick that not even Dahlia with her extensive makeup knowledge would be able to recreate them. His skin was pale and flawless, and if it weren't for the amusement in his purple eyes, I'd have thought him made of marble.

"I'm not here to hurt you," he growled, "but with a welcome like that, I might change my mind."

I struggled against him, which only served to amuse him more. He pulled my arms up above my head, and I thought, for a second, he was going to kiss me. Let him try. I'd bite his tongue right out of his mouth. He didn't, though. He merely waited, watching me silently.

It took me a good few seconds to put my thoughts in order to speak to him, but I had to wait until he took his hand from my mouth to say anything.

"I can see you have something to say, but until you promise me that you won't do anything stupid such as scream or spit in my face, I won't take my hand away, do you understand?"

I nodded as much as I could with a hand over my mouth. He lessened his grip, and I breathed in, grateful of the cold night air.

"What the hell do you think you are?" I hissed.

He laughed. "What am I? I think you already know." He tipped his head slightly to the side, exposing one of his pointed ears. "I think the more pertinent question should be, who I am."

I wasn't in the mood for games, but as he still had my hands clasped together over my head and the weight of his body on top of me, I decided that playing along was my only option at this point.

"Fine," I muttered through gritted teeth. "Who are you?"

He sat up, pulling me with him so that we were next to each other on the bed. Every part of me wanted to run for the door, but as I'd already seen, it would be a pointless endeavor.

"I, my dear, am your fiancé."

My stomach tightened as I tried to take in his words. The guy was obviously deranged. My fiancé?

"Didn't your parents tell you? They have come to the conclusion that you are old enough to marry, and I am the person they picked." He leaned forward and spoke in a low voice. "Apparently, I'm quite a catch! I had hoped to get to know you before we were formally introduced, but I see you need a little time."

The magical energy had me pinned to the spot, and yet, he was quite obviously insane. I didn't have the first clue why he was in my room, but his explanation left me in no doubt that I wasn't safe. Pulling myself out of his magnetic grip, I ran for the door a second time. This time, it opened at the first try. Pulling the door open, I screamed down the corridor loudly. As they had been trained, the two guards came pelting down the corridor, their swords raised.

"There's someone in my room," I gasped, trying to keep the tears at bay. The two guards ran past me, but when I turned around, the faery had gone. The first guard, an older gentleman with a receding hairline that even his helmet couldn't hide, checked the bathroom while the younger one checked my closet and under the bed. I knew they wouldn't find anything. However the faery had gotten into the room, he'd obviously gone out the same way.

"I'm sorry. I must have had a nightmare." What else could I say? A crazy faery had somehow magicked himself into my room, held a sword to my throat, and told me I was to marry him? It sounded crazy to my own ears. The elder of the two, a gruff-looking man with way too much ear hair making up for the lack of it on his head, nodded, and I noticed a roll of his eyes as he left the room.

"Well, sorry for taking you away from your night of excitement guarding the corridor," I hissed under my breath. Heat rose to my cheeks as the younger guard answered me.

"Don't worry about Jack. He's a miserable old coot at the best of times."

I lowered my head. "I'm sorry. I shouldn't have said that. It was unkind, and you both really did help me."

"Hey, that's our job. I'm here to keep you safe."

I looked up into the kindest pair of brown eyes I'd ever seen set onto a handsome face.

He smiled. "Are you sure you are alright? I don't want to leave you upset like this."

After everything that had happened, I felt soothed by his presence, but I could no more have a guard spend the night in my room than a faery. "I'm perfectly fine. I feel a little foolish, actually."

The guard glanced around the room again as though he thought I wasn't being honest with him. When he was satisfied there was no one in my room, he stepped outside. "I'm going to stand guard right outside the door tonight. If you need me, just call out, and I'll be in here in a flash."

He was so kind and concerned that the anxiety I'd been feeling fell away. If the faery did decide to come back, there was no doubt in my mind that the guard would be as helpless against him as I was. Maybe this guard was an amazing swordsman, but the faery had magic, and as I'd already seen, it was hard to fight magic without any of your own.

I thanked him, closing the door. Standing with my back to it, I could hear him settling down at the other side.

As I stepped forward, my foot stood on something

sharp. As I looked down, something glinted in the light. Picking it up, I saw it was an amethyst from the faery's sword. Anger filled me. Who did he think he was to just come into my bedroom unannounced and scare me half to death? I gripped the small jewel tightly and stormed across the room, anger filling my every pore. Opening the window, I hurled it as far as I could. Satisfied that it was far away, I turned back to the bed. The dent where he'd lain on top of me was still there. In a fit of anger, I pulled the covers taught, before hopping into bed.

He was no longer there. The strange energy he exuded was long gone, but the fear he'd produced, still pulled at my nerves. I couldn't expect the guards to help me, but there was no way I was going to be defenseless anymore. Tomorrow I would stop playing at sword fighting and start learning it for real.

...

A noise at my door made me jump. My sword was gone, and the candlestick I'd tried defending myself with was in pieces on the floor. Once again, I was at the mercy of whoever was on the other side.

My heart calmed a bit when I heard the voice from the other side. It was the young guard from the night before.

"Your Highness. It is morning, and my shift is coming to an end. I didn't want to leave without knowing if you were alright."

A smile played on my lips. The poor guy had spent the night outside my room, standing to attention, waiting for an attack that never came while I'd slept in a comfy bed, and here he was asking if I was all right.

I opened the door. Immediately, his deep brown eyes crinkled at the side. Just peeking out from below his helmet, soft brown curls flanked his ears. A small smile crept over his face. "Are you ok?"

I smiled back. "I'm fine. Thank you for looking out for me. I'm sorry to have been a bother."

"No bother at all. It was a privilege. Milo Kelly at your service." He nodded his head, and after giving me a lingering look, he set off down the corridor. I half expected him to turn around and say something to me, but he didn't.

Back in my bedroom, I dressed quickly before Dahlia could come to do the job. I didn't want to talk to her about what had happened last night. It was probably better she didn't know. There was only one person I needed to speak with, and if I wasn't quick, I'd miss him for the day.

I found him saddling up his horse in the stables, ready to go out to wherever he needed to go.

"Father, I need to speak to you."

He pulled a fur cloak around his shoulders and hopped aboard Talia, his horse.

"I'm in rather a rush. Can it wait until tonight?"

I stepped in front of the horse, blocking his path. "Not really. I need to know who it was you wanted me to meet last night. Why all the secrecy?"

My father sighed, "I didn't want to tell you like this, but your mother and I think it's time you settled down. I'm so very proud of you, my daughter, but you have your own ideas and plans; and while that is all well and good, it takes ambition and dedication to rule a kingdom. You are spirited, and that's what I love about you the most, but you need someone to guide you. To stand by your side. To help you on your journey."

I tapped my foot, getting more and more annoyed by the second. Why didn't he just come out and say it? That he had me promised to someone. Someone I'd never met before he'd somehow appeared in my bedroom in the middle of the night. I wasn't going to let my father off easily, though. I needed him to tell me outright what he'd planned.

"Who? Who do you want to guide me?"

He shifted in the saddle. "I really would have preferred to tell you this tonight with your mother."

"Tell me now," I demanded. I wasn't usually one to demand anything of my parents, but after having a stranger magic his way into my room, I'd changed my mind.

"Your mother and I think it's time you got married, and we've found someone who we think you'll like. He's not from Draconis, but he's a powerful man. Your mother tells me he's good-looking, though I wouldn't know about that sort of thing. I'm sure you'll like him."

"This man. Is he a fae by any chance?"

Now, my father really looked uncomfortable. "How did you...never mind. Yes, he is one of the fae. He's a powerful man."

"So you said. What if I don't want to marry him?" because I most certainly did not. I'd only just turned eighteen a few days ago. I didn't even want a boyfriend yet, let alone a husband and certainly not the kind of man that called my brother an idiot then snuck into my room in the middle of the night and threatened me.

"Why not give it a little time before making any hasty decisions? He's coming over for tea tonight. You'll get to meet him then. I'm sure you'll find him an agreeable sort of fellow."

Yeah, if you call holding a sword to my throat agreeable. I stepped back and let my father pass, frustration gripping me. Tears of anger spilled down my cheeks at the thought of what my parents were doing to me. Why had none of this been mentioned before now? I gritted my teeth. Dragon's breath, I really could go for a full-on tantrum, but what would be the point? My father was the king and what he said went.

I spent the day in my room, not wanting to talk to anyone.

My mother found me hours later, still in my bed. I'd spent the day reading and trying to pretend I didn't exist. At least, that way I wouldn't be forced to marry a faery jackass.

"What's the matter?" she asked, noticing the scowl on my face. My mother didn't like scowling, it gave people wrinkles.

"You loved my father when you married him," I stated it as fact. This was no question.

"Yes, of course. I still love him dearly."

"So why is it you are asking me to marry out of duty?" I huffed. "You didn't. I'm not ready for this, and I don't want it."

My mother sighed. Even that simple noise sounded beautiful like the pealing of bells or a breath of wind on a summer's day. "I see you have been talking to your father. Come with me, and I'll tell you our reasons." My mother opened the door to my bedroom and beckoned me out. "We are not doing this to you out of mere tradition. We are doing it to protect you."

"Protect me?"

"Azia, you are a bright young woman, and I know, in time, that you'll be perfect for the role of queen. I know that with a bit of schooling, you will run this kingdom beautifully with or without a husband."

"So why the arranged marriage then?" I asked, darting around her to the corridor outside.

She twisted her own wedding ring on her finger, a

gesture she always made when she was nervous.

"I didn't want to tell you this, and it probably won't even mean anything to you, but in the past couple of days, a dragon has been spotted flying over the moorlands."

She stopped there as though that explained everything. It did not!

"So? What does a dragon have to do with marrying me off at the first available opportunity?" The dragons usually stuck to the mountaintops. I used to enjoy watching them as a kid. Their serene beauty belying their fierce nature. They never usually came down as far as the moorlands, but if it was just flying and not bothering anyone, who cared?

She sighed and held the wall next to her as if to steady herself. She looked tired, as though this had been going through her mind all last night. Bringing her hand up to her throat, she began. "Before Draconis was at peace, the whole twelve kingdoms were at war, and there was nothing anyone could do to stop it. Even the government in Urbis that oversaw all the laws in all the kingdoms couldn't stop what was happening. There was a lot of dark magic. For years, those people who used their magic for evil were doing pretty much anything they wanted. It was part of that black magic that sent me into a hundred-year sleep."

I knew all this. The stories of my mother's sleep and the kiss that ended it were legendary, but I still didn't understand what that had to do with dragons...or me. I kept silent, knowing there was no point interrupting her. She would tell me.

"It was horrible, and it had gone on for so long that most people had no fight left. Dark magic weighs on you. It's like the worst kind of depression, but worse, because the people it affected didn't even know why they were depressed. No one was happy, and the people committing unspeakable acts were normal folk, turning to the dark out of fear, sadness, and desperation. Sadness creeps into your soul and burns it until you no longer feel, and it somehow becomes a part of who you are. It was like that in my youth and for a hundred years while I slept. In that time, the dragons came down from the mountains a lot. No one knows why. Maybe they were feeling the same things we were all feeling. The people in all the kingdoms were killing each other, so why not the dragons too? Like I said, a dragon has been seen down from the mountain for the first time since I married your father. It is an omen of the worst kind. You can't understand how awful it was. You could never imagine, because your whole life, you have only known peace."

A shiver of fear ran through me. My mother often told the story of how my father fought through a wall of brambles to kiss her, which woke her up, but she never talked about what happened before. I knew that an evil witch had cursed her and that the witch had gone long before my mother awoke, but she'd never mentioned the wars before and the dark magic. "I still don't understand. What has this to do with me getting married?"

She took my hand in hers. "Your father and I want to keep you safe. It was the kings and queens, the governors, the ministers, and presidents that were targeted before. I don't like to think that the same is happening again, but the man you are just about to meet is magic. He can protect you in ways that we can't."

He can protect me from outside dangers? So who was going to protect me from him?

"You want me to marry to keep me safe?"

She shook her head. "I don't really want you to marry, but if anything should happen to your father and me, I want to know you aren't alone. Remy will need care for the rest of his life, and Ash and Hollis are still children. You'll need help. You'll need someone who loves you by your side."

I sighed with frustration. There was no way the faery loved me. He'd only ever looked upon me with disdain and a hint of glee when he knew I was trapped. Hardly the recipe for a happy marriage. "The castle is full of advisors and men and woman who would step up in a heartbeat to help me rule a kingdom."

My mother nodded and took my hand in hers, and once again, we began to walk. "That is true. Our staff are some of the best, but unless they are family, this will never be any more than a job to them. Even our most loyal advisors leave the castle at the end of the day to go home to their own families. I cannot ask them to choose you or us over the ones they love. If you had a boyfriend already...that would be different, but you've never shown any interest in love."

We made it to the door to the drawing room. The man I was supposed to marry, the same one who had tried to kill me was inside. My mother had said that my father trusted him. I wondered how much he'd trust him if I told him where he was last night.

The fae was talking to my father as we walked in, but as soon as he heard us, his eyes turned to me. His hair was brushed back and the braids he wore tied behind. He wore some kind of ceremonial uniform. One I didn't recognize from any of the kingdoms. It was white with gold trim and amethyst colored buttons. He was off the charts beautiful. Even from across the room, he held me in his gaze. This wasn't attraction. There was no love nor chemistry between us. I didn't even like the guy, but right at that moment, I was drawn to him in a way I'd never been with anyone.

"There you both are." My father stood up and came over to me, breaking off my eye contact with the fae. Just like that, the spell was broken. The asshat had been using magic on me, some kind of attraction spell, and I'd very nearly fallen for it. What would have happened if my father had not blocked his path? It didn't bear thinking about.

"You both look beautiful," my father continued, kissing my cheek, before moving to kiss my mother.

"This is Caspian," he said, sitting back down. "Caspian, this is my daughter, the princess, Azia."

"Pleased to meet you, Azia." He stood and took my hand, kissing the back of it gently. A shiver went up my spine, whether through attraction or nerves or fear, I couldn't tell. Something was messing with my body... or someone was.

I pulled my hand from his. "It's very nice to meet you too," I answered through gritted teeth.

My mother busied herself with pouring tea into four cups, so I sat down, waiting to see what would happen next and wondering what I could do to drag myself out of this mess.

My father clasped his hands together and leaned forward in his chair. "We've been thinking of your future, Azia and..." He nodded to my mother as she handed him a cup of tea.

"She is aware of the reason Caspian is here," my mother butted in. "I've already explained the situation, and she is fully aware of what is going on.

"You're one lucky girl," Caspian said a smarmy smile

on his face. Beneath it, I could still feel the disdain he held for me. If he despised me so much, what were we even doing here? What a sanctimonious creep.

My mother tugged my father's hand. "Now that everything is out in the open, why not leave these two alone to get to know one another? We can retire to the orangery and drink our tea there." She gave my father a meaningful look, and he stood, taking her hand, and following her from the room.

Clenching my jaw, I breathed deeply through my teeth. I was once again going to be alone in a room with this jerk.

I opened my mouth to say something, words to the effect of "no way," but nothing came out.

Casting my eyes to the fae, I saw him, once again, staring at me. When the door slammed shut behind my mother and father, my voice magically came back to me.

"Stop doing that," I demanded, my finger outstretched, anger coursing through me. He was a manipulator and a magical one to boot.

He sat back on the sofa as languidly as any cat and crossed his arms, a smirk painting his face.

"But it's so much fun. Why not sit down? I promise to keep my sword at my side."

My gaze wandered down to his sword, and I remembered with great satisfaction that he had lost an amethyst from its hilt the night before. It was beautiful, but flawed, a little like its owner.

"I'm not marrying you," I hissed. He continued to watch me as I threw myself down on a seat away from him.

"I really should apologize for last night. I'm not in the habit of coming into girls' rooms in the middle of the night."

"And sticking a sword to their throat," I added for him.

"Quite, it's just that I've been watching you, and you are not quite what I expected of a princess— Sleeping Beauty's daughter, no less."

"Sorry to disappoint," I shot back.

"No, actually I like it. I was expecting some kind of up herself prissy girl obsessed by her own looks, but you are almost beautiful without caring. It makes a refreshing change. I live in The Forge, and beauty is the currency there. It's extremely boring."

He was getting close to getting a teapot to the head if he continued talking. I picked up a teacup and held it so tightly I was afraid it might smash under the force. At least then, I'd have something sharp to gut him with if the need arose. The thought of stabbing him with a sharp piece of broken china calmed me down, enabling me to speak to him evenly without screaming.

"I'd rather marry literally any other man in the kingdom than you," I growled. "And that includes a troll I once saw living under a bridge."

He roared with laughter. "I've been training as a warrior for most of my life. You'll find your parents think I'm the best man for the job. The deal is, how do you say...done." His eyes centered on mine, and once again, I felt my body reacting to him. Damn it!

The way he looked at me made my heart pound and my stomach churn in equal measure, but my brain wanted to clock the guy right in the nose.

"Look. I don't know what magic you are performing on me, but it isn't going to work." The truth was, his magic was affecting me in ways I'd never imagined. I just didn't want him to know that. My pulse raced every time I looked at him.

"What makes you think I'm performing magic on you?"

Damn. He'd backed me into a proverbial corner. I could hardly tell him that just looking at him made me weak and dizzy....and sick.

"Just stop, all right?" I said, slamming the cup back on the table and standing up, turning away from him so I didn't have to look into his eyes a moment longer. "I'm sorry you have come such a long way to meet with me," I said calmly, measuring my words, "and I understand that you and my father are friends, but I'm afraid I cannot marry you."

"So you've said," the faery replied, sipping on his tea. "What you have failed to tell me is why not."

Because you are a jerk of epic proportions?

"Because I'm already dating someone else." What had made me say that? I wasn't dating anyone.

The door opened, and my mother and father came back into the room hand in hand.

"How is everyone doing?" my mother asked pleasantly, expectation plainly on her face.

Caspian answered for me. "Azia was just telling me she can't marry me because she is dating someone else."

He was annoyed. I could hear it in his voice. I preferred it to the smug drawl he'd used before. "I traveled a long way to be here, and I was assured that this was set to go ahead."

My mother and father's eyes swiveled towards me.

"You're dating?" My mother asked in a shaky soft voice. She dropped my father's hand and clutched her own to her chest. Probably because I'd not told her before. Not that there was anything to tell. I didn't know any men beyond the castle walls.

"Who is it Azia?" My father asked in a sigh. He didn't seem shocked in the way my mother was, but the look of annoyance on his face was evident. This was not the way they planned the evening to go, but then again, it was hardly my idea of fun either. They'd dropped a huge bombshell on me, so now I was giving them a taste of their own medicine. The only problem was I didn't have an answer to give.

I fumbled around in my mind, trying to come up with a name. Any name.

"Milo Kelly!" I blurted out. My mother and father looked at each other.

"Milo Kelly? Who's he?"

3RD JANUARY

"All this time, I've hoped you'd find a nice young man, and now, at the worst possible moment, you tell me you're dating?" my mother lamented at breakfast the next morning. "Why didn't you mention Milo before?"

I'd spent the previous evening searching the castle for Milo to give him the head's up while my parents argued over what was to be done with me and placating Caspian who was pissed off with my little announcement. Dating Milo wasn't helping their cause at all. He was a guard, and although he worked in the castle, it was unlikely that he knew how to run a kingdom. Not that it had been adequately explained to me how the fae knew how to run a kingdom either. Thankfully, my parents had packed him off back to the capital, hopefully never to be seen again. I'd not found Milo, and now, it was a race to see who would get to him first. Me or my mother.

"It's new, and I didn't want to embarrass him," I fumbled, hoping that would tame her desire to go looking for him. She wouldn't want to embarrass her staff.

My mother waved my answer away while Ash and Hollis smirked. At sixteen and fifteen respectively, they both looked on the verge of becoming men, but their attitudes had a lot of catching up to do. The pair of them were enjoying this immensely.

"It's very unfortunate," my mother began. "You heard what your father said last night. We need someone to guide you. Someone who is a leader. Someone who..."

"Someone like me?"

My heart dropped as Caspian sauntered into the room, helping himself to a piece of toast and giving me a wink as he sat in the seat next to me.

My mother smiled at him, making me want to puke. I would have asked why he was here, but obviously, he'd not gone back to the capital as I thought. They'd invited him to stay. Dragon balls!

"Will you be with us much longer?" I inquired, trying to sound innocent and not in the murderous rage that I felt. "It's just a shame you've come so far and for nothing."

"I wouldn't say for nothing," he replied cryptically.

My mother buttered a piece of toast and passed it to him. "You may be dating this Milo fellow, but as you've said it's a new romance and most romances don't last," My mother said. "Caspian will be staying with us a while, and I'd like you to take some time to get to know him."

I shook my head in disbelief. "I don't want to get to know him. I'm dating Milo."

"Are you in love with Milo?" inquired Caspian. At the other side of the table, my mother watched curiously at what I was going to say. Ash and Hollis did the same. Only Remy continued eating his cornflakes like nothing important was going on. Turning back to the faery, I was ready to tell him that I was in the deepest love possible, but I could feel the tendrils of his magic poking at my mind.

"No. I barely know him," I said. Dragon balls! Why had I said that?

"Well, that settles it then. I'm sure your young man will get over it."

Mother, seemingly satisfied with my answer, shifted her focus back to her breakfast while I was left wondering what the hell just happened. Glancing over at the faery, he gave me a sly grin then poured himself a cup of coffee.

He'd made me say those words. He'd made me tell the truth. I'd been thinking it, but it hadn't been what I wanted to say. I hated him even more. It was bad enough that he crept into my room, but to mess with my own mind. That was other-level dragon crap.

"If you excuse me, I have to go and talk to Milo." I stood up from the table, throwing my napkin down in disgust.

"Let him down gently darling," my mother advised, giving me a knowing look. "Men are never very great when it comes to heartbreak."

Cursing the pair of them, I left the room, wondering how I was supposed to get myself out of this mess.

I wasn't going to marry Caspian, that was for sure, but I could hardly marry Milo either. For all I knew, he already was married. He probably had five kids at home. Searching the rest of the castle, I was forced to come to the conclusion that he wasn't at work today. I did, however, find the old guard he was working with the previous night.

"Have you seen Milo?"

The older guard narrowed his eyes. "He's not at work today. What do you want him for?"

I glared at him, and he quickly backed down. "I mean, is there anything I can help you with Your Highness?"

"Yes. Can you tell me where he lives? I need to see him."

The guard arched an eyebrow at this request, but I wasn't about to tell him why I wanted to see his workmate. The guy obviously didn't like me...or his job.

"He lives in Zhore. Three doors down from the Dragon Roost Inn by the town square. It's a green house, can't miss it."

The capital city of Draconis, Zhore was actually our nearest town. I say town because it was barely big enough to qualify as a city. As most of Draconis was barren, the land didn't support a lot of people, so while we equaled in size most of the other kingdoms, we were vastly underpopulated compared to them. Luckily for me, the center of Zhore was just a thirty-minute walk away from the castle.

"And does he live with his wife?" I inquired, causing the old guard's eyebrows to shoot up once again.

"If Milo has a wife, he's yet to mention it," he huffed.

I thanked him and headed out of the castle. It was a beautiful day, which belied the squirming in my stomach. Remembering what my father had told me about the dragons, I cast my gaze to the tips of the Fire Mountains. A number of dragons circled the top as they did frequently, but none came lower, leading me to believe that my parents were worrying over nothing. I wasn't strictly allowed to walk into town by myself without a guard. But I figured, seeing as both my parents had succumbed to insanity at the moment, and technically, I was going to see a guard and would be with him part of the time, there was nothing they could say.

I pulled my hood over my head, shielding myself from the villagers. It rarely snowed in Draconis except on the tops of the Fire Mountains, but it was cold, and the hood would shield me from prying eyes.

The town square was a mess, debris left over from the celebrations on New Year's Eve. As I watched, a young boy with a cart swept up the discarded decorations and other detritus left from the celebrations.

I found the Dragon Roost Inn quickly, and from there, it was only a matter of looking for a house painted green.

The architecture in Draconis left a lot to be desired, and the ones here in Zhore were barely any better than the ones in the rest of the kingdom. What they lacked in quality and workmanship, they made up for in originality. As metal was in abundance and wood was scarce, many of the houses were built using a lot of it. Milo's house was no different in that respect. Built from brick, it featured a metal roof and doorway. Metal shutters painted green were clipped open on each side of all the windows creating a pleasing effect.

I raised my hand up to the wrought-iron knocker shaped like a face with a ring through its nose, but then paused. I'd been so eager to come here and talk to him, that I'd not spent any time thinking of exactly what I was going to say. I could hardly tell him that we were dating now. He'd think I was weird. Worse still, he might feel obligated to pretend for fear of losing his job. It wasn't I that employed him, but my father, and yet, the guards were all told to follow my orders too. How could I even think of asking him to go lie to my father? The whole thing was stupid, and yet to not do it would mean I had no excuse to get out of marrying the faery. My not wanting to, apparently, was not enough of a reason, and although my mother had waved off my fake budding romance with Milo as less than nothing, she couldn't ignore him if we were in love. Could she? I sighed and realized that this wasn't just my life I was playing with. I didn't know Milo, but he'd helped me at a time when I needed him. I couldn't bring all this on him. It wouldn't be fair. I was just about to turn away when the door opened.

I'd not even knocked.

"I saw you deliberating about knocking," Milo grinned at me. "You should come inside before anyone sees you. Are you here alone?"

He took my hand and pulled me inside, giving a quick glance up and down the street before closing the door behind me. His hands were warm, but he let go and dropped into a bow immediately after the door clicked into place. "Forgive me, Your Highness, for my rudeness. I just didn't like you being out there alone. It's not safe for you."

"Please stand. You weren't rude; I was. I'm sorry to have bothered you, I..." my train of thought wandered as I took in the sight behind him. The walls were lined with pieces of art, all made from metal. An abstract sculpture made of curves and swirls filled the far wall, reminding me of the ocean, even though it was static. One of the other walls had sculptures of animals, and a third wall held all manner of swords, each one more beautiful than the last. My breath caught in my throat as I saw a sword not unlike the Fae's sword, although it held rubies instead of amethysts. The hilt was shaped into a dragon, the rubies making up the eyes. It was exquisite, unlike the plain swords worn by the castle guards. I immediately felt a connection to it like no other sword. It made my own stolen sword look like a child's toy. I took my coat off and laid it on the arm of his sofa, not taking my eyes from the sword the whole time.

"This is beautiful. Where did you get it?" I whispered, moving across the room and bringing my hand up to touch it.

Milo pulled it from the wall. "I made it myself. Would you like to hold it?"

The moment I took the hilt into my hand and wrapped my fingers around the metal, I knew that this sword was meant to be mine. It fit my hand perfectly, and when I held it out, I felt a power I'd never known before. I was no longer Princess Azia of Draconis; I was a warrior. A warrior who could rule the kingdom alone, who didn't need anyone by her side, let alone the slimy fae.

I waved the sword, thrusting it forward slowly, defeating an invisible foe and causing Milo to jump back.

"You aren't holding it right," he said, coming up behind me and taking my hand at the wrist. "I've seen you practicing in the fields behind the castle." He adjusted my grip and the position of my hand. His warm breath tickled my ear, sending goose bumps down my arm. I'd barely been aware of him, but in this close proximity, the thrill of the sword was now overtaken by the feel of his body against mine.

He must have realized at the same time as I did

because he jumped back and once again, dropped into a bow. "I'm so awfully sorry, Your Highness. I shouldn't have been so bold as to presume..."

"Please stop calling me Your Highness," I said, placing the sword back on the wall. I was reluctant to let it go, but it wasn't mine.

"My name is Azia, and it is I that should be apologizing. I shouldn't have come to your house. It could get you in trouble."

He looked up from his bow and stood up straight. "Trouble? I'm not scared of trouble, but I am interested as to why you would visit me."

My cheeks colored as I remembered the reason I'd come here. How could I tell him the truth? I couldn't. I'd have to figure a way to get it through to my parents that I wasn't marrying Caspian.

My brain whirred, but nothing came to me. "How much for the sword?" I asked, changing the subject instead.

It didn't matter how much he said. I was both rich, and I was poor. My parents had given me everything I could ever want, but there was no way they'd give me the money for this. Milo could give me a figure; I'd say thanks and then be on my way.

He walked back to the sword and once again took it from the wall. He held it out to me. "The sword is yours. It is my pleasure to give it to you."

I stared at him, shock racing through me. As the daughter of a king, I was accustomed to being given gifts. Any trip to foreign kingdoms usually resulted in a carriage full of presents, but this was something else. Milo wasn't a rich diplomat or a member of the royalty. He was a guard who used his artistic gift to make things. The rubies alone would be worth a lot of money.

"I cannot accept this."

Milo thrust the sword into my hand. "I made this sword after watching you practice one evening. The sun glowed red, silhouetting you, and the dragons circled low in the air. You were so wrapped up in what you were doing that you didn't notice them, but I did. As soon as my shift ended, I ran home and designed this. It took a few days to make it, but you were the inspiration. If anyone is meant to have this sword, it is you."

His words were beautiful, and yet, something he said reminded me of my father's own words.

"The dragons were circling low? Lower than usual?"

Milo arched a brow, probably confused at the subject change. "Yes, but they were still far above you. You were in no danger. You were wearing a red and gold robe and looked like you were commanding them. You were the queen of the dragons that day."

I remembered the robe he was talking about. It was a present from my mother. I'd only worn it one time, on my birthday. Milo must have made this sword recently.

"That's beautiful," I whispered, "but I cannot accept such a gift from you. I don't even know you."

"So let's change that." He took the sword from my hand once again and placed it on the wall. "I'll keep this here until a time you decide you want it." He stepped back and held his hand out for me to shake. "My name is Milo. I've lived in Zhore my whole life. My father worked in the mines, and my mother made jewelry from the metal that came from them."

"Your father worked in the mines?"

He began to laugh. He must have understood my confusion. Only dwarves worked the Fire Mountain mines, and they were fiercely protective of them. Humans were not allowed in there. It was said that they imbued a spell into every piece of metal that no other magical person could break.

“He was an intermediary between the dwarves and the humans and was only allowed in the entrance to the mines, which the dwarves made into a shop. Even after twenty-five years of working there, he never ventured in any further. The dwarves needed food and such to survive, and they only had precious metals and stones. My father was a necessary evil as far as they were concerned, but they treated him well, and as you can see, we were never short of metal to work with. He loved his job. He told me stories of the dwarves all the time, how they used to complain about anything and everything. I think he found them funny, but he did his job well. He was the only human allowed to work in the mines until the day he died. They asked me to take his job, but I’d just been appointed at the castle, and I love my job.”

“I’m sorry to hear about your father’s death. What about your mother? Where is she?”

“When my father died, my mother realized that life was too short. She’d spent her life working the metals that my father had brought home into beautiful jewelry to sell to people at The Forge and other kingdoms. She’d saved up enough to travel, so she cut out the middleman, loaded up our family carriage with her jewelry and some of the swords I’d made and moved to The Forge. I hear she’s living in a massive apartment there now, although some of her letters come from other places so I know she vacations a lot.”

“It sounds wonderful,” I said, noticing a clear box on a stand. Upon a red velvet cushion lay a beautiful ruby necklace. One of his mother’s I assumed.

“She’s enjoying life,” Milo said, taking my attention

from the necklace. "I might do the same thing when I've saved up enough, but there's not as much call for intricate swords here as there is for jewelry. The castle uses another supplier, and the guards use a basic design. It's cheaper that way."

"Yeah, they are nowhere near as pretty as yours, though."

Milo's face dropped. "I'm sorry. I didn't mean to offend the king. I wasn't calling him cheap. Getting the best price for swords in this climate is the better choice. I would have done the same if it were I. We live in peaceful times, and if I'm going to be honest, my swords are purchased more for decoration than for actual use, although you'll not find a stronger sword than the ones I make."

"Actually, my father thinks things are beginning to change," I sighed, sitting down on one of Milo's comfy couches. "He says that there is something in the air. You said yourself that the dragons were circling lower than normal. He thinks it's an omen of how things were before."

"Before he rescued your mother, you mean?" he asked, sitting beside me.

It figured he knew the story. Everyone knew the story. "Yeah. He thinks that he was only able to rescue her because the curse was already broken. I mean, so many other people tried to cut through those brambles before he did. Why did he get through when no one else could?"

Milo shrugged. "I don't know. My father told me that he had a line of people begging for the dwarves' metal every day for years, but when the brambles receded, people stopped coming. My father's workload cut by a half the day your father rescued your mother."

"Wow. I've only ever thought of the positives of that story. Did things get hard for your father then?"

He twisted on the couch, so he was facing more toward me. "Nah, he just tripled the price of the metals. People still came and bought it. It is magical to an extent, but those brambles had a strong curse, and even though swords made with the dwarves metal could cut through, they often grew just as quickly as they were cut, making it a pointless task to even try."

"Oh." Maybe my father was right, and he was lucky. Just what I needed, another thing to worry about. The dragons coming low in the sky was an omen according to my mother, but they'd done no damage, nor hurt anyone.

Milo must have seen the worry on my face because he scooted forward and laid a protective hand on my shoulder. "Listen. Don't worry about such things. I might have been exaggerating about the dragons. I don't really remember if they were lower in the sky than usual. They looked like they were, but it could have been a trick of the light or perspective."

I sighed. "I'm not really too worried about any curse or the dragons. I enjoy watching them. I find them beautiful."

"The queen of the dragons," he said again, smiling.

I laughed, feeling light for the first time since that jerk of a faery had turned up. It was nice to be with someone I could talk to away from the confines of the castle. The weight of the world was not as crippling as it had been just a few hours before.

"Not quite. I enjoy them from a distance...It's...It's my parents. They want me to marry someone I don't want to marry. They sprung it on me last night."

A look of comprehension dawned on him. "Ah, so

that's why you are here. You are hiding from your parents."

I shook my head, dreading his reaction when I told him what I was about to tell him. "I wish that were the case. It's much worse than that. I told them I couldn't marry him because I was dating someone else, and in a panic, your name came to me."

Milo's mouth twisted into a grin. "Are you telling me that the king and queen think we are dating?"

He lounged back on his sofa, as my cheeks once again reddened. Dragon's breath, this was embarrassing. I'd been so worried about embarrassing him, that I'd not put any thought into how embarrassing this would be for me. And it was. My cheeks were hotter than a dragon's flame.

"Maybe," I admitted. "Just a little. My mother wants me to break up with you."

"No way!" He clasped his hands to his chest theatrically. "I love you too much. You are my heart, my soul, my one true love." He pulled me from the sofa and spun me around the room as though we were at a royal ball. He was teasing me, of course, using the same line that had become famous when my father kissed my mother, awakening her from her long sleep. She'd said at the time he was her one true love and that it had been love's true kiss that had awakened her.

"Stop it," I admonished, laughing at the moment of silliness. We were no longer princess and guard. We were just two people having fun. It was embarrassing sure, but it was fun too. I'd never done anything like this before. Such behavior was not acceptable at the castle.

"You know, this calls for a drink," He picked up the coat I'd left on the arm of the sofa and threw it at me.

"Put your hood back on, we're going out."

I'd barely had time to cover my head when he took my hand and led me outside. It had gotten considerably darker, even though it wasn't even dinnertime yet. The bright skies I'd walked to town in were now filled with ominous dark clouds.

Milo noticed it too. "Looks like a storm is coming, but we have time for one drink. I'll walk you home after that. What do you say?"

Looking at the clouds, I guessed his estimate was wrong. The storm was almost upon us, but I'd rather walk home in the rain with him than through the dark streets without him. That way, if my mother caught me, I could tell her I'd been out on a date with Milo. She'd be more upset that I hadn't broken up with him than me wandering through the streets by myself.

The inside of the Dragon Roost Inn was darker than the thick clouds outside, making it clear that I wouldn't be recognized. I'd be surprised if anyone would see me at all. All I could see were various outlines of the customers.

"What do you want?"

I shrugged. I'd never been in a bar before, and the only alcoholic drink I'd ever partaken in was champagne at royal parties. "I don't even know what to order. You choose for me."

He left me in a booth and headed to the bar. It was quiet enough that he was served right away. The barmaid, a pretty woman with big hair and a slim waist, leaned forward. "Hi, Milo. What can I get you?"

"I'll have two beers, please. One for me and one for my friend."

The barmaid turned toward me, and I smiled, although I wasn't sure she'd even see my smile through the gloom, so I waved. She gave me half a smile back before her expression turned like milk gone sour. "Sure. I'll have to bring a keg up though."

I allowed myself a small grin. The poor barmaid was probably crushing on Milo, and here he was with a girl. I wondered how she'd feel if she recognized me as the princess.

I waited in the booth while Milo stood at the bar. Another man took the seat next to him and began a conversation. He talked much more quietly than the barmaid had, but my ears were keen, and I picked up the gist of the conversation.

"Who's the girl, Milo? I thought you were holding out for the princess?" The old man laughed, and I blushed. Milo was holding out for me? He liked me? No wonder he hadn't been angry when I'd told him what I'd said to my mother. Dragon balls. That complicated matters. I liked Milo. He was fun, and yeah, he was cute, but I didn't need a boyfriend. I didn't want one. I wanted to learn who I was before I even thought of sharing my life with someone else. That was the point of this whole endeavor in the first place.

The old man's words didn't seem to faze Milo, though. "It's my new girlfriend. I'd take you over to introduce you, but I wouldn't want to put her off her beer."

Dragon crap! Now he was introducing me as his girlfriend.

The old man laughed again as a flash of lightning struck, lighting the bar for a brief second. I almost screamed as the face of an old woman was illuminated in front of me. A woman with thick wrinkles and barely any teeth. The pub fell into darkness, but the woman was still there, standing just inches from me.

"You are new here," she cackled. "I've never seen

you before."

I tried to catch Milo's attention, but he was deep in conversation with his friend.

"I'm visiting someone," I said, pointing to Milo, hoping she'd get the hint and go away. She was very short, owing probably to the fact that she was hunched right over. There was nothing innately scary about her, but she put me on edge. A shiver ran down my back as she pointed a spindly finger at me.

"You are a woman of great power, but I don't think you know it. You parents. Who are they, Dearie?"

I tried to come up with a lie. She obviously didn't recognize me as the princess any more than Milo's friend or the barmaid had. I was spared having to pull something out of the air as she didn't wait for me to answer.

"Yes. I can see the power in you. It is like nothing I've ever seen before. Those eyes of yours—beautiful, but strange. I wonder if you see the power in yourself? You have a lot of hardship coming up young lady, but I don't doubt you'll fight it. There's something else I see in you, but I can't get a full picture. It's like you are not fully there. There's a lot of you missing. Scattered like leaves in the wind." The crash of thunder shut her up, and then thankfully, Milo returned with two beers in his hands.

He handed one to me. I glanced back up at the old woman, but she was already gone, slipping back into the gloom as quietly as she had appeared.

"Did you see her?" I asked Milo, shivering. He must have walked right past her.

He turned his head to look around the bar. "See who?"

How could he have not seen her? She'd been right

next to me when he slipped into the booth opposite me.

"There was an old lady with a hunch back. She said that I'd have a lot of hardship and that part of me was missing."

"You look fully intact to me," he said good-naturedly, taking a sip of his beer. "It sounds like Gladys. She's crazy but harmless. She seems to think she can predict the future and makes a little cash, but she's a phony. Don't worry about her."

I took a sip of the beer. It tasted like nothing I'd ever tasted before. The cold liquid ran down my throat almost making me forget the old woman's words, but part of what she'd said resonated with me. I'd never felt whole. I'd been loved my whole life. By my parents, my siblings. Even the public kinda, sorta loved me when my mother wasn't around to adore, but I'd always felt that there was something missing. It was probably to do with me being adopted. I guessed most adopted kids felt that way at some time or another, but it was more than that. It was like part of my entire being was ripped away from me. The old woman had hit the nail on the head. I didn't feel whole. I'd never felt that way.

Milo placed his beer down on the table and flipped a beer mat, catching it back in his hand. "I don't often come in here, but occasionally, I'll come in for a drink. What do you think of it?" Milo asked me.

"It's very dark," I observed. "And the barmaid has a crush on you." I left out the part where his friend had mentioned him having a crush on me and the part where I'd overheard him calling me his girlfriend. It was a conversation I was going to have to have with him, but now was not the time.

He spluttered a bit then regained his composure. "Lisa doesn't have a crush on me!"

I glanced over at the barmaid who was very plainly staring at us, her elbow on the bar, supporting her head in her hands. When she saw me looking, she stuck her tongue out and moved away to tend the bar at the other side.

"Really?" My mouth curved up to the side.

Milo raised his hands in the air in mock surrender. "What can I say? I'm irresistible."

Lightning flashed again, illuminating his face. He really was cute with his deep brown eyes and curly brown hair. Freckles dotting the bridge of his nose. In another life, he was someone I could consider as a boyfriend. If I wanted a boyfriend, which I didn't.

"So let's talk about this great love affair we are supposedly having?" he said, his head resting on his hands. "Who asked who out? Have we kissed yet? You know I just told my friend you were my girlfriend. I figured we may as well start the ruse now."

"Oh, Dragon's breath! Don't. It's embarrassing. I'm sorry I ever told you." I was glad of the dark covering the grin on my face. At least, he was honest about telling the old guy I was his girlfriend. It had put my hackles up, but he was just having fun with it...hopefully.

"I'm not. This could be fun."

Yep. Fun. That's what it was.

"You know my mother wants me to break up with you," I said, leaning in closer. "She'll come looking for you, and knowing her, she will warn you off."

A mischievous grin appeared on his face, and as he spoke, he raised an eyebrow. "We should have one last torrid night of passion before we break up then."

"You wish!" I grinned back at him, trying not to laugh. I was having so much fun. No one ever spoke to me this way. I was used to decorum and rules. Drinking beer and talking about torrid nights of passion didn't feature heavily in my daily life.

"I'm engaged to another man," I reminded him. "Or at least, I would be if it weren't for you."

He shrugged as if this piece of information was inconsequential. "So what? You aren't married yet. Let's go back to the castle. I'll tell your mother how you broke my heart into a million pieces and that I cannot live without you."

"You should," I agreed. "She'll probably feel so guilty that she'll find a job for you in another house and send you on your way with a lot of money in your pockets."

We both sobered up at my words. My mother would fire him. She'd have to. She couldn't have an old flame of mine working in the castle while I was engaged to someone else.

"I'm sorry," I continued. "I'd not thought of that before. I won't let her fire you. I'll tell her that it was something and nothing and that we are completely over. I won't give her reason to sack you."

"So you don't want me to tell her about our torrid last night together then?" he asked, picking up his beer again and taking a sip. He left a white mustache of white foam behind on his upper lip.

"Maybe you could keep down the theatrics a little," I grinned at him, moving forward, and wiping the foam off with my thumb. His eyes locked on to mine as I held my thumb up.

"Foam," I explained.

No. I wouldn't let my mother fire him. I'd play down the romance and try to make her see sense about the faery.

I finished my beer, which went right to my head, making me a little woozy. I wasn't used to drinking much at all. The champagne I did get was measured in such small glasses that I usually only got a sip of two. Now, I'd downed a whole pint of the amber stuff.

I opened my mouth to tell him that our romance was only for show and that I didn't want to date him…or anyone else, but a peal of thunder hid my words.

Outside, someone screamed, making me forget what it was I was about to say.

Milo stood quickly, taking my hand in his as all around us, people left their seats to see what was going on. We both ran outside into the street as a dragon shot a breath of fire straight at us. Milo shut the door just in time before we both got barbecued.

My father had been right. The curse was returning. The dragons were back.

4TH JANUARY

I woke up to an urgent knocking on the door. Opening up my eyes, I tried to get my bearings in the unfamiliar room. Next to the bed, a side table held a book about ancient swords. It was a book I would have liked to have thumbed through, but it wasn't mine. Outside the room, another door opened, and then Milo spoke. He wasn't speaking particularly loudly, but just like in the bar, I could hear every word. My hearing was becoming keener with each passing day, though I didn't understand why.

"She's here. She's safe. I'll go get her."

Heavy footsteps sounded, getting closer, and then the door to the room flew open. Pulling the covers up to my neck, my muscles tensed as I recognized the man entering the room.

"Father!"

"Get out of bed!" he ordered, through gritted teeth, his red face scrunched in anger, "Now!"

I'd never seen my father look so angry in his whole life. His knuckles were white where he held his sword, his cape saturated by rain.

When I'd pulled myself from the warmth of Milo's bed, he pointed to the front door of Milo's house, leaving no room for misunderstanding.

"You," he shouted at Milo as we passed. "Get your ass up to the castle. If you don't have a horse, one of the guards will take you." He nodded to one of the castle guards who grabbed Milo's arm and began to drag him to the door.

Outside, wind blew torrential rain right into my face, making it difficult to see. The storm of last night was still going strong. I was almost pushed into the black carriage, and when the doors were closed, I was finally able to speak.

"This isn't what it looks like, Daddy," I said, reverting back to the name I'd called him as a child.

"I'll tell you what it looks like," he bellowed, slamming the curtains of the carriage shut. "While the dragons were rampaging through Zhore, you were here with some strange man. Sleeping in his bed, no less! Your mother is so unwell over the stress that she's been ordered to go to bed by the court physicians."

My mother was unwell? I knew staying out would have worried her, but I didn't want to hurt her.

"I'm sorry, Father. I was only in town to talk to Milo. Mother asked me to break up with him and..."

My father grimaced and drummed his fingers on his knee. "Talk? In his bed? Please, Azia. It didn't look like you were breaking up with him to me. I wasn't born yesterday."

"But I..."

"Save it for when we get home. I'm in no mood to talk to you right now. I've been out all night knocking on doors looking for you. I thought you'd been taken. That's what they did, you know. The dragons. They took people. Young girls were their favorite."

My heart dropped. Of course, he would come to that conclusion. "I'm sorry, Daddy."

He huffed and turned away from me.

We made the rest of the journey in silence, anxiety eating me up all the way. I wanted to know everything about the dragons, such as, if my father knew why they had come down from the mountains and if anyone was hurt. I had to be patient and wait, and all the time, I knew Milo was behind us on horseback, being forced to come with us.

I tapped my toe against the carriage floor as the anxiety of the situation threatened to take over. My father must have been aware of it, but he didn't say a word. Maybe he couldn't hear it over the staccato beat of the pouring rain hitting the carriage windows. After what seemed like an age, we arrived at the castle. The portcullis shut behind us, only letting the guards through, though I couldn't say why. If the dragons were still active, it would be easy for them to swoop into the open courtyard. As it was, we only had the rain to contend with as we trooped from the carriage to the castle entrance hall. I followed my father, and behind me, Milo was brought in flanked by two other guards.

"Father, please let him go," I begged. "He's done nothing wrong. He was protecting me; that's all."

"Is this the young man you spoke of yesterday?" My mother's voice drifted across the hall. I turned to her, and my heart lurched. My father had said she was ill, but nothing had prepared me for the sight of her. Her usually flawless face was marred with blotchy skin, and dark circles painted the skin under her eyes. Her usually perfect hair resembled a bird's nest, something that I'd never seen once, and she looked about to pass out. I ran to her, afraid she might fall without assistance.

"You should be in bed," my father said, taking her other arm. She swayed a little in his arms.

"I couldn't go to bed knowing Azia was outside. I'm just tired; that's all. Thank you for bringing my girl home."

A tear fell from her bloodshot eyes, and she brought us both in for a hug. This was more disconcerting than the blotchy face. My mother never lost it in front of people, and as far as I could tell, half the guards were currently in the entrance hall, most of them with swords trained on Milo.

"Sorry to interrupt your majesties, but can someone tell me why my lad Milo here, has fifteen swords at his belly?"

I turned to see the grouchy older guard, who worked alongside Milo. Jack, somebody. He didn't hide the irritation of having his workmate held up.

"I found Azia in his bed," my father announced, both to the guard and to my mother, making my cheeks flame once again.

"So bloody what?" Jack said. A round of titters went round the assembled guards. I'd never been so embarrassed in my whole life. And if my nonexistent love life being blown completely out of context wasn't bad enough, Caspian walked into the room, eating an apple.

"My fiancé has been sleeping with whom?" he inquired, not seeming particularly bothered by the current state of affairs. He wasn't angry, not that he had any right to be, merely curious.

"I've not been sleeping with anyone," I shouted out. "I went into town to see Milo. Mother, you already know we are dating. I was barely with him an hour when the dragons came down. They were spitting fire. Milo very kindly let me sleep at his house until the threat passed. I knew you would be worried for me, but I had no way of letting you know I was safe. I could hardly send a message to you and risk the life of someone. I had to do what everyone else in Zhore did yesterday. I hid." My throat constricted as I spoke, and I was aware that everyone was watching. "And yes, I slept in Milo's bed, but as you saw yourself, Father, when you barged through his door, he wasn't in it. He slept on the sofa all night. He was a perfect gentleman. Now could you please let him go!"

My voice had risen by at least an octave, and I was bordering on hysteria. The whole scene must have looked a sight to any outsiders.

My mother obviously thought the same thing. "Guards, leave the poor boy alone and go and do your jobs. There's enough to do at the moment without holding one of our own up. Alec, did you order this?"

My father looked down at the floor, shame written on his face. My usual stoic father was certainly running the gamut of emotions today. Not that I could blame him. There was a lot going on. He'd certainly never treated me the way he had this morning before. It just wasn't like him, but the strain in his voice was evident with every word he spoke.

"I was worried," he said, turning to me. "I am worried about both of you. Azia, please forgive me. I'm under a lot of stress. The kingdom is going to rack and ruin today, and I acted rashly." He lifted his hand to his brow and began to massage his temples.

I moved closer to him and lowered my voice." It's ok, Father, but I think you are apologizing to the wrong person." I moved my eyes to the retreating guards.

Milo was the only guard in the entrance hall not moving.

My father turned to him. "Young man, please accept my most humble apologies." He held his hand out, which Milo stood forward to accept. It was a great honor to shake the hand of the king, and yet, Milo did it with grace.

"Perhaps we should all sit down and have a talk about everything that's going on," my mother said.

"Milo, please be our guest, and Caspian, you'll join us for tea?"

"Delighted," he purred, giving me a wink, which brought a bitter taste to my mouth. I was close to socking the guy in the face, but I held back. I was a princess, after all.

"I'll go and fetch Milo a towel," I offered, more to get away from Caspian's gaze than anything else. "He's soaked."

Milo followed me to the guest bathroom, and surprisingly, nobody stopped him.

I pulled a white towel embroidered with the castle crest from the cupboard and turned, ready to dry his hair.

He stood there in nothing but underwear, his almost naked body damp from the rain.

My heart pounded against my ribs, and my eyes widened at the sight of him. He was gorgeous. Because he had a cute face and curly hair, I'd not thought of him as someone to have such an amazing muscular body, but clearly, I was wrong. I cleared my throat, pulling the towel to my chest, trying to hide both the flush that was rising up my neck and my heart that seemed to be making an escape for freedom.

"I was going to dry your hair," I choked out.

He took a step closer and bent his head forward a little. If either my mother or my father walked in now, they would both ground me for a month, and Milo would lose his job. It would be pointless pretending this was all innocent when he was mostly naked, and I was rubbing my hands all over his body...his hair. I corrected my internal voice and pulled the towel over his head, trying to ignore the fact that below it, he had no clothes on except his underwear.

If Caspian walked in now, well, that would be another thing entirely. I'd get great satisfaction from seeing his face.

I rubbed Milo's hair vigorously, trying not to let this get any more intimate than it already was. I was already imagining the headlines in tomorrow's newspaper if we got caught. The dragons wouldn't get a mention. Besides, I reminded myself. I wasn't actually dating Milo nor did I want to. I wanted my freedom. Although, I could be persuaded to change my mind given the current situation.

I felt a tug and the towel came away from my hands. Milo quickly wiped down his body and made to get back into his saturated clothes.

"I think we may have a spare uniform. If you like, I can get it for you?" Yeah, please put clothes on before I do something stupid...like drool.

He looked up and gave me a smile. "That would be great, thank you."

When I hadn't moved, he raised his eyebrows.

Now was the time to tell him that I didn't want to date him in real life. Now was the time to mention that I only wanted him for show, for pretend to get out of marrying Caspian. It was unfair to him if he had a crush on me. If he knew that I wasn't ready to date in real life, then he could make up his own mind about whether to carry on the pretense. Now was the time...but he was so breathtaking that I couldn't get the words out.

I left the room and grabbed him a uniform from the storage cupboard off from the entrance hall. I was just about to pass it through the door to him when my mother caught up with me.

"Is Milo in there?"

I nodded, hoping that she wouldn't decide to go in herself to check up on him. Although, knowing my mother, she'd enjoy the display.

"Wonderful," she gave me a smile. "We are in the drawing room. Tell Milo to join us when he's ready."

I passed Milo the uniform through the door and headed to the drawing room, followed a minute or so later by Milo. He looked very handsome in his uniform. He took a seat next to me and took my hand in his, making me squirm. My mother noticed the gesture and pursed her lips, but she made no mention of it. I guess we had bigger fish to fry what with the dragon situation and all.

"Please excuse me," she said, nodding at Milo and trying to pull her hair back into something more presentable. "I was up all night. We have two major problems here. The dragons that affect all of us, including pretty much everyone in the kingdom, and the matter of Azia. That is why I wanted all parties involved here to discuss the matter. As one matter has directly arisen from another matter, I think we should discuss the dragons first. Milo and Caspian, normally, I wouldn't involve anyone outside of family in talks like this. They should be held between my husband and his advisors, but nothing is normal at the moment, and quite frankly, I think the king's advisors are running scared."

"I agree," my father said. "The dragons are definitely a problem we need to address first."

"Was anyone hurt, Your Majesty?" Milo asked. He leaned forward, resting his arms on his knees, showing great interest. By contrast, Caspian sat back and stared out of the window.

My father shook his head as he answered Milo. "No major casualties that I'm aware of, although I'm told there were a number of minor injuries from people tripping over themselves while running away. No one got burned, but I believe luck was involved. Now that the dragons are coming down the mountains, we will have to prepare."

I thought of the dragons that had been peaceful my whole life. Nothing about their sudden appearance made sense to me. Before yesterday I couldn't comprehend the thought of them causing havoc. They were such beautiful creatures, and if I was going to be honest with myself, I envied the way they lived, flying freely over the mountains. Many times throughout my childhood, I'd dreamed of being able to fly with them.

"How do we do that?" Caspian asked lazily. He didn't care one iota that dragons had invaded. He could scoot on back to The Forge whenever he wanted. I only wished he would.

My father put his head in his hands. I'd never seen him look so defeated before. He'd always spoken about how lucky he was to have never had to deal with any big problems during his reign. This was the first time he'd had to prove that he was the man in charge. Unfortunately, from where I was sitting, it looked like he was crumbling. Worry over my mother and then me only compounded everything, hitting him all at once. Without waiting for an answer, I spoke up.

"We need to set up some kind of alert system. A siren or something that could go off whenever a dragon is spotted lower down in the mountains."

My father shook his head. "That's all well and good, but the dragons are not really the main concern.

Before you were born…just before you were born, a reign of terror ended. Everyone over the age of twenty-five or so remembers how awful it was. The dragons were an omen. I can deal with them. I have an army that can go out and kill them all if need be. My men are trained in the art of combat. It's what's coming next that worries me."

The thought of my father's army killing all the dragons brought a lump to my throat. Yeah, they'd rampaged through the capital, but no one had been hurt. Before that, they'd kept to themselves, living peacefully in the mountains.

"Do you really believe that this is an omen?" I asked. I didn't believe in omens, and before this, my father had never been superstitious.

"Don't you feel it?" My father asked, directing his question to all of us in the room. "Something has changed. I can't describe it, but it's like nothing is quite right anymore."

Milo looked at me, and I shrugged.

"He's right," Caspian said, inspecting his nails. "There's been a huge magical energy shift. I'm surprised you felt it as a mere human, Alec."

My father flinched at Caspian's choice of words. Mere human! Who did he think he was talking to?

"I think it was just about time for something to happen," Milo said, diffusing the situation. "It is a blip, and that is all. If you find a way to deal with the dragons, everything will go back to normal."

"Actually," Caspian jumped in. "I cannot disagree more, Mikey. I'm a magic-user, and because of that, I can sense that the vibrations in the air are off. I cannot tell what has caused the shift, but recently, as recently as last week, there was an event that happened, changing the magical atmosphere. I don't know what it was, but there was a massive shift in the magical equilibrium, and I think it will be a mistake to discount it."

"It's Milo," Milo corrected him.

"Hmmm," Caspian replied, unbothered by his deliberate mistake.

Ignoring the fae's rudeness, I thought back to the past week or so. It had been a great week, and nothing about it predicted doom and gloom, as far as I was concerned. First, there was Christmas where we opened the castle grounds for people to join us to celebrate. After that, came my eighteenth birthday, which was mainly spent eating cake and opening presents and, finally, the huge celebration ball we hosted every year for New Year's Eve. No doom and gloom here, just parties and fun. Caspian had to be wrong. He was a manipulator at the best of times, and this was far from that.

"Let's just see how this plays out," I argued. "It could be something and nothing. For all we know, someone decided to climb the Fire Mountains and steal a dragon egg. That would set the dragons off, right?"

"That would be an excessively stupid thing to do," my father remarked, and beside him, my mother nodded her head.

"Yes," I agreed. "It would, but since when were people not stupid? We do stupid stuff all the time."

I purposefully looked at Caspian as I said this, but he'd gone back to gazing out of the window. I wondered for a second if I'd get away with throwing him through it.

My mother stood up, taking the floor between us. My father watched her like a hawk, ready to jump up and catch her in case she fell.

It warmed my heart. If I could guarantee a love like that, I might actually consider marriage. Not to Caspian, but to someone. My eyes caught Milo's and I looked down, worried he'd somehow catch my thoughts.

"The dragons have been coming down the mountain for a while," she said. "Last week, it was over the moorlands; last night, a couple of them rampaged through Zhore. What we don't know is why.

My father answered her. "Historical evidence suggests that it is an omen. Dragons hold a kind of magic that we humans know little about. They have only been known to come down the mountains in times of great stress."

"But it's the dragons causing the stress," Milo pointed out. "Apart from the two instances of them flying low, has anything else happened that could make you think that they are an omen?"

My mother held a hand to her head. "No. Nothing else has been reported. We could treat these as isolated incidents. Maybe, as Azia said earlier, someone was foolish enough to climb the mountains and disrupt them, but for the time being, we all need to be alert and prepare ourselves for the worst."

"I'll get my best men working on a solution to the

problem," my father added, standing up to move nearer my mother. He picked up a glass of water and passed it to her. "I'll get them to ask around and see if they have seen anyone trying to sell dragon eggs. As you all are probably aware, the sale of dragon eggs is highly illegal, but that only drives their value up. It is definitely conceivable that someone decided to flout the law to make some money."

"That seems the best option at the moment, Alec, thank you." She took a sip of the water. "Which brings me to the next matter. Azia, I love you. You are my only daughter, and I want more than anything for you to be happy. However..."—she turned to Milo—"and this is no reflection on you, Milo." Turning back to me. "You cannot marry a guard. I took the initiative to look at his records. He's only been a guard for us for seven months. Probation and training last a year. He is not qualified to run a kingdom. I need someone by your side who can protect you. If he'd completed a little more training, maybe we could consider it."

"I've trained my whole life in swordsmanship, Your Majesty," Milo said. "My father made swords using metal from the mines, and I followed in his footsteps. As well as making them, I learned how to use them."

"Keeping a kingdom safe is not going to be helped by one man with a sword," Caspian uttered dismissively, waving a hand in the air. "A leader has to know how to protect all his subjects, not just the ones he lives with."

"With respect, sir," batted Milo back to him. "I wouldn't think of Azia and her brothers as my subjects if I married her. I'd think of them as family."

Caspian narrowed his eyes, and I could see that the conversation was ruffling his feathers. Good! He deserved it.

"It's the same thing when you are in charge," hissed Caspian.

"He called Remy an Idiot!" I shouted, adding to the argument. "He held a sword to my throat!"

My mother stood in the middle, clutching her ears.

"Enough!" she shouted. "This is just like this last time. People fighting over nothing. It doesn't matter about who is wrong or right in this particular argument. Azia cannot marry a castle guard, and that is final. I'm sorry."

"And I'm sorry," Caspian said, the smug look firmly back on his face. "I didn't mean to be offensive to your son."

I noticed he didn't apologize for what he'd done to me.

"Get out!" she yelled at him. I'd never seen her lose it like she was doing. Caspian stood and gave her a brief nod before walking past her and heading out the door. It would have been a moment of celebration if my mother hadn't chosen that moment to fall to the floor. Both Milo and my father moved to catch her.

"I'm fine, really," she whispered as my father took hold of her and pulled her back into a standing position. "I'm just so tired."

My father and Milo each took an arm, and between them, they helped her out of the room and up to her bed, leaving me alone in the drawing room.

She'd screamed at Caspian, which was good, but she'd also said I couldn't marry Milo, which was bad... kinda. I had no intention of marrying Milo any more than I had of marrying Caspian, but if my mother had forbidden it, surely that meant I still had to marry Caspian. It didn't bear thinking about.

As I pondered over the subject in my head, I moved

over to the window and gazed out as I had done many times in my youth. Looking up, I spotted one or two dragons up by the snowy peaks of the tallest of the mountains. Up there, they looked serene, nothing like the ferocious beast with blazing red scales and a yellow underbelly that had blazed Zhore the night before. It had flown so close to me. Close enough that if I'd wanted to, I could have reached out and touched the tip of its wing. Once it had passed, Milo had taken my hand and rushed me back to his house.

The sound of the door opening again had me turning my head.

"Your mother is asleep," Milo said, standing by the door. He looked at me with a sheepish grin. "I'm sorry our plan didn't work. For what it was worth, I liked being your boyfriend for the past day, and it would have been the greatest honor to marry you."

"It's probably for the best," I sighed. "I've had so much fun with you, and I like you a lot, but I'm not ready to have a boyfriend. I want to see things, explore. I want to know who I am before I share myself with someone else."

"I can understand that," Milo said, taking a seat on the sofa. He picked up one of the untouched biscuits that my mother had brought in and began to chew it. "Maybe we could hang out sometime...as friends?"

A smile twitched on my lips. I could tell that now the pretense was over, it had taken a great deal of courage to ask that.

I sat down next to him on the sofa. "I'd love that. I really did have more fun last night than I remember ever having before."

"Until we were almost eaten by a dragon, you mean?" he teased, casually bumping my side.

"Actually, you running me back to your home and making pancakes for me was my favorite part," I said, remembering the evening before and how we'd stayed up late, eating pancakes with raspberry jam and chocolate sauce. Then I thought back to how I had felt when I was with him. "I felt safe with you," I whispered.

Milo sighed and looked right into my eyes. "It's a shame your mother doesn't feel the same way... I would have kept you safe, Azia."

I put my hand on his. He was warm, and touching him, even in such an innocent way had me wishing for more. "I know you would have. If things were different, maybe..."

"But you have to marry that buffoon."

I laughed at his choice of words. I had a feeling that Caspian would not like to be called a buffoon. He was one, but that didn't mean he had to like it.

I mulled everything over in my mind. "If only there was some way we could make my parents believe we are in love," I said idly. "Maybe if they could see that, they would change their minds."

"I could think of a way," he said softly. I was keenly aware his hand was still in mine.

He tightened his grip, which forced me to remember the night before when he'd introduced me as his girlfriend. This was all too real for him.

"But it can't be real, remember?" I said, pulling my hand back. "I can't. I just can't. I don't want a boyfriend. I'm sorry." I was playing with his emotions and felt dreadful.

Milo nodded. "I understand. No boyfriend. I already told you I get it. I could fake love you all you need and when the time comes... if you change your mind..."

"I won't," I said, a little too quickly. "Not for a long

time anyway. I want to travel first."

"It's fine. I was only teasing you."

He wasn't, and we both knew it.

"Where do we start then?" he said a little too jovially. It broke the tension that had been building between us. Now we were all business. It made things so much easier without worrying about emotions being added to the mix.

Where did we start? How should I know? I knew what love looked like. My parents were like walking Valentine's cards around each other. Songs were written about the love they shared for each other, but how could I replicate it? Everything they did was so intimate. They didn't stop gazing into each other's eyes for a second, and when they thought no one was looking, they'd often sneak kisses. I couldn't do any of that.

"How about we start by holding hands when my parents are around. That would show them we are in love. It would piss Caspian off to boot."

As though I'd summoned him, the fae walked through the door.

Taking me by surprise, lips pressed against mine. Milo pulled me towards him, wrapping one arm around my waist, the other cradling my face. He tasted of peppermint, and as his warm lips moved against mine, I felt myself falling into him, moving closer without the need of his arm to guide me. My mind screamed at how wrong this was. This was no fake kiss. This was as real as it got, but my body ignored all thoughts.

It was only when the door slammed shut, that Milo pulled back.

"That works too," I whispered, my heart hammering in my chest.

Across from me, Milo said nothing at all.

5TH JANUARY

I spent the night fretting over both Milo and Caspian. Yeah, Caspian certainly wasn't happy which gave me a sense of satisfaction. Promised to me or not, I didn't want him, and I'd been very honest about it from the start. Milo, on the other hand, was turning out to be the bigger problem. He'd kissed me for show, but there was nothing fake about the kiss. Echoes of it had peppered my dreams all night, and I could still almost feel the warmth of his lips on mine and the way my body responded to it. My first kiss, ever! It should have been a moment to cherish in my memory, not something that induced heart-pounding guilt. Although thinking about it had my heart pounding for other reasons too.

The whole thing was a mess. Why did everything have to be so complicated?

It was a relief when my father asked me to go out

on a ride with him. At least, I wouldn't be in the castle wondering, which of the two to avoid the most.

After saddling up the horses, we set out into the blistering cold day. Once again, thick white clouds threatened snow.

"Where are we heading, Father?" I asked, cantering out of the castle grounds to the bridge that would take us to the fields.

He galloped a little to catch up. This was something we did often, go for rides together in the warm weather, but today wasn't warm, and I had a feeling this wasn't a casual ride for fun.

"We are heading into Zhore, but first I need to check the base of the mountains." I opened my mouth to ask why when he spoke again.

"I hate superstition, but I cannot deny that the last two incidents involving the dragons have made me nervous."

I cast a side-glance at him. He looked forward, his face set in grim determination, his cheeks already reddening in the blistering cold.

As I breathed out, my breath made its own little clouds. It rarely got cold enough in Draconis to do that. "Do you really believe the dragons will bring about dark times? I don't really see the correlation."

My father shrugged, passing me slightly on his horse. "I don't want to believe it. I consider myself a rational man, but dark magic has ways of getting through. I'm hoping it is merely a human aggravating them that has caused it. That is why we are out today. I've ordered a long fence to be put up along the base of the mountains. It won't keep the dragons out, but it will keep any humans from going in, and hopefully, that will be an end to the problem. The mountain range is thousands of miles around, so I've tasked almost my whole army on it. Let's just hope that our neighbors don't intend to attack, huh?" He laughed mirthlessly.

He meant his words as a joke, but they left unease in my gut as I considered our one true neighbor. On one side of us stood the peaceful kingdom of Badalah. To the south, our kingdom bordered Urbis for a while, but Urbis didn't really count as a kingdom. It was controlled by men in suits and governed all the kingdoms to some extent. Any king or queen could make a law for their own kingdom, but first, that law must get passed by the governors in Urbis before it could be used. To our north and east, rugged coastline stretched for miles bordering the great sea. Badalah would never attack us. Their king, the great Aladdin, and my father had met many times and got on well.

My father picked up the pace once we rode past the pastures and out onto the moors. I raced to keep up with him, but the wind in my face as the first snow began to fall took my breath away. I usually only saw snow on the top of the fire mountains in the deepest part of winter, but every few years or so, a dusting of snow would fall making everything white for a few hours before it thawed and the landscape turned red again. Even the weather, it seemed threatened to prove my father right about dark times coming.

Eventually, we came upon a group of men and women clad in fur coats, working against the weather to erect the fence, which stretched out miles behind them. The few small snowflakes that had begun to fall turned into flurries as my father jumped down from his horse.

"How are things coming?" My father asked what looked to be the man in charge. He was a thickset man with furs wrapped around him tied by a belt that strained.

"It's going to take weeks," the man said gruffly. "If the snow keeps up, it could run into months."

My father glanced up at the sky. At least, the dragons remained hidden from us by the snow-ladened clouds. Pulling my arms around myself to keep out the cold, I listened in to my father's conversation.

"It won't snow for long. It hasn't snowed like this since..."

"Since the dark days," huffed the man. "I know, but I still maintain that this is a waste of our precious time and resources. With dragons attacking, we need to be in the towns and cities ready to fight, not stuck out here in this cruddy weather building a wall that a dragon could fly over."

My father sighed, moving closer to the man. I noticed that the other workers had now stopped what they were doing and were listening in to what my father had to say.

"I've explained my reasoning, Jacob. I don't believe the dragons are coming down here to hurt us."

"Coulda fooled me," Jacob said, folding his arms around his rotund middle. "I suppose they were breathing fire in the main town to keep us all warm, eh?"

Behind Jacob, some of his crew smirked.

My father held firm. "I understand your frustrations, but I've given you a job, and I expect you to do it. Liking it is optional."

I gave my father a silent cheer as he stood up to Jacob. Jacob, on the other hand, scowled, his face sour.

"I'd rather send all my people up the mountain and kill the bloody lot of them," Jacob responded. "If we do it at once, they won't know what's hit them."

My father shook his head and jumped back on his horse. "I've given you my orders. No one is to go up these mountains until we find out why the dragons are coming down. There will be severe consequences for anyone that disobeys my order."

With that, he turned his horse around and began to walk back towards the road that would take us to Zhore.

"Some of the people don't like the way I'm dealing with things," my father admitted once we'd trotted out of earshot of the fence crew.

"I can understand why he is upset, but he had no right to talk to you like that. Besides, I don't like the thought of anyone killing the dragons. This is all some big mistake. I honestly think someone disturbed them."

My father gave a low chuckle. "You really like the dragons, don't you?"

"I think they are misunderstood," I said, tugging the reins to the right to take us on the path to Zhore. "They've been peaceful for over eighteen years. Creatures don't change habits on a whim, not even dragons."

"I hope you're right, Azia," my father answered slowly. "I really do."

We rode in silence for a mile or so as the snow became heavier around us. "Why are we going to Zhore?" I asked.

"I need to show my face there," he explained. "Ninety percent of being a leader is presence. There is little damage, and those with injuries will make full recoveries, but people are scared. They need a leader to let them know that they will be alright."

That would have comforted me if I knew that he thought things would be all right, but he was flailing along with the rest of us.

It took longer than usual to reach Zhore, owing to the blanket of white snow. Despite the weather, hundreds of people came out to see my father, filling the main square like the audience at a somber music concert. While my father took to a stage to tell everyone about the fence being built, I walked around the square, glancing in the shop windows. I'd not prepared myself for the blistering cold and my fingers hurt.

As all eyes watched my father giving his speech, no one bothered me as I walked the perimeter of the square, checking out the shop windows as I walked, hoping to find one that sold gloves.

At the very back corner, away from the stage, I found a shop that looked like I might be in luck. Tucked away down a small dark alley away from the main square, stood a shop with a sign plainly saying Zhore Wool Shop. If it sold wool, hopefully, it would sell things made from wool too.

I headed into the alley, but when I came to the storefront, I saw something that made my heart seize with fright. There in the shop window stood a spindle.

I'd never seen one in real life before, but I knew exactly what it was. My grandfather had ordered all spindles to be burned when my mother was young. Once my father had become king, he'd ordered spindles to be made illegal. It had been a huge controversy at the time, putting a great many people out of jobs, but the people had forgiven him, knowing it was to keep their beloved queen safe. Well, most of them had. We had to import wool from other kingdoms now, and some of the people didn't like it.

Part of me wanted to run away from the thing, pretend it didn't exist, but my rational mind took over.

It was only a spindle, after all. A device for spinning wool. It was not harmful nor dangerous.

Taking a deep breath, I pulled open the door to the shop and walked in. Balls of wool in many colors lined one wall, and throughout the rest of the shop, to my relief were items made from said wool, including a pair of mittens. Picking them up, I headed to the till. Behind the counter, a tall, slim lady watched me warily as I approached. When I placed the mittens on the counter, she broke into a smile. Perfectly straight white teeth filled her mouth, and black-green heavily lidded eyes looked upon me, sending a shiver down my spine. Something about her put me on edge, but I couldn't say what. She was dressed perfectly normally with a purple shawl covering her shoulders, but her eyes bore into mine.

"Is that it, my love?" she asked, her voice brittle and croaky.

"What?"

"The mittens, dear. Is that all you want today?"

"Oh, yes," I said, feeling dazed. I handed over the little bit of cash I happened to have in my pocket and picked the mittens up. That was it. I'd gotten what I'd come for, so now it was time to leave. I'd almost made it to the door when the spindle caught my eye again.

I should have left well alone, but it intrigued me, and I had a strange compulsion to go close to it, to reach out and touch it.

"Is this spindle real?" I asked, turning back to the strange woman.

"Oh, yes, my love. How do you think I come to have so many balls of wool. It's the easiest way to make it."

"But it's illegal," I blurted out. "My grandfather ordered all the spindles to be burned many years ago."

Her expression changed at the mention of my grandfather, but she soon plastered on that white smile again. "Did he? It must have been before I moved here because I don't remember it. Besides. If I burned my spindle, how would I spin my wool? And if I couldn't spin my wool, how would I be able to sell mittens to young ladies such as yourself?"

I shook my shoulders. I didn't want to rob her of her livelihood by telling my father about the spindle. What harm could it do really?

"What harm can it do?" she said almost as if she read my thoughts. "Go and take a closer look. You can see for yourself how harmless it is."

I stepped towards the spindle.

"Go on, touch it."

I jumped. Her voice was right behind me, whispering in my ear. How had she moved across the shop floor so quickly? My mind felt thick with fog, but all I could see was the spindle, and all I could hear were her words.

"Just touch it, my love, and you'll see for yourself that it is nothing to worry your pretty little head over."

Urged on by her words, I held my finger out, ready to bring it down upon the spindle.

"Azia, there you are."

A deep voice made me jump, snapping me out of the fog.

I turned to the door of the shop where my father was waiting. "I've been looking all over for you. What are you doing in here?"

"I was just buying mittens," I said, holding the pair up to show him. My head felt groggy as if I'd only just woken up from a long sleep. I turned back to the woman to thank her for the mittens, but she stood once again back behind the counter, a sour expression on her face. Hurrying out of the shop, I followed my father to where we'd tied up the horses. It was only when we were halfway back that, I realized I'd not pointed the spindle out to my father. Deciding to let it go, I followed my father back to the castle.

When I got home, my mother greeted me at the door. She must have been watching out of the window for our return. She still looked dreadful, but at least, she wasn't in bed any longer.

"I'm sorry I missed you leaving this morning, Azia, darling, but I've had a lovely day with Caspian, and as time is ticking, I really think it's time for you to get to know him."

"He called Remy an idiot," I reminded her. "I don't want to get to know him."

My mother considered this for a second before guiding me back into the drawing room. This time no tray of tea and cookies greeted us. I guess it was so close to dinnertime that she hadn't bothered.

"I spoke to him about that," she said, closing the door behind her. "He says that you misheard him."

"Dragon dung!"

"Azia, please. Keep your voice down and mind your language," she admonished. "That's no way for a princess to talk."

I sat down on the sofa, and she took a seat beside me. "Maybe not, but I heard him perfectly." I knew I had. My mother took my hand in hers, reminding me how Milo had held my hand only yesterday before kissing me on this very sofa.

"As you say," my mother said, taking me away from the thought. "But he's spent a lot of time with Remy today. He even let him touch his sword, and you know how much Remy likes swords."

"He spent time with Remy?" I thought back to the time I'd seen him by the pasture watching Remy and I play sword fighting. He'd looked upon Remy with such disdain. He'd looked at me the same way. As though we were dragon crap on his shoe. Why did he want to marry me so much and why spend time with Remy? I hated to think of my brother playing with that jerk.

"Is Remy alright?" I hardly dared ask.

My mother tutted and brought up her hand. "Don't be silly, Azia. Of course, he's all right. I was watching them the whole time. He only let him touch the hilt of the sword, not the sharp end."

I wasn't thinking about the sword. Caspian used magic that messed with people's minds. Remy was defenseless against him.

"Now, what do you say about you two spending the day together tomorrow?" she asked lightly. "You could do something fun."

Yeah, like garrotte the ass with cheese wire. That would be fun.

"I kissed Milo last night," I stated in the hope this might sway her.

She pursed her lips and narrowed her eyes. The faint hint of laughter lines appeared in her tired face. "I heard," she said brusquely. "You will have to stop seeing him, Azia. It's the only way. Give Caspian a chance, he really has been a dream today, and he's awfully beautiful."

She left me no choice in the matter. What might have seemed like a simple request was not a request at all. It was an order. I nodded.

"Yes, Ma'am." It probably wouldn't be too bad as long as neither of us killed the other. Or if I killed him first. I could pass it off as an accident.

"I'll do as you ask, but that doesn't mean I will come back from our date wanting to marry him."

My mother brought me into a hug. "The way things are going, you may have to whether you like it or not. Now, go along and tell Milo it's over between the two of you. The longer you draw it out, the harder it will be for all involved, and I don't want a mopey guard protecting the castle at a time like this. The quicker he can get over you, the better."

I nodded my head, too depressed to answer, but when I left the drawing room it wasn't Milo I went to see, it was Remy. I needed to know he was all right after his day with the faery. Mother might have not seen anything, but that meant nothing when Caspian was involved. It didn't take me long to find him. He spent a lot of his time in the library. He could barely talk, but he knew how to read. He enjoyed books more than anything in the world. He loved adventure books the most, stories of swashbucklers and pirates. I think it let him escape from who he really was. He could pretend to be free of his own mind and body.

The library was also my favorite room in the house. Bookshelf after bookshelf filled with every book imaginable, from books on the history of Draconis to adventure books that Remy liked to read. I found him laid out on the library floor, a number of books open next to him. When he saw me, a grin crept onto his face.

"Aza, pira." He ran over to me and took one of my hands into his huge bear paws. Picking up the book he'd been reading, he thrust it at me, eager to share today's adventure.

"Pirates, arrgh," I said, making him giggle.

If only all my relationships were as easy as the one

I had with my younger brother. He never asked me for anything beyond reading to him, and he always made time for me.

"Arrgh," he replied, giggling and thrusting a make-believe sword at me.

I jumped back, my hands in the air, which only brought about more giggles.

He seemed ok. Maybe the day with the faery hadn't upset him, after all, and I was worrying about nothing.

"It's nearly time for dinner," I said, picking up some of the books he'd casually dropped all over the floor. "Can you help me put the books back on the shelves?"

He nodded eagerly, and between us, we picked up all the books he'd gotten out and placed them back in their places.

Hollis and Ash were already waiting at the dinner table as Remy and I walked in. Seconds later, my mother followed, hand in hand with my father.

Thankfully, Caspian was nowhere to be seen.

"Azia and Milo sitting in a tree," Ash started, and beside him, Hollis began to laugh as though this was the funniest thing he'd ever heard. Then, of course, Remy started laughing because his brothers were, even though he didn't know why.

"Aren't you a bit old for that?" I accused, throwing him shade across the table.

"Stop it, the pair of you," my mother admonished. "I'm tired enough as it is." She held her hand to her head as my father pulled the chair out for her.

"K.I.S.S.I.N.G.," Hollis added under his breath. It was a good thing my parents adopted me; otherwise, one of these morons would one day be running the kingdom.

After suffering through dinner, I decided to head

back to my room, needing to spend some time to think things through. Everything had suddenly turned so chaotic. I knew that transitioning from a child to an adult was never easy, but this was ridiculous. One week on from my eighteenth birthday and the entire kingdom had gone insane, not to mention my parents. If I'd have known turning eighteen would make everything so weird, I'd have stayed seventeen forever and just spent my days out in the pasture, practicing my sword fighting. My heart fell a little at the thought of it. I'd not been out with my sword in over two weeks. Practicing my sword fighting was the only time when I felt free. With a rush of excitement, I increased my steps, back to my room to pick up my sword. It was only when I entered my corridor that I remembered that Caspian had magicked it away the night he came into my room.

"Dragon balls!" I muttered under my breath.

"On toast?" a voice asked. Milo stood there in his position outside my room. This was his corridor to guard, so it wasn't infeasible for him to be there. The last time I'd seen him, we'd shared the most amazing kiss, and now that he stood in front of me, the nerves began to creep in.

"What?" I asked.

"It's a saying my father used to say. He got it from the dwarves. Dragon balls on toast. It was one of the few he picked up that I can repeat in front of a princess." He gave me a lazy grin

My lip quirked up at the edge, but his humor was not what I needed. I needed to vent my frustration, and fighting - even with an invisible foe was the only way I knew how.

"Are you ok?" he asked, catching my expression. I guess my smile didn't quite extend to my eyes.

"I was going to go and practice my sword skills, but I've er...lost my sword."

A look of comprehension dawned on his face. "Ah, so that's why you've not been out practicing so much lately."

My cheeks colored and I stared at the floor so as to not accidentally look him in the eyes. "Do you watch me a lot out there?"

"I don't make a habit of it, but sometimes I see you out of that window on the end of the corridor there." He pointed to the small round window.

"I thought I was well-hidden around the back of the castle. My parents wouldn't like it if they knew what I was doing, my mother especially."

He stood so close to me that I could barely breathe. The memory of the kiss fluttered into my mind, taking root there and making me want to run away. If only I hadn't enjoyed it as much as I had.

He nodded. "I think you are fine. I doubt any other windows show that exact spot, and your mother rarely comes up here. I've only ever seen her on this corridor once in the seven months I've worked here, and that was when Remy was sick."

"Well, then, I should..."

I pointed to my door. This was ridiculous. He was my guard. Actually, he wasn't even that. He was just one of a number of guards assigned to this particular corridor. I had no reason to feel shy around him...because that's exactly how I felt. Before the kiss, I was so sure I didn't want a boyfriend or husband. Even now, the day after the kiss, I was still sure, but something was different. Before the kiss, this whole thing was a fun game. Now it had turned serious, and like a freight train with broken breaks, I didn't know how to stop it.

He nodded slowly and gave me a look. The look someone gives you when they are being let down. A half-smile didn't quite reach his eyes. It pained me, but what could I do? He shouldn't have kissed me in the first place...and he shouldn't have been so damn good at it.

I closed my bedroom door behind me and breathed out a sigh of relief. I'd not even noticed I was holding my breath. When I'd let my heart rate drop to an acceptable level, I walked over to the window. Outside in the distance, the workers erecting the fence were still going at it. It was probably a different crew. My father said they'd be working day and night until the whole mountain range was fenced in. It seemed such a ludicrous proposition. The Fire Mountains took up the whole northeast of Draconis before they tapered off into the sea. They would need hundreds, if not thousands of miles of fencing. All to stop anyone deciding to climb up them to steal an egg.

I lay back in frustration, wondering what else I could do to calm my nerves. Jumping up, I decided to go for a run.

Outside, the snow was coming down thickly, laying a blanket of fine white powder. Not the best weather to run in, but it was either that or go stir crazy. Breaking into a jog, I lapped the castle three times, before stopping in the hidden space I usually practiced in. An area at the back of the castle that no one had any reason to venture to but me. Glancing up at the round window, on the second floor, I half expected Milo to be watching me from it, but there was no one there.

Bending over to catch my breath, I heard the damp crunch of footsteps on snow. Looking up, I saw Milo standing before me as though thinking about him had made him appear. He was holding the ruby sword. My breath caught at the sight of it.

He held it out to me, the sharp end in his gloved hand.

I looked at him, ignoring the excitement in the pit of my belly. If this was a gift of love, I could never accept it, but there was no expression on his face at all.

Taking the sword from his hand, I once again felt the power in the Dwarves' metal as though the sword and I connected somehow.

"Thank you," I whispered.

"I can only let you take this sword on one condition," he said solemnly. "You are an amazing swordsperson. I've watched you practice, but you lack training. Thanks to your father, I've been trained among the best. Let me teach you. Let me refine your talent and make you the swordswoman I know you can be."

Excitement flooded through me at the thought of it.

"Thank you," I whispered.

I doubted my parents would take too kindly to him training me, and if we got caught, he would surely lose his job. He must have thought the same thing because he took my hand and led me to the wall that surrounded the castle. At the back, a small door led to a wooded area. Together we stole through the door and entered the woods.

I'd never been in these woods before. I had never had reason to, so I let Milo lead me to wherever he wanted me to go. He stopped at an open area where the trees thinned out a little, letting the snow fall lightly through. Inside, a circle was drawn into the snow.

"This is our training area," he said, pointing to the circle. "I came here earlier and set it up."

I raised my eyebrows.

"I knew you'd come," he said with a grin, making my stomach squirm.

Next to the circle on a rock, sat two sets of protective clothes made of leather and metal.

"Will we be safe in here?" I asked. My fear was not for wolves or other creatures, but of a member of the castle staff strolling through and accidentally coming upon us. My mother would pitch a fit if she knew where I was...and with whom.

"No one comes here," he said, throwing one of the protective breastplates at me. "Put that on."

Pulling it over my head, I let it drop, hanging from my shoulders. It weighed me down. This would hamper my movements.

"Is this necessary?" I asked, pulling the buckles tight.

"I'm not going to take it easy on you, and I don't expect you to take it easy on me. I'm not teaching you to dance, I'm teaching you to protect yourself, to kill if necessary. That sword I've given you will slice a limb off as easily as it would slice a tomato. Seeing as I'm partial to all my limbs, I'd say that this is entirely necessary."

His words sent a shiver of nerves running through me, followed by a thrill of excitement. I'd been wanting this from the very first time I'd been allowed to watch my father's men training. The training arena stood within the castle grounds, and after that first time, I'd steal into it and watch them. It was there that I developed my love of fighting. I'd been practicing ever since, first with sticks as pretend swords, and then with the stolen sword from the armory.

Once our protective suits covered us, I picked my sword back up and waited for Milo.

"You're standing wrong," he said, walking toward

me. I let him position my arms and legs, trying to ignore the thrill of electricity running up my legs as he clasped each ankle in turn and moved them so they were about a foot apart.

He worked his way up, moving my body until he was satisfied.

"This is the strongest position. One foot slightly in front of the other, your body slightly twisted. You want to give your opponent the least amount of space to stab you. Hold your sword out in front of you, then swipe it to the side. That is your fighting space. You do not, under any circumstances, want your opponent in that space. I am going to attack you now. Don't worry, the armor will protect you. Your job is not to kill me; it is only to defend that space. I don't want to be able to get anywhere near you. Ok?"

I nodded. It sounded easy. Stop him getting close to me. I'd been doing the exact same thing metaphorically with no luck, but hopefully, I'd do better with the physical stuff. He bowed down, and I followed suit before readying myself in the stance he showed me.

"Go!" he shouted out.

My hand stiffened around my sword. I was ready.

Three seconds later, my sword was on the ground beside me and Milo's lips pecked my own, taking my breath away.

"What was that?" I asked him.

"I stole a kiss," he grinned. "Any other opponent would skewer your heart."

I doubted anyone would be able to find my heart, as it seemed to be doing a rumba around my chest.

Picking up the sword, I readied myself again, gritting my teeth in anticipation.

"Go!" I shouted. He ran toward me and this time

I dodged. He missed, but then from behind, he once again swiped my sword from my hand. When I turned, he stole another kiss.

Trying to keep the amused smile from my face and hide the fact that my whole body was trembling, thanks to his kisses, I picked my sword up once again.

"That wasn't fair. You cheated."

"I'm trying to kill you, remember?" he said, dancing around me. "I'm your enemy. Do you think I care if you think I cheated? I am alive, and you are dead."

"You really are going to kill me at this rate," I huffed, taking up the stance again. We practiced for hours, taking it in turns to "kill" one another. By the time our only light was starlight, he'd given me one hundred and thirty-three kisses. I'd not managed to strike him once.

"Let's call it a night," Milo said. "It's dark, and I have to get home." He placed his sword on the stone to pull his armor off, and that's when I saw my chance. Swiping his feet from under him, I elbowed him in the side so he toppled over. Without giving him time to recover, I dropped on top of him, pinning him to the ground below, my legs straddling his stomach. The tip of my sword rested right over the metal plate covering his heart."

"I killed you," I whispered.

"You cheated," he responded. "I'd already put my sword down."

"I'm your enemy out for the kill," I said, echoing his own words from earlier. "Do you think I care that I cheated?" I lowered my sword to his side and took my own victory kiss. This time it was not just a peck on the lips.

6TH JANUARY

"Let's go for a walk, shall we?" The fae held out his hand for me after breakfast.

I looked toward my mother, who yawned, then when she caught me looking, nodded her head.

"Fine," I capitulated. There was no way I was holding the guy's hand, though. He could walk next to me…or behind me…or off a cliff. Whatever.

"Interesting weather we are having," Caspian mused as we stepped out into the snow. "I was under the impression it barely snows in Draconis, but it's worse than a Forge winter."

"Hmm," I sighed non-committedly. Who cared what the weather in The Forge was like. "Why don't you head back there?"

I picked up my pace as we headed across the bridge out onto the pastures.

"You've not liked me from the start, but there's no reason not to," he began.

I cut him off. "Really? Because I can think of at least three reasons off the top of my head, and I'm sure if I thought a bit longer, I could come up with more."

"Please stop. I don't like playing games."

I turned to face him, annoyance filling me. He was beautiful without the sneer he usually wore, which put me off guard, but I was too angry to let a bit of gorgeousness get in the way. "Who's playing games? I've been very honest from the start with you. That's not game-playing."

I brought my hands up to my hips and gave him my best, prove me wrong look. Unfortunately, to him, the challenge was a red flag to a bull, and he was nothing if not bull-headed.

"The romance with your guard is fabricated, and that feels a lot like game-playing to me," he growled, bringing his face close to mine. His disdain for me was overwhelming, though I could also see desire in his eyes. I don't know which annoyed me more. "If I wanted to be messed around by women, I could have stayed in The Forge."

I swayed slightly on my heels and resisted the urge to kick him. "How did you... never mind. It doesn't matter. If you are somehow reading my mind, you'll see that I don't want to marry you." He'd also see that my fake romance with Milo was becoming more real by the day and the whirl of emotions that went along with that. It wasn't Caspian I saw when I closed my eyes at night. It was Milo. That was a problem to deal with later. Right now, dealing with Caspian was taking up all of my energy.

He narrowed his eyes. "I don't need to read your

mind to know that. You've made it very clear. I also don't need to be a mind reader to know about you and Milo. When I saw you kissing him the other night, you seemed genuinely shocked. If you two were dating, why would you be so shocked to be kissed by him? It was only a hunch up until now, but you've confirmed it. I can't read minds, by the way. Manipulate them a little, but not read them. Very few

fae can, but I can read clues. I like to watch people."

He smiled languidly as he caught me out in my lie. Dragon shit! I gritted my teeth and sucked in a deep breath, which froze in my lungs, causing me to cough.

The faery waited for me to stop coughing before continuing to speak. "Look, I know we've gotten off on the wrong foot, and I also know that it's mostly my fault."

"Mostly?" I questioned raising an eyebrow, tears running down my face from the coughing. I wiped my eyes on the back of my sleeve, hoping he didn't think the tears were something to do with him.

"Ok," he relented, putting his hands in the air. "It's all my fault. I've been insensitive and rude, and I've made mistakes. I came here because your father asked me to. He thought that he owed me for something I did for him a long time ago. That's why he offered you to me."

"You make it sound like I'm a pig in a meat market," I barked, narrowing my eyes at him.

"Hardly, but your father does owe me, and he thought I'd make a good husband for you."

Ignoring the squeezing sensation in my stomach, I asked him through gritted teeth why my father owed him.

He beckoned me onwards, away from the castle.

"We were friends many years ago, and back then, he asked me for magical help to get through the enchanted brambles that surrounded the castle."

I turned to him. "That's not what I was told. The curse had ended anyway. That's why he was able to get through the brambles when so many others had failed before him. He told me that cutting through them was easier than he'd been led to believe."

The fae nodded thoughtfully. "Maybe that's true, but why? What was it that ended that curse if not me? Only a couple of weeks before your father attempted it, someone died trying the exact same thing. Many people lost their lives in the attempt to save your mother. Your father found it difficult, but as you say, the brambles were dying. What was it that changed? That curse was never meant to be a hundred-year curse. It was meant to last forever, a testament to Derillen's power."

"Derillen?" I'd never heard the name before. "Who is Derillen?"

The fae kept his eyes ahead, looking into the distance as he spoke. "It seems I've spoken out of term. If you do not know that name, it is not my place to enlighten you."

Anger coursed through me. Why was it that every time I spoke to this man, I wanted to stick a sword through his ribs? I thought back to the dragon sword carefully hidden in my room and wished I'd had the forethought to bring it with me.

"Why won't you tell me?"

"It is not my place to," he said. "There is no point in getting angry with me. It is not I that has spent your whole life keeping secrets from you. Perhaps you should ask your parents."

I stalked off ahead in the snow. New snow dropped

constantly, transforming the landscape into a winter wonderland. I watched my breath in the frigid air, transforming me almost into the fire-and-smoke-breathing dragons everyone feared so much.

"Let's talk about something else," Caspian said, catching up. "We are to be married soon, and I would like to find some common ground with you."

I huffed. "I can't think of a single thing the pair of us have in common." I trudged ahead of him again, but something stopped me. As if a net had been thrown over me, I felt myself being pulled back, my feet making tracks in the snow.

When I ended up back next to him, he waved his hand and the invisible ropes pulling me disappeared.

I glared at him, ready to give him the tongue-lashing he deserved, but he spoke first.

"Actually, I think we have more in common than you know."

"Give me one example," I fumed, folding my arms across my chest.

He cocked his head thoughtfully before bringing his hand back up.

I felt the ropes around me again, but this time they crushed my arms to my chest and locked my legs together. Falling into the snow, I fought against the invisible bonds that had taken hold. Beside me, Caspian held out his hand, his fingers splayed, his mouth silently working his magic. If I had my sword, the dwarf magic in the metal would cut through the strands of magic like butter, but I didn't. I was defenseless.

"What are you doing?" I screamed, letting snow enter my mouth. Swallowing back the freezing water, I fought against my magical chains as the fae watched on with interest.

"I'm not trying to hurt you, but the more you move, the more painful it will be. Hold still and fight back properly."

Fight back properly? When I was free of his magic, I was going to knock his block off.

I squirmed against my binds as they cut into my clothes and bit into my skin. As soon as I became still, the pain subsided, and the ropes or chains loosened a little. More squirming and they bit down again.

"Let me go," I hissed through chattering teeth as the snow began to melt into my trousers, soaking me to the skin.

"Make me," he answered back, his teeth gleaming from the wide smile he gave me.

They would be the first to go, I mused, as I contemplated punching him right in his beautiful mouth.

"You aren't even trying," Caspian goaded, tapping his toe in the soft snow as he waved his hands around to keep the magic flowing.

"What exactly do you want me to do?" I hissed through chattering teeth.

He bent down until his face was close to mine. Not close enough for me to head-butt him, but close enough to see how much he was enjoying this. "I've seen something in you that excites me, but it looks like I'm going to be let down. I'm very rarely wrong, but it has been known to happen."

"What are you talking about?" I screeched. I was going to get hypothermia if I wasn't careful. Or if he wasn't.

"Magic, Azia. I'm talking about magic. I can feel it in you, but I wonder if you can feel it yourself." He pulled back his hand, and I found myself rising into the air.

When I was about six feet from the ground, he began to spin me around.

The world tumbled about me as I spun in the air.

"Stop it," I yelled as darkness appeared at the edge of my consciousness, threatening to make me black out.

"Make me," he yelled back.

Anger surged through me like never before. Fury raged, warming my belly. Make him? I was going to kill him, the first chance I got, my mother and my marriage be damned.

The warmth became energy, which became something else entirely. In front of me, the world toppled end over end, the mountains, becoming Caspian and then going back to the mountains again. While inside, I burned with sizzling energy.

With a primordial scream, I let the energy go before it burned through me. With a bump, the soft snow flew up beneath me, and I landed on the ground. With shaky legs, I stood. It took all my energy not to fall over again, thanks to the dizziness that engulfed me.

"I will murder you!" I muttered, holding a shaky finger out to Caspian's face. My feet wobbled, wanting to topple beneath me, and it took everything I had not to let them.

The fae had the gall to laugh.

"I wasn't wrong. I didn't think I was. You are magic."

His words pierced the fog in my brain.

"What?"

"You have magic in you. I didn't let you go. You fought against my magic. Now, I don't like to brag, but I'm pretty powerful. Not the most powerful in all the kingdoms, but it would take a lot of magic to be able to cut through those bonds that held you. You did that, my dear, not I."

"I'm not magic," I whispered, faltering.

"How do you know?" he asked, brushing my hair back over my ears. "You don't have the pointed ears, so you are not fae, but I suspect your magic is powerful. Maybe even more so than mine. You were adopted, so you don't know your birth parents. How do you know that you are even human?"

"Of course, I'm human!" I shouted at him, then proceeded to throw up all over his shoes.

It took a good few minutes of sitting in the snow before my head stopped spinning entirely. While I sat with my head in my hands, my ass getting soaked by the wet snow, Caspian performed spell after spell over his puke-covered shoes, trying to make them clean again. Eventually, he waved his hand over them and made them disappear, before conjuring a pair of boots from thin air.

When he'd put them on, he waved his hand at me. Below me, a picnic blanket appeared, and a warmth came over me, drying my clothes out immediately. I went from shivering and cold to warm and cozy in a second. He sat beside me and conjured up a large umbrella to stop the snow falling upon us. When he'd done that, he performed his last piece of magic and set out a spread of food for us.

Now that I'd calmed down and my head no longer spun, I decided to let him live. At least, until we ate. I'd consider it again once the food was gone.

He poured me a glass of wine and handed it over.

"A celebration for your first performance of magic. The fae always celebrate a child's first act of magic. Usually, it is when they are young, three or four perhaps. But I think that this merits a celebration even if you are not fae."

"I am human," I reiterated, taking a sip of the wine. The sweet nectar ran down my throat, warming me from the inside out.

The fae shrugged. "Maybe, maybe not, but how do you know?"

He'd already asked me that. It was obvious I was a human. What else could I be? "Because I look human. I feel human, and as you pointed out, I don't have any markings of being a fae. Apart from my title of princess, I'm as ordinary as it gets."

The fae shook his head. "That isn't true. I knew you were far from ordinary from the first moment I saw you. Magic attracts magic, and I felt a strong attraction to you that had nothing to do with sexual attraction. It was more than that, something magnetic. Now I'm not saying that I don't feel sexual attraction to you too. I do, but this is most definitely something different."

I blushed at his words. He was so forthcoming. I chose, however, to skip over the sexual attraction part and move back to the magic part of the conversation. "I only have it on your word that I am magic. I don't feel magic. You could have stopped your own magic, and I would have fallen into the snow exactly the same."

"True," he said, picking up a sandwich, "But I didn't. You did it all by yourself. Only someone of greater power than mine would have been able to do that."

I shook my head. "Surely, if I was magic, I would have noticed before now?"

"Not necessarily. Your power is greater than even I expected when I first met you. When you cut those bonds spinning you, I felt the heat in your magic. If I wasn't as strong as I was, it would have sent me flying. It might be worth talking to your parents. There are obviously things they haven't told you. I don't even know all the answers myself. When you were adopted, there was an announcement in the papers. It was only a matter of weeks after they married. They hadn't even gone on honeymoon yet. I asked your father once why they had adopted you so soon. They were still very young, only eighteen themselves. They had their whole life ahead of them. Your father wouldn't say more than the newspapers told me. Then, when they did go on honeymoon, your mother fell pregnant with your eldest brother. They became a family very quickly. I wonder if that had something to do with the questions you ask."

I contemplated his words. Like any other orphan, I'd thought about my birth parents from time to time, wondered who they were. I'd been told very little, though my mother had been honest with me from the start about it. At least, I thought she had been until today.

The reason I'd never probed further about my birth parents was that I simply didn't want to know. I was the princess of Draconis, the heir to the throne. How could I have come from better than that? I couldn't. I had two loving parents, three brothers and I lived a good life. I had fine clothes, I traveled a lot, and the pain of being given up when I was a baby? Well, I'd buried that deep long ago.

"If I'm magic, why can't I do anything?" I challenged. I waved my hand out in the same manner that he had as if to prove my point, and nothing happened.

"Magic is not just something people can automatically do. It is a learned skill even by those who possess it. You have to learn to channel it. Didn't you feel it when you broke my bonds?"

I thought back to the warmth in my belly. I had felt something. Something I'd mistaken as anger.

"Here," he said, throwing me an apple. "Turn this

into an orange."

I looked at the apple. It looked like any other apple, with shiny red skin. I could no more have turned it into an orange than I could have turned it into a horse.

"No."

"Look at it and envision the shape of it becoming more spherical. Imagine the color changing. Imagine a citrusy smell. Imagine holding an orange in your hand. And when you can see the orange in your mind's eye, do whatever it was that you did back there when you saved yourself from my clutches."

"I imagined stabbing you through the heart with my sword," I answered.

The fae gave a big belly laugh. "If you need to do that to make your magic work, then do it. Once you've mastered it, it will come a lot easier to you."

He pointed back to the apple in my hand. I did as he instructed. Imagining an orange was easy; what I struggled with was bringing all the energy back to my core. Anger at Caspian hurting me had set me off, but now I was no longer angry. Curious, unbelieving and slightly annoyed perhaps, but no emotion big enough to cause the same reaction as last time.

I pulled everything I had into myself. Closing my eyes, I could hear Caspian's words of encouragement. I no longer wanted to kill him, but I remembered how I felt when I did. The energy began to build, and this time, I let it, keeping it churning in my stomach. When I could take it no longer, I channeled it down my arm to the fruit. A bang, followed by something wet splattering my face caused me to open my eyes.

Caspian was covered in mashed up bits of apple, as was I. A black scorch mark was all that was left of the apple in my hand.

"Maybe you need a little more practice," Caspian said and began to laugh again. This time I joined in. "That's it for today. Learning magic is exhausting work, and you need to rest."

He wasn't wrong. My entire body ached with the effort I'd put in. He pulled me up by my hand and magicked the picnic, the umbrella, and the wine away. The snow that had been drifting around us, once again, began to fall on our heads.

"Do you want to go back to the castle or do you want to go on that walk we had planned?"

I glanced over his shoulder. The castle was not far behind him. We'd barely made it to the pasture where we first met. I surprised myself by answering that I did want to walk. Snow was so uncommon here, and now that I was warmed by both Caspian's magic and the wine, I found I wasn't ready to go back to the castle yet. Exhaustion aside, I wanted to see what else I could do. Exploding an apple was one thing, but it had no practical use.

"I told you we had something in common," Caspian said, taking hold of my hand. This time I let him.

"You and I are one of a kind."

"You said that I wasn't fae." I flicked my hair behind my ear to show him my perfectly normal-looking ears. "Remember?"

"Maybe, but you are a person of magic. It's up to you to decide if you want to find out exactly what it is you are. Humans don't have the ability to perform magic. If you ever see a human doing that, if you check his family tree, you'll find something in there. Maybe you are a witch."

"A witch?" A shiver passed through me. Witches had a bad reputation, although there were some known to be good. They used the magic of the earth in their spells. I didn't feel like I was pulling magic from the earth. Whatever my magic was, it came directly from me.

We walked lazily across the snow-covered fields, and for the first time since meeting him, I felt comfortable in his presence. We walked a couple of miles until we were at the base of the Fire Mountains, close to where I'd been with my father. The fence stretched as far as the eye could see in both directions, disappearing into the white of the snow.

Now that I could feel the magic, and understand what it was, I was eager to use it more. "I want to do more magic. I want to learn to do more than change fruit."

"Aren't you tired," he asked, but I could see the amusement in his eyes.

"Yes," I admitted, "but I want to keep going."

"Ok," he capitulated. "What is it you want to do? Make me fall in love with you, maybe?"

I pulled a face, I was sure was not attractive.

"You can't conjure love, no matter how much you'd like to," he added after taking a look at my face.

"That's good to know. I wasn't sure if I'd be able to hold myself back otherwise." I replied.

He gripped my hand tightly before letting it go. "Oh, I do enjoy a spot of sarcasm. What is it you want to learn then?"

I wanted to learn to fight. If I could learn with magic, the same I could learn with a sword, I'd be an invaluable member of my father's army whether he liked it or not. I didn't just want to learn, I wanted to be the best.

"Teach me magical combat."

Caspian sighed, not as excited about the idea as

I was. “You could have asked for anything. How to conjure money, jewels...anything.”

“I have all the money and jewels I want. I’m a princess,” I said, holding my hands up and waving them down myself. “Jewels hold no interest for me. Knowing how to defend myself in times of trouble. That’s what I want to know.”

“Defense?” He sighed again. “I suppose teaching you how to defend yourself is not the worst thing I could teach you. Fine, we’ll have a magical duel. Whatever you do, do not use your magic to kill. You are stronger than me, and I don’t want any accidents.”

“You’re good. I’m not feeling as murderous as I was a couple of hours ago.”

“How reassuring. Let’s aim to mark the other’s skin with paint. That way, no one will get hurt, and a winner will be clear. Pick a color.”

I thought back to the ruby sword. “Red.”

He nodded. “I’ll be purple. Stand over there and face me. When I say go, I want you to conjure little balls of red paint and fling them at me.” He waved his hand, and a clock appeared from nowhere and hung in thin air. “When the clock counts down to zero, time is up. I’ve set it for ten minutes. The winner is the one least covered in paint. Do you understand?”

I nodded and readied myself, getting into the stance that Milo had taught me the night before. I might not have been fighting with swords, but I was most definitely fighting, and I planned to win.

“I’ll give you a few seconds start, to get to grips with everything, but once you take your first shot, it’s every man for himself.”

He’d barely finished the sentence when an explosion of color hit his chest. Red bloomed, looking like a knife wound. With a grin, he pulled back his hand and launched his own paint. Pretty soon we were running around, launching paint at each other, giggling like schoolchildren. The snow resembled an abstract painting, but I was having too much fun to care. I screamed loudly, laughing as each blast of purple hit me. It was hard to tell who was the most covered in paint. Battlefield fatalities were less bloodied than him, and although I knew his blood was nothing but harmless paint, it didn't make the effect any less horrific. At least, the paint on me was purple and couldn't be mistaken for blood. If anyone came upon us, they wouldn't know what to think. Not that I was worried, the weather was taking a turn for the worse, and the snow fell more thickly. I was about to declare a tie when Caspian volleyed a number of purple globs of paint at me. I screamed again and readied myself to give back as good as I got, when the sky lit up a deep red, coloring the falling snow. Seconds later, a deep roar filled my ears. Caspian ran towards me and grabbed my hand just as the dragon appeared through the clouds. It's giant wings displaced the snow as it opened its mouth to roar again. The smell of burning sulfur filled the air as we ran, the dragon flying behind us.

"Do something," I screamed as another dragon appeared in front of us, blocking our path. The base of the mountains was to our left, which meant the castle was somewhere in front of us, but we'd walked so far, and it was impossible to see through the falling snow. There was nowhere to run to and nowhere to hide.

A blast of fire heated my side as we tried dodging the dragon in front of us. Above us, the snow stopped ominously. I didn't need to look skywards to know it was because yet another dragon was above us, blocking it.

"I can't," Caspian yelled back. "Dragon hide is thick. No magic can pass through it. If they see us fighting back, they'll barbecue us for sure."

But what else was there to do? We were surrounded by them. It was fight or die, and I wasn't ready to die yet. Pulling in the magical energy was easier this time. I had fear coursing through me, which was enough emotion to fuel the magic. So far, my magic had only exploded apples and conjured paint, so this time I'd have to dig deep. Neither of those things would save us from a pack of dragons. I wished for my sword. That would be the most useful, but no amount of wishing or trying to conjure it worked. The magical energy burned as it swirled around inside me, getting hotter and hotter with each passing second. It looked like I was going to fight fire with fire.

I pointed upwards, and a jet of fire rose into the sky, like a beacon, lighting up the snow and showing me just how serious our problem was. There weren't just three or four dragons. There were hundreds of them. The flames rose higher, but then something astonishing happened.

The dragons on the ground lowered themselves so their bellies touched the snow and the ones in the air came in to land, making the earth move every time one of them landed. Pretty soon, we were surrounded by dragons. When my magic finally gave up, my senses kicked in. We were in the dead center of hundreds of dragons, any one of which could kill us in a second.

My mind was in fight or flight mode, but my feet wouldn't move, tethered to the ground, not by magic, but by fear.

Caspian stood next to me, unmoving.

"What is happening?" I whispered

"I don't know. I've never seen anything like this before." The dragons nearest to us lowered their heads, and Caspian clasped my hand. We began to walk slowly through them, neither of us daring to run in case it spooked them. As we passed by, more of them lowered their heads to the snow. They weren't sick. Their eyes were open and followed us as we passed, but none of them made a move to hurt us. The ones behind us took to the skies, harmlessly flying upwards and the ones in front continued to bow. It was only when we had the castle in sight, and the dragons were long behind us that we began to run, stopping only when we were at the very edge of the pasture.

My nerves were wrecked, and it wasn't helping that Caspian was still covered in red paint and melting snow.

He was a picture of water and blood.

He waved his hand, and the pair of us cleaned up instantly.

"Thank you," I wheezed, not knowing what else to say. "Did you use magic on those dragons?"

He shook his head. "I told you, dragon-hide is impenetrable by magic. The only magic I saw was yours. What did you do?"

I shrugged my shoulders, aware that I was still shaking. "I didn't do anything either. I shot a flame up into the air."

"Well, that flame got those dragons to bow down to you. I've never seen that before. It's not natural for dragons to act that way. You need to speak to your parents about where you came from. You are more powerful than even I first thought. Not even the most powerful mages can control dragons, but, sweetheart... looks like you just did."

He held out his hand to me, but I couldn't take it.

I'd enjoyed the day. Well, up until the point a hundred dragons swooped in, but I still didn't want to marry him. Enjoying a day out was one thing. Forgiveness of the things he'd said and done, another, but the feelings that were growing for Milo were something else. I couldn't walk into the castle hand in hand with Caspian in case Milo saw. I'd not given any promises to anyone, but I had a feeling I was giving my heart to Milo.

"I can't. I'm sorry."

His face twisted into a sneer. "I hoped you'd changed your mind. We are getting married as per your father's decree whether you want to or not. I just hoped you would actually want to."

He stalked on ahead, making me run to catch up.

We were in the entrance of the castle before I caught up to him. I needed to thank him for such a nice day and for telling me something about myself that I hadn't even known. Guilt squeezed my heart, and I knew sorry wasn't enough, but I wanted to say it to him anyway. My mother never gave me the chance. She must have heard the door, and she came to greet us before I had chance to apologize.

"Did you have a nice day, you two?" she beamed.

Before I had the chance to speak, Caspian answered for me.

"There is no reason that Azia cannot marry me now. While we were out walking today, she told me that her romance with Milo was fake. The pair of them made it all up to fool you."

I glared at him with murder in my eyes. How could he do this? Just as I was beginning to like him.

7TH JANUARY

Overnight, the snow had softened, and the sky was clear when I woke up. I'd spent half the night angry at Caspian and the other half waiting for Milo to arrive. He'd not worked the day before, nor had he done a night shift. Therefore, he would be working today. I'd not mentioned anything to my parents about what happened with Caspian the day before. Only he knew about my magic, and only he knew about the dragons. I should have told my parents, at least, that part. My father should know, but I'd gone straight to my room and skipped dinner. After a couple of hours trying to do magic again, I'd finally given up and fallen asleep. I would tell my father about the dragons soon, but it was Milo I wanted to tell first. I wanted to show him my magic too.

The clock hands moved excruciatingly slowly as I waited for them to tick down to nine am when his shift usually started. The fear of him having been fired because of what the fae had told my mother rendered me almost immobile, but at five minutes to nine, I caught him walking past my room to start his shift. I pulled him into my room and closed the door behind me, locking it in case Dahlia or anyone else came to find me.

He kissed me, pulling me into his arms and the anxiety I'd been feeling all night melted away.

"I don't want a boyfriend," I murmured, but it was hard to really push the point home when I followed it up with another kiss.

"Are you ok?" he asked, pulling back, a quizzical expression on his face.

"Yes," I lied. "Why shouldn't I be?"

He glanced around the room. "I can smell burning. Was there a fire?"

I laughed. "Something like that." I lowered my voice. "I went for a walk with Caspian yesterday. My mother insisted," I added when his face dropped. "Anyway, the dragons came down the mountain yesterday. They surrounded Caspian and me."

Milo's eyes widened. "Woah, Azia! Thank the gods that you are all right. How did you escape? Did Caspian help you?"

I could see in his eyes that he didn't want to hear that Caspian had saved me. Luckily for him, he didn't have to.

"I saved us."

Before I could elaborate, the sound of my mother's voice came drifting through the door.

"Azia?"

Pushing Milo to one side quickly, I opened the door a crack.

"Sorry, Mother," I said, feigning a yawn. "I only just woke up."

"Azia, you know I deplore tardiness and breakfast has been laid out for ten minutes."

"I'm on my way," I singsonged, eager for her to leave should she see Milo behind me.

She held a hand to her mouth to cover a yawn, then turned and left, and I closed the door again.

"Sorry," I whispered, turning back to Milo. "I'll tell you after breakfast." I gave him a quick kiss then sprinted down the corridor after my mother.

In the dining hall, only my brothers were eating. "Where is Mother?" I asked Ash. "She only just came to get me."

Ash swallowed his cereal before addressing me. "Mother said she was tired and headed back to bed. Father is busy, and your boyfriend is with him. Something to do with dragons." He went back to his breakfast.

I assumed by boyfriend he was referring to the fae. I guess he told father about the dragons. I was surprised my mother hadn't knocked my bedroom door down to check if I was all right. I suspected that no one had told her. My father never kept secrets from her, but she'd been looking so ill recently that he probably didn't want to burden her.

At least, it solved the problem of having to tell my father about the dragons. Caspian was good for something, after all. When breakfast was over, I ran back upstairs.

"I'm glad you're here," Milo said when he saw me. He pulled me away from Jack and spoke again. "I've just been called to go outside. Your father knows about the dragons and wants most of the guards on outdoor duty today. I volunteered to check out the woods. I thought you might want to join me."

He looked at me so earnestly that I didn't have the heart to say no. Not that I wanted to say no.

I headed out first as not to arouse suspicion. With my mother asleep and my father out with the fae, it was unlikely anyone would see me slip out of the castle, but if they did, I would tell them I was going for a walk. I slipped out of the castle grounds by way of the door in the outer wall. I waited in the area we'd practiced fighting for Milo to arrive. Ten minutes later, and he was there, my sword in his hand.

"I hope you don't mind. I went into your room and picked up this. I thought you might like to practice what with there being dragons around. I still don't know how you survived them, but I'm pretty sure we are safe in here. The trees are too thick for dragons to get through."

He sat next to me on the rock. "So how did you escape the dragons?"

"I know magic," I explained, "I didn't know that I knew it, but Caspian showed me."

Milo's reaction was not what I expected. He stomped his foot down and turned away from me, his fists balled. "I don't trust that man."

I smiled at the ferociousness of his reaction. He'd barely ever seen the guy, and I'd talked so very little about him. This was jealousy. He was jealous because I was going to marry the fae. The smile faded from my lips. I was still going to marry Caspian. After what he told my mother, I would have no choice in the matter. My mother hadn't wanted me to be with Milo from the start, and now that she thought what we had was fake, she would never allow me to marry Milo instead. Not that I was ready to marry him either, but I'd rather share my days with the boy who kissed me first than that duplicitous creep.

"Let's fight," I said, picking up my sword and standing up. I turned him around to face me and kissed him lightly. Immediately his posture relaxed.

"We can't fight the way we did before. I couldn't carry out the armor we need. Today I'll teach you how to block, but we'll work slowly. That way, neither of us will get hurt."

We worked for hours, concentrating on posture before moving on to blocking. With each stroke of my sword, he showed me the correct way to block, first slowly and then when we'd both grown more confident in my ability, we speeded up. I wasn't set on hurting him, so none of my swipes were aimed at him, yet he danced around me, blocking each parry.

As my confidence increased, I began to copy him, until we were practically dancing around each other, the clank of our swords the only giveaway that this was no dance. Our swords were a blur as he threw in some attacks of his own. If we carried on this way, we would have no doubt slipped up and hurt each other, but a sneaky bit of tree root had me stumbling backward. Milo ran forward and caught my wrist. My sword fell to the ground, but I remained standing. He pulled me close until our faces were mere inches apart.

"You won," I whispered, my heart thumping in my chest. "What can I give you as the prize?"

He didn't answer, at least, not with words. He leaned forward and crushed his lips upon mine. All around us, snow began to fall again, but nothing mattered. Nothing at all but the here and now of the kiss with Milo and the realization that despite everything, I was falling in love with him.

Milo took my sword for me when it was time to go. We'd spent the whole morning practicing and then quite a bit of it kissing. I'd almost certainly missed lunch, and I was in danger of missing dinner too. I was surprised that my mother hadn't come looking for me. Perhaps she had but hadn't thought to check the woods. Why would she?

I left Milo and headed back into the castle, simultaneously feeling as light as a feather and broken-hearted at what I'd done and how my future was shaping up.

My heart had never felt so utterly bereft as it did now. How many times had I told myself over the past week that I didn't want or need a boyfriend? Falling for Milo had not been in the script at all, but now that our chances of dating were truly over, it made me want him all the more. Why hadn't I seen it from the start? Why hadn't I seen him? He'd been guarding my room every night for seven months, and it was only at the beginning of the year I'd really noticed him. If I'd thought to look up once in a while, I might have noticed him before. We could have been dating for months, and then, none of this would have happened. After months of dating, my mother would never try to force me to marry another man. Why had I been so stupid to let Caspian know that dating Milo had been fake?

My skin still tingled from where Milo had run his hand up my arm, my lips still felt the caress of his against them.

"Aza!" Remy shouted over at me as I stepped into the castle. He was sitting at the bottom of the main stairway, books surrounding him. When he saw I was looking at him, he waved his huge hand and beckoned me over. "Aza boo."

"Yes, I can see your books, Remy," I said only mildly impatiently. "You've been told about this before. Books belong in the library. You should only take one at a time." I moved forward and began to collect the books, but he grabbed my wrist.

"Aza, boo,"

"I'm picking them up. We have to take them back. Will you help?"

"No, Aza! Boo!" he strengthened the grip on my wrist and began to pull me upstairs.

"Remy stop. We've not picked up the books yet." I tried to pull against him, but he was too strong.

"Remy, let go!"

He shook his head and squeezed. Pain shot up my arm from where he squeezed me too tight. "Unsquash, Remy. Unsquash!"

He lessened his grip but didn't let go entirely.

"Is something wrong, Remy?" I asked, finally pulling my wrist from his hand. Giving it a rub to bring back the circulation, I looked into his eyes. I saw excitement in them. "Do you want to show me something?"

He danced up and down on the step, nodding his head. "Aza, boo."

"Ok, Remy, let's go." Sighing, I followed him up the stairs. He led me to the library.

The door to the precious books cabinet was open. It was the one part of the library that Remy was not allowed to touch, and he knew that. It was filled with books about the history of the Draconis Royal Family. Fear filled me as I realized the implications of this. Checking the books, I saw a space. One was missing.

"Remy," I said calmly. There was no point shouting

at him. It would only freak him out, and I'd get nowhere. A quick scan of the library told me that the book was nowhere in sight. I thought back to the books at the bottom of the stairs. Most of them had been left open. I wondered if one of those had been the missing book, it couldn't have been. The old books were bound in leather. The ones downstairs had all been paper. "Where is the book?"

"Boo," he repeated and took my hand. This time I let him. He led me over to a table at the other side of the library. Under it, was the missing book. Ducking under the table, I reached out for it, breathing a sigh of relief to find it still in one piece.

"Aza!" Remy jabbed a finger at the page the book was open on.

"Is this what you wanted me to see?" I asked him. He clapped his hands together and danced on his feet, a beautiful grin, splitting his face.

Looking at the title, I saw it was one of the older history books of Draconis. I'd never read it before because it was horribly outdated. The section Remy wanted me to look at was about royal laws.

At first, nothing jumped out at me, but then something caught my eye.

Regarding marriages of the first daughter of the king and queen, if she is the eldest sibling, and therefore, the heir to the throne, she must be found a partner to marry if she cannot find one herself. If there are two or more suitors, the law states that a competition must be held to determine the man who the princess will marry. Any man in the land may enter, but usually, it is only the two men in question. These competitions were rare as most of the young princesses found a man themselves, but in one particularly strange incident over three hundred years ago when the monarchy was still young, Princess Bethel chose two men, both of whom died in the usually brutal competition. She ended up marrying a complete stranger. It didn't do her any harm. She went on to have sixteen children with him. For more details on the competition, turn to page seventy-three.

I didn't need to turn to page seventy-three. This was my way out of marrying Caspian that didn't involve going to prison for murder! I pulled Remy's face towards mine and gave him a kiss on the forehead. I was finally free of the madness, and there was nothing my mother or father could do about it. It was the law, no matter how outdated and sexist, and not even they were above it. Changing laws in the twelve kingdoms was a tricky endeavor and could sometimes take years. The king had to put the law forward, and the lawmakers of Urbis decided to pass it or not. I doubted my parents would want to wait years for me to marry Caspian, so they'd be forced into upholding the law. "Remy! You are a genius!"

Remy did another dance on the floor, and this time, I danced along with him. I was free of Caspian.

A noise shifted my attention away from our little soiree. I placed the royal history book back in the cabinet and went to investigate.

Outside the library and all over, the castle buzzed with people. Servants and guards ran this way and that in a state of what I could only describe as panic.

If they were all running in one direction, I could understand it, but there seemed to be no rhyme or reason to the chaos.

Fear gripped me as I thought about the dragons. Had they come back? Were we being attacked?

"What's happening?" I asked a maid who was passing

by, with what looked to be a wet cloth in her hands.

"I can't tell you." She burst into tears and ran off towards the main staircase.

Following the maid to the second floor, the chaos was even more pronounced here. A gaggle of people stood outside my parents' room. Most of them worked at the castle. Some, I didn't recognize at all. They all spoke over each other, so it was impossible to tell what any of them were saying. The maid with the cloth practically screeched, making everyone move back. As the crowd moved, those at the back noticed me. A whisper went among them, and suddenly, they were all quiet and looking at me, pity filling their eyes.

"What is it?" I whispered, not daring to move. The path the maid had made between them widened to allow me to pass through.

With each step I took toward them, my heart rate increased, and as I passed, they all lowered their heads. Inside the room, my mother lay on the bed, her face ashen, her eyes closed. Beside her, my father held her hand as the maid mopped my mother's brow and someone I didn't know checked her pulse.

"Father..." I started, walking toward the bed.

When he looked over in my direction, a stab of fear clutched at my heart. He had tears in his eyes. I'd never seen my father cry. Not once in my whole life.

"She's alive," he said, holding out his other hand to me.

I glanced back toward my mother again. She looked like the mother I knew well. Gone were the dark circles under her eyes and the blotchy skin. She looked perfect in every way. Underneath the thin sheet covering her, I saw the rhythmical rise and fall of her chest as she breathed. Her eyes remained shut.

"What happened?"

"I don't know," my father said quietly. "She's not been feeling well for days. She came for a nap this morning, and when her personal maid came to wake her, she wouldn't wake up."

At this, the maid with the cloth burst into tears.

"I'm sorry, Your Majesty. Forgive me." She ran from the room, taking the cloth with her. I followed her with my line of sight to find the people still looking in. In my father's worry, he'd allowed the staff to congregate. I let go of my father's hand and marched to the door.

"Please leave us. We will let you know what is happening as soon as we ascertain the situation ourselves. Please carry on as normal. I'll meet you all in the grand hall at seven o'clock and fill you all in. Please pass the word to the other members of the staff and don't let word of this get out to the public." I closed the door. That speech was my very first act as a leader. My father was in no fit state to be a king today. He deserved a day off after eighteen years of service without one. I would take that meeting, and I would tell everyone what was happening. I'd tell my brothers too. Once I knew what it was that was happening myself.

"Do you know what is wrong with her, doctor?" I'd not been introduced to him, but it didn't take a genius to figure out who he was.

"Her vital signs are normal. Her breathing is normal, her heart rate is normal. It would appear that she is just asleep, Your Highness."

A thrill of fear passed through me. My father's face drained of the little color it already had. I'm sure that to literally anyone else, the fact that she was perfectly healthy would be a comfort, but my mother had been in this situation before, and that time, she'd not awoken for a hundred years.

"I've never seen anything like this before," the doctor continued. "I see no reason why she won't wake up. If you let me take her to Zhore, I could have my partners run tests on her."

"She's not leaving this room," my father uttered, his jaw clenched. "Get your partners in here if you must, but she stays."

The doctor nodded, taking his stethoscope and putting it in his bag.

"I'm not sure it will help. I don't want to be the one to say this, but I think this is a little out of my realm. I don't think this is an illness. I think this is a curse."

The anguished cries of my father rang through the castle. After eighteen years, my mother was Sleeping Beauty once more.

Heiress of Embers

8TH JANUARY

"Touch it, my dear. Touch the spindle. No need to worry." The beautiful young woman with startling black eyes that shone like dark diamonds with flashes of green urged. And the spindle itself. I'd never seen a piece of machinery so wonderful, so intriguing. So forbidden. It was only a contraption made to spin wool. Not harmful. But it was so tempting. I'd always been the good girl, kept to the straight and narrow, but this was something else. The woman had promised me nothing, and yet, she made me feel that this would be the answer to all my prayers if I only did the unthinkable.

I reached out, my forefinger extended, every fiber of my being, wanting...no, needing to touch it. The one thing I'd learned my whole life never to touch. Glancing back to the woman, she nodded her head, a smile on her face. A face with high cheekbones and a severity that came with the beauty she had. She mesmerized me with her strange horned headpiece and clear delight. I wanted to please her almost as much as I wanted to touch the spindle for myself.

A glint of light hit the needle, enticing me further. It was just so beautiful...so perfect.

"Do it! Do it, Azia."

I reached forward and touched the needle. A sharp pain shot through my finger, and I screamed out. Everything went black...

"Ouch!" My eyes shot open as I banged my head on my headboard. My breathing came raggedly as I took in my surroundings. I was in my room. Everything looked normal except for the bump appearing on my head. It was a dream. I'd dreamed about her, the witch that had cursed my mother. I wondered if my mother had been so taken by her when she fell into the spell. It had felt so real.

I didn't want to believe the doctor that my mother's sleep was a curse any more than my father did, but the fact remained that every doctor my father had brought in to see her had agreed that apart from the fact she was asleep, there was nothing wrong with her. None of them used the word curse, but they didn't need to. This happened to her the first time after she pricked her finger on a spindle. She couldn't have done that this time. Spindles didn't exist in Draconis anymore. They were illegal. Except...except I'd seen one just days before in a shop in Zhore. I'd bought my mittens in the shop. The shopkeeper had been urging me to touch the needle on that one too. Why hadn't I thought of it before? The shock of my dream brought back the memory with startling clarity, except the woman had looked different. I thought back to the woman I'd seen in the shop. She was older than the woman from my dream. My chest tightened as I wondered if I could have stopped all this by telling my father earlier. Jumping out of bed, I pulled my nightgown around me and tripped over my slippers in my rush to see him. Maybe I should have told him earlier, but I couldn't turn back time. I could only tell him what I knew now and hope he wasn't too angry with me.

I rushed out of my bedroom, smack bang into Milo.

"Where are you going in such a rush?"

His hand brushed my arm, and worry showed in his beautiful brown eyes. Jack eyed us curiously from the end of the corridor, causing me to speak in a hushed tone.

"I remembered something I saw last week that might help my mother," I said, pulling him away from Jack. "I don't know why I didn't think of it yesterday when all those doctors were going in and out."

Milo pulled me close to him. I guess he didn't care what Jack thought of us. "I'm so sorry about your mother, Azia. I wanted to come to you last night, but I knew you were with your parents, and then I thought you'd need your sleep."

I nodded. "I wish you had come to my room too. I barely slept, anyway."

It was an invitation. Who cared if Jack overheard. It didn't matter anymore. My mother was asleep in a curse, and my father was beside himself with stress. My life was falling apart, and nobody cared if I was going to get married or not.

He pulled me into a hug, holding me tightly, keeping out the world. It was all too brief.

I kissed him quickly and left him to work. The not having a boyfriend/fake boyfriend/not-so-fake boyfriend was not going well, or it was going too well. Who knew? The whole thing was complicated, but I knew that having Milo around was what I needed right now. The consequences of our new relationship were not something I had the brainpower to worry about at the moment. I found my father where I'd left him the night before, sitting in an armchair beside his own bed. He looked up as I closed the door behind me. His eyes were red as though he'd been crying, and the dark circles that had plagued my mother in her final days awake now rested under my father's eyes.

"I didn't want to disturb her," he said, by way of explanation, though it explained nothing at all. A horse could ride across the bed, and she wouldn't wake up. Still, my father was in pieces. He needed help, not logic.

"Why don't you have a shower and nap in one of the guest rooms for a while? I will stay with her until you come back."

He nodded slowly, pulling himself out of the chair. His clothes were the same clothes he'd been wearing the previous day. He'd not even taken off his boots. The bottom of his un-tucked shirt rested over the line of his belt, and one button had come open. After kissing my mother, he ambled past me, giving me a pat on the shoulder as he passed. I'd never seen him look so defeated.

My mother lay in peaceful slumber. Once again, she was Sleeping Beauty. I could well imagine how my father had fallen in love with her all those years ago, just by looking at her. I didn't believe in love at first sight. That was the stuff of romance books and fairy tales, but I could see why my parents were attracted to each other. They grew as a couple from there. I Sighed. Going to sleep and waking up with my soul mate would be so much easier than falling for my fake boyfriend and then having to marry someone I detested.

The only good thing about my mother being cursed was the fact that the fae had kept a low profile. I knew he was in the castle somewhere, but I'd not seen him since the curse took over. Of all the people in the castle, he would be the best one to speak to about the curse. He was the only person of magic in the castle. Correction. He was the only person of magic in the whole castle apart from me, but seeing as I only just found out I was magic, I was no use when it came to curses.

I tried to conjure up some magic over my mother's body, but nothing came of it. I felt too dull and depressed to muster up the energy needed, and I didn't want to explode her like I did with an apple only a few days before.

I sat with my mother only twenty minutes before my father returned. He'd changed clothes and showered, at least, but the pallor on his skin and the deathly tired look in his eyes remained.

I stood up to let him sit back down.

"I couldn't sleep," he mumbled, sitting back into his chair and resting his head in his hands. "How can I sleep knowing that your mother is deep in a curse? I don't know what to do, Azia. Last time kissing her was all I needed to do, but now when I try...nothing. Her eyelids don't even flicker."

I took a deep breath and psyched myself up for my confession. Now was the time to tell him what I'd seen the other day.

"When we were in Zhore, I went into a wool shop to buy mittens. In the window was a spindle. I didn't tell you sooner because I thought it was just for show. I didn't expect anything like this to happen. I'm sorry, Father."

My father licked his dry lips and sighed. "I don't think your mother visited Zhore yesterday, so I doubt that has anything to do with the curse, but I'll get someone to look. Thank you for letting me know."

"The woman behind the counter was strange," I added. "She wanted me to touch the needle. It felt like I was being compelled to do it. I would have, too, if you'd not walked in the shop."

My father's eyebrows furrowed. "It is a strange coincidence. I'll speak to the castle guards and ask if anyone saw your mother leaving yesterday. If there is a spindle there, it needs to be destroyed, even if it is harmless."

I jumped at the chance of leaving the castle. "Let me go. I know where the shop is."

He moved closer to the bed and gazed upon my mother. "There are things you do not know and things I promised her I'd never tell you. I do not wish to revisit the past, and yet it seems the past is revisiting me. I cannot let you go. I'm sorry. I remember the shop you spoke about though I don't recall seeing the spindle. My guards will find it."

I remembered how real it had all felt. How much I needed to touch the spindle. My dream. "Do you think the curse was meant for me, Father?"

My father took my mother's hand and looked my way. "I do not know, Azia. We are powerful people, and with power comes enemies. It is possible that someone out there wanted to recreate what happened to your mother all those years ago. You need Caspian keeping you safe now more than ever."

I resisted the urge to roll my eyes at the mention of the fae. "Don't you think it could be the same person who cursed mother before?"

"No," he said, standing up abruptly. "That woman is long gone. It is impossible."

"That woman? Who?" I knew whom he was referring to. I just wanted him to acknowledge it.

"I do not wish to talk about it," he said, striding over to me. "And I do not wish to talk about her."

I sucked in a breath, heart hammering at the name on my lips. "Is it Derillen?"

He looked me dead in the eyes. "I do not know where you learned that name. We never mentioned her to the press, but it doesn't matter. She is dead. She has to be. I do not wish to discuss the matter further."

"Ok, Father," I said quietly, nodding my head. "I'll find a guard and let him know where the wool shop is"

He nodded. "Thank you....and, Azia?"

"Yes?"

"I do not think this is your fault, and I do not want you thinking it is. I would have thought nothing of a spindle either."

I left him there, my mind swirling with everything he'd told me. Long ago, I'd thought my parents had been honest with me about my birth and adoption, and because I was happy, I'd never thought to question it. I was very young when they told me I was adopted, and they'd always assured me that, adopted or not, I was still the heir to the Draconis throne and just as important to them as Remy, Ash, and Hollis. By rights, the throne should have gone to Remy as the real blood-born son of the king and queen, but my parents had decided to treat me as they would as if I was born to them. I wanted to believe I wasn't part of this, but the weird compulsion to touch the spindle had been playing with my thoughts. Whatever my father said, I knew that this was something to do with me, and my mother had somehow gotten caught in the crossfire. I needed to find out who I was and where I'd come from, and my father would not tell me. It was also certain that I would go against my father's wishes. I'd never done it before, but there was no way I would mope around the castle like him. The problem of the dragons was nowhere nearer to being solved, no one knew what was wrong with my mother, and now we had a spindle to destroy. At the moment, my father was not capable of dealing with any of it, which left it to me. And I knew which guard to ask to come with me...

"Your father asked for me to come into Zhore with you?" Milo cocked an eyebrow.

"Not exactly," I hedged. "I made an executive decision, but seeing as he's in with my mother and everyone is too scared to bother him over trivialities, I figured it may as well be you as anyone else."

"Great!" he said, his eyes shining.

"I have a job for Milo," I shouted over to Jack, who watched us with curiosity. He frowned, knowing he'd be guarding the corridor alone, but there was nothing he could say or do about it.

As soon as we were in the stables and away from the prying eyes of the castle staff, I took Milo's hand in mine. Illicit, and yet it felt so right. My engagement with the fae had still not happened and hopefully never would. Maybe when this mess was all over, we could go back to how everything used to be, and I could decide whether or not I wanted a boyfriend.

"Don't you think it's weird?" Milo asked as he heaved himself up upon one of the castle horses.

"What?"

He waited until I'd mounted my horse to continue. "So many things going on at once. I've heard the phrase 'I've not seen anything like this in eighteen years' so many times this past week, mostly from Jack, but I've heard it from others too. The townsfolk are gossiping, and it isn't good. They say that things are going back to how they used to be, and it scares them. I'm sorry to say this, Azia, but they need a leader, and your father isn't up to the job at the moment. Not that I'd expect him to be in his situation, but..."

I sighed as we headed out into the cold. He was right. I'd been so caught up in everything going on in the castle that I'd not thought about the townspeople or the state of the kingdom. It stood to reason that everyone was scared. Giant dragons were invading every other day, and the queen was back under her curse. I hurried a glance up into the sky, but clouds obscured the peak of the mountains, and I couldn't see the dragons.

"I've been thinking of the flip side to that," I said, trotting along the path that would lead us to Zhore. "Everyone is talking about things going back to how they used to be, but no one has mentioned why things changed for the better all those years ago. One minute everything was horrible, and then overnight, everything became rosy."

Milo pulled to the side of the road to skirt around a muddy patch where the snow had thawed. "You know, I'd not thought about it like that before, but you are right. The change back then must have been as startling as it is now. Your father broke your mother's curse. Maybe that had something to do with it."

"He did," I said, following him around the muddy patch, "but he told me that the curse was already weakening. He was able to get through the brambles much easier than anyone else. Why? My father was no one special before then."

"He was your mother's true love," Milo pointed out.

I rolled my eyes. "Oh, please! He'd never even met her before that day. He only knew of her beauty through legends. No one was alive that remembered her. And have you seen my mother? Every man who meets her falls in love with her instantly. At best, he kissed her without permission. It was practically abuse."

Milo laughed as I caught back up to him. "Your parent's story is the most romantic story ever told, and you've turned it into a felony. I think it's sweet. Maybe they really were made for each other, and it was love at first sight. Have you thought of that?"

"Love at first sight is a fallacy," I huffed. "It doesn't exist."

"Doesn't it?" He turned his brown eyes to me and gave me a meaningful look that made my stomach flutter.

Zhore town square looked so much different from the last time I'd seen it. The decorations from New Year's Eve had long been cleared away, and now it was perfectly clean. Clean and empty with a light dusting of snow. In a marked difference to a few days ago when my father had given a speech, there wasn't a soul to be seen. The shops were all closed, many of them shuttered up.

"What's going on?" I asked nervously.

"I told you people are scared. No one dares open their shops. No one dares go outside. Those that aren't frightened of the dragons are scared of the curse. Last time the whole castle was cursed, but people wonder if this time it will hit the town too, or even the whole kingdom. Everywhere is closed but the Dragon Roost

Inn. It's making a roaring trade. People are drinking to forget."

I swallowed back a small laugh. At least someone was having some good luck amidst all of this.

I walked the horse over to the dark alley at the back of the square and dismounted. The shop with the spindle was still there, and in the window, the spindle stood where it had before.

"This is it," I exclaimed, my pulse running faster at the sight of it.

Dismounting, I tied the horse up and wandered over to the window. As I had felt before, a strange feeling came over me. This time I recognized it for what it was. Magic. Cautiously I beckoned Milo over.

"Do you feel that?" I asked.

Milo glanced around him as though this feeling would suddenly materialize out of thin air.

He shrugged his shoulders. "Feel what?"

Maybe I could only feel it because I was magic too. Maybe it didn't affect him the same way it had me, but it was there. Its suffocating presence squeezed at me, wrapping itself around me like a blanket of invisible fog.

"Never mind," I said, taking his hand. "Let's get that spindle."

"Go in?" he looked at me with a puzzled expression. "It's empty. I can see from here that there is nothing in there. They probably packed up and moved at the first sign of trouble. You can't blame them. I mean, who would be stupid enough to put a spindle in a shop window? Especially in this climate."

My eyes widened. "Are you being serious? The spindle is right there." I pointed through the shop window even though we were but inches away from it.

He let go of my hand and moved towards the window, placing his face right up to the glass, the way a child might gaze into a sweet shop.

"It's empty, Azia. It looks like there's not been anyone here for a while."

He was staring right at the spindle, and he couldn't see it. I wondered if my father had seen it when he'd come looking for me the other day or if he'd only seen me in an empty shop.

A thrill of fear shot through me as I took in the repercussions of what I was seeing. If Milo couldn't see it and I could, it meant one thing. That the spindle was there for me. My theory that this had more to do with me than my mother intensified.

I hesitantly pushed on the shop door, and it opened easily. The shop looked as it had before with wool and woolen items filling the shelves. The buzz of magical energy intensified as I walked through the door.

"Let's go. Milo said, taking my hand again. This place gives me the creeps."

Just then, a woman appeared behind the counter. It was the same woman I'd seen before, but this time, she couldn't be more different. Her shawl had transformed into a cape, the hat on her head shaped into two horns. This is how she had appeared in my dreams. Younger, more fearsome. Panic gripped me as she pointed her finger.

"You," she shrieked. "You did this! This is all your fault."

A ball of green magic appeared in her hand, swirling hypnotically. She leveled it at Milo and threw, hitting him square in the chest. As it hit him, he turned to stone. Unmoving, unblinking.

"Milo!" I screamed, but he didn't answer...couldn't

answer.

"What have you done?" I screeched.

She cackled and pulled on her energy again. Feeling for my own magic, I tried to recreate the same as I'd done out on the moor with Caspian, but it wouldn't come. In the grips of fear, I couldn't pull my energy inside, so I did the next best thing. Pulling my sword from my side, I charged her. There was no fear in her eyes, only amusement, but as the sword pushed deep into her belly, her eyes opened wide.

"Mark my words, I will get you," she hissed and then turned unto purple and green smoke, evaporating in the air. The shop around me fell away until all there was left were empty shelves and cobwebs that looked like they had been there for years.

"This place needs a good clean is what it needs."

I turned to find Milo looking as good as new, wiping dust from a shelf. He'd not even noticed he had been petrified. Behind him, the storefront was empty. The spindle was no longer there.

"Did you see that?" I choked out, but I already knew his answer.

"See what?"

His eyes roamed the empty shop, searching for something that he couldn't see.

I took Milo's hand, thankful that it was warm and real. He hadn't seen the magic, but I sure had. Whoever this woman was, she was connected to my mother's curse, and not only that, she now wanted me.

"Come on, let's go."

Milo studied me through curious eyes. "Where?"

"We are heading back to the castle," I replied, dragging him from the shop. "There's someone I need to see."

~

I found Caspian in the drawing room, a bag by his side. He was dressed in a powder blue waistcoat with gold trim and a gold fob watch on a chain leading to his pocket.

"Are you leaving?" I asked, though it was obvious he was.

"Yes," he muttered. "I've booked tickets on the Urbis Express from Zhore for this afternoon. You've made it very clear that I'm not wanted, and as your mother is sick, I feel that my time here is done. You have your wish granted, Azia."

I hated the next words I would speak, but I spoke them anyway. "Please stay. I need your help."

He tutted and waved his hand as though I no longer mattered. "I see. Now that you need me, you want me to stay. I'm nobody's pawn, not even yours, princess."

My stomach churned. He was right, and I could hardly deny it, but I needed him. He was the only connection I had to a magic world, a world in which the evil woman from the wool shop had tried to hurt me. I sat next to him on the sofa.

"I met a woman today..."

"How delightful," he growled.

"She was a witch," I replied, ignoring his sarcasm. "I think she was the same witch that put my mother in a curse, and I think she was the same witch that did it the first time. I think it was Derillen."

He sat toward me, his lips bared. "If it was Derillen, you wouldn't be here to tell the tale."

I matched his pose, leaning in toward him. I wasn't about to be threatened by him. "I saw her, and I did survive. She was tall and thin with a cap of horns."

I saw a momentary flicker of fear in his eyes. “It’s not possible. She is dead.”

“Why would she have an interest in me?”

He stood and picked up his bag. “I’ve said too much. None of this is my business. I tried helping your father eighteen years ago, and I’ve tried helping him now, but I can plainly see that my use here extends only to being a fount of knowledge to you. I’ve already told you to speak to your parents, now good day, I have an airship to catch.”

He made to walk, but the door to the drawing room opened before he could reach it. My father walked in. When he saw Caspian, his expression turned into one of surprise.

“Where are you heading, my friend?”

Caspian turned and indicated me. “Your daughter has made it perfectly clear that I am unwanted here. I’m heading back to The Forge. At least there, people have manners... Well, some of them have.”

My father cast a warning glance over Caspian’s shoulder, directed at me. He then turned his attention back to his friend. “Caspian, you are more than welcome to stay here in the castle, despite what my daughter thinks. I wouldn’t hear of you leaving us.”

Caspian held up his hand. “Your offer is kind, but I see no reason to stay. I’ve already told you, I cannot break the curse on Briar Rose, and as marriage to your daughter is no longer on the table, my time here is done. Farewell.”

“Nonsense.” My father clapped him on the shoulder and led him back to the sofa. “Who said anything about marriage being off the table? I know that Briar Rose was having the staff here look after you, but I believe they will continue to do so in her...absence. We planned for you to marry Azia, and you will." He paused for a minute, his finger up to his lips, deep in thought. "The wedding will happen three weeks from today. I'll get my staff to prepare. I'll tell Briar Rose. If there is anything she will wake up for, it is our daughter's wedding."

A surge of nausea took my breath away. "But Father..."

"But Father nothing," he began, his tone changing to one of anger. "You've disobeyed me more than once this week. I know you went to Zhore, despite me forbidding it, and I know you went with that Milo chap. I've got enough on my plate without having to worry about a wayward daughter. Your mother wanted you to marry Caspian, and so do I. I never wanted to force you into marriage, Azia, but with your wilful ways, you've forced my hand. The wedding will go ahead. I suggest you spend the next three weeks getting to know Caspian because you'll soon be living with him."

"But..."

"Don't," he warned, leveling a finger at me. "I am the king, and the last time I checked, you are my daughter. You will do as I say."

I lowered my head in submission. "Yes, sir."

"Good."

My stomach churned, but anger at my father shouldn't stop me from telling him what I saw. My mother's life was at stake.

"I saw a woman today," I said. "She had a spindle. I saw her use magic. She turned Milo to stone, but when I stabbed her with my sword, the spell on Milo was broken."

The anger in my father fell away and was replaced with concern. "What did she look like?"

"Alec," Caspian cautioned.

I took a deep breath as I recalled the woman and how she looked now. "She was tall with horns and angular cheekbones."

My father turned on the spot, running his hands through his hair. "No."

"Your daughter could have been imagining it, Your Highness," Caspian said, narrowing his eyes at me.

"I wasn't imagining anything," I persisted. "She turned to smoke when I stabbed her."

My father stormed out of the door. I followed quickly, Caspian behind me.

"You," my father barked at one of the guards. "Round up all my men. All the Draconis Army. I want every single man out looking for spindles. Scour the whole kingdom. I will not rest until every last one is in the courtyard and on a bonfire. " He turned to me. "Azia, you can go to your room. I don't want you coming out until I say so."

He stormed off up the stairs as the guard ran outside to alert the other guards.

"What's happening?" I asked, fear gripping me. "Is the witch that cursed my mother back?"

Caspian drew me into a hug that was strong and surprisingly tender for such a jackass. He stroked my hair. "Let's hope for all our sakes she's not, princess, because last time no one could defeat her. No one at all."

9TH JANUARY

I sat on my bed, gazing out of the window, sorrow filling my soul. Exhaustion crippled me, but sleep had only happened in fits and starts, and every time I closed my eyes, I saw her face. The witch, with her heavily contoured face and cheekbones like knives. Why had my magic not worked?

I patted the sword on the bed next to me, running my fingers over the beautifully shaped metalwork. It, too, was magic, but the magic it possessed wasn't mine. It belonged to the dwarves. It had been them that had turned the witch to smoke, not anything I had done. I was surprised that I was still allowed to keep it. I'd even briefly mentioned it to my father the night before, but he'd not said anything, and so, I'd brought it back to my room and slept with it by my side.

A small knock on the door took my concentration

away, and a quick look at the clock told me it was only a little after four am. I guess I wasn't the only one who couldn't sleep.

"Who is it?" I asked quietly.

"It's me."

I leapt out of bed, knocking my sword to the floor with a clatter. Opening the door, I pulled Milo inside and brought him into a kiss. I'd hoped he would come to my room last night. If I was going to be honest with myself, that was part of the reason I hadn't slept. I was betrothed to one man, but my heart now belonged to another. My father had ordered me to marry Caspian, and after the wedding, I would be the dutiful daughter and wife and be true to him. I owed it to my parents. They had taken me in as a newborn and made me a princess. The heir to the Draconis throne. They had given me a wonderful childhood and everything I could ever dream about. In exchange, I would do as they wanted. Up until then, though, I was nobody's but my own.

Milo kissed me back, his lips crushing against mine, matching the urgency. This kiss had to say it all because I would break down if I had to say it in words.

Milo's arms held me, pulling me into him, our bodies fitting together like puzzle pieces. My hand ran through his hair as I held onto him, fearful of letting go in case this was our last kiss.

He lay me down on the bed, his body on mine. An unwanted image of when Caspian had done the same thing flittered through my mind. Except he'd been pinning me down with a sword to my throat.

"I'm engaged," I whispered, blinking back the tears.

Milo pulled back until I could no longer feel the weight of him on me. I sat up to find him hunched over on the bed.

"I didn't expect you to say that after pulling me into your room and kissing me like that," he sighed.

"I don't want to be."

He looked up and took my hand in his. "I know you don't, but it's probably for the best anyway."

I furrowed my eyebrows. "What do you mean?"

"Your father has ordered all his men out to look for spindles," Milo explained.

I already knew that, but it never occurred to me that Milo would be one of the men to go.

"You're leaving?" I asked. I had so little time with him until my wedding that I couldn't bear him going away for any of it. I needed him.

He nodded. "That's what I came up to tell you. I've been assigned to one of the towns, but I won't know which one until I leave. I was going to ask if I can be kept in Zhore so I could still see you, but I guess it's best if they send me somewhere far away if you are marrying Caspian."

My heart bottomed out. "I don't want you to go." What had I done? Now not only was I going to be marrying the fae, I was also going to lose Milo for the three weeks I had left. "It's not fair."

Milo shook his head "No, it's not, but life never is fair. We get what we get, and it's how we deal with it that counts. "

"I planned to spend the next three weeks with you," I explained. "I had it planned out. We were going to go into the woods and practice sword fighting every day and..."—my voice choked up—"I planned lots of kissing."

"Is that when you are getting married? In three weeks?" The look on his face damn near broke my heart.

I nodded slowly.

"Then, it is right that I leave," he said brusquely, standing up from the bed. "You will be safe. Jack is staying here to guard the corridor. He's been told not to let you out of your room. I thought it was because of everything going on, but now, I see it's so you don't sneak out to see me."

He walked to the door. I ran after him, catching his arm.

"There is a chance I won't have to marry him," I whispered as he spun to face me. "Remy found a chapter in an old book about a competition for the princess's hand in marriage."

"I remember. You told me before, but I think it is too late for that. I'd hoped that it would never come to that, and now, I don't think it will. I would have fought for you, Azia. I would have fought with everything that I had, but I'm not sure you want to fight anymore. Maybe The fae will give you everything you need."

He closed the door behind him, and I broke down. Tears cascaded down my face as I flung myself onto the bed.

He was wrong. I wanted to fight. I wanted Milo, but how could I go against my father's wishes when the whole kingdom was falling apart?

Another knock on my door had me stumbling out of bed again. I wiped my tears on the back of my sleeve in a very un-princess-like manner and opened the door. My heart fell as I found Jack there instead of Milo.

He held out a flower. "Milo asked me to give you this," he growled. "I don't like it, mind you. I don't like it one bit, and it's good that he's gone. I told him it would lead to no good, you being a princess and him being a guard, but would he listen? Youth today!"

I took the flower from his hand. It was a poppy. No poppies grew around here and certainly not in the winter, but he'd found it anyway. Maybe he'd bought it from one of the expensive flower shops in Zhore. They imported flowers from other kingdoms. This one probably came all the way from Floris, the kingdom famous for its flowers. I thanked Jack and closed the door, my heart in pieces.

Two hours later, I had another knock on the door. This time the door opened without me answering, and Dahlia bustled in.

"Are you still in bed?" she asked. "Lazy girl, come on. Let's get you bathed."

"I don't want to bathe," I huffed, but Dahlia ignored me as she so often did, and from the small bathroom, I heard the taps being turned on.

"Heartbreak doesn't give you an excuse for being dirty young miss," she admonished, coming out of the bathroom with a towel and throwing it at me.

"Who said anything about me being heartbroken?" I picked up the white towel and sat up.

"No one, but I'm not blind. I might be old, but these eyes are as good as yours. I've seen you sneaking out with that young guard of yours, and this morning, I saw all the guards being sent off to look for spindles. I also heard on the grapevine that your wedding to that charming Mr. Caspian is being planned."

"You know about that?"

"Know about it?" she exclaimed. "I'm the head of the planning committee."

I sighed, falling back on the bed. "I don't want to marry him, Dahlia. I don't love him. I don't even like the guy. He's a creep."

"That's as may be," she said, pulling me out of

bed so she could straighten the sheets, "But he's very handsome. Very, very handsome. You are a lucky girl."

I rolled my eyes. "Hmph. He's an idiot, and he's nearly as old as my father."

"I'd wager he's a lot older than that," she said as she fussed with my pillowcase. "Fae age differently than we human folk do. He doesn't look it, though. He'd pass for being in his early twenties with that fine physique of his... and oh, that hair!"

Her eyes misted over as she spoke.

"Dahlia!" I snapped.

"Sorry. I got carried away with myself. I have to say you are wrong about one thing, though. That man is no idiot. He's a smart cookie. I saw him with a suitcase yesterday. He said he was leaving to head back to The Forge. He said he had a ticket booked on the Urbis Express and everything."

"Yes, so?"

She ushered me into the bathroom and turned off the taps.

"That suitcase. I picked it up to take it back to his room for him, and I'm telling you now, it was as light as a feather."

"What do you mean?" I asked, though I had a suspicion I already knew.

"I mean, it was empty. He'd not packed at all. He had no intention of going back to The Forge."

"Why the stinking...rotten...double crossing..."

Dahlia laughed as she pulled my nightdress over my head. "He'll keep you on your toes will that one, and that's half a marriage right there. You want someone who will excite you. Life will never be boring with that one around."

I splashed down into the bath, letting water drip all

over the sides. I was going to kill him. Excitement? I would slice his head off way before I got to my honeymoon night. I wanted to please my father; I really did, but if I was going to survive my first week of marriage to that creep, I would have to be in a different room from him. We would, quite literally, kill each other.

"You know..." I shouted back through the open door to my bedroom where Dahlia had gone to tidy up. "If I don't marry him, that means he's available. Maybe, he'd like a beautiful maid by his side?"

"Get away with ya! I'm an old woman. What would he do with the likes of me? He's got rich blood, that one. Oh, if wishes were pennies, we'd all be rich."

She drifted off into song, leaving me to soak and think of everything she'd said. Caspian really was good looking. Fantastic looking. Carved by the gods gorgeous, and yet, he drove me crazy.

I wasn't ready for marriage. All I'd ever seen of it was my mother and father, and they pranced around like newlyweds all the time. I couldn't see Caspian and I being like that. Tempestuous was the best way I could think to describe a marriage with Caspian, and that was being nice. Bloody awful was the real term I was thinking of.

He didn't even want me. He wanted power. Maybe he wanted to overthrow my father. It wouldn't surprise me. He wasn't beyond lying and subterfuge to get what he wanted. I'd seen that for myself.

"Urgh," I said, which turned into a gurgle as I lowered my face into the water. If wishes were pennies...I'd be a mermaid like the people of Atlantice, and I'd never get out of this bath ever again. As it was, I wasn't a mermaid, and lying with my head under the water would drown me, so I had to come up for air eventually.

After my bath, I let Dahlia choose my clothes and dress me. I usually fought her every step of the way, preferring to choose my own clothes and dress myself, but this morning, I didn't care what I wore. What did it matter when I was nothing more than a prisoner in my own room? When she was done, I sat by the window as she brushed my hair—another job I hated having done for me.

Outside, hundreds of guards crowded around the courtyard. One of the men I recognized as Gerard, the man who trained the guards and was the highest in command of the army. He was shouting orders, getting everyone into groups. Next to him, stood Jacob, the man who'd argued with my father about the wall being erected around the Fire Mountains, a grim expression on his face and his arms folded across his chest. He didn't look any happier with the thought of going out to find spindles than he'd been about erecting a wall. He was the type of guy who wanted action, and in his case, that meant taking his men up the mountains and killing all the dragons. As I watched, another group set out on horseback. I looked for Milo, but I couldn't see him amongst all the other young men with helmets on. As the men set out, the number in the courtyard became smaller, and I was forced to realize that I'd already missed him. He'd already gone, and with him, my heart. It wasn't a dangerous mission, and yet, my nerves were on edge as though something bad was going to happen.

"You were around when my mother woke up the first time, right?" I asked Dahlia.

Dahlia had been my maid my whole life. She'd also been my governess when I was very young before my parents brought in tutors for my brothers and me. If anyone knew anything about Derillen, it was she.

"I wasn't one of the staff here at the palace that was cursed along with your mother," she replied. "They were all given a pension for life and told to leave and have fun. It was a generous settlement, by all accounts. They were given the option to stay if they desired, but none did. They'd all given enough service, and they had enough money to live the rest of their lives comfortably. Your grandfather was a very generous man. I was hired just after that. Your grandmother hired me."

My grandparents had died when I was young. I barely remembered my grandmother at all.

"She was a lovely lady," Dahlia continued. "Busy, though. She was in charge of filling the castle with staff again. Your grandfather might have been generous, but he wasn't very clever. He let all his staff go at once, and so, your grandmother spent weeks trying to find staff again. My first few weeks here were hectic. I was doing about eight people's jobs already when you came along."

My curiosity peaked. "What happened with that? Did my parents go to an adoption agency?"

She stopped tugging my hair for a second. "I don't know, lovey. I was cleaning the rooms one day when I was handed a baby. I don't know where you came from. I do remember how surprising it was. Your parents were still in that lovely honeymoon phase. They never left their room except for food."

I blushed at the thought of my parents on honeymoon. Their love was already barf-worthy.

She began tugging at my hair again, pulling through the knots. "I remember thinking it was odd that they'd adopted so soon after marriage. Barely three weeks after the wedding. But I was just a maid. I didn't ask questions. They were wholly unprepared for you, too. They had nothing. No crib, no clothes apart from what you were wearing, and that was no more than a cut-up piece of blanket. I wrapped you up warm and took you to Zhore with your mother. She bought you the best of everything that day. She might not have been prepared, but already she was in love with you."

"Why wasn't she prepared?" I asked perplexed. "Surely, if she'd adopted me, she would have gotten everything ready?"

Dahlia shrugged. "As I said, it's not really my place to say, but I got the impression that she wasn't quite expecting you."

I mulled this over. How could she not be expecting me? I didn't know much about adoption processes, but she must have known. How does anyone adopt someone without knowing? The more I thought of it, the more I realized that Dahlia was right. My mother was meticulous about everything. There was no way that she would not have had everything ready for a baby. Yet another mystery to figure out.

"What happened after that?"

"Eventually, they decided to hire a nanny, and as I'd already been looking after you, I volunteered for the job. They still wanted me as a maid, so I took on both jobs and have been doing them ever since. A few months later, your mother fell pregnant with Remy, and life went on."

She was cut off by the sound of shouting outside. Standing up, the pair of us gazed out of the window. Dahlia grabbed my shoulder and brought her free hand up to her chest. The dragons were back, and this time, they were angry.

As we watched, guards rushed at them, only for the

dragons to retaliate, breathing their fire, smoking the warriors and knights.

I screamed as a group of knights got the full effect of the flames, falling to the ground, still on fire long after the dragon's fire had ended.

"Please don't let Milo be in there!" I whispered to myself, tears coursing down my cheeks.

"He set out a couple of hours ago, lovey," Dahlia assured me, gripping my shoulder tightly. I could only look on in fear as the dragons skimmed the ground, knocking over knights, burning everything in their path.

"I have to do something!" I cried, grabbing my sword from under my covers.

Dahlia's eyes widened at the sight of it.

"Now, where do you think you are going with that?"

"I'm going to fight!" I'd beaten the dragons before, and I'd do it again. Last time, I'd used magic. This time, I was going in with a sword. I'd use both if that's what it took.

"You stay right here!" Dahlia demanded. "I don't think your father would want you to..."

I didn't listen to the rest of the sentence. I was already out of the door. What I hadn't anticipated was Jack blocking my way.

"Move," I ordered sternly.

"Sorry, Your Highness, but his Majesty's orders are to keep you in here safe. Where is it you wish to go?"

"She wants to go out and fight the dragons," Dahlia told him. I could have fought him. I would have won too. He had more training than I did, but I was younger, and I was desperate. The thing was, I didn't think my father would take too kindly to his daughter killing one of his guards. Deciding against it, I ran back to my room, bolting it from the inside before Dahlia could follow. If I couldn't help on the field, maybe I could help from a distance. I'd produced a tower of fire that had made the dragons bow down before. There was nothing to say I couldn't do it again from my window. I flung the window open, just in time to see the dragons flying off into the skies. The fight was over. The pasture was littered with the bodies of men. At least twenty were burned beyond recognition. Many were injured. More still ran out to help in the fight. They would be of no use, beyond helping the injured and taking away the bodies of the dead. I scoured the men for my father. He wasn't there. Unlike Milo, who would blend in with all the others because of his uniform, my father would be easy to spot in the crowd. He wore the uniform of a king, not a guard.

A banging on my door rattled me. Pulling back the bolt, I saw Dahlia. Behind her stood Jack.

"Go and look at what has happened!" I screeched at Jack. "You are keeping me in here, but look at what is happening. Does my father even know?"

Jack strode past and glanced out of the window, his face paling from the scene below. I chose his moment of shock and ran out of the room. I wasn't going to fight anymore. There was nothing left to fight, but I would tell my father. His men needed him now more than ever.

I found him exactly where I thought he'd be, holding the hand of my mother.

"I told the guards to keep you in your room," he began when he saw me.

Out of breath, I wheezed. "The dragons have attacked. Some of your men have been killed...outside."

He stood up and strode past me out of his room. I followed along in his path, almost having to run to keep up with him. Outside in the courtyard, the non-injured men were already bringing in those that weren't so lucky. Embers floated in the air like fireflies. The injured were being brought into the castle. Those that didn't make it were being laid out next to each other. The smell of burning flesh invaded my senses, making me want to throw up, but my father stood tall. If he noticed the wretched looks on the faces of the burnt men or the stink of the charred remains, he didn't show it. He called to one of his men. When the man turned, I almost fell over in shock. It was Ash. Ash dressed in the uniform of a knight. The only distinction between his uniform and that of the others was a plume of red feathers coming out of the top of his helmet.

"Yes, Father?"

"Get someone into Zhore immediately. I want all the doctors, physicians, nurses, and healers brought up. As many as you can find. We'll also need someone to deal with the bodies. They will need identifying, and their relatives will need to know."

"Yes, sir," Ash saluted. When had all this come about? Ash was only sixteen. Why was he wearing a knight's costume, and why was he not acting like the snot-nosed kid I knew and loved?

"About the dragons?" he asked.

My father sighed. "I don't know. I had hoped that the sightings were just flukes, but now, they are killing. I always respected them and knew when to leave well enough alone, but it seems I am being forced into doing something I do not wish to do. Gather your best men, and I'll see them tomorrow about going up the mountain. You are in charge of that. I want only my best warriors up there, but they have to know what they are letting themselves in for. Get Hollis to help you. I want them all here by tomorrow. Let's sort this mess out first, though."

Ash saluted again. Hollis was here, too? He was only fifteen. Why were they knights when I was older than them? I knew they were taking the knight's training, but all this time, I thought it was just to keep them occupied.

"I'll do it, Father," I said, standing forward. "I'll go up the mountain." Fear gripped me at the thought of it, but I had a weapon no one else did. I had magic.

My father glared at me as though he'd only just realized I was still there.

"You should be in your room."

"No! If Ash and Hollis are fighting, then I want to, too. You can't lock me up because I'm a girl."

My father sighed through gritted teeth. "I'm not locking you up because you are a girl, Azia. I'm locking you up because I love you, and I don't think you are safe."

And my brothers were? Both of them had just narrowly missed being barbecued.

"But..."

"But nothing. Either go up to your room, or I will get someone to carry you up there."

I stood my ground. This wasn't the ideal time to be arguing with my father, but it was too important not to.

He nodded his head at someone behind me, and two sets of arms grabbed hold of me. I screamed and writhed against them, but these were big burly men. Even though my sword was at my side, my arms were held in such a way that I couldn't get to it.

"Make sure she gets to her room safely," My father said to them. He turned to walk away.

"Fine, I'll go to my room quietly," I screeched. "No

need to have these two take me."

He turned and considered it a moment, then nodded his head.

Turning to the side, he shouted to someone who turned out to be much worse than the two burly guards.

"Caspian, my friend. Please, will you escort Azia back to her room and make sure she doesn't get lost along the way."

Caspian looked up from one of the injured men. He was performing some kind of spell on his burned leg. As I watched, the skin on the man's leg healed. When he was done, he came towards me and took my arm.

"With pleasure."

I walked with him through the castle, my mind whirring, my nerves in tatters. It was as if my whole life was a lie. First, I was magic, and no one knew; then, I find that I'd suddenly appeared out of nowhere as a baby, and now my younger brothers were knights. Ash and Hollis, the two least knight-like people I'd ever met. Although I had to admit, I'd seen a strength in Ash's eyes I'd never seen before. Maybe he needed something like this to finally become a man. Maybe they both did. It royally sucked that I couldn't join in, though. My father had told me it was nothing to do with me being a girl, but, of course, it was. I was only a girl, fit for dresses and parties, and marrying the first guy that would have me because I was too frail to do anything alone.

Anger surged through me, and when I got to my room, I pulled my arm from Caspian's and slammed the door in his face, bolting it once again for good measure.

I could only watch on helplessly from my window as the men below did what they had to do. Far up in the skies, the dragons circled harmlessly like they had done for years.

I wondered what had changed to cause previously peaceful creatures to suddenly turn violent? It wasn't an omen, I was sure of that. It had nothing to do with superstition. Something else was at play, and I was going to find out what.

I didn't care what my father said. I would go up those mountains, and I would figure it out for myself.

10TH JANUARY

My stomach rumbled as I got together everything I would need for my trip. There wasn't a lot to pack, just my sword plus some warm clothes. It was cold at the bottom of the mountains. I needed to prepare myself for a lot worse at the top. If only I had burn resistant clothes, too. That would help, but in my closet of pretty dresses, I had no such thing. I could have asked Caspian to conjure me some up, but that would mean waking him at three am, and he was bound to ask questions. It was pointless, anyway. If the dragons wanted to fry me, no amount of clothes would help, fireproof or otherwise. They'd just sizzle my head instead.

With my backpack crammed with extra layers, I stole down to the kitchen. Getting past Jack had been easy.

It was dark, and I'd walked quietly down the corridor in the opposite direction to where he usually sat. He'd not seen me. He was asleep. Getting out of the castle was another matter. I couldn't count on all the other guards to be asleep. As it was, the castle was almost empty. Most of the guards were out on various missions, and in a twist of irony, the worst situation the castle had been in for eighteen years meant it was at its least guarded.

I knew the kitchen staff worked early, but I hoped that three am was early enough to miss them. The kitchen was empty. I pulled some food out of the fridge and made up some sandwiches, two of which I ate. I'd barely eaten the day before, and I was starving. Food had been brought up to my room, but I was too angry and pig-headed to eat any of it. My mistake. I needed the energy to complete today's climb. I figured it would take me at least five hours to get near the top. When I got there, that's where my plan ran out. I wanted to see the dragons without them seeing me. I wanted to try and figure out what was wrong without upsetting them.

Pulling some chocolate bars and a flask of tea into my bag, I stole out of the kitchen and into the night.

I slipped out of the back gate into the woods where Milo and I had spent hours practicing sword fighting. I only hoped that all that practice would come in handy. Fingering my sword to make sure it was still there, I felt a moment of reassurance. I strode through the woods purposefully, not daring to stop or even to consider how dangerous my plan was. I should have left it up to my father's men, but I knew that it was something more than an omen or the dragons coming down the mountain for no reason. In my heart, I knew something much deeper was in play, and the only way to figure it out was to head up the mountain. My father's men would go in there, all noise and bluster, and get themselves killed without being any closer to finding out what was going on. I might not have a set plan, but I knew I would play this a lot more carefully than any man in a suit of armor could do. I was not only going to come out of this alive, I was going to come out of it a hero, and if I had to kill a dragon or two...well, so be it.

At least, that's what I told myself as I crept up to the wall, blocking me from the mountain. I could have tried to come up with a way to climb over it, but I could see in the distance that it had not yet been completed. Of course, it hadn't. It would take months to surround the mountain, and many of those tasked to the job had been sent out to look for a spindle instead.

Finding a way up the first part of the mountain was easy. Paths worn away by generations of hikers drifted up the first part of the way. They didn't go very far. Even before the dragons decided to come down to the moors, hikers were not stupid enough to venture very far. Pretty soon, I was higher than the castle, and I could see for miles. Snow-covered most of Draconis, so I couldn't get a good view of the normally red and purple landscape, but I could see Zhore in the distance with a number of other small villages dotted around. Seeing the kingdom before me made me think of Milo. He was out there somewhere. I'd been so worried about him leaving, but the truth was, he was much safer than me. While he was asking old ladies about spindles, I was out conquering dragons. As long as he didn't run into Derillen, which I doubted he would, he would be fine. Caspian was adamant that the woman in the wool shop couldn't possibly be Derillen, but I knew in my heart it was.

The gradient steepened as the terrain of the

mountain changed. Snow-covered heather gave way to grey, craggy rocks, which I would have to climb. I pulled myself from rock to rock, finding paths when and where I could. Mostly, it was just scrambling rather than full-on rock climbing, but I had the snow and ice to deal with, too, which made every foothold treacherous. After three hours of climbing, I took a break and pulled out one of the chocolate bars I'd pilfered from the kitchen. I was still a couple of hours from the top of the mountain, but I wasn't taking any risks after what I'd seen the day before, so I sat under a rocky outcrop and tore open the chocolate. A blanket of snow covered Draconis, but the sky was clear, and the sunrise gave the blanket of snow a pinkish glow. Taking in my surroundings, I noticed a small door, incongruous to the landscape around it. I was curious until I realized what it was. I'd never seen one before, but I'd heard of them. It was a dwarf door, one of many hidden on the mountainside. The main entrance to the dwarf mines lay about five miles east of the castle, but the mines themselves stretched out throughout the Fire Mountains. These doors allowed access to and from the mines, whether for emergencies or just for the dwarves to admire the view, I did not know, but I knew to leave well enough alone. I was already on my way to fight one creature; I didn't want to start a fight with other creatures too.

For a start, they had more weapons than I did. Putting the chocolate wrapper back in my bag, I set off again. The incline was getting steeper, and my going was slower. With each step, my lungs strained, and my muscles burned like dragon breath. The air was thinner up here, something that I'd not thought about when I planned this little quest. Breathing became something I had to think about something I had to consciously put effort into rather than something I just did. At the rate I was going, I would end up killing myself, long before the dragons got to me. If I didn't expire from lack of oxygen, I was likely to slip on an icy rock and fall to my death.

I was just beginning to think this whole thing was a bad idea when a brilliant blue dragon flew right over my head. It circled around before coming in again, and this time, it dove right towards me.

I grunted at the force of the dragon's talons as it gripped me, pinning my arms to the side. The little air I'd managed to breathe left me as it squeezed tighter. We flew upwards, going at a much quicker pace than I had managed alone.

I struggled in its grip, straining to get air into my lungs as the smell of burning and sulfur filled my nose.

When it had reached its destination, it dropped me. I fell only two or three feet, but the shock of it had me tumbling over and over. Something blocked my path, causing me to come to a standstill. For a second, I felt relief until I saw what I'd come up against. It was the leg of another dragon. A dragon that was craning its head around to see me.

My heart beat so quickly, I could feel the rush of blood through my eardrums, and a shiver went down my spine. Looking around, I realized I was in some kind of hollow. A thrill of fear passed through me as I saw bones littering it. Big bones. Scrambling to my feet, I ran, trying to get away from the beast. In a riot of storm and smoke, other dragons, ten or more of them, circled around what I could only describe as a giant nest, all of them fixated on me. None of them moved in to attack. They just watched intently as I pulled myself up the curved edge of the nest to the rim. When I looked over, it became apparent why none of them had gone for me. I was hundreds of feet up with a steep drop below me. A fall would kill me instantly. I was in a dragon's nest, and not only was I their dinner, it seemed they were going to play with me first.

Turning, I saw the dragon I'd originally backed into. A huge red beast with long eyelashes and big teeth, although its mouth was closed. With my back to the rim of the nest, there was nowhere for me to go. My options were to jump over the edge to my death or to stay and have it eat me alive, burned to death, or pulled apart by sharp talons. None of those options appealed, but as fear was gripping me to the floor of the nest, it seemed my nervous system would decide for me.

"Dragon balls," I hissed, pulling myself right to the edge. Below me, another couple of dragons flew. They were so low down that they looked tiny, and yet from the castle, they looked so high up. My hand gripped the edge, and something cold touched against it. My sword! I had my sword. I also had magic. Magic had saved me from the dragons before, it could do it again, but while I dialed back my nerves, the sword would have to do. Pulling it out, I leveled it at the red dragon. Immediately, the surrounding dragons flew closer, but the red dragon shot warning looks at them, and they flew back again. Was it warning them off so it could eat me itself?

Remembering my stance, I moved cautiously towards the dragon. It watched me closely but made no move. It could have roasted me at any point, but it chose not to, and when I was within hitting distance of it, and it still hadn't moved, I was left immobile with indecision. My nerves had dropped a little. If I'd wanted to, I could have reached forward and pet its snout. I was here to kill it, or at least I thought I was, but no. I'd come up here to understand the dragons. I couldn't understand anything if I killed them. It blinked as I stood right in front of it, probably wondering what my next move would be.

You and me both, buddy, I thought.

I didn't know what to do, but killing it was no longer an option. I could kill in self-defense, but I could never attack something that was not attacking me. Instead, I did the unthinkable. I put my sword away and bridged the distance between us. Taking a last step, I held out my hand and touched the tip of its nose. It closed its eyes and then opened them again. This creature was no threat to me.

"We wondered when you would come to see us."

My heart pelted around my chest at the voice behind me. There had been no one in this nest a minute ago, I was sure of it. I turned to find a man, or at least, he was almost a man. The top half of his body was human if you could call a man with long blue hair human. Brilliant blue scales that shimmered in the sun covered his bottom half. His legs were the legs of a dragon, and I knew this was the dragon that had brought me up here.

"You are a...What are you?" I'd asked the fae the same question only a week ago. He didn't take too kindly to it. Hopefully, this man would understand my confusion. Unlike Caspian, who had growled at the question, this man smiled widely in response. He came forward and held his hand out for me to shake.

"I am Vasuki, the king of the dragons, and you are my new queen."

I must have stood there, my mouth hanging open, because he carried on talking.

"Things in your world are changing, and in turn, they affecting ours."

"I can't be your queen," I bleated. "I'm already in a fake relationship with someone I've inadvertently developed a crush on, and I'm almost, not quite, but probably engaged to someone else. My love life is tangled enough without turning my weird love triangle into a love square."

Vasuki laughed, though there was no joy in it. "I apologize for laughing, but you misunderstand me. I am already with a partner. Although we do not follow the human constructs of marriage, I am very much partnered with her for life, and she is the love of my life. I do not wish for your body, nor your soul. I only wish your council and your magic."

"I'm not too sure I can give you those either," I said, confusion in every word. "Can you tell me what is going on?"

He moved forward and took my hand. He was so unthreatening that I let him. On my other side, my other hand was taken by someone else. It was the red dragon with the huge eyelashes, but now she was a beautiful woman, or at least, half-woman for she was scaled from the waist down like Vasuki. Her hair was a magnificent crop of ombre, ranging from orange at the root to flaming red at the ends. The pair of them were so beautiful, they took my breath away, and the sooty smell followed them, even after their change.

"This is Emba," He said, introducing the red-headed woman to me. She smiled a dazzling smile and nodded her head slightly.

"Things are changing in your world," Vasuki repeated. "Normally, we do not care about the goings-on of humans, but unfortunately, it has invaded our world. Not once have we allowed a human up here, but you are different. We are hoping...I am hoping that you will do us a service."

I pulled back from the two of them, remembering the charred remains of the guards being lined up in the castle grounds.

"You killed people," I choked. "You killed the castle guards. My father is gearing his men up to come and attack you."

Vasuki threw a knowing look at Emba before turning back to me. "That was not us...at least, it was none of my doing. Please hear me out. I am no threat to you, nor is my dragon clan. I will promise you safety and safe passage back down the mountain if you listen to what I have to say. It is as important for you as it is for us."

I nodded my head slowly. It was hardly as if I had any choice in the matter, but I let that slide. I was intrigued by what he had to say.

"A couple of weeks ago, a massive shift in magical energy occurred. I doubt if humans felt it, but magical beings are sensitive to such things and dragons probably more so than most. I feared that things would go back to how they were many years ago. I felt a darkness that was all too familiar to me. I hoped that it was nothing, that the change was just some natural shift in energy, but then the humans started coming. Many years ago, we were hunted almost into extinction. Humans were afraid, angry. People were hurting other people, all because of the darkness, and they didn't stop there. Greed was prevalent. Humans came up the mountain. They stole from the mines, and they stole eggs from us and hunted us as trophies. The darkness affected us too, and we began to fight back. It was only when the princess of the people woke up from a slumber that things got better for us. Her father, the king, made the journey up the mountain himself and made it clear that he was outlawing dragon hunting. He told us we would be free, and as long as we stayed on the mountaintops, no one would bother us again. He was true to his word until the darkness came back a couple of weeks ago. The humans blamed us, although we know no more about it than they do."

"The king was my grandfather," I told him. "The princess who slept is my mother. She is cursed once again and now lies in slumber at the castle."

A curious look passed between Vasuki and the red dragon.

"That cannot be," he said, confusion in his voice. "You are not the same as him."

"I'm adopted," I explained. "My parents adopted me eighteen years ago."

Comprehension dawned. "Ah, I see. That makes sense. You are a lucky woman. Your grandfather is a good man."

"My grandfather died many years ago."

Vasuki bowed his head. "I'm sorry to hear that. My condolences. We do not keep up with what happens down there unless it affects us directly. As I said, it became illegal to hunt dragons, and until now, we have not been harmed. Unfortunately, in the past two weeks we have had many instances of humans coming up the mountain. Our eggs are being stolen again. Lives are being lost. I wanted to come down and speak to your grandfather, but my kind is not welcome down there, as you can imagine. I had planned to wait a week or so more, keeping extra guard over our eggs, but some of the dragons disobeyed my orders and took it upon themselves to give the humans a warning. I did not ask them to do it, and they will be punished for their actions. I do not believe in an eye for an eye. That way, everyone ends up blind. We are a peaceful people and do not wish to harm humans."

"My father has been erecting a wall to keep people off the mountain, but it will take months to build, even with all the men he has available."

Vasuki smiled curtly. "It seems your father is a good man as well. Please tell him we mean no harm, but we cannot have more humans on the mountain. I will talk to the dragons responsible for killing your guards, and I will make it clear that I don't want it to happen again, but I cannot chain them down. They are angry and mistrustful of humans. The dark energy is making everyone edgy."

"I can understand why," I said. "I'm sorry that we humans are doing this to you. I can ask the media to tell the people you are shifters. I doubt anyone would want to steal your eggs if they knew that."

Vasuki shook his head roughly. "That is where you are wrong. Dragon eggs are valuable, but Dragon shifter eggs are the most valuable of all. We are a rare species, and our eggs are priceless in certain markets. Only your grandfather knew the truth about us. I have to trust that you will keep our secret and only tell your father and no one else."

I nodded. "If you are sure."

"I am sure." He paused before speaking again. "May I ask you why you came up to see us? I see that you are carrying a sword that bears our image. A high honor, indeed, although I would expect nothing less from our queen."

There he went again calling me his queen. He had

yet to explain why. "I came up for information. I had a feeling that you had something to do with the shift in magical energy, but now I know you do not. Why do you keep referring to me as your queen?"

Milo had called me the queen of dragons a few times, and now it seemed he wasn't wrong. The irony of it didn't escape me.

"Do you not feel it?" he asked, gazing at the air around him.

I felt a lot of things at the moment, but whatever it was he was referring to, no, I didn't.

I shrugged, not knowing how to answer.

"You have a very deep connection to us," he said. "The magical ability you showed the other day drew our kind down from the mountain. You called to us. There is something I must tell you that you may not already understand. You said earlier that you were sorry that we humans did this to you. That's how you phrased it. We humans. You are not human. You are something much greater."

I blinked, unnerved by his words. "What do you mean I'm not human?"

I mean, what else could I be? I looked human, I talked like a human, I walked like a human. I'd already established that I wasn't fae and there was no way I was a witch or a vampire. He was wrong. he had to be wrong...but...

Caspian had said something similar. I was magic, a skill that humans didn't possess except the mages of Enchantia. Was it possible I was from there originally? Why would my parents adopt me from a place so far away when there were plenty of orphans here in Draconis? But then, I couldn't be a mage either if Vasuki was right. Mages were human. He was saying I wasn't.

"My eyes!" The gold ring around my irises had always marked me apart from others.

"Yes, your eyes are unusual." It was Emba who spoke. I'd not heard her speak before. Her voice was rich like honey, and she had the same accent as Vasuki." I have never seen anything like them. We do not know what you are, but we know you are special. It is foreseen that you will bring prosperity to our kind."

"Foreseen?"

She nodded. "We have a limited sense of the future. We do not see things as such, but we feel the vibrations rippling back. We are in for dark times, but there is a hint of the light in the distance. We believe that you are part of that. We feel a great affinity to you, one that has nothing to do with the fact that you are royalty."

"Indeed," Vasuki agreed. "We would not have known your royal status unless you told us. You are a queen of the people, as well as a queen of dragons. We bow down to you."

"I don't understand," I said.

"Neither do I," Vasuki admitted. "I cannot answer your questions, and I am sorry. All I can tell you is that your magic draws us to you. You are very special to us though I don't even understand it fully myself. We rarely bow down to others, but our bond with you is strong."

As he spoke, the other dragons that had been circling flew in and dropped their bellies to the ground as they did before. Looking around, the sight baffled me, but I now felt a kinship with them I'd never thought possible. Not that I'd thought dragon shifters were possible either. Just then, a smaller dragon nudged me harmlessly in the back of my leg with its snout. It was the most beautiful dragon I'd ever seen with brilliant iridescent purple scales that changed color in the sunlight. It looked up at me with mischievous eyes and made a cute little barking growl sound.

"Yes, Nyre," said Vasuki to the little dragon. He pronounced the name Ny-ree. "You may take her back, but fly straight back, you hear? Don't go too close to the castle. You won't be safe, but your small size will make it harder for the castle guards to see you."

The small dragon half-hopped, half-flew up and rested on my shoulder. It was barely bigger than a puppy. How was it supposed to fly me down the mountain?

The red dragon stood back up from her kneeling position and kissed my hand. "My daughter has always had a fascination with the human world, and even though you are not human, you are still part of it. I think she likes you. It would be a great honor to us if you let her take you down the mountain."

"You mean, fly on her back?" I asked, looking at the small purple dragon on my shoulder nervously. I doubted I'd fit on its back.

"No. Nyre will know what to do. She is a proficient flyer and stronger than she looks." Vasuki said. "I trust that you will pass on my sincere condolences at what my brethren did to your people. I will do my utmost to stop it from happening again. If your father is building a wall, I will pass the message on to the perpetrators. If he and his men come up the mountain, I will set defenses, but will not attack first. I will, however, fight back if need be."

I nodded as Nyre nudged me again. She hopped up and down on my shoulder impatiently. "I will keep your secret too."

"Thank you. You are welcome here whenever you want, but the rest of your people are not. Be safe, young princess."

Before I had time to answer him, Nyre's talons bit into my backpack, pulling me into the sky. All I could do was grip onto the straps of the backpack and hope neither of them broke.

I'd expected a calm flight down the base of the mountains, but Nyre had other ideas. She flew with me in the opposite direction, over the peaks of the mountains. I should have felt scared, but like Vasuki had said, I shared an affinity with her as if I could almost read her thoughts. She didn't want to hurt me; she wanted to show me things. She wanted to have fun. I whooped as she spun into a dive before leveling out. My heart raced almost as much as Nyre did, but I was having the time of my life. The view was like nothing I'd ever seen before, and I saw parts of Draconis that I'd never been to. Red mountains emerged out of the snow, giving me the most impressive scenery. We flew for hours, over secluded villages and hidden valleys, and before I knew it, the sun was beginning to lower in the sky.

"I have to get home," I said to her, and she nodded, before turning in mid air. My stomach rumbled. I had food in my back pack, but as she was holding on to it, I couldn't get to it to eat and so by the time I could see the castle, I was starving. She came into land at the other side of the woods where no one would see her. No doubt there would be men on patrol looking out for dragons and the woods was the safest place I could think for her to land.

I'd only just touched down when an arrow flew past me, almost grazing my ear. Nyre launched herself from my back. taking off into the sky, flying quickly away as more arrows followed her.

"Stop it," I shouted at the shadow in the woods. I couldn't see who it was, but I could clearly see the bow in his hands.

The man stepped forward out of the woods. "Azia?"

My heart skipped a beat when I realised who it was. "Father?"

"Get back to the castle at once!" He demanded, pointing sharply at the path through the woods that would lead me back home.

"But I have something to tell you," I began, but he cut me off.

"At once!" he barked. "Don't make me repeat myself again."

He marched behind me as I walked, not letting me speak at all. When we got to my room he opened the door for me.

"I've been out looking for you all day," He hissed as I walked past him. "Don't you think I have better things to do than go looking for you? Your mother is sick, the people are frightened, my guards don't know what to do next and that's only the ones that survived the dragon attack."

His voice got louder and louder with each syllable.

"I couldn't deal with any of it. I couldn't be there to comfort the bereaved families and I had no time to organise a killing trip up the mountains, and why? Because of you!"

He shouted the last word.

"Jack," he barked. "Come here. I want you standing outside this door all night. she is not to come out at all, do you understand?"

He slammed the door shut behind me, leaving me trapped in my very own prison, with no hope of escape.

I'd not even had the chance to beg him not to go up

the mountains and kill the dragons.

11TH JANUARY

I found out very quickly that not even Dahlia was allowed to come to my room to visit. My father himself brought me my food, but he wouldn't stay long enough to let me talk. The strain in his face was evident as he dropped the tray of food on my side table before slamming the door shut behind him. I could do nothing but stare out of the window and wait for the men to return, men which included both my brothers. My brothers aged fifteen and sixteen. It boiled my blood that Ash and Hollis were out there, doing something important for our kingdom and they weren't even of age yet and here I was, the heir to the throne, locked in my room and engaged to someone I didn't even like.

As if he could sense my grumbling (and yes, he probably could) Caspian knocked on my door in the early afternoon. I opened it quickly.

"What do you want?" I asked, not even bothering to put on any airs and graces. He was about as welcome as dragon rot.

"I came to see how you were and bring you chocolate."

"Great," I said, snatching the chocolate bar from his hand. At that point I would have liked to slam the door in his face, but he'd managed to sidle past it and was already in my room.

I didn't say anything. I guess I was too annoyed with everything else going on to care about my feelings towards him. Sitting down on the bed, I tore off the chocolate wrapper and tore a chunk of chocolate with my teeth.

"I came to tell you that I've started arrangements for our wedding. It will be a glorious affair."

My heart dropped further at his words. I'd been so caught up in everything else, I'd not even thought about the wedding. Who even cared about a wedding when my father was starting a war with the dragons and my mother was cursed and Milo was out there looking for a witch. It kinda made the thought of wedding favours and bridesmaid dresses seem ridiculous.

"I'm not doing it." I replied plainly, laying back on the bed. "It's a ridiculous notion."

"Your father doesn't think so," Caspian argued, sitting on the end of my bed.

I grimaced at him. "My father is not himself. He doesn't know what he's doing. He doesn't really care if I marry you or not, he's only making me do it because my mother is cursed and he thinks that's what she wants."

"But he is making you do it," Caspian countered.

I sat up to face him, bringing my feet up away from him. "My mother and father barely know you. You helped my father all those years ago, but you said yourself that the curse was already beginning to wane so in reality you did nothing. You did nothing then and you are doing nothing now."

"On the contrary," he replied, inching slightly closer. Any closer and I was going to kick him off the bed. "I've been to see your mother. I saw her when she first fell into the curse, but last night your father asked me to perform some spells to see what was wrong. I wanted to see if there was anything I could do to help her."

The tightness I'd been carrying around in my chest lightened considerably at his words. "And could you?" I held my breath. If anyone could help her it was him.

He licked his lips as he thought how to word what he was about to say. "It is indeed a curse that is binding her to sleep, but I don't think it's as simple as that. She is not just sleeping. I believe she is bound to the Dream Realm."

I raised a brow. "Dream Realm?"

"We all dream," he said. "Most of us about banal things. Occasionally we have strange dreams. I myself once dreamed I turned into a toad.

"If only," I retorted through gritted teeth. "Get to the point."

"It's these strange dreams we have that take us into the Dream Realm. Unlike the normal dreams of family or whatever, the strange dreams are like postcards of our visit to another world. It is a place that many visit without realising it's real. Very few stay more than a few minutes. We wake and the Dream Realm falls away. Whoever cursed your mother put up a block when she was in the Dream Realm. Stopped her from exiting. That, I believe is how this particular curse works."

I tried to get my head around what he was telling me.

"So she is in another world, lost?"

He shook his head "I doubt she is lost. This is a world she knows well. She spent a hundred years there already. She just can't find the exit."

I heaved a deep sigh. I had a choice, either believe the lying toe-rag or throw him out of my room. As I had very little else to do with my time beyond lay on my bed and grumble about my situation, I decided to hear him out.

"She's never mentioned another world before," I said, pulling my feet even closer to me.

This time he didn't follow. "I bet she hasn't. The Dream Realm is not a nice place. There are no rules there and the landscape is made up of other people's imaginations."

"So it isn't real then?"

"Oh, it's very real," he insisted. "It will feel as real to your mother than the real world does to you. She will be able to see, hear, smell, touch. Much of it will be familiar to her as she will have formed a lot of it with her own mind. Just because it's constantly evolving, doesn't mean it's not real. I'm not a master of the art of sleep, but I know someone who is. She studied Morpheus at the university in Urbis."

"Who's Morpheus?"

"Morpheus," Caspian said, "Is the god of sleep and dreams. The Dream Realm is his domain. He likes his fun...his dark fun."

Our kingdom had many gods that people worshipped, and I didn't believe in a single one of them. I'd never heard of Morpheus. Maybe Caspian was making this all up so I'd marry him. I wouldn't put it past him. The whole thing sounded like total boohickey.

"If the Dream Realm exists," I asked, uncertainty in

my voice. "What's to stop me, or anyone else from going in there in our sleep and pulling my mother back?"

"It doesn't work like that."

No, of course it didn't. Why would anything be so simple?

"Morpheus is a trickster," he stated, staring right into my eyes, giving me an involuntary shiver. "The person you see in there might be your mother, but it also might be a trick by Morpheus. He's not a nice guy and yet he's a God so there's nothing anyone can do. If your mother is trapped in his world, whoever did it must know him. He wouldn't trap anyone without someone very close to him asking him to, but once he has them, he'll play with them."

Bile burned at the back of my throat. If he wasn't telling me this as some weird joke, the thought of it was horrific. It was hard enough knowing my mother was a sleep, but knowing she was also trapped in some kind of Dream Realm with a crazy god made everything a lot worse.

"Derillen?"

Caspian shook his head. "I know you've said it before, but I don't think Derillen is the person behind your mother's sleep this time. I think it's a copy cat. The person you think you saw was copying her. Anyone could get a horned headdress made up."

"Think I saw? I did see her and I don't understand how this is so hard for you to believe."

Caspian sighed. "I really didn't want to get into this with you. Derillen went a long time ago. She was extremely powerful. Probably the most powerful witch that ever lived. No one could defeat her, not even me."

"Which makes it more likely that the witch I saw is her."

"Actually, I think it means the opposite. Something defeated her back then. She was relentless. She wouldn't just disappear without someone making her. I just don't know who. I can't think of anyone with that much power. She took it from the gods themselves. I think Morpheus knew her and told someone else how to block the exits to the Dream Realm."

"I need to get my mother out, Caspian," I whispered, swallowing back the lump in my throat.

He brought his hand to his chin thoughtfully. "There is a way to get into the Dream Realm from ours but I do not know it. My friend studied dream lore for a long time. I could ask her to come here."

Hope rose in my chest. "Could you?"

He nodded "I will send word to her, but she will not be able to get here soon. She lives in Urbis. It's quite a journey, even on the Urbis Express."

I thought of the huge sky ships that occasionally passed by in the distant sky. I'd never travelled on one, but I'd often wondered how nice it would be to travel so high up, to see the kingdom from above. I'd had a taste of it by flying on Nyre yesterday and I wanted more.

"I appreciate it, thank you."

Caspian took my hand and for the first time, I didn't pull away.

"I owe you for everything I've done to you," he said. "What I did was wrong. I wanted your mother to like me and I wanted to marry you. I shouldn't have betrayed your trust, just to get what I wanted, but I didn't know what else to do. I hoped that if I could only get you to marry me, then maybe love would come after."

"Tell me honestly," I started, looking right into his eyes. "You talk of love and specifically of my love, but you never talk of your own. Do you love me?"

He looked at me intently, those amethyst eyes boring into me. "I cannot say I feel love. I barely know you, but I feel a connection and I feel a strong attraction to you that I wasn't prepared for. I came here to help your father out. I wasn't expecting to even like you, let alone love you, but I've seen things in you that I've never seen in anyone else. You have a bravery like no one I've ever known. Your father told me that he caught you flying in the talons of a dragon yesterday. I cannot even begin to understand how you managed something so dangerous without getting hurt or killed. I also cannot comprehend why you would want to do something so reckless, especially after what the dragons did to your father's men."

I sighed. "Is my father still mad at me?"

"Of course he is. Would you expect anything different?" he arched a brow waiting for my answer.

"The dragons aren't as bad as everyone thinks," I said, remembering my talk with Vasuki the day before.

"All evidence to the contrary."

"Just because some dragons hurt my father's men, doesn't mean that they all did." I wanted to tell him about Vasuki and the others but I'd been asked not to and Caspian had betrayed me once too often for me to trust him completely.

"No, maybe not, but they've done enough damage. I know they are fascinating creatures. I, myself would like to know more about them, but that doesn't mean you should put your life at risk to study them. Maybe their behaviour is directly related to your mother's curse, maybe not, but killing yourself to find out won't help the kingdom and it won't help your mother. You are best staying in here where your father knows you are safe until this all passes."

I sighed. “I don’t want to stay in here. I’m being punished. I don’t want to be a princess locked in a tower, waiting for a knight to save me. I want to be the knight and I want to save everyone else.”

“And that...” Caspian said, standing up, “is half the problem. That’s the reason your father won’t let you out. He can’t trust that you won’t go and do something crazy like you did yesterday. I have something for you. I didn’t want to give it to you like this, but I don’t see there being a better time in the next three weeks.”

He bent down to his knee and produced a box. When he opened it, I saw the most gorgeous ring in white gold with a huge amethyst set in the middle of it. It was the amethyst from his sword. The one I’d thrown from my bedroom window in the previous week.

“I don’t want to ask you to marry me, I already know your answer, but I hope you’ll wear it anyway. It belonged to my mother.”

When I didn’t move or speak, he left the box on my bed and walked to the door.

“I’ll speak to my friend about Morpheus,” he promised and then left, shutting the door quietly behind him.

Picking up the box, I laid back on the bed. It really was a beautiful ring. My mother would love it. I thought back to what Caspian had said about Morpheus. I’d never heard the name before, just as I’d not heard of Derillen before last week. There was so much happening, so many new names, so many people involved and yet none of it really was new. This had all been in play before I was born and instead of coming to an end, had merely been paused, ready to start again, bringing the horrors back.

Derillen was where this had all started. I’d learned her name. I’d even seen her and yet I knew nothing about her. My mother had never really talked about her life before her big sleep. The story of my father meeting her and saving her eclipsed everything that came before and whenever I'd asked her about it, she'd brushed it off saying it didn't matter anymore. But it did matter. If only I'd pushed her on the subject, maybe I'd have an idea how to solve all these problems now. If I could get to Derillen and stop the darkness she was spreading, everything else would fall into place.

I slipped the ring on my finger. It fitted perfectly. Of course it did, I expected no less from Caspian

Sighing, I pulled it off and placed it back in the box that I put on my nightstand. I couldn't think about weddings and rings. My mother was still cursed and the kingdom was falling apart. I didn't even know if my father's men had attacked the dragons. I'd been watching from my bedroom window, and I'd not seen anyone venturing up the Fire Mountains, but that didn't mean they hadn't. It only meant that I'd not seen them.

I closed my eyes and wished for sleep even though I wasn't tired. I needed to know if Caspian's story about the Dream Realm was true. It took over an hour of tossing and turning, but eventually the darkness eclipsed the light and I found myself dreaming. I was flying with Nyre again but below me the kingdom was strange and distorted.

"Go down there," I whispered and Nyre fell into a dive so steep I had to hold on for dear life. We hurtled towards the ground at an astonishing speed. It was too quick. We were going to crash. I fell out of my bed with a scream.

My door opened.

"Azia, what happened?"

I stood, blinking the sleep from my eyes. Milo stood

before me. After a moment of confusion, I saw that he was real and the Dream Realm had escaped me. I fell into his arms, exhaustion passing through me. Tears prickled my eyes.

He brought his thumb up and wiped them away.

"What's going on?"

Looking over Milo's shoulder I saw Jack watching us.

"It's okay Jack. I've got this," Milo said, following my line of sight to the old guard.

"His majesty won't approve," Jack huffed.

"It's okay Jack," I said, pulling Milo into my room. "Milo's job is to protect me. I won't be able to run away while he's here."

"That's not what I was worried ab..."

"Bye Jack." I closed the door and pulled the bolt across for good measure.

"You shouldn't have done that," Milo said, keeping his voice low. I smiled for the first time all day.

"I know, and I know I don't care. I'm just glad to have you back." I pulled him into a hug and immediately my fears fell away. Everything felt better when Milo was around, even if nothing really had changed.

He held me tightly, running his hand up and down my back, comforting me. I never wanted to let go, but if Jack was to tell my father that Milo was here, he'd be right up here demanding Milo leave.

I pulled apart from him and sat down on the bed. "Did you find any spindles?"

Milo shook his head in frustration. "No. Not one. The whole thing was a waste of time. I've spent the last two days terrifying elderly ladies while I searched through their houses on order of your father. No one has any spindles anymore. If the witch has one, she is long gone and has taken it with her. It was more than likely made out of magic anyway and if it was, we will never find it. I spent the whole time thinking about you."

"You did?"

He nodded and took my hand in his. His face was pale, lined with worry. "There's something I have to tell you and I don't know how."

His shoulder slumped as if the weight of the world was upon him. A thrill of fear ran through me.

"What is it?"

"I was in the teams scouting around Zhore and the other nearby towns. That's why I'm back so soon. I didn't have too far to go. Here..." He pulled out a copy of a newspaper and handed it over.

It was the Draconian Sentinel, the Draconis national paper. I'd not read the paper in days and now that I could see the headline, I realised why. It had been hidden from me. It was an announcement of Caspian and my wedding on the date my father had said. My hand went to my throat as I read the announcement. The whole kingdom was invited to a party I knew nothing about, to which I was the main guest. I threw the paper down in frustration.

"He gave me a ring today," I said pointing to the box that still sat on the nightstand. He must have known about this announcement and didn't say anything. "

I stood up and paced the room. "Why are they reporting this when the whole kingdom is falling to pieces?"

"I don't understand it either," Milo said. He sounded so defeated. "I thought that the dragons would take up more column space but I suspect that your father has something to do with this. Maybe he thinks that the kingdom needs something to look forward to. Zhore is already preparing for the party. The town square was being decorated when I left."

"I don't want to marry him."

"I know," Milo replied softly. He stood up to face me and pulled me to him. "And I'm not going to let you. I told you I'd fight for you before and I meant it. If the law states that a suitor can win your hand in competition, then I'll fight for you. I know what I said when I left, but I was wrong. I missed you so much and realised what an ass I'd been. I'll always fight for you."

I'd completely forgotten about the book that Remy had shown me. So much had happened since then. I guess I thought that my father wouldn't push a wedding on me with so much already going on. How wrong I was.

"Azia." Milo looked right at me. "I don't want to lose you. I know we barely know each other and I know that I don't have a ring or the blessing of the king, but if I win this competition, will you marry me?"

It was my second proposal in just over two hours. It was probably a kingdom-wide record. I'd gone over eighteen years without anyone being interested in me and now I had two men, both of which I'd only just met, willing to fight for my hand in marriage. Well Milo was, but I guessed that Caspian wouldn't want to lose face. He was a warrior. He would fight too.

"Wait here," I said, unbolting the door.

I strode right past Jack who tried stopping me.

"You are not to leave the room," he said, holding his sword up.

"Don't you think that's overkill, Jack?" Milo said behind me.

"No, not really," Jack replied. "She sneaked past me once already. I can't let it happen again. The king will have my job."

I pushed the sword away from my chest with my finger. He was all bluster. My father would be much more upset if one of his guards turned me into Swiss cheese than if I got out of my room again. "It's my father I'm going to see," I said to him. Please come with me if you don't believe me."

Poor Jack looked nervous as I strode purposefully past him. I didn't turn around, but I could hear two sets of footsteps following me. One from Jack who didn't trust me and one from Milo who had ignored my order to stay where he was. I'd not wanted him with me when I confronted my father and demanded a competition, but as I walked I realised it made sense for Milo to be there. Technically anyone could enter, but only Milo and Caspian would.

I didn't want to have a competition. I was too busy. I had the dragons to worry about, not to mention this Morpheus character that Caspian mentioned, that I still wasn't sure was real or not. But if I didn't at least propose a competition, my father would have me married off before I had chance to do anything about either of those problems, and despite everything that Caspian said, He'd probably keep me at home like a good little wife.

My first stop was my father's bedroom, but it was empty save for my sleeping mother and her own maid.

"I'm looking for my father," I said to the maid. "Do you know where he is?"

She shuffled her feet nervously. "I believe he is in the main hall talking to his men. A lot of them are back today."

I nodded my thanks and once again brushed past Jack.

He looked no happier to be following me than I was

of having him follow me.

I found my father exactly where the maid said he was.

The great hall was filled with men but the overall atmosphere was one of defeat. None of these men had found a spindle and they never would.

I saw Caspian in the corner talking to one of the men. When he looked up, I beckoned him over.

"Did you send word to your friend yet?" I asked.

"Of course. As soon as I left your room.." His eyes flickered down to my hand.

"I see you are not wearing my ring yet."

"Actually, that's why I'm here," I said. "Please come with me."

My father seemed surprised to find his daughter with three men in tow. "What's this?"

"I tried to stop her sire, but she's a wilful one," Jack pointed out.

My father sighed. "And that's exactly why I asked you to guard her." To my side, Jack sunk back. I would have felt sorry for him if he wasn't so intent about keeping me locked in my room.

"I do not want to marry Caspian," I said. I turned to Caspian. "I'm sorry. The ring you gave me is truly spectacular, but I cannot marry you because you gave me nice jewellery."

"Not this again," My father huffed. "I'm well aware of your thoughts on the matter. Indeed, you've not stopped telling me them , but as I've already told you, you have no choice and I do not wish to discuss this matter with you again. As you can see I'm extremely busy with my men. As soon as they all get back from looking for spindles I'm sending them up the mountains."

"I do have a choice and it's the law," I said, standing

my ground. I brought my hands up to my hips. “Remy found it in a book.”

My father raised an eyebrow? “What has Remy got to do with this?”

“Everything! He found a book of old Draconis laws. One of them states that if there is more than one suitor for the heir to the throne, a competition should be held to decide between them.

“More than one suitor?” My father blustered. It was clear that he didn’t want to be having this conversation, but tough luck, because I was going to have my say. “That’s preposterous,” he added.

“I agree,” Interjected Caspian, pushing forward. “I’m the only person that has asked you to marry me!”

“Actually, that’s not quite true,” Milo said, standing forward. “I just asked her.”

Caspian’s face dropped. “You can’t.”

“He can,” I said. “I never accepted your proposal. You gave me a ring, but you can see for yourself that I’m not wearing it. I’ve not accepted any proposal and seeing as my father would not let me accept one from Milo, it will have to go to competition.”

My father brought his hand up to the back of his neck and closed his eyes. “I don’t know of this law. I’ve never heard of it.” He spoke through gritted teeth.

Just then, Remy’s voice echoed through the hall.

“Aza!” He ran towards us, the book of laws in his hand. He passed it to my father.

“Page thirty two,” I said, a self satisfied smile on my face. I gave Remy a wink who beamed at me.

My father turned the pages.

Caspian bridged the gap between him and my father. “You can’t listen to this Alec? Just because something is written in an old book doesn’t mean it’s true. Besides you are the king. You make the laws."

My father found the right page and read it quickly.

"It's true, I do make the laws..." he said, slowly.

"But it's Urbis that passes them," I added, raising my eyebrows in triumph. "And changes in law can take months...years even." I folded my arms and gave Caspian a smirk.

Beside me, my father sighed. "Fine. If this is the law, then so be it. We will have a competition but let it be known that I'm not happy about this. I have way too much to deal with, without this nonsense too."

"You could just let me wait until I'm ready to be married then pick who I want," I said.

He shook his head. "No. The wedding will go ahead. It's already booked." He looked to Caspian. "I trust you can win this."

He then snapped at one of the guards who ran right over.

"Go to the editor of the Draconian Sentinel and let him know that the wedding is still on, but we don't know the groom yet. Tell him that the last post was a mistake. You'd better tell him that we are abiding by law and holding a competition for the princess's hand in marriage."

He threw me a look of agitation and threw the book back to Remy before storming out of the room. Caspian followed, trying to get him to change his mind.

"Good job Remy," I said, pulling my brother into a hug. He squeezed me tightly, but this time I had company in his arms. He'd pulled both Milo and Jack into the hug with me. Next to me, Milo smiled, but the squashed face of Jack next to him showed only an expression of pure terror.

"Unsquash Remy," I grinned and Remy let go.

“What now?” asked Milo.

“Now? I guess we read this book thoroughly and figure out exactly what to practice for the competition.

12TH JANUARY

I woke early as the first light of dawn trickled sunlight through my curtains.

I'd spent hours practicing swordmanship with Milo in my room the night before and now my body ached. Muscles I didn't know I had burned, but if it meant I was getting better and Milo was getting better, I could survive a little pain. It had taken my mind off everything else going on. Things I couldn't control. The dragon situation, Morpheus, my upcoming wedding. I didn't want to think about any of it and so I didn't. I practiced sword fighting till I was too tired to do anything else.

No one had come to my room to drag him out so he'd stayed late, leaving me with a kiss way after dark. I jumped out of bed and opened the door expecting him not to be there, but he was. Dark circles blotched under his eyes, but when he saw me he broke into a delicious grin.

He moved forward and kissed me.

"My shift finished half an hour ago, but I didn't want to go without seeing you first."

"I'm surprised you are still working in this part of the castle."

"Me too," Milo said, lowering his voice. "but I stayed for my shift and no one complained. Well, Jack complained, but he always complains." He gave me a beautiful smile. "He left an hour ago."

He nodded his head towards another guard who had taken up a spot. This one was new. He was also mean looking and huge. My father really didn't want me to leave it seemed. When he caught me looking he gave me a leery grin.

"I have something to show you," I said to Milo, ignoring the other guard. "Do you think you'll be able to come see me later?"

"Show me now?" he asked, stifling a yawn.

I pulled him close and whispered in his ear, not wanting the other guard to hear. "You are tired. Go home and sleep. You need to be more awake to see this."

I'd deliberated all night about breaking my promise to Vasuki. I'd promised to tell my father about him and not tell anyone else. I'd failed miserably on the first part. My father didn't want to hear anything to do with Dragons. And here I was wanting to tell Milo about them. I needed to tell someone. I wasn't even going to tell him, I was going to show him.

He gave me a brief kiss goodbye and left. The other guard glared meanly so I shut the door, only to have it opened a few minutes later by Dahlia.

"You're dressed already," she said, noting the dress,

I'd just pulled on.

"Always a tone of surprise," I said back to her.

"Well at least let me brush your hair," she said, bustling into my room. "I wouldn't want you putting me out of a job now." I stuck my tongue at her and sat on the chair, facing it out to the moorlands. It was too cloudy to see the peaks of the fire mountains, but I imagined the dragons were flying around as they always did.

"Have you ever heard of Morpheus?" I asked as she ran the brush through my hair, tugging the tangles out. I wasn't sure I could believe what Caspian had told me.

"He's one of the gods...God of sleep, I think," she mused aloud. "I don't know. There are so many of them. I don't know how people keep up with who they are worshiping these days."

"Don't you believe in the gods, Dahlia?" She'd never mentioned them, and I'd always took her as a non-believer like I was.

"It's all stuff and nonsense if you ask me. How can there be so many gods? It doesn't make sense. People believe what they want to believe. They believe whatever suits them."

"That's what I thought, too, but..."

"But?"

"Caspian was talking to me about a world run by a god named Morpheus, and I'd never heard of him before."

Dahlia tutted. "Well, the fae are a law unto themselves. They follow their own rules. I have to say, I'm glad that you are not being forced to marry him anymore. I don't like him much. "

"You've changed your tune," I said, remembering how she'd practically drooled over him last time he was mentioned. "Why not?"

"I've heard rumors that he's not nice to the staff. I know I'm not supposed to talk ill of your parents' guests, but I'm not sure either of them knows him like they think they do. Yes, he's utterly gorgeous, but that doesn't account for much now, does it?"

I gave her a wry grin

Dahlia thought the same of him as I did now that she'd finally seen past his pretty exterior. It was nice to have her on my side, even if she was practically yanking my hair out as she talked about him.

"Do you think Milo has a hope of winning against Caspian...in the competition I mean?" I assumed she already knew. Very little escaped Dahlia when it came to matters in the castle.

"I don't know. I've not seen either of them fight," She said, gathering my hair up and beginning a braid. "They've got quite a bit of competition too, so who knows really."

My ears pricked up. "Competition? What do you mean?"

"You don't think it's only them interested, do you? Once the story broke of the competition, every man in the land wanted in."

"What?" I asked queasily as she wrapped a ribbon around the end of the braid.

"Yes," she answered cheerfully, unaware of the nausea rising in my stomach. "Your father has been fielding inquiries all day. I don't think he's very happy about it. He's passed it to the castle admin staff to deal with, but they are swamped too."

"Other people want to marry me?" I gulped.

She moved around to get a look at my hair from the front. "Oh, yes. There's a line a mile long outside the castle wanting to join in."

"No!" I stood up and wandered to the window. As she had said, a line of men stretched as far as the eye could see. One of them saw me and pointed up to the window. Suddenly, I had the eyes of hundreds of men looking my way. I shut my curtains quickly.

"This was only supposed to be for Milo and Caspian," I croaked.

"Yes, well, if you open a can of worms, you have to be ready for the birds."

I sat back in my chair, feeling faint. I'd had enough on my plate juggling two men that I didn't want to marry; now, I had a whole army of them.

"Why would anyone want to marry me?" I squeaked.

"You're a beautiful young lady, Azia. Why wouldn't they?"

"No one looked twice at me a couple of weeks ago," I argued.

Dahlia went to my bed and began to pull the covers straight. "I'm not sure that's true. You've always had your admirers. My son often asked about you when I went home. He's always had a crush on you."

"He has?"

"Yes. He was first in line to join the competition this morning. I told him he was a fool, but he wouldn't listen. I just hope your father doesn't come up with something too awful for it. I wouldn't want him getting hurt."

This wasn't supposed to happen," I complained. "I don't even want to get married. I'm only eighteen years old. I want to travel and see things. I want to know what it's like to be me before I know what it's like to be a part of someone else.

"I was married with a child on the way at your age," she said, plumping my pillows. I didn't have the opportunities you have. You are a princess. Just because you are married, doesn't mean you can't experience life. It just means you'll share those experiences with someone else. Besides, rumors about that fae chap of yours aren't the only ones going around the castle. I've heard that you are getting very close to that young guard.

I felt the blush rise to my cheeks. So the castle staff were talking about me. Didn't they have enough to talk about?

"I really like Milo, but he knows I don't want to get married so young. He's only doing this competition so I don't have to marry Caspian."

She put the last of my pillows back and placed her hands on her hips. "You have a great opportunity here. You have the best men in all the land lined up outside wanting to marry you, not to mention two in the castle."

"But most of them will only want what comes with the position," I sighed. "The castle, power, money."

"True," she nodded, "but the bravest will win."

"No, the best fighter will win, but will that necessarily be the best husband?"

"No, I guess not," she agreed, picking up a duster and beginning to dust. "Maybe your father will come up with a fair competition. I know he's under a lot of stress at the moment, and he's making some poor decisions, but I really do believe he has your best interests at heart. He will make it fair, and you never know, you might find the love of your life in all of this."

"I doubt it," I sighed, sitting back in the chair. I could no more imagine finding the love of my life than sprouting an extra head and turning green. "How is my father anyway? This must be an awful nuisance for him."

Dahlia pursed her lips. "You could say that. He's not happy at all that you've brought this on him. He has enough on his plate as it is with your mother being cursed and the dragon problem to deal with. I'd stay out of his way for a few days if I were you. I don't think you are his favorite person at the moment. "

My heart already ached with everything I had to deal with, and now, I'd hurt my father.

"That will be easy," I sighed. "I'm confined to my room. I can't leave even if I want to."

"Actually, that's not quite the case," Dahlia smiled. "That's why I'm here. I'm to make you look presentable."

"Presentable for what?"

"Your father wants you downstairs for a photoshoot with the Draconian Sentinel. Apparently, they've sent a photographer who is refusing to leave until he gets a photo and an interview."

"Why doesn't my father get the guards to throw him out? "I asked appalled.

"Because then the press will print a story that your father is under duress. Remember, he has a kingdom to run, and he's got to be a good leader while everything around him is falling apart. Let's just hope he's not going to stick around for the interview, eh?"

My stomach dropped at the thought of the mess I'd made. I couldn't see a way out any more than my father could, and now, it was going to be printed in the Draconis national newspaper.

Could anything worse happen?

Just then, there was a knock at the door. It opened without me moving to it.

"There you are!" Caspian walked in uninvited. "Your father asked me to escort you to the grand hall."

I looked at Dahlia. She shrugged her shoulders.

Just great! I stood up and walked past Caspian. There was no point pretending I cared anymore. As I passed, I slipped the ring box into his hand.

"I'm sorry," I whispered. I wasn't sure if he even heard me.

The great hall was in chaos, and any thoughts that my father might not be there were quashed. He looked so tired as he fielded questions from all over the place. There was no coordination, and it was difficult to tell who was who. I couldn't even see the photographer in amongst all the men.

Pushing through, I climbed the small stage to my father's throne.

I leaned down and whispered in his ear. "Go to bed. I've got this."

He shook his head, but he didn't move. His eyes were glazed over, the look of a man too exhausted to move.

"Gentlemen," I shouted to the rabble. When the noise didn't abate, I coughed then tried again, this time, shouting loudly.

"Gentlemen!"

This time a hundred pairs of eyes looked my way, and a light flashed. So the photographer was in there somewhere.

I'd given my first speech only a few days previously, but that was to the staff. This was my first time giving one to complete strangers, but with everything going on, it was about time I stepped up.

I cleared my throat and began to speak. "I appreciate you all coming here. It means a lot to me that you would all want to be considered to be my husband. I wasn't expecting such a turnout, but I am grateful to all of you. You are my father's loyal subjects, and therefore, you all mean a lot to me. Unfortunately, I am only one person, and I cannot marry you all."

A titter of laughter went around the hall as more men filtered in.

"As you probably already know, the kingdom is under a lot of strain at the moment, and it's not possible to see all of you today. Instead, I'd like all of you to write your name on a piece of paper along with your address to register your interest in the competition."

I motioned for one of the guards to fetch some pens and paper. "We will send you a personal invite a few days before the tournament, and we will print instructions in the Draconian Sentinel. Until then, I ask that you write your name quickly and leave us to come up with the rules of the competition. "

I asked the guard with the pens and paper to take them outside. They could line up there. One by one, they trooped out until there were only a few people left. A man with a notepad and one with a camera stayed behind.

"Dahlia," I said, my heart still thumping from having to talk to so many people. "Please, will you help my father to his room while I give an interview for the Sentinel?"

My father rose. "I don't need any help. If you'll excuse me, gentlemen, it's been a long day."

Dahlia followed him anyway. Only Caspian remained.

"Is your father sick?" The reporter asked. He was already writing something in his pad. "He said it's been a long day, but it's still early morning."

"My father is perfectly well. He's just got a lot going on, as you can imagine. However, we are not here to talk about my father, we are here to discuss the competition. It will be held the week before the wedding. I have no information on what the competition will entail at this time, but the winning suitor will be the one to marry me."

"What if you don't like the winner?"

What if, indeed. "Then I shall marry him anyway as the law states. The competition will weed out anyone not suitable to the life of the queen's court. He will never be king. When I ascend to the throne, he will work alongside me, but will never be my equal, nor will he ever be above me in position. Not many men would like to be in such a position, so a word of warning to all the men that enter. This will be the life you will live, always second. I have no more answers, so if you'll please excuse me, gentlemen."

I walked past them with my head held high, ignoring the stares from the reporter and his photographer. That should cut down on idiots thinking they would be able to rule the kingdom by marrying me.

The castle was quiet as I walked back up to my room. When I got there, Milo stood outside. Without stopping, I grabbed his hand and pulled him down the corridor.

"Come with me."

"Where are we going?" he whispered as I spirited him through the castle. My father was asleep, and my mother cursed. I was the eldest child, and, therefore, the person in charge, but that didn't mean I wanted to be stopped by any member of staff brave enough to question where I was going. The big mean guard was absent this morning, but that didn't mean that there wouldn't be others like him.

Despite what my father said he wanted, I wasn't planning on spending the last remaining free days of my life locked in my room as though I'd done something wrong. I cared about this kingdom, and I needed to do something to help—anything. I didn't even know what, but I wasn't going to help anyone by sitting on my bed moping.

I took us out of the back entrance to the castle and across the grounds to the little door through the back wall. A thick brass lock held it tight to the frame.

"Now what?" Milo asked.

I turned to him and kissed him quickly on the nose, before expertly climbing up his body. He soon got the idea, clasping his hands together to give me a leg up the wall. When I was at the top, I leaned down to help him over.

"Are we going to practice?" he asked as we walked quickly through the small wooded area.

"No. The time for practice is over. It's now time to start doing."

We emerged into the sunshine at the base of the Fire Mountains.

"Doing what?"

I took his hand and began to lead him to the part of the wall I'd walked around last time. My father's army hadn't managed to build any more of it, and like everything else in Draconis at the moment, it had ground to a standstill. "I don't know yet," I replied cryptically, "but I know someone who might."

We climbed a little way before I felt comfortable enough to use my magic. I'd kept this part of myself away from Milo, afraid that he might think there was something wrong with me, but I couldn't keep it in any longer. I was magic, and even though I wasn't sure exactly how to use it, I knew it was worth figuring it out. Maybe one day I'd be able to help my mother. It only ever seemed to work when I was close to the dragons, but that was fine as I could already see a couple of them flying high above us.

“Watch this!” I said, before pulling my hand from Milo’s and closing my eyes.

I concentrated for all I was worth, pulling all my energy to a central point deep in my belly before letting it blast out of my hands and spiraling up into the cloudless sky.

The people would have been able to see it. Even as far away as Zhore, but it didn’t matter. As long as the Dragons saw it first.

“Azia?” Milo asked, grabbing my sleeve. I ignored him as best I could, even after the pulling on my sleeve became all the more insistent.

“Azia!” He was louder now, but I was in the zone. When he tugged me so hard, we both collapsed to the ground, the beam of magical light disappeared.

It happened so quickly. Milo jumped to his feet and pulled out his sword, ready for a fight. My heart raced for a second before realizing who it was he was up against. A flash of purple in the corner of my eye told me my friend was here. I pulled myself up next to Milo, and this time, it was my turn to pull on his sleeve. “Put your sword away. That’s Nyre. That’s who I brought you here to see.”

Milo turned to me, a look of disbelief on his face, but he didn’t lower his sword. “You brought me to see a dragon? Are you serious?”

I nodded, then waved at Nyre, who landed next to us as Milo watched on with mild concern. He didn’t sheath his sword as Nyre skipped towards us and flew up onto my shoulder like she had before.

“Woah!” I held my hands out at Milo, who’d readied himself for attack, his sword aloft and his mouth a perfect o shape. “She’s a friend. Milo, this is Nyre, Nyre this is Milo. His bark’s worse than his bite.”

Milo gazed at me goggle-eyed as Nyre pranced on my shoulder, before hopping over to Milo's. He'd ducked, but not in time. Nyre had got him. She wanted a stage to dance on, and he was it. I laughed as she hopped up and down on his head playfully. When Milo saw he was in no danger, he relaxed. Nyre hopped back over to me as Milo put his sword away.

If he thought cute little Nyre was scary, wait until he met Vasuki and Emba and the other dragons. He was in for a shock, but I wasn't going to spill the beans.

"Do you think you can get one of the others to come fly us up the mountain?" I whispered in Nyre's ear. I didn't want Milo hearing. It would spoil the surprise.

She tightened the grip on my shoulder as she prepared to launch herself upward. Or at least, I thought that's what she was doing before I found myself flying up into the air with her. She swooped and grabbed Milo with her spare talon and began the ascent to her mountaintop home.

Color drained from Milo's face as we flew at a dizzying speed upward. He didn't say a word, and I think that was only because he would throw up if he dared to open his mouth

I thought we'd fly into the nest we'd flown into before, but Nyre carried on flying over the other side of the mountain to a valley I'd not seen before. A small river twisted through it flanked by huge houses dotting the scenery.

"Where is this place?" Milo whispered, his voice almost lost on the wind. I had to strain to hear him, but I got the gist. I had no answers for him. Dragons were everywhere. I didn't know where we were. As we got closer, the houses became more pronounced. Each of them was made in a haphazard manner with what looked like found objects, and all of them had two doors. One normal-sized and another huge door. My mouth went dry as I noticed we weren't alone. The dragons in the air had begun to follow us, and as we neared the ground, the ones down there dropped whatever it was that they were doing and followed suit. Behind me, Milo gripped me tightly as we ended up the head of a parade of angry looking dragons.

I'd gone against my promise to Vasuki not to bring another person here. On the other side of the mountain, it had seemed like a good idea, but now that we were surrounded, I was beginning to rethink my decision. Not that I could do anything about it. We'd already landed. There was no going back.

Milo pulled out his sword again the moment Nyre let go of him.

I let my hand fall on his and softly lowered it. "They are not a threat."

I hope.

One of the nearest dragons bared its teeth, saliva dripping from its large jowls.

"Are you sure?" Milo hissed. "Because I'm beginning to feel like dragon-breakfast."

Gazing around at the dozens of eyes watching me, I began to wonder if I hadn't overestimated my welcome here.

Inside me, my body responded to the dragons the way it had when I'd been out with Caspian. My magic or whatever it was began to stir. I'd spent so many hours trying to recreate it with no success, but now, it was churning, boiling away inside me. I threw it out, sending a beacon up into the sky. This time rains of hot pink and purple fell like cherry blossoms in spring. As they had before, the dragons dropped to their bellies, bowing down to me.

Milo gripped my hand tightly as the whole village of dragons came thundering down.

Between them walked a man and woman, if you could call them that. I bowed my head as Vasuki and Emba walked hand in hand through the crowd of dragons.

"What's this?" Vasuki asked, eyeing Milo.

My stomach had been in knots, but Vasuki didn't appear to be angry, merely curious to the stranger beside me.

I held my breath as I introduced Milo.

Vasuki walked forward, his hand extended. Beside me, Milo hesitantly held out his own hand. To give him credit, he stood tall and firm, though I could see a small tremor in him. I should have warned him before, but I was afraid he might not come if I did.

"My father wouldn't listen to me," I said as Emba pulled Milo into a hug. "I tried, but he is under a lot of strain, and he thinks I'm causing trouble. I've told no one else. Milo didn't even know until I brought him here. He is the only one who listens to me. I'm sorry if I have gone against your wishes."

I bowed my head to him.

Behind him, someone growled. It was the green dragon from earlier, but now, he was transformed into a grizzly beast of a man. With his green hair and scaled skin, he looked more moss than man. He also did not look impressed.

"Darius, know your place," Vasuki growled back, and the man took a step back. "This is our queen, and this is her guest. Respect her as such."

Darius growled again and stalked away, disappearing into a nearby house.

"Queen?" Milo whispered, arching his brow. "Do

you want to, at least, give me a hint at what's going on here?"

"Remember when you called me Queen of the Dragons?"

He nodded.

"Well, it turned out you were right...sort of."

Turning back to Vasuki, I bowed again.

"I come to ask your guidance. I have no one to help me, and there are people I'm not sure I can trust. I do trust you, however, and I'd value your honesty."

"I am nothing if not honest. Bluntly so, at times. How can I help you?"

"I've have been told of a place called the Dream Realm. I wonder if you know of it?"

"I have heard of such a place," he confirmed. "We do not worship gods in the way that you humans do. There is no dragon god. We believe that we are the higher beings. That doesn't mean I do not know of them. However, I am not the best person to ask of such a place. You must know people better than I who can tell you about it. What about that fae I saw you with the other day. If anyone knows about the gods, it is he."

"He was the one who told me about the Dream Realm, but he is the one I can't trust. I fear I'll have to travel to find someone who knows. I am sorry for taking up your time."

"I already told you that you are welcome up here any time that you desire. Your friend here also, but only with you. I request that you don't bring anyone else up here. I have been more than fair with you even though you went against my wishes. There is only so much I can do to keep you safe. You saw how Darius reacted to your presence. I am not his keeper, and there is only so much he will take."

"I understand. I promise I will not tell another soul about you, although, as you requested before, I will try and get through to my father. He is having a difficult time. He still wants to send his men to the mountaintops to kill you all. I've not had a chance to talk him out of it. I don't think he really wants to hurt any of you, but the people are looking to him to take action, and he is a broken man. He knows not what he is doing now since my mother fell asleep."

"I understand. Things must be hard, and I do not envy him. I will keep this information away from Darius, but I'd like you to do me one more favor. "

I nodded enthusiastically. I owed him as much.

"Can you send a beacon of light up as a warning if you see anyone climbing the mountains? It will give us time to prepare. I will make my people safe by hiding them rather than fighting back, but the women nest on the mountaintops and are the most vulnerable. I do not want a war with your father. I will extend this as a courtesy to you for the time being. Is there anything else I can help you with, my queen?"

I was about to say no, but then Derillen popped into my mind. "You were around eighteen years ago. I've asked my family and my servant about my history and about that of my mother. I only get half-truths. Do you know where I came from?"

He shook his head. "I have told you before that I do not pay attention to what happens down in the human world. There was a shift of magic at around that time. It has shifted again recently. We are heading for dark times. My magic only extends to the changing of my shape. I am no fae and no magician."

"My magic only works at certain times too."

"Ah, now that, I can tell you about. I do not understand

why. It is clear that you are not a dragon shifter with us, but your magic has elevated you to your position. I believe it is the magic of the dragons, and therefore, only works when we are around. I feel your great power, but I believe it is limited. We are naturally drawn to you and the light that comes from you. No other person has been able to do that, but that does not mean you will be able to do anything else. Of course, I could be wrong. "

He hesitated for a second. "Actually, there are other magic users in Draconis that might help you to understand your powers. It's a long shot. They are as mistrusting of humans as we are, but they have their own brand of magic."

"Who?"

"The dwarves," Milo answered for him.

"You are correct. They live beneath us in the depths of the mountains. We do not like to mix with them, but we have a mutual arrangement. We protect them from humans up here, and they provide us with gold. It is a mutually beneficial agreement, but that is all. We do not socialize, and I cannot promise you will find what you are looking for."

"Thank you." I didn't hold out much hope that the dwarves would be able to help us, but I had no other leads to go on, and as Vasuki said, they were magic users.

"If that is all, I will take you back down the mountain. Night is drawing near.."

It was indeed getting darker.

He shifted quickly, allowing Milo and I to jump on his back, which was a marked difference to the way Nyre flew us. Less terrifying for a start. He dropped us off near the base of the mountain, leaving us to walk the last part.

We'd not learned much, but at least, Milo finally knew my secret. A secret I'd hated keeping to myself.

In the woods, he stopped me.

"What?"

He cleared his throat. "I can probably get us in to see the dwarves. Humans generally aren't allowed in their mine, but they know me. It's possible that they will talk to you. I don't know what they can tell you, though. They don't care about human gods any more than the dragons do."

I sat on the boulder we'd used to drop our armor on before and dropped my head to my hands.

"I don't know what else to do, Milo. I have my father trying to get me married and hundreds of men wanting to marry me. My mother is sick, and no one believes me that it's Derillen. They all think it's some copycat, but I know it's her, and I know she wants me. I've been told lies about my history all my life, and I don't know who I can trust anymore."

I felt the tears begin to sting my eyes.

He pulled my face up so I was looking right at him.

"You can trust me. I don't know anything about Derillen, and I can't do anything for the queen, but I'm going to enter that competition, and I'm going to win."

I nodded my head slowly.

"And until then, I'll be right by your side while we try and figure out what is going on."

He kissed my cheeks, wetting his lips with my tears.

He spoke with such earnestness, but how could he compete with over a hundred men? I was going to end up married to a total stranger.

"If you are going to beat this thing," I said, my voice wavering. "We will need to practice." I pulled my sword out and stood up. With a smile, he did the same, matching my stance.

We had no armor with us, so we couldn't try too hard without the risk of hurting each other. I didn't even know if sword fighting was one of the things my father would add to the competition, but if it was, I needed Milo to be the best.

We spent hours like that, just the two of us with our swords and our freedom. When it became so dark, we could no longer continue, so we walked back into the castle. I half-expected my father to be waiting for me, but he wasn't. I kissed Milo quickly outside my bedroom door and shut it behind me.

"You've been out a while."

My heart lurched, and my breath caught in my throat. In front of me, the bolt on the door closed of its own accord.

Turning, I found Caspian lying on my bed, a smug grin on his face.

"I thought we'd established that you were not to come into my room without permission," I said, storming over to him.

"I remember, but I thought you'd want to know. I've found out how to get into the Dream Realm."

13TH JANUARY

Breakfast was a miserable affair with both my mother and father missing. Ash and Hollis had wolfed down their food and had left, leaving only Remy and me.

He sat gazing at his bowl, an empty stare down at the food he'd not touched. That wasn't like him at all. Remy loved food, and yet, he'd not even picked up his spoon.

"You okay, Remy?"

He looked up, dazed as though he'd forgotten I was even there.

When he spoke, his voice came out in a whisper. "Mama."

My heart dropped. He missed our mother. Of course, he did. The castle was in chaos, and Remy didn't understand what was going on. I'd been so preoccupied with my own problems that I'd not thought about Remy. Standing up, I rounded the table and brought him into a hug.

"It's going to be alright, Remy. Mama is asleep. Would you like me to take you to see her?"

He nodded his head, and a little of his sparkle came back. Had no one thought to take him to see her in all this time? It broke my heart to think how confusing all this would be for him.

"Can you eat your breakfast first? Momma likes to know you've been eating properly."

He obediently picked up his spoon and began to spoon the cereal into his mouth, bringing a small smile to my face. I made a mental note to pay more attention to him. He had his own member of staff just as I did, but she was only to help him get dressed and bathe and get to bed. Unlike myself and my other brothers, it had been my mother who had taken most of the responsibility for Remy. There'd barely been a minute in his whole life that he hadn't had her at his side, and now, he'd gone over a week without her.

"Come on, honey," I said once his cereal was finished. Taking his hand, I led him up to our mother's room. Knocking quietly, I opened the door. I expected my father to be there, but it was only my mother's maid. She dropped a book she'd been reading onto my mother's nightstand and looked towards us guiltily.

"It's ok," I said. "I don't mind you reading. We are here for a visit."

"Very well, Your Highness." She stood and curtseyed.

"How is she?" I asked, although it was obvious. There was no change in my mother. She slept as soundly as she had the last time I saw her.

The maid stood, picking her book up and lowered her eyes. “Still the same, I'm afraid. I've been moving her position to prevent bedsores, but I'm not sure there is anything else I can do for her. I wish there was.”

I nodded my head. “That's fine. Thank you.”

The maid walked past us, leaving just Remy and me in the room with our sleeping mother. She looked like an angel in sleep. Her perfect face rested peacefully. I hoped that wherever she was, whichever part of the Dream Realm she was in, it was a nice place. Caspian hadn't mentioned much about what it was like except to say that her exits were blocked.

“Mama,” Remy said, approaching her cautiously. He stroked her face the way I'd seen her do to him a thousand times.

“She's asleep, Remy,” I told him. “She worked so hard looking after us and being the queen that she needs a lot of rest.”

He looked at me and nodded. I wasn't sure if he really understood. It was hard to tell with Remy, but I could see the grief in his eyes. He pulled the covers back quickly. My heart started to race as I wondered what he was going to do. He climbed in next to her and snuggled up next to her body, closing his own eyes.

“Are you tired, Remy?” Had he even been sleeping himself, or had he lain awake as I had, worrying about everything? I had no way of knowing, but he looked so sweet and comfortable snuggled up to her that I didn't have the heart to move him. I wondered if somewhere my mother could feel him beside her. I hoped so. I hoped it would bring them both comfort. I pulled the cover back over both of them and kissed Remy's cheek. A small smile came to his lips.

“I'll let you nap here and come back for you later,

okay?"

He nodded his head almost imperceptively and closed his eyes.

I left him there, feeling a little bit better about having ignored him for the past week and headed through the castle to somewhere I never expected I'd ever voluntarily go. I went to Caspian's room.

After throwing him out of my own room last night without hearing him out, I figured I probably should go and find out what he had to say. If there was any way of getting my mother out of the curse she was in, I'd do anything, even if it meant listening to Caspian.

"Hello," he said, opening his door with the same smug grin on his face he'd been wearing the night before. "I knew you'd come to me, eventually."

I bit back the vomit rising in my throat and gave him a smile of my own. It wasn't one of pleasure.

"Shut it, buster. I'm here to find out how I can save my mother, and that's all."

He tapped his fingers against the doorframe. "You didn't seem to care last night when you were unceremoniously throwing me out of your room."

"I was tired, and I was angry because of you," I said, my anger rising. Every conversation I had with this guy made my blood boil. I took a deep breath and plastered on a smile. "I've calmed down now, so if you'd please let me know."

He wavered. "It's a pity..."

I sighed. "What's a pity?"

"I thought you were here for something else," he said, raising an inquiring eyebrow. "I thought you wanted my company." His smug grin widened.

Sanctimonious bastard!

"I'm not sure how I can say this without offending

you, but seeing as I don't care about your feelings, I'm going to go right ahead and say it anyway. I do not want your company. I've never wanted your company, and I see no reason why I would ever want your company."

"Well, then," he said, his hand dropping from the doorframe to the door handle. "I see no reason why I should tell you what I know."

I pulled out my sword and held it to his throat.

"Is this reason enough?" I said. This time, the smug grin was all mine.

He held his hands up and backed into the room.

"Tell me what you know," I growled.

Quick as a whip, his sword matched mine, knocking it away from his face.

His grin returned, but I'd been practicing with Milo and was better than I'd ever been. He seemed surprised as I came back from his defense, recovering quickly.

His eyebrows rose, but the grin remained. "I see you've bettered yourself. What fun. I do like an opponent who can fight back."

Every thrust I gave, he parried. We were now equally matched. "We both know you can't kill me," I said, sweat forming on my brow as the exertion of keeping up with him was beginning to wear me down. He was good, really good, and I wasn't better than him. Not yet, but I would be.

"We do, do we? I don't recall signing anything," he said.

"Sign this!" I shouted out, slicing through the top layer of his immaculate jacket. He looked down at the rip, surprise filling his eyes.

Now, he really came at me, and it took every bit of effort I had not to fail under the pressure. It was like fighting a whirlwind, and everywhere my sword was, his was there ready to knock it down.

I panted, as the fight became something it was never meant to be. Dangerous. I'd only meant to scare him, not to injure, but I could see by the look in his eyes, that we were both beyond that point. This was a fight to the death.

Dragon balls, my father was going to kill me himself if Caspian didn't. What a ridiculous position to find myself in.

"I surrender!" I said, pulling back and narrowly missing the sharp end of his sword. Almost instantaneously, I found myself lying flat on my back on his bed, him lying on top of me. His hot breath came quickly, a sign that he was as exhausted by our fight as I was.

"Get. off. me!" I growled, shoving him in the belly with my hand. Unfortunately, my sword was in my other hand.

"I don't know," he mused. "Why should I?"

He had a point. He had me completely at his mercy, and I was in no position to make demands. Damn it all!

"Because if you don't, I'll slice your head off so quickly you'll be looking at your back from the wrong angle."

Caspian craned his head around to see who was speaking, and I looked over his shoulder to see Milo standing in the doorway, his sword held aloft.

The weight on me lessened as Caspian stood up, his hands in the air.

"Just a little fun and games," he said. I sat up and gulped down a couple of breaths.

"Actually, Caspian was going to tell me how I can find my mother. He says he knows how to get into the Dream Realm."

"I suggest you talk then," Milo said, cocking his head

to the side to indicate the bed. He pressed his sword to Caspian's chest to give him no option but to sit back on the bed. I jumped out of the way as he sat down.

A sneer came over Caspian's face. "I could defeat you with magic right now. I don't even need to pick up my sword to fight you."

It was true. The first time he'd come into my room, he'd made my old sword disappear with a wave of his wand.

I stood up in front of him and considered being nice to him, then I decided against it. "Look, Caspian. You've come here as a guest of my father. I don't think he will take too lightly to you fighting his guards, not to mention his only daughter. One word to him, and he'll have you packing your bags. I suggest that if you want to stay here and still be included in the competition to win my hand in marriage, you tell me what you know."

He seemed to consider my words. I had no clue why the guy would want to marry me. He clearly couldn't stand me. Perhaps, it was about power. Whatever it was, he backed down.

"There is only one way into the Dream Realm from the outside without dreaming, but you will not find it in this kingdom. It is not in a set place, so it is hard to find. Only Morpheus himself can open the portal."

"So how do we find it?" I asked, biting back a curse. I was getting more and more frustrated by the second.

Caspian shrugged, the grin creeping back onto his face. "That's where your problem lies. You need to find Morpheus."

"How?" Milo asked.

Caspian shrugged. "I don't know. He's a god. He lives in a place that we mere mortals cannot get to. Only in death do we travel there."

I sucked in a deep breath and tried hard to refrain from hitting him square in the nose. He was enjoying this a little too much.

"So you are telling me that to save my mother from dying, I have to die first in order to enter the portal to the Dream Realm and then come back to life once I return from it?

"No," he replied. "Once you are dead, you are dead. There is no coming back. The dead are not able to enter the Dream Realm at all. Dead people don't dream."

I stood, frustration running through me. "Let's go," I said to Milo. "This guy is wasting our time."

"You could, however, try and find him when he is in our realm. The mortal realm. Maybe if he is feeling generous, he might let you into his domain."

"How do you even know this? You said you'd ask your friend."

"And, so I did," he answered.

"You told me your friend lives in Urbis. That's three days' journey on the Urbis Express or longer by train."

"I have many ways to contact my friends, none of which I wish to share with you. Why do you care anyway as long as you get the information?"

I did care because it was awfully convenient that he had "ways" to speak to his friend, who was days away. It didn't lend much credibility to his story.

I walked toward the door.

"You won't find him anyway," Caspian continued. "It's extremely rare that the gods come down to the mortal realm. It's not unheard of, but it's rare. Even then, you could speak to him directly and not even know it's him. The gods don't like to make their presence known. They are masters of disguise. You could look for him forever, and never find him."

He was still giggling as I slammed the door shut behind me.

"What a jerk!" Milo said.

"Do you think he was lying?" I asked. I wanted Morpheus to be real, just so there was something I could do. Some way of bringing my mother back. I was willing to latch onto anything, even if it came from that lying scumbag.

Milo shrugged. "I don't know. I never held much stock with Gods and religion."

"I guess there's one way to find out."

I strode down the corridor so quickly that Milo had to run to keep up with me. "Hey, where are you going?"

"I'm going to my room to pack. I can't stay here anymore. You heard him. I have to find Morpheus. If there's a chance that Caspian is telling the truth, I need to know."

"Yeah, I heard him. I also heard when he said it would be impossible to find him. What about the competition?"

I turned to face him. "I don't want anything to do with the stupid competition. You know that. I never did. I don't want to get married. Not even to you."

I saw his face drop a little, and I realized how harsh I sounded.

"I'm sorry. You've become so important to me these past couple of weeks. I like you a lot. I can't imagine a life where you are not in it and one day, yes I'd like to get married. I can see a beautiful wedding surrounded by our friends and family. Your mother will create a lovely tiara for me, and my parents will be there looking on proudly. I can see your face full of love, and I can feel the happiness in my heart. But none of that will happen if I get married in a couple of weeks when my father wants me to. Marriage to you would fill me with joy, but not like this. Not because I have to. We don't even know each other. We've been dating for less than two weeks, and most of that was fake dating. There's every chance you won't win anyway. There are so many entries. Who knows what will happen?"

"I love you," he said, breaking my heart into pieces.

Tears coursed down my face. I leaned forward and kissed him slowly. It would have to be enough. He had loved me for a long time. I'd only just met him.

He held my hand. "You don't have to spend your life looking for Morpheus, you know. There is another way."

I smiled, grateful for the change in subject. I wasn't ready for declarations of love. I wasn't ready for any of it.

"We only have to find Derillen," he explained. "She is the one stopping your mother from leaving the Dream Realm, according to Caspian, right?"

I sighed. "Yes, but she could be anywhere. Where would I even start?"

Milo took my hand. "Where would we start? I'm coming with you. At least, you know what she looks like. With Morpheus, we don't even know that."

I nodded. What he said made sense. "Where do we start?"

"I guess we start where your dragon friends told us to. We start in the mines."

I wiped my tears on the back of my sleeve. Had my mother been around, she would have told me off, but she wasn't around. We walked back through the castle, hand in hand. I didn't know what I could do, but I was determined to do something. My father collared us as we entered the long corridor that led to my room. Nerves took over as I realized I'd gone against his wishes... Again.

"There you are. I've been searching the castle for you. I thought I'd told you to stay in your room?"

"I'm sorry, Fath..."

He waved my words away. "Never mind about that now. I'm up to my eyeballs with stress over this competition you've gotten everyone into. No, don't apologize again. I've hardly been the exemplary father I should have been. Stress, you know. I'm the one who should be apologizing. A good night's sleep has done me a world of good. Anyway, I've looked through that book of yours, and the details of the competition are very vague. It seems to involve a lot of fighting. I was thinking of asking Caspian to sort it out, but then I realized that it would hardly be a fair fight if he's one of the competitors. My advisors are all busy, and I have had no time to do anything, so I want you to do it."

"You want me to plan the competition?"

Hope rose in my chest as I took in his words. If I was in charge of the competition, I could sway it in Milo's favor. I knew where his strengths and weaknesses lay, and he could help. I just wouldn't have to let my father know that.

"I'll do it."

From the corner of my eye, I saw Milo giving me a funny look. Only minutes before, I was ready to leave the castle before the competition took place.

"Wonderful," Father said, handing me a sheet of paper covered in scribbles. "Here are some notes I made, but the rest will be up to you. You'll have to coordinate things with my secretary and the press. This needs to be finalized within the week if we have any hope for getting it sorted out in time. I think I'm going to have to ask you to plan the wedding too. I know it's a lot to ask. Caspian was going to do it, but it's a bit unfair to ask the chap to plan a wedding that might not be his."

"Thank you, Daddy," I said, giving him a kiss on the cheek. He was back to his old self. Lack of sleep and excessive stress had turned him into someone I no longer recognized, but the old king was back.

"I need to speak to you about the dragons," I said, glad that I'd finally caught him in a good mood. Vasuki and the others had been playing on my mind the whole time, but this was the first time I'd been able to get my father to listen to me.

"What about them?"

"I've met them." I held my breath as he took the information in.

"I'm aware. I saw one carrying you, remember."

And so he had. He'd fired arrows at Nyre. "Nyre is just one of the dragons I've met."

"Look," he said, holding up his hand to me. "I'm well aware you went up the mountain without my permission. I'm also aware that the dragons are shifters. Your grandfather told me before he died. Why do you think I started the wall? However, they still attacked my men."

"Not all of them," I argued. "It was just a few. They are angry."

"Well, they wouldn't be the only ones now, would they?"

"People have been going up the mountain to steal eggs. The leader, Vasuki, doesn't want to attack."

"I don't really wish to speak to you about this. Please don't take me for an idiot. I know a lot more than you think I do, but my loyalty is to my men, my people. They attacked us. I don't have all my knights back yet, but when they all return, I will be sending them up the mountain."

"But..."

"No more, Azia." He turned and walked away.

"It's a fight for another day," Milo said. "The knights might not be back for weeks. Draconis is a huge kingdom."

I nodded. He was right.

I thought you weren't interested in this competition.

"That was before I realized we could make it so you win. Yeah, I'd like to wait, but this way, at least, my father is happy, and I won't break his heart by running away."

"One other good thing has come of all this," said Milo taking my hand.

"Yeah?"

"Your father didn't send you back to your room. He seems to have forgotten that he grounded you for the rest of your life. We can go to the mines without having to sneak out the back way."

I gave him a grin, and the pair of us stole out of the castle. We did end up taking the back way, anyway, mainly because it was the quickest route.

"There are small doors all over the mountain," I said as we strolled through the woods.

"You don't want to use one of them," Milo replied. "They don't like humans, and they especially don't like humans going where they are not wanted. There is only one way you will get to speak to them, and that is by walking in through the front door."

"They have a front door?"

Milo laughed. "Yes. How do you think my father got in to work every day when he worked with them? He didn't climb the mountain. About three miles from here, there is a front door. Anyone can enter. It's basically a shop with a back entrance to the mines. The shop is where my father worked. He was the go-between for the dwarves and the humans. They didn't like to speak to us mere humans, so my father had to do it. It was a necessity for them, and they tolerated him. I think they even grew fond of him after a while. I was allowed in the shop sometimes. They know who I am. Whether they will listen to me or talk to me is another matter."

"Won't they talk to me?" I asked. "I'm the daughter of the king, after all."

"That means nothing to them. They don't have the same rules as we do, and they recognize no one as their king. Don't worry. I think I'll be able to get us an audience."

We came out of the woods. I blinked as the sun filtered into my eyes. Milo pointed out the road we would have to take. It was a little more than a track that skirted the base of the mountains. My father's men had gone back to work on the wall because it now stretched further than before.

"We won't be able to climb up to see the dragons for much longer," I pointed out as we began the trek that would take us to the mine entrance.

"You'll always be able to get up there, remember? Your friends will fly you up."

"I guess," I answered. "It seems an awfully long way to go. How did your father travel there every day from Zhore?"

"My father took a horse."

A horse! Why didn't I think of that? It would have made the journey a whole lot quicker. It was then, I remembered something better.

I pulled my magic into myself. It was useless in

any other way, but it was great for getting dragons to come to me. I was getting better at it too. I thought of Nyre only. There was no point bringing the others down here. Vasuki had been kind to me so far, but I doubted his patience would last if I asked him to carry me places. Nyre was small, but she'd already heaved Milo and me up the mountain. She would bridge those miles in no time. Plus, she was so eager to help. A small jet of light escaped my hands, shooting up into the sky. A small dot appeared circling it, getting lower and lower until the purple scales of Nyre's armor became more apparent.

"We are traveling by dragon?"

I shrugged. "Why not? My father has use of all the horses, and I'm yet to get one of my own. This way, I won't have to bother anyone."

"Anyone, but your friend!" Milo tipped his eyes to the pretty young dragon that landed next to us.

"Nyre, would you mind taking us to the entrance of the Dwarf mines?"

Nyre jumped up and down in excitement. I nodded towards Milo to come to me. This time, I held his hand as we were hoisted up into the air. It would have been better if she was big enough to have us sit on her back, but she was still too small for that. Maybe I should have called for Vasuki or one of the bigger dragons, after all, I thought as my fingers turned white from being gripped so hard.

"I guess I shouldn't put anything to do with heights in the competition," I said, laughing at Milo's expression. His eyes were firmly clamped shut.

Nyre landed us on the ground with a soft bump. Milo sucked in a couple of deep breaths, and his face gained back the color that had drained from it when we were flying.

Once she saw we were fine, she once again took off into the sky. I watched her for a few seconds as she circled around up high.

"I think she'll wait for us," I said to Milo.

The entrance was nothing like I expected. I'd expected another door like the little wooden doors I'd seen dotted around the mountains. Or maybe a huge wooden door with a keep out sign on it and lots of bolts. As it was, it looked like any other shop, with windows full of metal objects. Armour and jewelry sparkled in the midday sun. Yes, it was like any other shop, but it was built right into the very base of the mountains. A sign above the entrance chiseled right into the rock, said Mine Shop.

"They don't actually make all this stuff," Milo explained as we walked through the entrance. "A lot of this was made by my mother. That sword over there is one of mine." He pointed out a sword. It was gorgeous, but nothing as grand as the dragon sword he made for me.

"They paid us extra to work with their metal for the storefront. All they do is supply the metals and gems. The people who buy it get to do what they want with the metal once it's bought. The dwarves don't really understand things like jewelry or swords, but they do know it's what the people want. They are simple folk. They mine the metal, imbue it with magic, and get food in exchange."

"People buy metal with food?"

"Yes. The dwarves don't want money. They don't like to leave their home, so they wouldn't be able to spend it. Besides, they literally have gold. What they don't have is a means to feed themselves. They cannot forage or garden. They hate being out in the sunlight. So they sell their metal in exchange for food or whatever else it is they might need. Sometimes, they will accept cloth for clothes. Don't be fooled that they are getting the raw end of the bargain. They know how much their stuff is worth, and they price accordingly. An ounce of gold can cost a whole cow. One imbued with a certain magic can cost upwards of a whole herd of cows. They are famous and get people from all over all the kingdoms not just ours."

Inside, the shop was dark, and nothing like the modern outside would have led me to believe. If anything, this is how I expected the place to look, with roughly hewn walls and an air of dampness. The smell of sulfur permeated the air. I wrinkled my nose and checked out the shop. Along one wall was a glass counter with ingots of different precious metals in it. Behind the counter, a tall reedy man stood. He was talking to another man in a hood. They were haggling over the price of something.

"I'll give you a goat for it," the shorter man said, pointing to one of the smaller ingots.

The tall one shook his head impatiently and clucked. "You know I cannot accept that. The dwarves would fire me on the spot if they thought I was giving away their metal."

The smaller of the two sighed. "How about two goats and you throw in a couple of gems?"

"Hmm. How about two goats, we forget the gems, and I give you a smaller ingot?"

"Fine," the smaller man grumbled. "I'll take the ingot and bring the goats back tomorrow."

The tall man raised an eyebrow.

"Okay, okay, I'll come back with the goats first." The man shuffled past us, his face a look of pure misery.

"Still the hard-ass, I see," Milo said. The man's expression softened immediately.

"Milo. Good to see you." He held out his hand to Milo's. "You are not here to take my job, are you, because I happen to know the Dwarves will have you back in a heartbeat."

"Not this time, Lou. I'm actually here to introduce my friend to the dwarves."

Lou held his hands up. "You know I can't do that. They don't speak to..." He stopped as soon as his eyes landed on me. Half a second later, he fell into a bow.

"I'm sorry, Your Highness, I didn't recognize you for a moment. Please forgive my impudence."

I bit back a grin.

"It's fine. I only come here in need of your help."

Lou stood tall and rubbed his hands together. "I would love to help you. Unfortunately, I know for certain that the dwarves will not let you in. They bow down to no one and recognize no royalty the way we do. I'm most awfully sorry. If there was anything I could do, I would," he said apologetically.

"Tell the dwarves that we think the princess is somehow connected to the change in magic," Milo said. "We are not here just for our own benefit, but for that of everyone."

Lou wavered. "I'm not sure I can do anything."

"Come on, Lou. You know as well as I do that the dwarves will be feeling the magical vibrations. I can't feel it, but I've heard from enough sources to know that there has been a massive shift in magical energy."

"Well, they have been talking," Lou said uncomfortably. "I don't really like to listen in to be honest,though."

"Is Goethe here? Can you tell him Milo wants to talk

to him?" Milo turned to me. "Goethe is the one dwarf that I've met. He's the one who asked me to stay on when my father died. He owes me."

Lou sighed, then walked past us and changed the Open sign to Closed on the door. I'll go fetch him, but don't expect him to be happy about it. He's been in a grump for the last two weeks."

"How can you tell?" Milo laughed. "He's always in a grump."

"Yes, well, he's worse than usual. Take a seat, and I'll go ask him if he wants to see you. I wouldn't hold your breath, though. Sorry Your Highness," he said again, looking my way and giving a little bow as he left through a tunnel at the back of the shop.

"Do you think this Goethe will be mad?" I asked.

Milo took my hand and gave it a squeeze. "Probably, but I wouldn't worry. He's always mad. It's his go-to response to everything. He's a big baby, really. Don't let his grouchiness fool you."

"Hmm." I sat back and twiddled my thumbs. Seconds later, a small man with more wrinkles than a prune and way too much skin waddled out.

"What?" he barked at Milo. "I thought we'd finally got rid of you."

Milo stood and walked over to the dwarf. "Not a chance, old man. I'm actually here for your help."

"So I hear," he grumbled. "Although, I don't know what you think I can do to help."

"We think you know something about the change in magical energy."

"So?"

"So, my friend Azia would like to know what you know. She thinks her family might be involved in some way. Her mother was the woman who was cursed."

Goethe turned his face to me. "The queen is cursed again? I should have known. You two had better come with me."

Lou's mouth dropped open as we trooped past him into the dark tunnel.

The stench of sulfur intensified as we walked into the gloom, and this time, it was my turn to be nervous.

"I've never once been let down here," Milo whispered. "My father was not allowed either. This thing must be huge if they are letting humans in."

"I'm not letting humans in; I'm letting you two in. That's different." Goethe barked.

I giggled until I remembered Vasuki's words. You are not human. I'd pushed them to one side, marking them as ridiculous. Of course, I was human, but did Goethe think the same thing? I'd not mentioned to Milo that particular part of the conversation. Maybe it was just the way he'd said it. Milo was human, after all.

The smell of sulfur intensified, the deeper we walked into the mountain, and the temperature climbed.

My sense of unease along with it.

"Is it safe?" I whispered, trying to keep my volume below that which Goethe could hear.

I was not successful.

"Yes, it's safe. I don't eat humans on Tuesdays," he barked back.

I looked at Milo, who grinned and shrugged his shoulders.

"Today is Monday!" I mouthed

Ahead of us loomed a huge room filled with bright flames, which probably accounted for the soaring temperature. How Goethe and the other dwarves managed to work in such temperatures was beyond belief. It was not this room we walked to as we veered off into a smaller tunnel. After walking for what felt like a mile, we finally stopped at a thick wooden door. Goethe brought out a large brass key and thrust it into the lock. Inside the room was a table and on the table, a small box.

"This has been waiting here for you for eighteen years," Goethe said, indicating the box. "I was beginning to wonder if you were ever going to come back for it."

Milo walked towards the box. "My father left something for me here?"

"Not you." The dwarf nodded his head to me. "Her. Her mother left it."

14TH JANUARY

I couldn't sleep. My mind was still whirring with everything I'd learned yesterday, which was precisely nothing. My questions hadn't been answered, but more questions had been thrown my way. Goethe knew nothing about the shift in energy, nor did he say much about the dragons. What he did tell me was that a box had been there since I was a newborn. When he told me my mother had left it, I thought he meant my birth mother, that maybe she was leaving some kind of clue for me to find her, but now, over twelve hours later, I knew that was ridiculous. Why would my birth mother leave me a clue to who she was in a mine? A mine to which humans rarely ventured? She wouldn't, and of course, she hadn't. The box had been brought here by the queen, just a day or two after the day she adopted me.

My parents celebrated my birthday on December 28th, which was the day they adopted me, but they thought I was a few days old by then, so my birthday was probably on the 24th or 25th. I had no real way of knowing. I pulled the box out from under my bed, where I'd stashed it the night before and opened it again, afraid that I'd imagined the whole thing.

There, just as it had been the night before, sat a stunningly beautiful ruby necklace. I'd never seen anything like it before, and even Milo, who had a mother who made jewelry, agreed that it was one of a kind. Hundreds of rubies set in gold. My mother had all the money in the world, and yet, I couldn't imagine why she would leave something so beautiful in the mines. I couldn't imagine her going to the mines at all, but I could hardly ask her why. She was still asleep.

All Goethe could tell me was that it was full of powerful magic, though he didn't know the extent of it. He'd been too wary of it to touch it, and so it had sat in the box, locked in the room for eighteen years. I held it up to my neck and glanced at myself in the mirror. It really was the most exquisite piece of jewelry, but I couldn't feel the power Goethe had said was in it. I clasped it around my neck, waiting for something magical to happen, but the room remained the same. I wondered if my own magic would be enhanced by it and if I would be able to do something more than call the dragons. But even with my concentration on full, I was not able to conjure so much as a teacup...or a teabag. Not even a tealeaf. I was beginning to suspect that maybe these magical beings were in on some kind of weird conspiracy to make me think I was powerfully magic when I wasn't. So I could summon dragons. Maybe that wasn't a difficult thing to do?

Unclasping the necklace, I placed it back in the box and ran my fingers over the intricate metalwork. This was a part of my history, but I didn't know what it represented.

It made me want to know more about my history. It seemed that everyone knew about my past but me. The natural person to ask would be my mother, but she was asleep. My father had flat out refused to tell me more than I already knew, and Dahlia was remaining tight-lipped on the subject. I couldn't shake the feeling that somehow my past was related to all that was going on. It couldn't be a coincidence that I arrived just after the worst part of history was over, nor that things happening to me now indicated that it was repeating itself. I'd never been magic before. So why now? Why when my mother was cursed, and the darkness was coming back?

I jumped out of bed and dressed quickly. My father had relaxed the rules about me being in my room, but he was on an emotional knife-edge, and there was no telling when he'd fall back into his foul mood. Thankfully, Vasuki had kept to his word, and the dragons had kept to themselves, although that was probably because my father hadn't attacked yet. I still had to figure out what to do with the competition and my wedding, but that didn't seem as important as finding out who I was.

Remy was the only one at the breakfast table when I got there. His mood was greatly improved from the previous day. I wondered if my father had let him sleep in his bed all night like he had done when he was a young child. Remy used to suffer from night terrors and would wake up screaming at all hours. My mother used to take him into bed with her, where he would sleep soundly. He gave me a joyful wave as I walked into the dining room.

"Hi, Aza,"

"Hello, Beautiful," I said, kissing his forehead and swiping a bit of toast from his plate.

"Ha oh,"

"Sorry, Remy, of course, I meant handsome. You are the most handsome."

He seemed satisfied by my answer and went back to tucking into his eggs.

I ate my breakfast more slowly, pondering who best to ask about my history. No one in the castle, that was for sure. If my father got wind of what I was up to, he'd only be mad again. So who? It had to be someone who was around when I was small. Someone who remembered me being brought to the castle from the adoption agency.

There was no one I could think of. The only people I really knew were the people who worked in the castle and some of my parent's friends. They were a no-no too. I couldn't trust them not to tell my father.

"Ok, Aza?"

I looked up at Remy, who had the most worried expression on his face. He was mirroring my own expression.

"I'm fine Handsome. I'm trying to think of someone who knew me when I was little...when we were little." Remy was only eleven months younger than me. We grew up together, almost as twins.

"Olly Polly."

Remy clapped his hands as though he'd just done something really clever, and he had. He was a genius.

Olivie Polmer, or Olly Polly, as Remy called her, was Remy's governess when we were small. She was a sweet young thing with ringlets of bright red hair. Remy was always transfixed by her. She left when I was ten as she was pregnant and wanted to be a full-time mother. Just as Dahlia had been, she'd been in my parent's service when Remy was born. She was a secretary or something, but she became Remy's governess. She cried the day she left. She and Remy had a special bond, and even now, she visited a lot and bought presents for Remy's birthday. She was almost family, even though she'd not worked here for seven years.

"Do you want to go and visit her?"

Remy bounced up and down in his chair and clapped his hands violently. I had to stand up and hug him to calm him down. He had a tendency to over-excitement, and especially so when Olly Polly was involved.

After breakfast, I told my father I was taking Remy to Zhore. It wasn't a lie. Olivie lived there with her husband and four sons. I just declined to mention why I was going. My father was too preoccupied to ask why anyway. He was knee-deep in paperwork. Waving a hand in my direction, he murmured an okay.

"Just take a guard with you. I don't want you two going out alone."

I ran back upstairs to ask Milo if he wanted to join us, but when I got there, Jack announced that Milo had the day off.

I either had to find another guard to go with us and risk them telling my father where I'd been, or I could disobey my father's orders...again.

A quick look at Jack told me that the second option was the most preferable. I knew where Milo lived. I could go and see him first. Then technically, I'd have a guard with me. Yeah, I was stretching the truth, but it was for the greater good.

Remy was ready and waiting in the entrance hall, as

giddy as a schoolgirl. I noted that he'd got changed for the occasion, wearing a bowtie. He'd been made to wear one once for some formal occasion or other, and Olivie had mentioned how suave he was with it on. He'd was six years old at the time and had to be told what suave meant. I'd never seen him look so pleased with himself. He wore that bowtie all the time, and even now, over a decade later, he still pulled it out when Olivie visited... or when we visited her.

"Looking very suave," I said, using the term he'd come to associate with the bowtie. He grinned from ear to ear, as pleased as punch with himself, even though he'd paired the bowtie with a sweater and shorts.

After sending him back to his room to change into long pants, I took his hand and left the castle quickly before my father could put much thought into where we were going and stop us. Olivie was my only chance to find out who I was without father finding out. She hadn't worked for us for years, and I trusted her to keep a secret. She still kept the secret that it was I that accidentally broke my mother's favorite looking glass by kicking a ball at it when I was eight years old. She told my mother a gust of wind had knocked it over.

The walk to Zhore was long and uneventful, and yet, I couldn't shake the feeling that something was going to happen. The weather was dull, with gray clouds but, thankfully, no more snow. Looking up towards the Fire Mountains, I couldn't see the dragons. It wasn't them that I was worried about, though. No, it was something else, something I couldn't quite put my finger on. Maybe it was just the darkness that everyone was talking about. The shift in magical energy. Maybe it was nothing, and I was paranoid. Who knew?

Milo was surprised to see me when he opened the

door. He was even more surprised to see Remy, but he invited us both in.

I told him quickly what we were doing, and so he decided to accompany us

Olivie lived in a quiet part of town, away from the hustle and bustle of the main streets. Her little cottage had a garden, and though the soil here was not exactly ripe for growing things, she'd made the most amazing space out front with pretty stones and cacti. All of it was under a layer of snow as we walked up the path.

The door flung open before we'd even had a chance to knock. A whirlwind of red curls launched herself at Remy, followed by four little red-headed tornados.

Remy hugged them all, carrying Olivie's youngest inside with him. I didn't know why, but Remy never had to be told to unsquash around Olivie's children. He was delicate with them, and they loved him almost as much as he loved them.

Olivie brewed up some tea while the three of us played with her young children.

"To what do I owe the pleasure?" she asked, placing the tea tray on a table and ruffling Remy's hair.

He responded with a wide smile.

I picked up a cup of tea while I deliberated what to say. In the end, I decided to go with the truth. "I'm here about my adoption. I want to know where I came from."

Olivie's face drained of all color.

"You four," she shouted at her kids. "Go upstairs and play for a bit."

There was a chorus of oh, Moms, but eventually, with a little help from Olivie's husband, all four of them went upstairs, leaving just the four of us.

"I was never asked, specifically, not to tell you anything. I was asked not to tell anyone, but as it's you..."

"My mother is asleep, my father is up to his eyeballs in stress, and I've no one else to ask."

She lowered her eyes and nodded. "What is it you want to know?"

"Anything. Which adoption agency they used, where they picked me up from...anything."

"I don't know about the first. There is only one adoption agency in Zhore as far as I know, but it was never mentioned. You kind of just appeared one day. The king and queen acted like it had been planned for a long time, but they were flustered and unsure of what to do. Your grandmother helped out a lot, but I had the feeling she didn't know that this was about to happen either. It was like we all woke up one day, and there was this new baby...except..."

She'd basically told me the same thing as Dahlia. I appeared from nowhere. "Except what?"

"I was doing a night shift the night you came. Your parents didn't pick you up from an adoption agency. You were delivered to the castle."

This was new. Why would an adoption agency drop a baby off in the middle of the night?

"There's more," Olivie continued. "I watched a woman bring you to the castle door and knock. She spoke to your parents for quite some time on the doorstep. I remember thinking that you must be awfully cold. It was a mild winter that year, and you were wrapped up warmly, but it was still winter, and I could see you were very tiny."

"Did my parents know you saw them?"

She shook her head. "No. I never told them, and I don't think anyone saw me. It was about two am, and I was looking out of one of the kitchen windows. The carriage that brought you was parked close to it, but I could still see past it to your parents..."

She hesitated.

"There's something else isn't there? Something you've not told me."

She took a deep breath. "It's something I've never told anyone. Not even your parents."

"What?"

"There wasn't just one baby in that carriage. I heard another baby crying."

Another baby. I wasn't the only one. Somewhere out there, I had a twin.

HEIRESS OF EMBERS

15TH JANUARY

"Your father wishes to see you. Get out of bed." Dahlia's urgent tone drifted through my dreams of children with golden rings around their irises, children that called to me but were just out of reach. Children that I knew, or at least I felt, I knew.

They evaporated like smoke on the wind as the first tendrils of light invaded my consciousness as Dahlia cruelly opened the curtains, letting the morning in.

I pulled the cover over my head, hoping that if I ignored her, Dahlia would leave me alone. My whole life felt like a lie, and my father was the last person I wanted to speak to. He was one of the people who perpetuated that lie. My mother was the other, but as

I could hardly be mad with her right now, I was saving all my anger for my father. My father, whom I'd loved with my whole heart and respected. My father, who was the most wonderful man I knew until the beginning of the year and the return of my mother's curse. Actually, no, his spiral into awfulness had started before that with the plan of marrying me off to a stranger who was at least twice my age and was, at best, a complete jerk.

Dahlia never did have much time for self-pity and whining. She didn't ask me again. She just pulled my covers off, leaving me on the bed, cold in only my nightgown.

The sound of my bath running reminded me that she wouldn't let up until it got to the point where she would literally drag me out of bed and plonk me straight in the bath.

I tried to grab back the memories of my dream, but it was too late. The children were long gone and, along with them, the warmth of wellbeing that I'd gripped to throughout the night.

I shivered as I pulled myself from the comfort of my own bed.

I'd barely slept a wink of sleep, and the few moments I had snatched were punctuated with dreams. Dreams of the brother or sister that I'd just found out about. Someone who looked like me. A twin.

I loved all my brothers, but I'd never really fit in. I was the ugly duckling in a group of beautiful swans. Ok, that was taking it too far, but I didn't look like them. I pulled my nightshirt over my head and settled into the bath, my mind still whirring with the thought that I had a real sibling out there. I had so many questions and no one to ask. Olivie had told me as much as she knew, but it didn't amount to much. She didn't know if my twin was still in Draconis or was somewhere else in another kingdom.

I remembered something Vasuki had told me a week or so earlier. He'd said that I wasn't a whole. That I was a part of something bigger. I don't think he truly understood what that meant any more than I did, but now it made sense. I wasn't a whole. I was one half of a set of twins.

I'd always wanted a sister. Growing up with three brothers had been fun, but I'd have liked another girl to play with. Of course, my twin could easily have been a boy. I wondered if he had golden rings around his irises like I did. If I wasn't the only one.

Rushing downstairs, taking each step two at a time and ignoring the maids who gave me dirty stares as I whipped past them, I raced to my father's office. I found him exactly where I expected to, eyebrows deep in messy paperwork with red rings around his eyes that told me he'd had yet another sleepless night. I wasn't in any mood to feel sorry for him. He'd kept a secret so huge that I was nowhere near close to forgiveness.

He looked up when I entered, paperwork still in his hand. "Azia, you're here. I wanted to speak with you abou..."

"I need to talk to you first," I said, butting in angrily and slamming my hand down on his desk. A few of the papers fluttered, but the huge stack held firm. I would never have done such a thing in the past, but things had changed. I was way past caring what anyone thought of me, and that included my father, the king.

"What is it, Azia?" His voice was weary, the voice of a man with the weight of the world on his shoulders. There was no anger in it, but I could see he didn't need yet another problem to deal with. If it wasn't such a huge deal, I would have left him to his work, but it was a huge deal.

“Why didn’t tell me that I had a brother or sister?” I asked, holding him in a cold hard stare.

He raised an eyebrow in askance.”I rather thought you would have noticed on your own.”

“I’m not talking about Remy or Hollis or Ash. I’m talking about the night I was brought to the castle when I was a baby. Why did you only take me in? Why separate me from my twin?”

He sat straight up in his chair and eyed me with surprise. “What are you talking about?”

“I know,” I replied. “There’s no point hiding it from me any longer. I know I have a twin.”

He shook his head slowly. “I’ll overlook the fact that someone has been filling your head with nonsense, and I’ll pretend that you are not being incredibly rude right now. Sit down, and I’ll tell you what happened the night you came to us.” He indicated a chair for me to sit in.

“We’ve never hidden anything from you, Azia. We decided right from the start that you were our daughter and that you were as important to us as if you were ours by blood. We even made the decision to pass the throne to you rather than one of our natural-born children. If that doesn’t show you how much we love you, I don’t know what will. We also decided to tell you right from the start that you were adopted. You’ve always known. I can tell you about the night you came to us if that will make you feel better.”

“So tell me,” I snapped, taking a seat opposite his.

He waited until I was completely seated and comfortable before he spoke. A frisson of excitement ran through me. I was finally about to find out where I was from. Maybe even who I was.

"Your mother and I were newlyweds," my father began. "Your mother made it no secret that she wanted children. I would have liked to have waited and spend a little time alone with her first, but she was adamant. We adopted you very early on in our marriage. Probably too soon, though I have never regretted it. Not for an instant. You were loved as if you were our own, right from the start."

Nice. Sentimental even, but this isn't what I needed to hear. I needed facts. "I was told that when I was brought to the house, there was another baby. It was heard crying."

He held my gaze. "I don't know of any other baby, Azia. There was never any other child. There was only ever you. Not long after you came, your mother fell pregnant with Remy. He, along with Hollis and Ash, are our biological children. Your mother always told me she was so glad we adopted you, or she'd be in a house filled with boys."

Frustration gripped me. "So why was another baby heard crying?"

My father rubbed his temples and sighed. "I don't know, Azia. Perhaps the adoption agency people were on their way to deliver another baby to another set of parents. It doesn't mean that the other baby was your twin. Plenty of infants are born in Zhore. Does that answer all your questions?"

I nodded slowly. He was right. Of course, an adoption agency might very well have been carrying more than one child to more than one set of parents. Why hadn't I thought of that? I'd not thought of it, because it didn't feel right. It didn't explain the gnawing in my gut when I thought about another child. It didn't explain my dreams. It didn't explain the fact that I felt less than whole.

"Well then," he said, going back to his paperwork. "I'll need you to finalize the plans for this ridiculous competition you've decided to stage. The Sentinel has been on my case, and all my administrative staff are busy fielding calls about what's going to happen rather than doing the job I pay them for. It really is a nuisance."

"I'm sorry, Father," I said, standing up.

I swirled the new information around in my mind as I walked back to my room. It was entirely plausible that Olivie had heard another baby that had nothing to do with me. Maybe it was a pipe dream, a delusion of an adopted child that there would be others out there who looked like me.

Still, it didn't sit well in my stomach. My father had all the answers, but I didn't believe him. There was nothing he said that didn't make sense, but there was a tell in his eye as he spoke. The way he blinked a little too rapidly. The way he rubbed his fingers together as he told me that I was the only baby. Taking a detour, I headed not upwards to my bedroom, nor to the library to come up with plans for the competition, but down to the rooms beneath the castle. We had a wine cellar down there that I was sorely tempted to visit, but there was also something down there that I needed to see more. The royal vaults.

A huge metal door hid rooms upon rooms of treasure and gifts given to the royal family for generations. My brothers and I often played hide and seek down there before Hollis accidentally knocked over and smashed a vase worth a fortune. After that, the royal children were banned, but I was no longer a child. and what was more, I didn't need a password to get in. The vault was guarded by two armed guards, plus the keeper of the vault, who was more of custodian than guard.

Having had no reason to come down to the vault since the vase incident, five or six years before, I'd only seen the keeper of the vault in passing since then.

Taking the steps two at a time, I came to a stop by the antique wooden desk in front of the huge metal door flanked by two guards in uniform.

"Good morning," I said, nodding to them before turning my attention to the keeper. He eyed me suspiciously, looking up from a huge book filled with entries of all the people who had been in and out of the vault and the times, dates, and reasons for each visit. Next to it, sat a pot of ink and a well-used quill.

He was meticulous and proud of his job. He also hated me and my brothers for bringing shame on him when we'd broken the vase. He took looking after the contents of the vault very seriously.

"Your Highness," he said, giving me a wary smile and a small bob of the head. "How may I help you this fine day?"

Wisps of thinning white hair covered his head, with bald patches shining through. He'd been here a long time, and it showed. His ink marked hands were covered with paper-thin skin, which showed his age. Not that he needed to be particularly fit or strong. That was the guard's job, which was just as well considering he looked like he'd throw his back out just picking up a pen.

"I'd like to go in the vault, please, Hestor."

Pursing his lips, he appeared to be pondering my request. I held my breath, waiting for the inevitable rejection, but it seemed he'd softened in his old age. He picked up a quill and dipped it in his ink well before writing my name in his book next to the time and date.

I would have preferred to have no account of this, but people came into and out of the vault all the time, so it wouldn't be long before my name was hidden down the list.

"And my I ask your reason for visiting the vault today?" he asked, raising a watery eye toward me. "I'm assuming that hide and seek is no longer on the agenda."

My mouth twisted up at the corners. He was teasing me. Maybe he wasn't the miserable old git I'd pegged him for all those years ago.

Not wanting to tell him the real reason, I made something up on the spot. Something I hoped sounded believable.

"There is to be a photoshoot of me for the Royal Competition for the Draconian Sentinel. I'd like to make it an official photograph, and I believe I should look regal. I'd like to take one of my mother's necklaces."

Licking his lips, he held the quill to the paper but paused. "And is there nothing suitable in your mother's room for you to borrow?"

Shaking my head, I readied the lie on my lips. My mother kept a lot of jewelry in her room. She hated coming down to the vault, but some of the jewels we owned were too precious to have lying around. The more formal jewelry, along with the expensive pieces and the royal crown jewels were kept down here behind lock and key.

"There is a piece I had in mind, and I can't find it in her room. I don't really want to be messing around in her things as she sleeps."

I put on the saddest face I could muster, hoping to appeal to his sympathy. My mother was cursed after all.

"I quite understand," he replied, licking the end of the quill then writing the word necklace down in the book. "As you require something of such value, I will be required to come into the vault with you and send you on your way with one of the guards until the necklace is brought back safely."

Panic shot through me. The last thing I needed was having Hestor follow me through the vault.

"That isn't necessary. I know where the necklace is. I can find it myself."

"Nevertheless," he said, pulling his bony body into a standing position. "My job is to keep the vault and make sure nothing goes missing. Having a thing of such value will put your own life at risk too, Your Highness. Besides, I need to write the tag number down in my book so nothing goes missing."

Damn. I'd forgotten that everything down there was tagged and cataloged with a number.

He pulled a key from a chain around his neck and inserted it into a lock holding the huge vault door shut before turning a small dial with numbers on it. He shielded it from my sight as he turned it left and right. A click indicated the vault was unlocked.

The two guards pulled it open for us with a high-pitched creak, and a wave of musty air hit me in the face, making me cough.

Hestor shuffled in, leaving me to follow in his wake.

The vault was separated into sections. Large items of value, such as furniture and statues, were cataloged and stored in a large room to the right. The higher up maids with clearance would often come down here to remove items to change the look of the palace at my mother's whims. I followed Hestor to a massive metal cage where he, once again, pulled the key out and unlocked the door that would take us to the most restricted part of the vault. The place where the jewelry was kept, the home of the crown jewels and paperwork of national importance. Not many had clearance for this part of the vault, and I was surprised that Hestor even contemplated letting me in. But then again, he knew as well as I did, the emotional state of my father right now, and though I'd played around down here in the past, I was an adult now and a member of the royal family. He probably thought it wise to just let me do what I wanted. Not that he trusted me completely. He walked right next to me the whole time, not taking his eyes off me for a second. Not wanting to arouse his suspicion, I went straight to the glass cases with necklaces in them. I didn't care which one I took. It didn't matter. I pretended to deliberate over them while trying to come up with a plan to get to the paperwork.

I knew where the family documents were kept. On the other side of the cage was a huge office with two leather chairs, a desk, and rows upon rows of cabinets. Most were filled with documents relating to the kingdom, but one end was reserved for family matters. The problem was, how was I supposed to get the documents while Hestor was watching my every move?

I fingered one of the necklaces. There was no way Hestor wouldn't notice me crossing the room and rifling through the documents, and if he did see me, he would run straight to my father.

Picking the necklace up, I held it to my neck before putting it back in its case.

I was just about to pick up the next one when a crash made me jump.

Hestor's head swiveled quickly towards the source of the noise.

It was a maid, trying to pick up one of the larger chairs from the other side of the main room.

"You shouldn't be trying to carry that by yourself!" Hestor shouted before muttering under his breath, "Silly girl."

He ran toward her, waving his arms around.

I made use of the diversion, running silently to the desk. Reading down the cabinets, which were all labeled in the same handwriting as Hestor's book outside, I came to the cabinet that said family documents. Four drawers full of the royal family history, but they had dates on them. The top drawer was the most recent. taking a quick peek at Hestor, who was busy arguing with the girl, I pulled the top drawer open. My heart fell when I saw no documents, but a safe instead. A safe with another combination lock on it.

I sucked in a breath, my heart hammering. Hestor wouldn't be with the maid for long, but there was no way he'd tell me the combination.

I stepped back and closed my eyes. My father would have picked the combination to this lock. There was every chance that Hestor didn't even know it. This safe was a personal safe and had nothing to do with the rest of the kingdom. This was for family.

Taking a deep breath, I held my hand out to the lock. There was only one conceivable number I could guess. If I was wrong, I'd never get it right. I turned the dial, this way and that, putting in four numbers. 1004, my mother's birthday. The safe clicked, and the door opened.

At the other end of the room, I could hear Hestor calling in the guards to help him with the chair. This was my only chance, and I had to be quick.

There was very little in the safe, so I pulled the lot

out. On the top, was my parent's wedding certificate. Below it, were the birth certificates of both my parents, Remy, Hollis, and Ash. Beneath Ash's birth certificate, I found nothing else. That was it. I rifled through them again, but again I came up with only the six documents. My pulse raced as I checked out the rest of the safe. There were my grandfather's ring and a bundle of letters tied together with a pink ribbon. Stashing the documents back, I pulled out the letters, but a quick rifle through them was enough to see that they were love letters between my parents from the early days in their marriage when my father had to go on royal trips without her. I quickly scanned a couple, but it was plain that they weren't about me. My name was mentioned a couple of times, but only my father asking my mother to kiss me and Remy goodnight for him. I guess they were written when we were young. Apart from a lot of declarations of love, there was nothing in there that would tell me about my past.

Which begged the question. Where was my birth certificate, and why wasn't it with the others?

Even if I was a found child with no birth certificate who'd been handed into the adoption agency, there should still be records of my adoption. But there wasn't. I didn't exist anywhere on paper.

"Sorry about that, Your Highness."

Hestor trooped back into the caged room just as I grabbed the first necklace. "I'll take this one. Thank you." I rushed past him, taking the necklace with me, my emotions in turmoil.

"Just a minute," he called out. "You can't go without a guard!" I halted on the stairs to the main floor of the castle. If I ran off with the necklace now, he'd be on my case forever. Even though I was desperate to be off, I waited for him, tapping my toe on the stone slab floor.

"You know what," I said, handing him back the necklace as he wheezed through the vault door. "I've changed my mind." The last thing I needed was to have a guard following my every move. Especially considering what I planned to do next. "I'll just take one from my mother's room after all."

He gave me a curious look but didn't question me as I bounded up the stairs and away from the vault.

I had no identity. I was no one. I belonged nowhere. I may or may not have had a secret brother or sister. I wanted to march back into my father's study and confront him, but then he would know I'd been snooping. Besides, if he found out, he'd almost certainly stop me from doing what I planned to do next. Actually, scrap that, he would definitely stop me.

I ran up the stairs to my room to pick up a shawl that would cover my head. Where I was going, I didn't want anyone to recognize me. As I came up to the corridor, I ran straight into Dahlia.

"There you are," she said in a testy tone. "I've scoured the castle looking for you. Where have you been? Actually, never mind, as long as you're here now. Come with me. I have a job for you."

"I was going to...go for a nap." I didn't want Dahlia to know where I was going any more than I did my father.

"It's nine o'clock in the morning!" she said, grabbing my hand. "I'm sure you can stay awake long enough to help me with this little task. You can nap after we are done."

The little task turned out to be a fitting for my wedding dress, followed by the planning of the wedding itself.

"Is this really necessary?" I asked as a seamstress

measured me. "I don't even have a husband-to-be yet."

Dahlia nodded. "Yes, it's necessary. The wedding is coming up in a couple of weeks. and you might not have a husband-to-be yet, but you will have. You need a dress. Once we've done here, we'll be doing a cake tasting and then picking some wedding flowers. I asked Caspian to come and help."

My face contorted into a look of distaste. "Why?"

"Because he will probably be the one to end up marrying you. As much as I'll be cheering my son on at the competition, he's an oaf, and I doubt he'll make it through the first round. He was only considered for the competition at all because I put his application in the yes pile when the secretaries weren't looking."

"There is a yes pile?" I asked. I'd not put much thought into the admin behind the competition. "That must mean there is a no pile."

"Of course, there is," she said, holding a material sample up to me. "Satin or silk?"

"I thought the competition was open to everyone. How is there a no pile if anyone can enter?"

"Silk, I think," she said, handing the sample to the seamstress who was now writing down the measurements in her book with a pencil.

"We've had over fifteen thousand applications. There just isn't time to have everyone enter. It would take weeks if not months."

"Fifteen thousand?" I asked weakly. "Fifteen... thousand!"

"Yes, that's what I said."

"No sitting down!" the seamstress screeched as I tottered. "We are not finished yet."

"What do you think about pink for the bridesmaids?" Dahlia asked, holding up another sample. My mind reeled with the sheer size of this thing, and my stomach groaned from the lack of breakfast. I'd been so busy, I'd forgotten to have any.

"I don't care," I said. "How are these fifteen thousand men being whittled down?"

"Oh, it's not just men. We've had plenty of women apply too."

I rolled my eyes. The whole thing was a joke. I almost regretted opening up the competition, but if I hadn't, I would have definitely had to marry Caspian. The way things were going, I wasn't sure what was worse. I still hadn't come up with what exactly the competition would entail. A sneaky part of my mind wondered if I could get away with requiring that the competition could only be won by someone whose name was Milo. But knowing my luck, there'd be a thousand Milos entering, and most of the others would change their names. Urgh!

"So how do these people end up on the no pile?" I questioned, ignoring the pink samples Dahlia was waving at me. Whatever way it was, I was going to make sure a few more would be added.

"Well," she began, sorting the pink samples from the purple. "First of all, anyone under eighteen has been immediately disqualified. My son is almost eighteen, so I doubt anyone will notice. Anyone over the age of sixty, too."

"Ah-ha!" I said, jumping on it. "That rules out Caspian. He's a fae and fae are all really old." Probably.

"I checked with him," Dahlia tutted. "He's fifty-one, but he doesn't look a day over twenty-five does he?" She swooned. "I don't know why you didn't just marry him when you got the chance. He's delectable."

"I thought you didn't like him now?" She changed her mind more often than she changed her underwear when it came to Caspian. She'd caught him out in a lie only last week and told me that she thought him untrustworthy. Now she thought he was delectable. I couldn't keep up.

"Not really," she admitted, "but he's a dream to look at, and that's half the battle."

"Hmm," I said unconvinced. "What else?"

"We took the women out too. I don't want to be sexist, but I have a feeling that you'd prefer to marry a man?"

I'd prefer to marry a troll over Caspian, but I nodded my head anyway. "Is that it?"

"No. They had to be physically capable of coming to the castle on the day of the competition too, but that's about everything. It's whittled it down to just over nine hundred, but there are still applications coming in."

"Great," I barked. "Nine hundred men, only two of which actually know me personally, and one of them I detest."

"My gorgeous bride to be!" I swiveled my head to Caspian, who had just walked in the door. "Are you finished in here, because the caterers have just brought in the cakes, and I must say, they look delicious."

Breathing back despair, I knew I wasn't going to be able to put my plan into action today. It would have to wait. I was still going to find out who I was and where I came from. I'd just have to eat a lot of cake first.

16TH JANUARY

After an excruciating day spent with Caspian yesterday, I was all the more determined to get out of the castle today. I went for breakfast as normal, not wanting to arouse suspicion. Once again, it was only Remy and I at the table. At least, he'd perked up a bit. He ate his food quickly as though he didn't have a care in the world. Of course, he didn't. He knew nothing of what was going on. The only thing he understood was the fact that our mother didn't play with him anymore. I could see the sadness in his eyes, and yet, he went about doing things the same as always. His governess had stepped up to the role of mother. I'd seen her spending more time with him than usual. It wasn't the same, but she was doing a brilliant job, and at least, I didn't have to worry about him on top of everything else.

"Aza. Go Zor?"

My heart flipped when I heard his question. He was asking me if I was going to go to Zhore, and that's exactly where I was planning to go. If Remy had figured it out, then so would someone else. But how did Remy know? I'd told no one, not even Milo. I'd not even seen Milo since deciding to go.

"Olly Polly,"

"Oh, you want to go and see Olivie again?" I breathed out a sigh of relief. He wanted to repeat our trip to see his old nanny again. "Not today, buddy, I have things to do."

He cast his eyes downward, tugging at my heartstrings. "I tell you what. When I'm done, we'll spend the evening together? I'll read to you."

He grinned up at me, his face brightening immediately. "Ya, Aza."

I smiled, the first smile I'd managed in days that wasn't plastered on for the sake of other people. "I'll come find you, ok?"

He nodded enthusiastically.

Taking an apple from the fruit bowl at the center of the table, I headed out of the castle, going the back way through the garden door.

I was going to Zhore, but I wasn't going to see Olivie. She'd already told me everything she could. I couldn't trust my father to tell me the truth, so I was going to have to find the truth out for myself. I was going to the adoption agency.

I knew of it vaguely in the way I knew where other buildings were in Zhore. As an adopted child, I should have had more curiosity about the place, but it had never really registered as somewhere I might like to visit. Not until now, at least.

I took the quickest path to Zhore that wouldn't lead me directly to a member of my father's guard. It meant jumping over some walls and running through fields, but the cloak over my head wasn't much of a disguise, and I needed for no one to find out.

I contemplated heading to Milo's house first. I'd never walked around Zhore or any other place on my own before, but this was something I needed to do myself.

The adoption agency was part of a children's home in one of the quieter backstreets of Zhore, a beautiful, faded-yellow building with flower baskets hanging by the door. They were currently empty other than a dusting of snow, but I remembered them as being filled with blooms of purple when I'd passed by in the summer when I was in a parade. I'd taken note of the sign outside, the Zhore Home for Children and Adoption Agency, but I'd filed it away in the back of my mind, not realizing I'd need to know it so soon.

I stole in, quietly making sure no one on the street was watching me. The street was quiet, and no one paid me any mind as I hurried through the front door. A long corridor led off ahead of me with an open reception area to my right.

"How may I help you?" asked a woman with graying hair and glasses that hung around her neck on a chain. She was the quintessential grandma figure with soft features and kind eyes. Perfect for someone working in a children's home.

My heart beat quicker as I realized I was about to find out who I really was, where I'd come from, maybe even who my real parents were. "I'm here about adoption," I said, keeping my voice low. I felt ashamed to be even asking after how well my parents had treated me.

"Specifically, about finding an adopted person's birth parents."

"Of course," she replied with a smile. "Anyone over the age of eighteen is able to come back to us and look at their notes. Of course, sometimes the child's birth parents give false names or don't leave a name at all. I wouldn't want you to be disappoint..."

I pulled my cloak down, exposing who I was. She stopped mid-sentence and dropped into an awkward curtsey, half on and half off the chair.

"Your Royal Highness, it' is an honor."

I stepped up to the counter that separated us and spoke in a quiet voice.

"As you can probably understand, I'd prefer to do this in private."

The sound of a child laughing came along the corridor, making both of us swivel our heads and was quickly followed by an adult's voice shouting, Timmy, after him.

"Yes, of course..." the receptionist said. "Follow me."

She pulled a door in the counter open, and I stepped through to her side. She took me through a door labeled Office, closing it behind us.

The cozy office was everything I'd hope for in an office for a children's home. Photos of kids and babies lined the walls along with thank you cards and letters. Potted plants lined the window sill behind the desk, and a row of cabinets stood against the right hand-wall,

"You asked about adoption. Who did you want to find out about?" she asked, indicating a seat for me to sit in. "Some coffee? Tea perhaps? I could ask my assistant, Jeanette, to bring some."

"That won't be necessary, but thank you. I'm actually here about me."

Confusion knotted her face as she sat in the only other seat in the room. "You?"

I nodded my head and tried to ignore the flutters of excitement in my stomach. I'd been here. I'd spent the first few days of my life within these walls. "Yes, I'd like access to my files, please."

She shook her head. "I don't understand. I have no files on you."

Her words hit me like an out-of-control carriage.

"But, I'm adopted," I said as though that was all she needed to know.

She nodded slowly. "Yes, I know, but you were never here. You never passed through our doors."

I knotted my eyebrows together. "Are you sure? It was about eighteen years ago. I was very tiny. A newborn. I was probably born in late December."

She sucked in a breath and drummed her fingers on the desk as she spoke. "I've worked here for twenty-five years. I remember the news reports about your adoption like it was yesterday. I also remember discussing it with some other staff members, and if you'll forgive me, we all said it was a shame you didn't come from here because your father would have made a nice donation."

Her cheeks turned pink at the admission, and I was positive she was telling me the truth. But I'd trusted people before, and I needed to see for myself.

"Please, may I look in your files?"

She nodded quickly, standing from her chair and hurrying over to the filing cabinets. "Usually, I don't let anyone come in and look at the files. They have to be either one of the parents involved or one of the children, and even then, we have protocol. I hope you understand I'm letting you look because you are a member of the royal family."

"Thank you," I said, feeling guilty. I was going against everything she stood for, but she was too afraid of saying no to a royal. She opened one of the cabinets and pulled out all the files from the year I was born, fanning them out in front of me on the desk.

"Please, can you take the year after ones out too. I was born in this year but was adopted just after. There's a possibility I may have been put in the wrong file."

It was unlikely, but I didn't want to miss something important for the lack of thoroughly checking.

"They are listed in date order," she explained. "The next filing cabinet along has copies of the same files but in alphabetical order. I assure you the files are exact copies, though."

I sighed, knowing I'd have to go through both. I couldn't chance missing something.

"I have a list of all the names of the children and the parents if you would like to check that first," she said, bringing out a thick leather-bound book. "It only holds the name of the adoptive parents though and not the name of the birth parents. That information is only in the files."

I thanked her and pulled the first pile over to me. There were only five adoptions in the last month of the year I was born, so the daunting task I had thought was actually not so bad. The first file was a baby boy born in the first week of October. The next three were girls, but they looked to be sisters aged three, six, and seven. The last was another baby boy. None of them was me. I moved on to the next pile and checked out the first two weeks of January. This time, there was only one, a nine-year- old boy.

"Is there any way a file could be missing?" I asked in frustration.

She shook her head and held the book she was looking at out to me. "No mistake. You can see here the names and ages of the children that left us around that time. They all corroborate the files."

Frustration overwhelmed me. I had to be from here—just had to be; otherwise, where had I come from? I couldn't have just appeared out of thin air.

"Were you in charge back then?" I asked. "Was there a chance that someone higher up than you kept it secret? I mean, what with my parents being who they are? My adoption could have been written down somewhere else."

She shook her head again. "I'm sorry. I told you, I remember that time like it was yesterday. Your adoption dominated the papers. It was huge news so soon after the royal wedding. There were no babies brought to us in December or January that year. None in November either. We did have a baby girl come in late October, but she stayed with us until she was adopted in the summer. I happen to know her still, so that couldn't be you either. As you saw for yourself, the only babies we adopted out in that time period were boys."

"Is there another adoption agency in town?" I sighed. I needed to get to the bottom of this.

She shook her head, a look of almost pity in her eyes. "No. I'm sorry. We are the only one. There is one about three hundred miles south in Jeeka, but that's the nearest one to us. I know the woman who runs it. I could send a letter to her if you like?"

It made no sense. Why would my parents travel three hundred miles to Jeeka when there was an adoption agency here? She'd just told me that there was a baby girl living here in the winter of the year I was born. Why didn't they take her?"

"No, thank you. Did my parents ever come and visit the agency here?"

"No," she shook her head again. "I would have remembered."

Once again, I was left without answers, and now I had hit a brick wall to find them. I couldn't think of a single reason my parents would travel to Jeeka without first visiting this agency. So the question remained. Who was I, and where had I come from?

"Maybe I will have that coffee after all," I said to the woman feeling utterly dejected. Either no one knew about my birth and adoption, or if they did know, they weren't telling. I had a feeling that this woman was telling the truth. She had no reason to do otherwise, and she seemed genuinely surprised by my questions.

"Of course." She gave me another curtsey as she left me in the room alone. I trusted her, but while she was out, I decided to look through her other files. The book that still lay on the desk told me nothing, and a quick check of her desk drawers brought up no secrets beyond her love of cheesy romance novels. All the cabinets were unlocked, and a quick peek in all of them brought up nothing more than more files. Years of babies' and children's information. Every baby but me.

By the time she came back five minutes later with a mug of coffee and some biscuits, I knew that I'd find out no more here. I did consider a trip to Jeeka, but even as I thought about it, I dismissed the idea out of hand. It made no sense for my parents to travel three hundred miles when there was a perfectly good orphanage here. It made no sense because they hadn't. I'd come to them from somewhere else, but where, and more importantly, how could I find out?

As I sipped on the coffee, I pondered my next move.

Someone had to know something about my birth. I had a birth mother and father out there somewhere, but I could hardly ask them. They had not come and asked after me in eighteen years...at least, I didn't think they had. My own parents couldn't help. My mother was asleep, and my father wasn't being entirely honest. Dahlia refused to help me, and so there was nobody left to ask.

Leaving the orphanage had me feeling even more dejected. It had been a colossal waste of time. I walked through the streets of Zhore, my hood over my head so no one would see who I was. I wanted to hide from everyone. It was only when I was almost at the edge of town when inspiration struck. The newspaper! They knew everything, and anything they didn't know, they would do anything to find out. The headquarters of the Draconian Sentinel was in the main part of town, just a few streets over from Milo's house. I couldn't go and ask the press if they knew about my history, but Milo could.

Running through the streets as the snow once again began to fall, I came to Milo's house and knocked on his door. I'd not seen him at the castle for days, so the likelihood was that he would be working today, but he opened the door. When he saw it was me, he pulled me inside.

"What's the matter?" he asked, the worry in his eyes, matching my own state of excited panic.

"So, the world is falling to pieces, right?" I began in a wheeze, pulling the cloak off.

He took it from me and hung it on a hook. "I guess you could say that," he answered slowly. "Yes."

"And we think it has something to do with my history, " I continued in an excited babble.

Milo shrugged. "Maybe."

I ignored the reticence in his voice and answer and told him what I knew.

"I wasn't adopted from the only adoption agency in town," I began, then proceeded to tell him everything I'd learned in the past few hours, which was precisely zilch.

"I want you to go to the Sentinel and ask to see everything they have on my adoption. I can't go because they'll plaster my face across the front page."

Holding my fingers up to perform air quotes, I spoke again. "Princess seeks truth in adoption scandal."

Milo laughed. "Okay, I see your point, but why would they let me look at their records? They don't know who I am."

"It doesn't matter," I explained. "Their records are open to the public. I know because my parents and I took a tour of the building when it added a new extension last year. They told me all about it. There's a huge room with files, and anything that's not undergoing an active investigation anymore can be viewed by anyone who wants to see it. The best part is, no one will know. There are rows of files, and as long as you don't sneak them out, no one will be the wiser."

"Okay, I'm going," Milo said as I hurried him out of his own house. If my father came here again and found me here alone, he would skin both Milo and me alive, but it was a risk I was willing to take. Besides, there was nowhere I'd rather be than Milo's comfy house away from the madness that was the castle at the moment. Here, I could sit back on his sofa and read his books, admiring the intricacy of the weapons on the walls. Here, there was no one to annoy me, no one to demand that I go here or do that. There was no one here at all, now that Milo had left, and that was the way I liked it. Peace with only my thoughts for company.

At least, that's what I hoped, but less than half an hour after Milo had left, there was a knock at the door. I hadn't even realized how worked up I'd been, but the sound of the slow knock, spiked terror in my heart. After a few deep breaths, I reasoned that if it was my father's guard out looking for me, he would have rapped on the door with much more force.

Frowning, I walked to his door, wondering if I should open it or just wait. Rocking on my feet, I waited, deliberating my next course of action. I had no reason to open the door. Whoever it was, was not here to see me. They would be here for Milo, and Milo wouldn't be back for at least an hour. Deciding to pretend there was no one home, I turned on my heel, but the knocking came again, more insistent this time.

"I know you're here, Azia."

My stomach tensed at the sound of my name. No one called me by my first name beyond my immediate family. To the staff and to the public, I was always addressed as Your Highness. I didn't like it, but that was just the way it was. The only staff member beyond Milo that addressed me as Azia was Dahlia, and that was only because she'd been with me for so long. I knew without certainty that this was not Dahlia behind the door.

Gulping back a breath, I made the decision to leave the door closed. Derillen was still out there somewhere, and although she'd targeted my mother again this time, I knew in my gut that she wanted me.

As I turned to walk away, the door burst open, sending a flurry of snow in its wake.

The shiver passing through me had nothing to do

with the cold, however, and everything to do with the wizened old woman standing at the door. It was the woman who'd spoken to me in the Dragon Roost Inn over a week ago. The one who'd told me I was full of power and then promptly disappeared. Gladys something. I'd forgotten about her because not long after, a dragon had flown down the street blowing fire. That was enough to put anything before it from my mind.

"Aren't you going to invite me in, Deary?" she asked, shuffling past me and not waiting for an answer.

I tried to block her, but something stopped my feet from moving, whether magic or fear, I did not know.

She ambled past, not a care in the world, and sat down on the sofa where I'd been sitting mere moments ago.

"Are you coming in or not, Deary, because that pile of snow is only going to get bigger the longer you stand there."

Feeling down to my side, I realized I'd left my sword at the castle, not thinking I'd have a need for it. Milo's walls were filled with swords. One of those would have to do.

Closing the front door, I ran back to the living area and pulled a sword from the wall, leveling it at the witch.

"Get out of here," I said with a shaky voice.

She looked up at me through watery gray eyes. "Why ever would you point a sword at me, Deary? I'm here to help you."

I held the sword firm. "I don't need your help, Derillen."

I swear, I was seconds from ramming the sword through her heart when she began to laugh. A creaky laugh of old age.

"You think I'm that witch? No wonder your heart is

racing nineteen to the dozen. Come sit beside me. I'm no witch, and I'm certainly not Derillen. I'm a seer. My name is Gladys."

I hesitated. Derillen was hardly likely to tell me the truth about herself, especially when the sharp end of a sword was inches away from her heart, but then if she was a witch out to kill me, why hadn't she done it already?

I remembered the cloying tendrils of magic trying to invade my brain the day I was in the wool shop. The urgency in which I desperately needed to touch the needle of the spindle. I felt none of that now. Fear, perhaps, but it was all me. This woman was not compelling me to do anything, and the low hum of magic did not reside within her. I lowered the sword and sat in a chair opposite her. She might not be Derillen, but she knew who I was, and I was way past trusting anyone these days. I kept the sword at my side, firmly gripping it in my hand.

"You knew I was here."

The old lady nodded. "I did. Since the moment I met you, your power has intrigued me. I did not know who you were back then. I only thought you were a friend of that boy, Milo. I've seen you a lot in the newspaper since. I never saw you before because you were always standing behind your mother in the pictures. Why was that?"

"Erm...My mother was...is Sleeping Beauty. No one wants to see me when she is around."

The old woman nodded thoughtfully. "You put yourself down. You are a pretty young thing. Certainly, Milo seems to think so."

I blushed at the sound of his name. I knew he liked me. He showed me all the time, but it was different hearing it from someone else. It made it all the more real somehow.

My nerves around this woman faded somewhat. Not enough to loosen my grip on the sword, but enough to listen to what she had to say. And calling me a pretty young thing aside, I felt that she might be able to tell me something.

"Thank you. May I ask you why you are here?"

"I came to warn you, child," she said, sitting forward on the sofa. "Who you are is connected to everything that is going on around us."

"I know. I figured that out, but I don't know who I am. I'm adopted, but no one seems to know where I came from, or at least no one is telling me. Do you know?"

She shook her head. "I do not know where you came from, but it isn't from around here. You were born a long way from this place. Your aura doesn't resonate like the others. You are a displaced child, taken from your home."

She made it sound so much more spooky than adoption, but she was right. I did feel displaced.

"My mother and father adopted me when I was a newborn," I explained. "They didn't even know exactly how old I was. Just a few weeks at most."

"And you never wondered why?" she asked, raising her eyebrows. "Even adopted children know their own birthdays."

"I want to know," I said urgently. "I want to know everything."

"Of course, you do," she replied, nodding her head slowly. "How about you whip me up a cup of tea, and I'll tell you what I know."

With my heart beating faster, this time with the

thrill of excitement rather than fear, I walked into Milo's kitchen and made us both a cup of tea. As the kettle boiled, I kept my eye on the old woman. She sat, hunched over, her gnarled hands on her knees. She was tiny on the sofa, and yet appearances could be deceptive. I already knew that Derillen could change her appearance. I brought the cup out to her, which she accepted gratefully.

As I sipped on my tea, she began to talk. It was almost as if she was telling a story rather than telling me things about my life.

"I cannot tell you anything about your birth," she said, "but I know that you are special. Much more special than a mere princess. You have power that you don't even understand yet, and as the days and weeks pass, it will only grow stronger. I told you before that you are only part of a whole. You will need the other parts to reach your potential."

"I think I have a twin," I said, sitting forward, sloshing my tea everywhere.

Excitement flooded through me at the thought this woman might shed some light on it.

"Hmmm, maybe, maybe not. I cannot say."

Right. Maybe not, then.

"You are a long way away from that which will bind you," she continued. " You will soon be going on a long journey to find out who you are. You will face untold dangers, but you will have a friend by your side."

"Milo?"

She thought for a minute, then shook her head. "I cannot see clearly, but you will trust this person with your life and your secrets. Milo is not the one."

I thought of all the people who I would trust with my life and my secrets. It wasn't a huge list. Milo was the only person I could think of who fit the bill beyond Dahlia, and I couldn't see her coming on a journey with me.

"The kingdom will become very dark," she continued. "We are coming up on a grave time indeed. You, yourself, will not be able to stop the forces gathering power, but I believe for every dark force, there is a person who will be able to combat that force. I wonder if you are a part of that?"

She drank the rest of the tea down and stood up. Without a goodbye, she began to shuffle towards the door, leaving me with no real answers and only more questions.

"Hey, wait," I shouted out. "What do you mean? What will happen to me? I'm a part of what?"

"I cannot foresee everything. Your path is not yet written."

Frustration gripped me. She said she'd tell me things about myself, but I was left feeling more confused than ever before.

"You said I was born far away. Can you guess where, at least?"

She laughed her croaky laugh. "Of course, I can guess, but guesses will not help you. It would have had to have been a place of great power. Somewhere where your birth parents could hide you. Have you not ever thought about why your birth is surrounded in secrecy? Maybe that's the part you want to concentrate on rather than where you are from."

She shuffled out into the street, soon to be lost in the swirls of snow. A clap on my back made me jump a mile.

"Milo," I screeched. "You made me jump."

"What are you doing out here? You'll catch your

death of cold."

He ushered me back inside and closed the door behind us. Noting the two empty cups, he raised an eyebrow.

"Who was here?"

"You remember the old lady from the pub? Gladys? She came to talk to me. She said she knew all about me, but then waffled on about power. I'd hoped she would tell me where I was born and who my real parents were, but she didn't really tell me anything at all."

"Well, maybe she didn't need to," he said, sitting me down on the sofa before sitting down next to me. "I think I've found something out."

Excitement hit me once again. "You know?" I held my breath, hoping that the pieces would finally fit into place.

"Not exactly. Please don't get too excited yet. I managed to speak to someone who was a reporter around the time you were born. The whole kingdom was so excited to have a new princess, especially after the excitement of your parents' wedding, not to mention the waking of the princess and your grandparents. No one even thought to question where you came from or why you were adopted so soon after your parents married. They were only eighteen and nineteen years old. They had all the time in the world to have children of their own."

"Yeah, I know all that," I replied impatiently. "So, what else did he say?"

", it turns out our reporter friend was new to the job. He was young and eager to please. He thought the whole thing was suspicious. He went to the editor of the newspaper and said that he wanted to find out exactly who you were, but he was shot down."

"Why?" I asked appalled.

Milo shifted on the seat. "Apparently, the editor didn't want him snooping around and spoiling it. He said that the kingdom had seen enough sorrow, and he didn't want the reporter to bring the people down. The people only wanted good news, and the good news was selling papers. Thankfully for us, the reporter decided to go and investigate on his own."

"So, what did he find?" I jiggled impatiently.

"He interviewed a great many people. He didn't go to the obvious places like you did. He never went to the orphanage. He spoke to those people who worked night shifts."

"Night shifts?" Now, I was really confused.

"Yeah. Apparently, you weren't at the castle one day, and then, you were the next. No one saw you being brought to the castle. No one saw your parents going to pick you up. It was like you suddenly appeared one night."

Everyone I'd spoken to about it said the same thing.

I clapped my hands together excitedly. "And so he spoke to people who might have seen me being brought into the castle. Genius."

"Exactly," confirmed Milo. "He said he interviewed more than two dozen people with no luck, but then he struck it lucky. An old man was out stealing apples from an orchard just beyond the gates of the castle on the night you arrived. He hid behind a tree as a carriage passed. He heard a baby crying inside. More than one baby."

"I already know that. Remy's former nanny told me that she heard another baby, too. I'm sorry I should have told you that part."

Milo waved it off. "That's not all. He said that he saw

who was driving the carriage."

"Who?" I asked, my voice laced with anticipation.

"There were two of them. A young woman and an old woman in a cloak. He followed the carriage up to the castle and then peered through the portcullis.

"It was the old woman that brought you out of the carriage. The younger one stayed inside the carriage the whole time. She walked you to the front door and spoke to your mother and father. He couldn't hear what was said, but she spoke to your parents for about ten minutes before jumping back in the carriage and racing back through the castle gates. He caught a glimpse of the younger woman as they barreled past him. He said that she had tears streaming down her face."

"That was all?"

"Yes. That's all. The old man has since died, and it was never printed. I'm sorry I couldn't find out more."

I kissed him lightly on the cheek. "You found out everything. You found out that my real mother didn't want to let me go. She loved me."

He wrapped his arms around me and brought me into a hug as tears began to fall down my face. "Actually, there was one more thing. He said the carriage looked like one of those from Urbis."

17TH JANUARY

I awoke to an urgent rapping on my door.

"Who is it?" I yelled out from under my covers.

"It's me."Oh, crap. Caspian.

"I think we should spend some time today working on our wedding," he shouted back through my bedroom door. "We didn't get nearly enough done the other day."

I rolled my eyes and dragged myself out of bed, wrapping my robe around myself.

"*The* wedding," I said, opening the door to him. "Not our wedding. There have been thousands of applicants for the position of my husband. Any one of them could win."

Caspian sneered and waved his hand dismissively. "Just a formality. I am the best swordsman there is, and beyond the guards at your castle, the people of Draconis aren't known for their fighting skills."

"Maybe, maybe not, but I wouldn't count your wedding favors just yet. I can't work with you on the wedding." I made to close the door on him, but he slipped his foot between the door and the frame. "I have to plan the competition," I reminded him.

"I don't know why you are bothering," he said. "It seems like a total waste of time, but if you must. I'll ask that lovely maid of yours to help me."

"Go ahead." Dahlia would probably love the idea of spending another day planning a wedding with Caspian, and if it kept the pair of them out of my hair, then all the better.

Kicking his foot back, I slammed the door, not wanting to speak to Caspian a moment longer. I had too much running through my mind, and I'd made it very clear that I didn't care one jot what the wedding was like. I didn't care about the dress, flowers, food. None of it. How could I even begin to care about any of that stuff when I didn't even care for my husband-to-be? Heck, I didn't even know who my husband-to-be was.

Dressing quickly, I made the decision to go to the library. I had the competition to plan, and that was much more important than the wedding. I needed to make it in such a way that Caspian didn't win.

Plus , at the back of my mind, I knew that all of this would be for nothing. The competition, the wedding, all of it. I would plan it like the dutiful princess I was, but I wouldn't be here to see it.

I was going to go to Urbis. After hearing that I might have been born there, it was the only possible lead I had, and I'd never forgive myself if I didn't go and check it out. I couldn't ask my father's permission. There was no way in this kingdom; he would let me travel alone to Urbis. I could have asked to bring Milo with me, but my father was already suspicious of him. No, I had to do this alone, and I had to do it without anyone knowing. The castle was going to be full of reporters next week. All here to write about and take pictures of the competition and the preparations leading up to it. Preparations that had not yet started.

If I handed my father a full list of what I planned to do for the competition, then he would not suspect anything. I hated leaving him, especially with my mother the way she was, but I was doing nothing here to help. I couldn't wake her up any more than the constant stream of doctors that saw her every day.

But...if all this really did have something to do with where I came from, then it was my duty to find out what. And if I could find a way to save my mother and maybe find my real mother at the same time, then fantastic.

Remy was already in the library, absorbed in his adventure books, as usual. He grinned at me when he saw me walk in and waved a book at me. I had to sit and read with him before doing anything. He wouldn't leave me alone for a second if I didn't. Half an hour later, when I'd read a few chapters of a book about the pirates of Skyla, and he'd acted out the swashbuckling parts with much glee, I finally pried myself away and found the book where Remy had originally found the information on the competition. The book, named *Winning the Legend* was so old that the leather binding it was beginning to crack, and the gold lettering on the spine had faded to almost nothing.

I opened it, flicking carefully to the page that mentioned the competition. It was so vague. It seemed there needed to be three parts. Part one had to be a game of skill, part two had to be a game of logic, and part three had to be a sword fight to the death.

Pulling a pencil and paper to myself, I wrote swordfight to the death in capitals.

I wondered how that would go down? If we killed all the men who had applied, we'd look like barbarians. It would make things easy for me, but I figured I should come up with something a little better. I didn't really want anyone to die on my behalf.

Milo would have been a good person to help me with this, but he was working today, and Jack wouldn't be too pleased if he dashed off with me again. There was no way I'd be able to take him away from his post without Jack tattle-telling to my father. And, of course, my father wouldn't be too happy about one of the contestants helping me. No, I was in this on my own, whether I liked it or not

Part one. A game of skill. But what skill? Nothing Caspian was good at, that was for sure. I could rule magic out then. I should also stipulate in the rules that anyone caught using magic would be disqualified for cheating.

I thought of Milo and his strengths. He was a good swordsman, and no matter what Caspian said about the men of Draconis, I wouldn't want to count him out. He could rival Caspian with his sword skills, but could he beat him? I sighed. I just didn't know. Caspian could still beat me in a swordfight, something that irked me no end. Anyway, swordfighting was the final part of the competition. The first part had to be something else.

I thought about the sword that Milo had made me. It was beautiful. I couldn't ask the competitors to make swords, it would take too long, and we'd need so much metal and way too many tools, but what if we had them make something out of clay? It wasn't exactly Milo's area of expertise, but he was artistic and could turn his hand to anything. Caspian, on the other hand, had made nothing but trouble since being here. And piles of clay could easily be brought in. The makers of the best statues or pots would qualify for the next round. As I wrote pot in my notebook, a thought occurred to me. I gave a giggle and erased the word pot and added the word princess. If they were fighting for me, they could make me. They could design a figurine that looked like me. The ten closest ones would get through. That would certainly whittle the pool down.

Chewing a hangnail, I moved to the next part. Logic. I probably should come up with some really clever logic puzzle, but I wasn't particularly good at them, and if I couldn't come up with anything clever, how would I expect others not to know the answer straight away?

I sat back in my chair, watching Remy. He was soundlessly acting out a part in his book, a sly smile on his face as he thrust his hand forward, killing some imaginary foe. When all this was over, I was going to take him to Skyla. The stories of pirates he read about were fiction, but I'd heard reports of pirates really sailing the waters around there. Not that I wanted him to actually meet a pirate, but he would be thrilled to just see the place where they lived. Part of Draconis bordered the ocean, but mountain ranges made it almost impossible to reach. We had no pretty sandy beaches that some of the other kingdoms boasted, and seaside villages on the Draconis coast were few and far between.

I decided to leave that part and move to the final part. A battle of swords. There was no way I was going to do that. I couldn't have someone's blood on my hands.

Besides, as Caspian kept boasting, Swordfighting was one of his greatest skills. Pondering my other options for a second, I wrote down the word wrestling. Still not ideal, but the competition must have some form of combat, and wrestling was the safest I could think of beyond thumb wars, but my father would never go for that.

After another ten minutes of thinking, I wrote the word question under part two and left it at that. My father could come up with some crippling brain teaser. He was better at that sort of thing than I was.

Taking the paper out of the library, I headed down to my father's office. He sat quietly, a stack of papers on his desk, black circles under his eyes.

"What is it, Azia?" He sighed, his voice weary.

"I've finished planning the competition, Father." I handed over the scrap of paper I'd written on. He took it and looked at it, reading it quickly before turning it over to look at the back as though there would be something more written.

"Is this it?"

I nodded.

"Part two says answer a clever question."

"That's right."

He handed me back the piece of paper. "Please stop playing games and take this seriously," he admonished, massaging his temples. "This is your doing, and you need to be the one to sort it out. I have enough going on without having to worry about this competition."

I bowed my head. "I'm sorry, Father. I'll do better. What is it you are working on? Maybe I can be of help."

He shook his head. "You'll help by sorting that out," he said, pointing to the paper he'd just given back to me. I'm in the process of bringing the best doctors in all the kingdoms here to look at your mother. It's not as easy as you'd think. Plus, that wall has become a bugbear. A lot of our people want me to go and kill the dragons instead of building a wall, and so, I've got people feuding, my own staff turning against me. Jacob is practically threatening to start a revolution over it. The whole thing is an utter nightmare."

I jumped on his words. The last time I'd spoken to him about the dragons, he'd been adamant he was going to send his men up to attack. "You aren't going up the mountain, then?"

He shook his head slowly. "I want to. Killing the whole bloody lot of them will solve a huge problem. They've been nothing but a headache, but I need my men in case something else happens. A lot of them are still out looking for spindles, another bloody waste of time. As long as the dragons stay up there, I'll leave them alone. If there is another episode like the one last week, I'll have them up there in a shot. My whole army. Jacob keeps on at me to do it. He's not happy spending his days building a wall."

This Jacob character was really beginning to irk me, but at least, it meant I could breathe easy about the dragons now. Vasuki promised to keep his dragons under control, and my father wouldn't attack unless they did. One headache resolved. Now, if only I could resolve the other million problems I had.

I bade my father farewell and headed back to the entrance hall. A huge weight had been lifted from my mind. A weight I didn't know I'd felt so heavily. I shouldn't care about the dragons as much as I did. I barely knew them, but Vasuki had been right when he said we shared an affinity. There was something about them that called to me, and for whatever reason, they had made me their queen. I felt it, too. My magic only worked around them. I'd tried a hundred times to perform magic in their absence, but nothing had worked, despite Caspian telling me how powerful I was.

"Ah, there you are..."

I swear that man could read minds.

"Hello, Caspian. I already told you that I can't help you with wedding stuff. Do whatever you want. I don't care anyway," I said, walking past him quickly.

I waved my hand dismissively in his direction as I passed, hoping he'd get the hint that I didn't care to speak to him about the wedding or anything else, but in his usual Caspian fashion, he didn't.

"Actually, I wasn't here for that," he said, skirting around to face me. "My friend is coming, and I'd like to make sure she is welcomed nicely."

"Excuse me?" I stopped and raised my eyebrows.

"Well, you do have an awful attitude about you most of the time, and that sour face is enough to turn anyone off. Not me. I find it rather hot when you scowl, but I'd like it if you could be a bit nicer to her."

I planted on a smile to hide my anger and clenched my fists tightly by my side.

Through gritted teeth, I spoke. "I meant, what are you doing, bringing your friends here? This isn't your castle, and may I remind you that you are a guest here... an unwelcome one?"

"Fine!" he said, turning on his heel. "I'll send Charlotte back to Urbis after her three-day trip to get here.Only I thought you'd want to speak to her as she is renowned on the subject of Morpheus."

He began to walk away, knowing full well I would call him back. "The friend you told me about?" I shouted at him a little louder than I intended. My voice echoed around the entrance hall.

He turned. "That is the one. If you don't mind, I'll borrow a horse to ride into Zhore to the Urbis Express station and tell her myself that she isn't wanted. I think she'll be a little peeved. After all, she only came here to help you, but we all know how your wishes come before anyone else's."

"Okay, I'm sorry," I said, a little quieter this time. "I'd love to meet her. I'll come with you to Zhore, and I'll get the kitchen staff to make her a welcome meal."

"That's what I thought," Caspian said, his sly grin returning to his face. "I'll meet you in the stables in ten minutes. Hurry up, though, I wouldn't want to have to set off without you."

I fumed all the way to the kitchen. Caspian was becoming more insufferable by the second, but I needed to see his friend. I wanted to know if Caspian had been telling me the truth or if it was just some elaborate scheme to be able to stay in the castle. He was having it easy here. I don't know what his life was like in The Forge, but he had a cushy existence here. Not that I could say much. I lived this way, but this was my home.

Ten minutes later, we were saddled up and ready to go. The snow was really coming down again, and the dreary skies matched my mood well. I barely spoke to Caspian as we trotted down the road, but despite my murderous feelings toward him, I felt a flutter of excitement...no hope, in meeting this friend of his. I wasn't convinced that he was telling me the truth. I could never tell with him, but if this woman proved to be trustworthy and knowledgeable, then there was a chance...a slim chance I would be able to find Morpheus and the entrance to the dream world. If I could do that, I'd be able to find my mother and free her from her mental prison. My father had only just told me he was bringing in the best doctors from all the lands, but I already knew that it was a pointless endeavor. I think he knew that, too, but he felt as powerless as I did. If finding doctors helped him get through this, then I was all for it. Maybe they would be able to help him if not my mother.

I'd only ever seen the Urbis Express from a distance. When we traveled for royal visits, we only took the royal train, or sometimes, if it wasn't too far away like Badalah, we took horses and a carriage. I'd often looked to the skies and seen the large airships flying overhead and wished I was on them. It must be so wonderful to be able to fly above the kingdom in the comfort of a seat rather than in the talons or on the back of a dragon.

The huge airship was already in dock, and people were beginning to disembark. Despite the massive proportions of the ship, the part that held people was actually very small, only holding up to twenty passengers plus four crew members at a time. It made it an extremely expensive way to travel, which only the elite could afford. My family could afford it. Indeed, there was a special section on every Urbis express reserved for royalty and high-up dignitaries, but my mother was scared of heights, so we never used it.

I scanned the people heading towards us as Caspian jumped down from his horse. I was looking for an incredibly attractive fae, so I was surprised when the woman he hugged was human and average looking. Her medium brown hair was tied back, and she wore no makeup. Her clothes were smart like a business woman might wear, and nothing like the over-the-top attire that Caspian chose to wear on a daily basis.

I jumped down from my horse as Caspian brought

her over.

"I'm very privileged to meet you, Your Highness," she said, dropping into a low curtsey.

"Oh, don't bother with all that, Charlotte," he said airily. "It's only, Azia. She doesn't need bowing down to."

Charlotte's eyes opened wide, and her bushy eyebrows shot up under her messy bangs.

"It's okay," I said, holding out my hand for her to shake and kicking Caspian's calf at the same time with my boot. "Caspian is right. We have no need of formalities here. We are all friends."

"Well, I'm very excited to meet you," she said, giving me a shy smile. "I couldn't believe it when Caspian told me you wanted to meet me. I never thought my degree would come in useful. My parents thought I was silly to take it, but look at me now. Heading to the Draconis Castle with the princess herself. That'll show my parents, eh?"

I laughed at her enthusiasm. Despite my reservations at her being Caspian's friend, I liked her a great deal already. A lot more than I liked Caspian, but then again, that wasn't saying much.

Caspian helped her onto the back of his horse, and the three of us made our way back to the castle.

Charlotte's mouth dropped as I escorted her into the castle. She gazed about her as I took her coat, her eyes drifting from place to place as she took it all in.

"It's so beautiful," she murmured.

"It's home, and you are very welcome here," I said. "I've had some food put out for you. Are you hungry?"

She nodded enthusiastically. "I'm famished. I couldn't afford to buy much food on the Urbis Express. I've only eaten a couple of sandwiches and some apples for the past few days."

"I've had a room made up for you. If you want to put your bags in there and then come back down to lunch."

She grinned and gave me the thumbs up as I asked a maid to take her to her guest room.

Caspian and I sat in the small dining room, waiting for her.

"Charlotte seems nice," I said, absently. The food had already been brought out buffet style, and the smell was causing my stomach to jump. I'd not realized how hungry I was.

"She's very knowledgeable. Anything you want to know about Morpheus, she will be able to tell you."

"How do you know her?"I asked genuinely interested. She didn't seem like someone Caspian would spend time with.

"I spent some time in Urbis a few years back, and we met then. I liked the fact that she was different from the girls at The Forge."

"I remember you saying the same thing about me once." I grinned, picking up a carrot stick and taking a bite.

"You are nothing like Charlotte," he said. I didn't have time to question him on what he meant because Charlotte chose that moment to walk through the door. She'd changed into a pretty but understated pink dress, and her hair was now down. She was a bonny girl with a sweet face that had an innocence about it.

"This looks yummy," she stated, taking in the spread of food.

I watched her as she ate. She took little bites out of everything, almost like a squirrel would. Every time Caspian spoke, her eyes would dart over to him.

"Charlotte took a course in the Gods at Urbis

University, but Morpheus was her specialty. She knows more about Morpheus than anyone," Caspian said. At this, Charlotte's face lit up like a beacon.

"Not really," she said, smiling shyly. "I'm sure there are other people who know more than I."

"I doubt it."

Charlotte positively beamed at his words.

"So," she said, talking to me. "Caspian tells me you want to know about Morpheus. He's already told me your situation."

"Do you think you'll be able to help me?" I asked.

"I'm not a mage. All I can do is tell you what I know."

"Which is a lot," said Caspian

"Which is a lot when it comes to Morpheus," she said.

I was eager to hear what she had to say. Anything that could help my mother.

Before she spoke, the door to the dining room opened. "Have you finished the competition yet?"

I looked to the door to where my father stood. His eyes bulged from lack of sleep, and his hair stuck up at all angles. He looked crazed.

"Not yet, Father, but..."

"I've just had a messenger from the Sentinel up at the castle again. I promised it to them yesterday."

"But Father..."

"But father, nothing. You promised me this morning that you'd get it done, and here I find you having a tea party. I'm going to bed. I've not slept for thirty-six hours straight. I need this done by the time the paper goes to press. They gave me a deadline of five o'clock."

Without another word, he slammed the door behind

him as he left. A glance at the clock told me I had a little under two hours to come up with three parts to this stupid competition. If only he'd listened to me about Charlotte and why she was here, he would have slept more soundly, but I didn't have the heart to go running after him. If he was going to bed, it was kinder to leave him be.

"I should go and do what he wants. I've been putting it off," I explained. "I'm so sorry, Charlotte."

"Would you like me to help you?" Caspian asked.

"No. Why don't you take Charlotte for a tour of the castle grounds? The weather's cleared up a little."

"Oh , yes, please," she said, practically bouncing out of her seat."I'd love to."

I left them both with a smile on my face. Charlotte's crush on Caspian was obvious. Insane, but obvious. Her eyes barely left him the whole lunchtime. He, on the other hand, hardly looked at her at all.

I really hated the fact I had to wait to hear what she had to say about Morpheus. I don't know what scared me the most. My mother being in a coma, her being cursed, or her being locked in a dream realm by some crazy god, but if I knew what it was, it would bring me closer to being able to deal with it.

I went to the library expecting to find Remy there. It was quiet, but his books still lay on the floor where he'd left them. I picked them all up and shelved them, before opening the cabinet with the special books in it and pulling the one with the contest in it out.

After reading it for what felt like three hundred times, I sat back in the chair and closed my eyes. This was too hard.

I looked at the piece of paper I'd scribbled on earlier. The clay thing was a good idea, and the fighting seemed to be mandatory, whether I liked it or not.

I just needed a question that Caspian would never be able to answer, a question that Milo would jump on. Nothing too obvious. Not that it really mattered as I was planning on not being here anyway, but if it did get postponed and I did get forced to go through it at some later date.

And then it came to me. With a grin on my face, I wrote it down.

"What is the name of the Queen of Dragons?"

18TH JANUARY

Charlotte was already sitting at the table when I came down for breakfast. She sat up in her chair and gave me a bright, breezy smile.

"I'm so glad you are here. One of your staff members woke me up and told me that breakfast was served, but I thought that I'd come to the wrong place when there was no one here."

"It will get very noisy soon. Just wait and see. I have three brothers who love food. In fact, I'd eat now before they come down and eat it all... Caspian thinks that my mother's curse is actually something to do with Morpheus," I said, trying to bring the subject around to the reason she was here.

"From what Caspian tells me, it possibly is the case. I'd have to see her, of course, but if it's like the curse she was under before, then I'd say Morpheus has a hand in it."

"How do you know Morpheus had anything to do with the curse before?" I asked. "A witch called Derillen performed the spell originally. I think it's Derillen again this time."

The door opened, and Caspian walked in.

"Azia thinks a lot of things," Caspian explained to Charlotte, "but she's very rarely correct."

Charlotte pushed his arm. "You are such a monster. Don't be so rude."

"Yeah, Caspian. Don't be so rude."

"You love it!" he said, swiveling his eyes to me.

"I'd agree with you if you were right," I snapped back.

"Let's assume it's the same person doing this..." Charlotte said, steering us back to the original topic of conversation.

"It's not," butted in Caspian.

"We'll let's, for the sake of argument, say it is," Charlotte continued. "I don't know much about what happened to your mother back then. It's a little before my time. I was only five when she woke up. I did write about her in my dissertation, but I didn't cover much. My hypothesis was that Derillen had somehow become friendly with Morpheus, and Morpheus had closed the entrances to the dream world for your mother. Other people could enter and leave, but your mother was lost."

"You see, that's the part I don't understand. How come other people could come and go, and my mother couldn't. Why couldn't she go with them."

"it's not that simple. We all have our own exit and entrance. We get there through dreaming. If we didn't, we'd wake up after a nap in someone else's head. It is possible...nay, probable that your mother is seeing these other people. If you've dreamed about your mother, it's possible that you have actually seen her, but like most dreams, we wake up and forget straight away. Occasionally, we remember our dreams, but usually they are strange. That's the dream world. It is a strange place. Morpheus likes to confuse."

"So, if I dreamed about my mother, I could talk to her?"

Charlotte shrugged. "It's possible she will see you and be able to talk to you. You might have already even been speaking to her every night, but unless you remember the dream, you wouldn't even know it."

My mind was blown by the thought of it. If Charlotte's hypothesis was right, I could spend my nights speaking to any number of people and not even know. It was a strange thought and one that didn't sit well in my stomach. I grabbed a sandwich and bit into it, chewing as I considered the implications of it.

"If you remember the story, your mother's curse was to kill her not to make her sleep. Derillen gave her the curse when she was a baby, but it didn't come into effect until she was seventeen years old. That gave your grandparents plenty of time to find other people of magic to stop the curse. The problem was that once a curse is given, only the original curse giver can break it."

I sat forward, intrigued. She knew more about my mother than I did. I'd not really been told this part of the story, just the bit about her waking up.

"Your mother was sent into hiding for the first part of her life, even though many people of magic told your grandfather that no amount of hiding could keep her from the curse. He didn't believe them, or he didn't want to believe them, so your mother barely saw her own parents throughout her childhood. Meanwhile, your grandfather hired every mage he could get his hands on. At one time, believe it or not, Draconis was the most magical kingdom, even beating out Enchantia, where most of the population is magic to some extent. "

She took a pause as she sipped on her tea. "There was almost an explosion of magic, but even then, they couldn't stop the curse, only lessen it. They made the curse so that if your mother pricked her finger, she would only fall asleep, not die."

"Which she did."

"Yes, but they made it so she would only fall asleep for one night. She was supposed to wake up the next day with nothing more wrong with her than a sore finger."

"How do you know all this?" I exclaimed.

"I told you. I used your mother's story as part of my dissertation. I spent four years studying Morpheus, and your mother's story is one of the more fascinating parts of my research."

"So where does he come in?"

"Well, " she said, clapping her hands together, "Derillen knew she had been beaten. The curse would still happen, but it would barely affect your mother at all. She was angry, but against so many people of magic, even she, with all her power, could do nothing. Nor dare she do any more curses with all the mages and fae looking after the young princess. But our Derillen was cunning. She knew a way around it. She somehow got to Morpheus, and between them, they cooked up the plan to close your mother's exit."

"How did she find Morpheus?" I asked.

Charlotte shrugged and rolled her eyes at the same time." That's where it gets difficult. I don't know how she found him. The gods don't live on the mortal realm.

They do visit from time to time, but they spend most of the time wherever it is that gods live. There is no way to get there. Only the gods themselves can come and go. There have been many reports of people meeting the gods throughout the ages, but Morpheus is a slippery character. He is a master of disguise and can shift himself into any shape. I could be Morpheus, and you'd never know. Caspian could be him."

"I'd make a great god," he said, putting his hands behind his head.

Ignoring him, I asked Charlotte another question. "If he is so hard to find, how did Derillen do it?"

"I don't know. I've never been able to find out. She was a very powerful witch, which might have helped. Morpheus is drawn to power. If she went looking for him, there is a chance he heard about her and made himself known to her."

"Could we find him? I mean, is there a chance I could find him?"

She shrugged again? "I don't want to give you any false illusions. You will be very lucky if you do find him. Even then, you'll have to have something he wants in exchange. He won't open the portal to the dream world for just anybody."

"Is there a way for us to find this portal without him?"

"No," Charlotte answered, shaking her head. "It's not in a fixed place. Morpheus conjures it up when he wants to visit the dream world and when he's done, the portal disappears. It could be anywhere, and it's only open when he's in the mortal realm. If he decides to spend the next fifty years in the realm of the gods, we'll never be able to find him."

The whole thing seemed impossible, but there was

no other hope for my mother. No medic or healer would be able to help her. It was either find the witch that cursed her or find Morpheus to unblock her way back. As I had no clue where to start finding either of them, the whole thing seemed pointless.

"So, I should give up."

"You do have more pressing matters," Caspian cut in. "Namely, your wedding to plan."

I noticed Charlotte slump as he mentioned the wedding.

"I've never met him, and believe me, I've looked. That's why I moved to Urbis in the first place. The sightings of him have always been there. He doesn't seem to travel to other kingdoms. If you are going to find him, Urbis is the place to be, but like I said, I've spent four years looking for him, and I've never met him...or at least I don't know that I have. There is a chance I met him and didn't know it."

She must have seen my crestfallen face.

"Look. You are prettier than I'll ever be, and that will give you the upper hand. He likes beautiful women."

She was putting herself down. She was pretty, just in an understated way. I watched as she slid her eyes to Caspian in the hope he'd contradict her on her level of beauty. Of course, he didn't. He was happy to talk about how clever she was, but he was blind to her. Idiot.

"I'm not sure I like the idea of you going to find him if that's the case," he said. "You are mine, and I'm not about to share you with some god."

Double idiot!

"I'm not yours," I reminded him, seeing the stricken look on Charlotte's face. "I've never been yours, and I'll never be yours."

"You will if I win the competition."

"If you'll excuse me." Charlotte stood up quickly, her face turned away from Caspian so he couldn't see her tears. "I've eaten a little too much. I think I should go lie down for a bit. Thank you for the food. It was lovely."

She dashed out of the door so quickly, I didn't have time to stop her.

"She barely ate anything," Caspian commented.

I glared at him. "You really are stupid, you know that?"

He sat up in his chair, giving me a what-did-I-do look.

I dashed out the door up to the room I'd had made up for Charlotte. I knocked on the door, but I could hear her sobbing quietly inside.

"It's me," I shouted through. A few seconds later, the door opened a crack. Before she had chance to speak, I said what I wanted to say.

"He's an ass. You know that, right?"

She opened the door a little more and let me come in.

"I'm sorry I ran like that. He's not the idiot. I am. I've been in love with him since the second I met him."

"I hate to break this to you, Charlotte, but he's easily the most awful person I've ever met."

"He doesn't think that about you," she said sadly, sitting back down on the bed.

"He's an obnoxious creep. Why on earth do you like him?"

"He's weird around you," she said. "He's not normally like this. Yeah, he's always been full of himself, but look how gorgeous he is. He's perfect."

Moving on...

"Weird how?" He was weird to me all the time, so I didn't know any different.

"He's not so cocky with you."

I laughed so hard I almost fell off the bed. "If this is him not being cocky, I'd hate to see him usually."

"He really likes you. The way he's acting is just for show. I've never seen him like this. He's always been cocky, but I've never seen him be rude before. I met him in my freshman year in a bar in Urbis. I was drawn to him right away. I'm not really a bar dweller, but I was out looking for Morpheus. As soon as Caspian walked in, he was surrounded by women trying to get his attention. I thought at the time he might be Morpheus. He has the same traits. Beautiful, confidant. When Caspian got annoyed at the constant attention-seeking, he slipped out the back. I followed him and let him hide in my apartment. "

"Uh, huh."

"It wasn't like that...okay, maybe it was. I was no better than those other girls, I wanted him just as much, but I guess I was cleverer."

"I still can't get over him having a swarm of girls after him," I said.

"He's popular in Urbis... He's popular everywhere, really."

"Not around here, he's not."

She gave a wry smile. "I think you are the only girl that hasn't fallen for his charms, which is ironic, really."

"I'm yet to see any charms. He's tried to kill me twice."

"I doubt that. This is the first time I've seen him actually like someone."

She sounded sad. "I don't see what you are seeing. He treats me awfully. I admit he can be nice sometimes, but he usually messes it up."

"He wouldn't be this insistent on marrying you if he

didn't want to."

"I thought he wanted to marry me because he wanted power."

Charlotte shook her head. "Do you even know who he is?"

Now it was my turn to shake my head. "What do you mean?"

"He is a member of the Urbis government. He's the president of magic and magical beings. Basically, any laws pertaining to magic have to be signed off by him before they can become laws. He might not be a member of royalty like you, but in some regards, he's already more powerful politically than you'll ever be."

My mind reeled with this new information. Caspian served in the Urbis government. Charlotte was right when she said he had a lot of power. Even my parents had told me he was powerful, but I thought they meant magically. The leaders of each kingdom were governed by the government in Urbis. Mostly, Urbis left the eleven kingdoms to their own devices, but sometimes, they waded in when they felt something wasn't being done right. He was giving up a lot to be here with me.

"It doesn't matter. I dislike the man so much that I opened up a competition to all the men in Draconis to marry me. It was either that or marry Caspian."

She giggled at this. "I bet that didn't go down too well."

"Not at all. He hates it, but tough. I don't want to marry him."

"I'd do anything to be like you. You really are beautiful. It's no wonder he likes you. I've known him for four years, and I don't think he's even noticed I'm a woman."

I looked down at my clothes. I was happiest in my

scruffy clothes so I could go out and practice fighting, but Dahlia usually managed to make me half decent every morning, whether I liked it or not. Today, she'd put me in a pretty blouse and skirt combo. She'd even managed to do something with my hair.

I looked closely at Charlotte.

"I think I can help you. You need some Dahlia treatment."

"What's that?" she asked, eyes wide.

"You'll see, but first of all, tell me more about Morpheus."

"Like I told you before, I've never seen him, but if you want to find your mother, finding him is the only way. You'll have to be clever, and you'll have to seduce him. You'll also have to go to Urbis. He's not once been spotted outside of the city."

I nodded. I'd already made my mind up to go to Urbis. I was born there, or at least I think I was. It was like everything was coming together, and the path I needed to take was an obvious one.

"If you do decide to come to Urbis, you are very welcome to stay with me. My apartment is small, but I have a spare bed. It's the least I can do after your hospitality."

"Thank you. I might have to take you up on that. How do you know all this? I mean, how do you know that the dream world exists, and how do you know that Derillen found Morpheus and got him to close my mother's exits?"

"I know of Morpheus because I dreamed about him once. I've always had lucid dreams, which makes me more susceptible to him. He came to me when I was in the dream world. He was so beautiful, I knew right then I wanted him . He told me his name, but then he left me alone. I woke up completely in love. I'm not a religious person, but I'd heard about the god Morpheus. It was then, I decided to learn more about him at university. There have been many sightings of him over the years. Some, I'm not sure are true; but some, I believe.

"As for Derillen, I stumbled upon her story in my second year. As I was researching Morpheus, I looked for any articles that were about sleep. The fact that Derillen had the ability to stop your mother waking up was what made me know that Morpheus was involved. No one is more powerful than the gods. Not fae, not mages, not even witches. The gods are about as powerful as you can get, so if anyone was stopping your mother from waking up, I knew it was him."

"Do you have concrete proof?"

She shook her head. "No, but I know everything there is to know about sleep, and there are only two ways to stop someone waking up. Either kill them or lock them in the dream realm. If your mother is still breathing, it has to be the latter, and if it's the latter, it means Morpheus is involved. There is no other explanation."

I tried to think around her reasoning. "What about illness? People in comas don't wake up."

"People in comas don't wake after a hundred-year sleep, not having aged a day either."

True," I conceded, "but could it be that she is in a coma now?"

"I don't know for sure, but Caspian told me that your father has had her looked at by many doctors, and they all agree there is nothing wrong with her. If there is nothing wrong with her, then she's trapped. There's one way to tell for sure."

"There is?" I wanted to believe her so badly, but I was the type of person that needed proof rather than guesswork. Even four years of study wasn't enough unless I could see it with my own eyes.

"I'd need to see her, and then, I can tell you if it's a coma or not."

The maid was by my mother's bed as I entered her room. She held a book in her hand as she had the last time I'd been to visit.

"I've been reading to her," she explained. "I thought maybe if she could hear a soothing voice, she might respond to it, you know."

"Thank you," I said, giving her a warm smile. Behind me, Charlotte whispered that a freight train could go through the room, and my mother wouldn't hear it.

The maid gave Charlotte a funny look as she walked around us to leave the room. No doubt she'd go straight to my father to tell him that I was here with a strange woman, not that it mattered. By the time my father came up the stairs to find out what was going on, we'd already know what was wrong with her.

"My father has hired the best physicians and healers in all the land. They'll all be arriving soon. The castle will be full again."I took my mother's hand. It was so cold.

"Just like your grandfather did all those years ago with the mages and fae, not that all the people of magic in the world would be able to help her if I'm right." She looked me in the eye. "I hope I'm wrong and that this is something else. Then those healers will be able to help her."

"I hope so too," I said. "So what do we need to do to tell if she's in a coma? Some kind of spell?"

Charlotte gave a small mirthless laugh. "I'm not magic. I'm originally from Arcadia, and there are not many people of magic there. No. This is something much more simple. If she is in a coma and you pull back her eyelids, you'll see her pupils. Most coma patients don't react to light. Some do."

"So what happens if she isn't in a coma? If she's cursed?"

Charlotte leaned over my mother and gently put her thumbs on her eyelids. "If she's in the Dream Realm, she'll not have any pupils at all." She pulled back her eyelids.

I looked down. Pain gripped my chest as my worse fear was realized. All I saw were the whites of her eyes. My mother was definitely cursed.

19TH JANUARY

"Dahlia asked me to tell you that there is a reporter from the Sentinel waiting to speak with you," Milo said after my good morning kiss. "Oh, and she said to dress up nicely...her version of nicely, not yours. She said they are waiting in the main hall, so hurry up."

"Urgh!" I sighed as I opened my wardrobe and pulled out a dress. I had too much going on to care about reporters. I had a trip to Urbis to plan. There were way too many reasons for me to go there now. I needed to find out who I was, but I also had to save my mother from Morpheus's clutches. The only way I was going to get close to doing any of those was to travel to Urbis.

I'd sent the three parts of the competition to the Sentinel by way of one of the castle staff a couple of days before, so I expected that was the reason they wanted to see me. I'd also done it without showing my father first. I didn't want to give him any more reason to make me do the whole thing again. I had too much on my plate to worry about a competition that I had no intention of holding, and my father was equally as busy. I was doing him a favor, really.

"I'll leave you to it," Milo smiled, "But maybe we could do some more sword practice when my shift ends?"

"Sure thing," I replied as he shut my bedroom door behind him.

I pulled out a beige dress that matched my mood perfectly and pulled it over my head. After running a brush through my hair and tying it back with a ribbon, I was ready to face whatever the Sentinel reporter had to throw at me. He'd no doubt want a couple of pictures, and for that, I should have put on some makeup, but I just wanted to get the whole thing over and done with as quickly as possible. I needed the time to plan my trip before I went out with Milo. I couldn't ask for his help because I wasn't planning on telling him I was going. He'd only try and stop me. The only person I was planning on telling was Nyre because I was planning on taking her with me. I'd be spotted if I tried getting to Urbis on the Urbis Express or on the train, which left me with three options. Walk, go on horseback or fly, courtesy of my little dragon friend. Nyre was the quickest option.

The main hall was packed with people, all of which turned their eyes to me as I entered.

"What's going on now?" I whispered to myself as I walked between the men, for they were almost all men. The only woman in the whole room was Dahlia, who bustled towards me when I walked through the door.

"What's going on?" I asked, though I was sure I didn't really want to know.

"Didn't Milo tell you? The Sentinel people are here. They want to do a feature as a way to build up excitement for the competition next week."

"You're telling me they sent this many reporters?" I asked as she hustled me up to the raised throne area.

"Don't be silly. The two in the front row are the Sentinel reporter and photographer."

"So, who are the others?" I asked, gazing over the heads of all the men. There were so many of them. Hundreds.

"They are the people we've selected for the competition. We invited them here today to meet you before they compete for you."

"Oh, you did, did you?" I asked weakly. So much for planning my getaway. I wouldn't even be able to practice my sword fighting with Milo at this rate.

"It wasn't just me. It was the castle administration team."

"What did my father say about this?" I inquired, looking around the hall. He was nowhere to be seen. Neither was Caspian or Milo. I knew Milo was working, but I had no idea where Caspian was when all this was going on. Hopefully, asking Charlotte out on a date so I could cancel this whole thing. Dahlia shrugged and moved back without answering my question.

"I'll do a quick interview afterward," the Sentinel reporter piped up, "but first, we'd like to get some shots of you talking to your suitors."

"Great," I said, not doing a good job of hiding my sarcastic tone.

"Andrew, first!" Dahlia said as I sat down in my father's throne. It was the first time I'd ever sat in it, not that it brought me any joy to think about it. I'd prefer to be literally anywhere than right where I was.

"This is Andrew," Dahlia said, bringing a shy-looking boy up to me. He didn't look much older than me, and the way he kept his eyes down told me he was nervous about meeting me. You and me both, Buddy.

"Andrew is my son," Dahlia said proudly, giving me a wink and pointing to him. "He's perfect," she mouthed silently behind his back. I smirked. The poor kid looked like he was about to lose his lunch.

"Hi, Andrew. I've heard a lot about you," I lied. All I'd heard were complaints that he wasn't doing as well as he could be in school.

"Really?" he said. His voice was almost a whisper. I talked to him for an excruciating two minutes while the photographer snapped away. The poor guy could barely string a sentence together and replied to everything I said in monosyllables.

"He's just a little shy," Dahlia explained as she ushered him off the stage. "You'll need to go through the rest more quickly or we'll be here all day. Just a how do you do and on to the next." What followed was no better. In nine hundred men, I would have thought I'd like at least one of them, but between the oafs, the men who forgot to speak, the men that thought they already owned me, not to mention the man who asked when his coronation would be, I was thoroughly bored and annoyed by the time it came to eat. To my chagrin, all these men had been invited to eat, and tables full of sandwiches were brought in.

There was no escape for me. Every time I tried to leave, Dahlia was there, reminding me of my duty. In the end, I grabbed a sandwich and sat on the floor in the very back corner of the room behind my father's throne. It wasn't ideal, but at least, I was mostly shielded from view, and no one else was allowed up here, so I'd get a little peace before it would all start again in the afternoon.

A shadow loomed above me. I was all set to tell them where to go when I looked up and saw Caspian with a tray full of food and a couple of glasses of wine.

"I thought you might want a bit more than a soggy sandwich," he said, sitting down and putting the tray between us. It was filled with fruit and pastries. My stomach grumbled at the sight of it.

"And I thought this might help you get through the afternoon," he said, handing me the wine. I took the glass from him and downed it in one go while he picked up a pastry for himself.

"You know, I never thought I'd say this, but you are looking quite the catch compared to the competition."

His mouth curled up at the edges in a picture of smugness.

"You brought this on yourself," he reminded me. "You could have had this." He indicated his body.

"You are hot," I agreed, probably because the wine was strong, and it had already gone to my head.

"There's still time. We could call this off. We could elope..."

"I could throw myself out of my bedroom window," I said, taking Caspian's wine and downing that too. If I was going to have to repeat this morning, I was going to do it drunk.

"I mean it. I could go and speak to your father right now. I know it's what he wants. He's sick of all this as much as you are."

He swept his head toward the rest of the hall, where nearly nine hundred men were eating.

"I suppose you can't be much worse than the guy whose feet smelled so bad that I almost threw up on him."

"Let's do it then," Caspian urged.

"You are forgetting one thing," I said, "You are a total ass, and I hate you."

"Hate is such a strong word," Caspian lamented, but the smile was still firmly on his gorgeous face. Urgh. Two glasses of wine, and my brain had completely given up.

"You are in love with that Milo chap, huh? Do you really think he can beat me?"

"He kicked your ass before," I reminded him of the time in his bedroom. "I see no reason why he won't be able to do it again. Besides. I'm not in love with him. I'm not in love with anyone. I just like him a lot. A lot more than you anyway."

"So you aren't in love with him? Well then, you won't mind if I do this." He leaned forward, and before I had time to react, he was kissing me. My mind was outraged, but my drunken brain wouldn't get my body to work quickly enough. My mind was saying move, but it felt so good, and the room spun around me.

Slap! Caspian brought his hand up to his cheek as I slapped him hard.

"How dare you!" I hissed, glaring at him.

"I notice it took you more than a few seconds to pull away," he remarked, grabbing another pastry. "And I didn't feel any resistance. In fact, I would say that you rather enjoyed it."

With that, he popped the pastry into his mouth, gave me a wink, and walked away, leaving me on my own, hiding behind my father's throne.

"Insufferable jerk!" I said loudly to no one in

particular. The worst part was, he wasn't wrong. I had enjoyed it. I'd enjoyed it much more than I wanted to admit. Damn the fae!

He stood watching me all afternoon. Everywhere I looked, I could see him in the corner of my eye. His smart pale blue outfit stood out amongst the grays and blues and browns that the other men had elected to wear. I hated that I'd enjoyed kissing him, that it had been exciting, passionate, and forbidden, hidden behind my father's throne in a room with nine hundred men, all of which wanted to marry me. I couldn't even tell anyone about it either. If I told my father, he'd insist I marry the fae. If I even hinted that I'd kissed Caspian to Dahlia, she'd be ecstatic once she got over the fact I wasn't going to marry her beloved son. And I really couldn't tell Milo. Sweet, beautiful Milo, who didn't deserve this. I'd told him time and time again that I didn't want a boyfriend, all the while stringing him along, kissing him at every available opportunity. And I loved kissing Milo. It was a beautiful thing, and when our lips met, it was just right. Perfect. I was at home. But with Caspian, it had been full of raw danger, excitement, and a whole host of negative emotions that were currently swirly around my mind. My stomach did the same, thanks to the wine that I was most definitely not used to. I swear I was slurring my words by the time I'd managed to speak to all the men. After an extremely brief interview with the Sentinel reporter I hurried up to my room before anyone else could take more of my time. To my relief, Milo had already left for the day. He must have seen what was going on and realized I wasn't going to be able to put in any practice that day. I would have to tell Milo about the kiss. It was only fair, but I wasn't in any fit state to do it now. I yawned as I sat on my bed and tried to put my feelings together. It was no use. My feelings for Milo eclipsed anything I'd ever felt before, and yet I could still taste Caspian on my lips. I remembered clearly the feel of his lips on mine.

"Urgh," I cried out in frustration, falling back on my bed and pulling a pillow over my face.

I probably would have stayed that way all evening if it wasn't for the tapping on my window. Looking up, I saw Nyre outside.

I opened the window, and she hopped in quickly. A minute later, she was sitting on my bed in her transformed form as naked as the day she was born.

"Here," I said, throwing her a robe. She laughed as she pulled it around herself, covering her body with the soft downy night robe. She snuggled into it before looking up at me.

"You humans are so uptight. We don't wear clothes up on the mountain."

I made sure my bedroom door was closed as she paraded up and down in front of my mirror, gazing at herself in the robe. I'd have to throw her a pretty dress next time.

"That's as may be," I said, "but down here, we do, and if anyone was to walk in, they'd get quite a shock to see a naked woman on my bed."

"A naked dragon!" she stated but grinned at me, all the same.

"What can I do for you, Nyre?" I asked. The truth was, I was glad to see her. I didn't have any female friends, and beyond my mother and the female staff in the castle, I didn't know any other girls.

"Nothing. I thought I'd come down and see how you are holding up. My father has all the dragons on guard, ready for attack from your father. The plan is to make sure everyone is down in the settlement apart from the egg layers. Dragons have laid eggs in nests for generations because the altitude is good for them."

I sighed and sat on the bed. "I don't think my father is going to attack the dragons anymore. The people of Draconis want him to, but he's got a lot going on. He's trying to bring in the best doctors from the other kingdoms for my mother, and all his attention is there at the moment."

"Well, that's great news...Not about your mom, but about the doctors. Do you think they will help her?"

I shrugged my shoulders. "I don't think so. She isn't sick. She is cursed."

I told her about Derillen and Charlotte's theory of where my mother was. Just thinking about Charlotte brought back the guilt of kissing Caspian. She was completely besotted with him. Milo wouldn't be the only one upset by the kiss earlier. I finished my story and broke down in tears.

"No frowns, babe," Nyre said, bringing me into a hug. "Dragons don't cry."

"I'm not a dragon," I reminded her.

"No, you're the freaking Queen of the dragons! My father says so, and so it must be true."

I snorted a laugh as my tears dripped onto her shoulder, dampening the robe.

"I kissed an asshole."

"Ew." she crinkled her nose up, pulling away from me. "I hope you are not speaking literally because you know I'm not into that shit, right?"

I cracked up again, and the tears that had felt so real turned to tears of laughter.

"I was talking about a guy. The guy is an asshole."

"Ooh. " she sat forward, her hands clasped together,

excitement about the change in topic coloring her features. "Which one? The fae? I know you're not talking about Milo. That guy is about as far from asshole as you can get."

I'd forgotten she'd seen me with Caspian once. The first time I'd used my magic, I'd been out with him, and the dragons had flown down out of the sky to bow down to me.

"That's the one," I said, nodding. "He kissed me today, and I feel like shit because of it. I'm not sure Milo will forgive me."

She weighed my words. "He's super hot, but if you say he's an asshole, then he's an asshole. Let's break this down, shall we? You say that he kissed you. Did you initiate it?"

I shook my head. "No. I didn't even want him to kiss me. I was a little tipsy."

"Well, there you have it," she said, clapping her hands together a little too excitedly. "You didn't want him to kiss you, and you were too drunk to fend him off."

She made it sound so cut and dried as though I wasn't somehow to blame for the mess I'd found myself in.

"Hmmm," I sighed. I wanted to believe her, but the fact remained I'd enjoyed it. Despite me hating Caspian, despite me wanting to shove a sword through his gut every time I spoke to him, I'd enjoyed kissing him.

"Urgh!" I said, throwing away the mental image. Every time I closed my eyes, there he was. "Let's not talk about him. There's something else I'd like to talk to you about. Actually, I'd like a favor from you. "

"Ooooh," she said, sitting up. "What is it? You want me to distract Milo while you secretly run to Caspian's room? I'll do it. Milo is cute, too." She threw me a wink.

"Keep your hands off Milo," I grumbled. "And no, that's definitely not it. I want to..."

Nyre jumped up off the bed as someone knocked on the door.

"Who is it?"

I'd not bolted the door. Whoever it was could walk in at any moment if they wanted. I waved my hand at Nyre to motion to her to hide. Dahlia wasn't known for waiting for an answer, and Caspian had been in my room uninvited a little too often to trust him to wait outside until I opened the door.

"It's me"

So it was Caspian. Beside me, Nyre jumped up and down in a little dance and clapped her hands together. I threw her a warning and pointed to the bathroom. She smirked as she left the room. I waited until she'd closed the bathroom door before opening the bedroom door to Caspian.

"What is it?" I asked, opening the door a crack.

"Can I come in?" He turned to look at the brute my father had hired to stand at the end of the corridor. Jack and Milo were obviously not working today.

"Nope."

"We can do this out in the corridor if you prefer. I'm sure your father would love to hear our conversation about the kiss."

"Come in," I hissed, pulling him in and shutting the door behind him.

"There was no kiss," I said, not bothering to hide my irritation. "I want to forget it ever happened."

He moved close to me, his eyes boring into mine. "Oh, but it did happen. It happened, and you enjoyed it." The way he looked at me stirred something within me, and his magical energy radiated from him. An image blazed in my mind of his lips against mine as we illicitly hid behind my father's throne. The tingling from his energy centered on my lips causing me to bite down.

"I did not," I said, taking a step back. Of course, he followed.

His breath warmed my neck as he spoke. "You asked me once if I could read minds, and I told you I couldn't. That was true, but I can read bodies. I felt you pushing into me as we kissed. I sensed your heart beating faster, your blood pumping for me."

"You're wrong," I said, gulping as his energy increased.

He inched closer, his face almost touching mine. He inhaled slowly, making my entire body tingle as his breath tickled my neck below my ear.

"You're heart is beating faster now. I know when a woman is turned on. Do you think I've not done this before? Do you think your body isn't giving me clues? Your body temperature is rising, your heart pounding, your breathing is deeper. You can tell me you don't want me with your mouth, but your body tells me otherwise."

"My body is going to give you a swift kick between your legs if you continue," I growled, but by gods, he was right. My own body was betraying me, and I couldn't back up any farther. My calves were already touching the bed. Any farther backward, and I'd be flat on my back, a position I'd been in one too many times as far as Caspian was concerned and one I had a feeling he'd be happy for me to be in again.

"Whatever you say, princess, but in another week when I win that competition of yours, you'll be mine to kiss whenever I want...whenever you want."

He kissed my neck, sending my body into rhapsodies, before turning on his heel and stalking out, shutting the door behind him. It took a few seconds before I could get my body to move to bolt the door.

"Swit swoo," Nyre came out of the bathroom, a huge grin on her face. "Are you sure you don't want me to be a diversion for Milo while you and Caspian get it on?"

I threw a pillow at her as I tried to bring my breathing down to normal levels.

"I can't stand the guy," I said to her. "So he makes me hot, but he'd cut my throat in a heartbeat if there was something in it for him. Milo isn't like that. Milo would go to the ends of the earth for me."

"But Caspian makes you hot..."

Damn the dragon and her logic!

20TH JANUARY

Today was the day I was going to leave for Urbis. I'd wanted to do it yesterday, but Nyre had flown off before I'd even gotten a chance to speak to her about it. My plan was to go down to breakfast as normal and make sure everyone saw me. And that included Milo. I wanted to tell him where I was going, but I knew he'd want to come along. He would insist on it, and Nyre was too small to fly the two of us for long distances. If she was bigger and we could travel on her back, then maybe, but as it was, I was probably pushing it, asking her to take just me. I'd leave him a note and tell him how sorry I was. He'd understand...hopefully. With any luck, I'd find a way to stop my mother's curse, and best case scenario, my parents would be so overjoyed, they'd forget this whole wedding thing. They were only insisting on it because of some weird omen of dark times. I'd had enough people telling me that there had been some huge magical shift for me to believe it had happened, and I couldn't deny all the horrible stuff that had been going on in the past few weeks. But my mother's curse was part of that. If I could cure her, then maybe I could cure all of it. And I had a feeling that if I could find my birth mother and uncover the circumstances of my birth, then everything would unravel, and we could get back to how things used to be. I could date Milo and take my time getting to know him rather than being rushed into marriage. We could travel together and see the kingdoms rather than live with the threat of being torn apart, which is what was happening here. My only option was to go, and this was the day I was going to do it.

Milo wasn't stationed outside my room when I left, which was probably for the best. If I saw him, I'd probably break down and cry right in front of him, and he'd know something was going on. I didn't want to say goodbye to him. It felt too final. With luck, I could do what I set out to do within a couple of weeks tops. There would be no need for goodbyes, I'd be back before he knew it. I'd already written the letter telling him where I was going and who with. There would be no need to tell him why. He already knew why.

My father was at breakfast, which was unusual. In fact, the table was filled with people. All three of my brothers were there, as were Caspian and Charlotte. It seemed they were all waiting for me. For a second, I wondered if this was an intervention, but as I sat in my chair, they all began to tuck into their food.

I watched Caspian eating. Why did he have to be so damned gorgeous? Just being near him made my heart flutter, my fists clench, and my stomach turn. The thought of the kiss we shared yesterday flittered through my mind. It had been so good, phenomenal, in fact! He'd taken me to new heights and dropped me to new lows. How was it possible that one person could elicit so many reactions? He was fraying my nerves. He caught me looking and threw a wink my way, sending my stomach into another loop-the-loop. Color crept into my cheeks, so I turned to my father instead. I really did not need to be thinking of kissing Caspian.

"Why are you eating with us, Father?" I asked, more to steer my mind away from Caspian than anything else.

"Can't a father eat with his family?" he said, piling his plate with food. It was the first thing I'd seen him eat in weeks.

"Of course," I said, spooning some porridge into my own bowl. "It's just unusual, that's all."

"I know I've been absent of late," he said, adding some raspberries to his plate. "That's why I wanted to come to breakfast with you all. I've been so preoccupied that I've been putting my family last when I should have been putting you first. Isn't that right, Remy?"

He shuffled Remy's hair, who gave him a thumbs up while dripping his own porridge onto the table.

"Plus," he added, "if I hadn't come to breakfast, I wouldn't have met the lovely Charlotte here."

I refrained from reminding him that he'd already met Charlotte. He'd been too busy balling me out to notice. I wondered if anyone had told him why she was here. I didn't want him to know. The thought that my mother was somehow lost in some weird dream world was horrific, and he was dealing with enough. Hopefully he thought she was just visiting.

"You seem happy today," I mentioned hesitantly.

"I've got the best doctors in the kingdom arriving today, plus one from The Vale, one from Aboria, and I've even managed to snag a mage from Enchantia who is renowned for his work on curses. I'm positive your mother will be up and with us by dinnertime tonight."

I glanced across at Charlotte, who shook her head almost imperceptively. She didn't believe a mage or any amount of doctors could cure my mother. She didn't say anything, though, she just continued to eat.

"It wouldn't do to get your hopes up this early, Alec," Caspian said.

My father glared at him, and he recoiled. "I mean, I'm sure you're right, and these physicians will be able to help, but if they can't, it doesn't mean there isn't another way to save her."

He looked at me as he spoke.

"Exactly," I agreed.

"Nonsense," my father argued."Why would we need another way when I have the best? The best of the best."

So Charlotte and Caspian hadn't told my father her theory, which was just as well. It only strengthened my resolve to get to Urbis as soon as possible. If he was right, I wouldn't need to go, but I knew in my heart he wasn't. In a few hours, he would be heartbroken all over again. I couldn't bear it.

"We'll get her back Father," I said. "No matter what happens, we'll get her back."

After breakfast, I ran upstairs to pack. The sooner I left, the better. Once I was packed, I'd call Nyre down from the mountain and ask her to come. I pulled open drawers and took out clothes for the journey. It was cold here, so I needed lots of layers. I'd pulled out and refolded half my suitable clothes when there was a knock on the door.

"Hi, it's me, Charlotte."

After throwing all my nicely folded clothes in a heap at the bottom of my wardrobe, I opened the door.

"Hi, Charlotte. What can I do for you?"

She shuffled her feet nervously. "You told me the other day I needed the Dahlia treatment. I was wondering if you'd mind if she helped me today?"

I thought of all my clothes I'd have to refold and of all the doctors coming to see my father later. "I'm sorry, I don't have time right now. Maybe later?"

I felt bad, knowing there would be no later. She would find out I had left, and then she'd go home to Urbis... Urbis! She lived in Urbis. If anyone could help me there, it was her. I knew no one else there. If anyone would be able to help me in the weird walled city, it was her.

"Ok," I said, changing my mind. "Come with me. We need to find Dahlia."

A couple of hours playing dress up with Charlotte would give me the perfect excuse to learn about Urbis from her. I'd been to the city a few times, but always as a royal visitor. I needed to know the real city if I had any hope of finding my birth mother...or of finding Morpheus.

Dahlia had stationed herself in one of the castle admin offices. Well, it used to be an admin office. She'd had the desks and filing cabinets taken out and surrounded herself in wedding stuff. A small table overflowed with bridal magazines, and fabric samples covered the floor along with reams of ribbons, flowers, and goodness only knew what else.

"It looks like a wedding shop exploded in here," I commented, stepping over a pile of wedding favors.

"Half the kingdom is invited to the wedding," Dahlia said, pulling some magazines away from me as I stepped over to her. "Not to mention the royals from other kingdoms. It needs to be perfect. Draconis hasn't had a royal wedding for over eighteen years."

I rolled my eyes. "Why are so many people invited?"

She stared at me as though I'd just offered to cut her dog into pieces and serve it up instead of wedding cake.

"This is so pretty," Charlotte said, picking up one of the bridal magazines and holding up a picture of some model in a white dress.

"That was in my top ten, too," Dahlia beamed. "The seamstress has already started on the dress, but I guess we could ask her to change it a little. I like the long train. What do you think, Azia?"

I shrugged my shoulders. Who cared?

"Actually, I was wondering if you'd have time to help Charlotte here. She'd like a new outfit and her makeup redone.."

"I'm sorry," replied Dahlia, extending her arms out, indicating the mess around her. "I'm up to my eyeballs in wedding planning, and seeing as the bride refuses to help, I'm doing most of it myself."

She looked at me pointedly as I gave her my best ha-ha face.

"Charlotte is going to be my bridesmaid," I lied. "I'd like to do a trial run with her makeup."

"Oooh," Dahlia stood up quickly, sending a stack of invites toppling over. "In that case, come with me." She took Charlotte's hand and pulled her out of the room. I followed, expecting to end up in my room, but instead, she took her to my mother's dressing room.

The huge room was where my mother often got ready for parties and events. She wore no make-up most of the time owing to her natural beauty, but she enjoyed going all out when she got the chance.

Dahlia pulled out a chair in front of a mirror for Charlotte to sit in and pulled out her extensive makeup palette.

"It will make a refreshing change doing makeup on someone who actually wants it," she said, casting a meaningful glance my way. I rolled my eyes again.

"Can you get her a dress out?" Dahlia said, ignoring my eye-rolling. "Not one of yours. You have nothing bridesmaidy. Your mother has a collection of dresses she's never worn in that closet there." She was right. My mother was constantly being given expensive clothing as gifts, most of which she never wore. The things she liked, she kept in a closet in her room. Everything else went in here. She made it very clear to the castle staff that they could borrow any of the dresses they liked.

Pulling open the closet, I rifled through the dresses. They were all made with my mother in mind, but Charlotte was tall enough and slim enough to pull them off.

"What color?" I asked, figuring I'd try and get it right the first time rather than waste my day rifling through dresses.

"Red," both Dahlia and Charlotte said at the same time, then dissolved into giggles.

Charlotte was better at princessing than I was. I pulled a red dress from the closet and wondered what my mother would make of all this. She would love a daughter whom she could sit with and brush her hair whilst discussing new fashion trends.

"This one ok?" I asked, holding it up to the mirror.

"Beautiful," Charlotte said breathily.

I sat on a chair and waited as Charlotte was

transformed from the mousy thing she was into a goddess. Dahlia really did know what she was doing. Charlotte sat patiently as Dahlia worked on her, but the excitement in her eyes as she was replaced by a woman of stunning beauty was clear to see.

I'd never had warm fuzzies from having my makeup done, but then again, to me, it was an obligation, a ritual I had to go through as the royal princess. To Charlotte who had nothing, this would be a treat. I almost envied her, her excitement in something I found dreary.

Once the makeup was done, Dalia began to work on Charlotte's hair. Pulling it from the ponytail it was in, Dahlia brushed it straight before beginning the process of braiding it into an elaborate up-do.

"How about leaving it down?" I asked, catching a glimpse at my watch. I'd wanted to set off for Urbis early, but the day was quickly getting away from me.

"You need something special for your wedding," Dahlia said, pulling some diamond hair clips from her pocket.

Right, Charlotte was my bridesmaid.

An hour later, and Charlotte was ready to put the dress on. With Dahlia's and my help, she shimmied into the dress.

"Woah," I mouthed as I took in the vision of beauty in front of me. How had Caspian not noticed her before?

"You just need shoes and jewelry," Dahlia said. "Let me see what I can find."

"I have a necklace," I said. "You get the shoes, and I'll be back in a minute."

I raced out of the room and through the castle. The necklace my mother had left with the dwarves was still hidden in its box under my bed. I'd not brought it out since bringing it home the previous week.

The necklace was mine, a bit of my own history, but it was near useless to me sitting under my bed, and no matter how pretty it was, I couldn't think of a single reason I'd need to wear it in the near future. Royal parties were a little thin on the ground these days, with my wedding being the only thing penciled in on the royal calendar. I could hardly wear a ruby-red necklace with a white dress. Not that I planned to be around long enough to attend my wedding anyway.

When I got back to the dressing room, Charlotte and Dahlia were in the middle of the extremely important task of matching shoes with the dress. Her feet were a size smaller than my mother's, so Dahlia was reduced to scrunching up paper to fill the ends.

"We'll have to order something for the actual wedding," she said as she slipped a shoe on Charlotte's foot. For a second, it reminded me of the story of the queen of Arcadia, Cinderella, who came to rule because of a shoe. I was willing to bet Cinderella didn't stuff her glass slipper with paper.

"Here," I said, passing the jewelry box to Charlotte.

She almost did a jig up and down on the spot in excitement. It was wonderful to watch. Her eyes opened wide with wonder as she opened the box. Inside the ruby necklace shone brightly, almost illuminating her face, but instead of the red they were before, now the rubies had changed into sparkling diamonds.

"Holy shit!" she breathed.

"Dragon fire!" I murmured at the change in the necklace.

"Beautiful," Dahlia mouthed.

We all spoke at the same time, but it was Charlotte's expression that interested me the most. The awe in her face had turned into something else, something bordering on shock.

"What is it?" I asked, pulling the box from her hands and gazing at the diamonds twinkling back at me. They had certainly not been diamonds before.

"How do you have the necklace of the gods?"

"What?" Dahlia looked at her with a perplexed expression, matching the turmoil inside me.

"I've seen this necklace before," Charlotte said, looking up at me, "but never on a human."

I snapped the box closed quickly. Suddenly it had become something I didn't want anyone to see. Something that elicited questions.

"Where did you get that from?" Dahlia asked, giving me a suspicious glare.

"I found it in the vault," I lied, hoping she wouldn't go down to check. "I guess it was given to my mother as a gift."

She nodded, seemingly satisfied with my answer, but I could see Charlotte wasn't.

"What do you mean, not human?" I whispered to her.

"These necklaces were given to people of high importance from the gods. Before now, I've only seen high fae wearing them. They hold powerful magic. I learned about them in my research."

I thanked her quickly, my mind whirring, and rushed the necklace back to my room.

Caspian had told me I wasn't a faerie like him. Of course, I wasn't. I didn't have the pointed ears of the fae, and yet, this was another hint that I wasn't human. If the gods gifted these necklaces to the fae, who else did they give them to? It was yet another mystery I needed to find out. I hid the necklace under the bed as someone knocked on my door. I opened it to find

Charlotte.

"I'm sorry if I upset you back there. You ran off awfully quickly."

"You didn't," I lied. She didn't need to know that my mom had left this for me. I knew for sure, my mother wasn't a faerie, nor was she any other kind of magical creature. No the necklace might have been left for me by my adopted mom, but it had come from my birth mom. Maybe that's why my mother had hidden it away with the dwarves.

"Who else but fae owned these necklaces?" I asked her.

She shrugged, belying the interest in her eyes. "I don't know, but you can bet they would be powerfully magic. I think there's one in Enchantia."

Well, that made sense. Enchantia was the most magical of all the kingdoms.

"A mage owns one?"

"I believe so. My research didn't stretch to the mages of Enchantia. They aren't given out willy-nilly, not even to royals. I'm surprised that someone gave theirs to your mother, even if she is a queen."

A myriad of thoughts ran through my mind as I considered the necklace and how it had come to be in the dwarves' mine. Nothing made sense anymore, and something that should have sparked such joy only made me more nervous.

"Not half as surprised as I am," I said under my breath, linking my arm with hers. "Come on, let's go find Caspian. You're going to knock him out in that dress."

After scouring the castle, we finally found him in the dining room, waiting for dinner.

"Ah, there you are," he said as we walked in. "I've

been meaning to come and find you. The Sentinel posted a picture of me, and I'm not sure you are going to like it."

Beside me, I felt Charlotte tense up. She looked absolutely stunning, and Caspian hadn't even looked her way.

"I don't care about what The Sentinel prints," I said, "Don't you think Charlotte is looking beautiful today?"

He grimaced, then cast his eyes at Charlotte.

"That's a nice dress," he commented, before swiveling his eyes back to me. "Now, what do you want to do about The Sentinel?"

Charlotte ran from the room, and I could hardly blame her.

"You are a total asshole, you know that, right? This is the second time in as many days you've done this," I snapped.

As I ran out of the room after Charlotte, I heard him shouting out behind me. "What did I do?"

I found Charlotte in her room, sobbing her heart out.

"The guy is an asshat, you know that, right?" I said, sitting beside her on the bed.

She smiled through a snot-streaked face. I stood up and found her a tissue, which she accepted gratefully.

"I just thought if I was beautiful, he'd want me."

"If you dated him, you'd have to fight for the mirror. The only person he thinks is beautiful is himself."

"He thinks you're beautiful."

"Purlease. He wants me because of who I am. He wouldn't give me a second glance if I wasn't a princess. Besides, he's only marrying me as a favor to my father. I don't even think the guy likes me very much. He keeps trying to kill me."

"I doubt that," she said. "That's his way of showing

love."

"His way of showing love is to kill his partner? What is he? A praying mantis?"

She laughed again. I left her to get out of her dress and take her make-up off and headed back to my room.

Looking down at my watch, I realized that the day had flown by, and my plans of heading to Urbis would have to be put off again. I didn't want to set off in the dark, and the evenings drew in awfully early in the winter. Closing the bedroom door behind me, I retrieved my messed up clothes from the wardrobe and began the laborious task of refolding them all. Less than a minute later, a knock at the door interrupted me.

Thinking it was Charlotte, I opened the door, but it wasn't Charlotte. Milo stood there, his face like thunder.

He threw today's newspaper down in front of me and walked away. When I looked down, I saw a picture of me on the cover. A picture of me and Caspian. We were kissing.

21ST JANUARY

Milo stood just outside my door, guarding it. It was his job, after all, but I knew he'd rather be anywhere but where he was. I'd hurt him badly, and no amount of talking to him had changed things. I'd brought him into my room, but there was no explaining away the photo of Caspian and I kissing. How the photographer had managed to capture the shot without either of us seeing, I'd never know, but he had, and now, the whole kingdom could see what a wretch I was.

I was lost to him now. It damn near broke my heart, but considering what I was about to do, it was probably for the best. Happily ever after for us was never in our future anyway. This heartbreak was always going to happen to both of us, it had just come sooner than expected.

Opening my window, I tried to drive thoughts of Milo from my mind. It was too painful to bear. Holding my hands out, I concentrated my magic. A small beam of light shot straight upward. My fear was that the guards in the courtyard would see me and come rushing up, but none of them even turned their heads my way, and I held the light.

I thought that maybe the dragons hadn't heard my call, but five minutes later, one of them landed on my window sill. The one I'd called for. Nyre ruffled her wings then hopped through the door. She'd transformed into her part-human self before the window was even shut.

"You ok?"

I nodded, running over to her, my forefinger extended over my lips.

"We have to whisper."

"Oh, wow. So exciting." her eyes widened. "What's happening? I love secrets."

It's not a secret exactly, I whispered, throwing a t-shirt at her to cover her bare chest. Her breasts were covered by her locks of long purple hair, but if anyone were to come in, they would wonder why she was in my room completely naked. The bottom half of her was almost more dragon than human with her iridescent purple scales, so it didn't really matter about covering her up there. Not that she seemed even the slightest bit bothered about her nakedness.

"You do realize that if I put this on, I'll only rip it to shreds when I transform back, right?"

I rolled my eyes and realized she was right. It must be awfully inconvenient being a shifter. Not that I'd seen any of them clothed when I was on the top of the mountain. Who needs clothes when you have beautiful scales and long hair to cover your wobbly bits, right?

She pulled the shirt over her head, not bothering to free her long hair from the neckline as I would have done. She looked remarkably cute in the thing. Much cuter than I ever had.

She picked up a book I'd left half-read on my bedside cabinet weeks before and flicked through the pages, absorbed in it as I often was with books. That particular book had sat there unloved and unlooked at for weeks, worry having taken over my nightly ritual of reading. I remembered it was a good book, but if anyone asked me now, I wouldn't be able to even begin to recall what it was about.

She appeared to be reading the words, but I wondered if she even knew how to read. Pulling the book away from her seemed cruel, but I had things to do. Things that couldn't wait. Carefully, I took the book from her hands.

"You can have this if you like."

Her eyes went wider still, elation plain on her face. She pulled the book back and hugged it to her chest.

"Thank you," she mouthed, her lips crinkling up at the side.

"I was wondering if you'd help me."

"In exchange for this beautiful paper thing?" she asked, holding the book up.

"No. The paper thing, the book. It's yours either way."

She nodded thoughtfully. "But you want help?"

"Yes. I need to get to Urbis. There are many ways to travel there, but I don't want anyone to stop me. Not even the king knows I want to venture there."

"You want me to take you on an adventure?"

I nodded. "I do. I could catch the train or Urbis

Express, but both of those are public transport, and people would recognize me. I could take a horse, but it would take days to get there. I need to get there soon."

"Sounds good to me. Ooh. I've never been to a big city before. Do you know how to get there?"

Now that she'd mentioned it, I had no idea how to get to Urbis. I knew it was southwest of Draconis, but that was about it.

"Not exactly, but we could follow the train lines. The main line goes there. I know because I've traveled there in the royal carriage before."

"Can't you just travel in the royal carriage again?"

"Not without my father finding out."

She bounced on the bed, clapping her hands. "Well, goody for me! I get to come on the adventure. What is it we are going for?"

"I want to find my mother."

"I thought your mother was sick?" she asked, cocking her head to one side

"Not my mother, my birth mother. I think I was born in Urbis, and I need to go there and try and find out for sure."

"And you want to stay how long?"

I'd been thinking about my trip for a few days. Ever since I'd found out from Milo that I was born in Urbis, going there had occupied my every thought. Not only would going there give me a chance to find out about who I was and where I came from, it also meant I might just be able to solve another problem I had. I could hide out in Urbis while the competition was going on and miss my wedding. Yeah, my father was going to go ballistic. My leaving would do him no favors, but if I could find out what had happened to my mother, and figure out a way to save her, he would soon forgive me.

He wouldn't care a jot about an abandoned wedding if my mother woke up. The competition was in a week's time and my wedding a few days after that. I figured it would take about four or five days to get to Urbis, but it was only a wild guess. I'd always slept on the train and never paid any attention to how long each journey took.

"Ten days. Four days there, Four back and maybe one or two in Urbis itself. I have a little money. Enough to stay in a hotel or something."

"You call this a little money?" she asked, taking in the grandeur of the room. It embarrassed me the way everyone thought I was rich because of the stuff I had. Okay, yes, I had a lot of fine things that cost a lot of money, but it was all useless if I didn't have the freedom to go with it. I had to stash money away to get the small amount needed to spend ten days in Urbis. I had to smash a childhood piggy bank, which I'd had since before I could remember, and even then, it was barely enough for a couple of days in a hotel. I couldn't sell any of my things, nor could I use them to buy other things like food. So I'd spent the last few days searching the castle for cash. For a place as filled to the brim with riches as it was, it was surprisingly difficult to find any actual cash. Going back down to the vault was not an option. I'd already made Hestor suspicious once this week, and I could hardly do it again. So I had to be more creative, searching down the backs of sofas and into the pockets of my parents' coats hanging in the closet. Okay, yes, it was stealing, but I found such small amounts in each place I looked, my father wouldn't notice anything missing. It took a full three days to gather the amount I had, and I wasn't sure it would be enough, but I was counting on Nyre being able to forage for a lot of her own food, and while we were out in the countryside, maybe some food for me too.

"I don't know much about Urbis," Nyre said. "But I think it will take a lot longer than four days. I will have to rest. I'm not a train or an airship. I'm a dragon. I will need to take frequent rests, and I will need to sleep. Am I right in thinking you slept on the train when you went before? Because I can't carry you while you sleep. When you sleep, I'll be sleeping too."

She was right, of course. I'd assumed she would be this relentless machine, but she was a living creature.

"I guess we will take longer then...maybe two weeks?"

"And you'll not want to fly over any towns or cities. People will see us, and word will get back."

I slumped down on my bed. In my active imagination, this had all been so easy. Find money, call Nyre, and just go. Now, she was filling my head with problems I didn't even know I'd have, and what was worse, she was right about every single one of them.

I'd only packed a small bag, thinking I'd not be gone too long, but it looked like I'd have to rethink the whole thing.

"Would you mind waiting until I repacked. It won't take a minute."

"I can wait for you, but you will need to wait for me too. I cannot just leave the colony. My father would come looking for me."

Vasuki! I'd forgotten about him too. My mind was just such a mess of things that my plan was a total disaster.

"Maybe I shouldn't do this..." I said, feeling dejected. Maybe I should accept my fate and marry whoever won the competition. It would keep my father happy if nothing else.

"Don't be silly. We can do this. I'll come back tonight."

I nodded. There was something about Nyre that made me feel better about the whole thing. She quickly turned back into a dragon, ripping the t-shirt to shreds as she had predicted and flew out of the window.

The door bursting open behind me had me turning my head.

"Who were you talking to?"

Caspian strolled into the room as though he owned the place. Something he was particularly skilled at.

"How dare you come into my room." I cast my eyes down to the bed, knowing I'd hidden my sword underneath it.

He followed my line of sight.

"Don't worry. You will not need your sword. I only came in because I thought you were in trouble. Who was it, by the way? Do you have someone hiding in the bathroom? It didn't sound like a man, but one can never be too sure."

"I wasn't talking to anyone," I snapped back as he wandered over to the bathroom door and peered into the bathroom.

"Hmmm. What a mess you keep your room in," he said, picking up a piece of the remnants of t-shirt that Nyre left behind. "When we are married, I'll expect you to keep your home much better than this."

I strode over to him, pushing against his chest. "If you don't like my house, feel free to leave…Any time."

I slammed the door in his face, anger surging through me.

I spent the afternoon outside in the woods where I'd been practicing with Milo. He wasn't outside my door when I left, and I didn't ask Jack where he was. I didn't want to know. If Jack told me he'd gone home, I knew

I'd run to his house and drag the pain out longer than necessary for both of us.

Without Milo, fighting seemed pointless, with only the snow to keep me company, but anger spurred me on, forcing me to carry on the practice. I was almost as good as Milo now. I'd proved that. I was a match for him. I fought invisible foes all afternoon until hunger forced me to leave the beauty of our fighting place and move indoors.

After a quick change of clothes in my bedroom, I headed down to dinner. I had plenty of time before Nyre was to come pick me up, so I decided to eat my fill. I didn't know when I'd be eating again.

For the first time in what felt forever, my whole family was at the dinner table. The only person missing was my mother. Her empty seat was all the more obvious now that the others were filled.

"Where have you been all day?" My father asked as I sat down in my place. Immediately, a servant brought over a plate of meat and vegetables.

"I was outside getting some fresh air, Father."

"In this weather?" he indicated the window where the snow fell freely. I would need to take some warm clothing with me if I were to survive.

"I like the snow," I answered, digging into the food. My belly was happy with the warmth.

"At least, we won't have to worry about the dragons in this weather," Hollis said. "They'd be mad to attack with the snow the way it is."

I paused and looked up at Hollis, who continued eating.

"Attack?"

My father waved his hand dismissively. "Not to worry, Azia. The dragons are quiet once again. We've not had an attack in over a week. The wall is still being erected to keep folk out. Maybe that's all they wanted."

"But we still need to be vigilant, Father," Hollis added." Just because they haven't attacked for a while, doesn't mean they won't attack."

"They won't!" I said, a little too urgently. Both my younger brothers' eyes swiveled my way.

"And how do you know?"

I was saved having to answer by my father chipping in.

"She doesn't. I don't want to hear any more about the dragons. I've done all I can with them. I've got enough on my plate at the moment without all this nonsense. Your mother isn't getting any better. The doctors I've had brought in have been looking at her all day, prodding and poking her, and none of them can find a damned thing wrong with her. All of my troops are back, and not a single spindle has been found. And now, I've got this bloody competition to worry about. The reporters are hounding me every second of the day, and quite frankly, I'm sick of it all!"

He stood up, throwing his napkin down on the table and stormed out, his face as black as thunder.

"It really would have been easier if you'd just married Caspian, "Hollis said.

"Are you blaming me for all this?"

"You did start this ridiculous competition," Ash added. "It's taking up so much of Father's time that he can't concentrate on the important stuff."

"And my life isn't important?" I shot back. "Would either of you married someone you hated out of duty?"

Both of my brothers nodded their heads. "I would do anything for my kingdom," Hollis said proudly.

Standing up, I glared at him. "Well, look who's

suddenly all patriotic. Three weeks ago, you couldn't have cared less, but now that Father has made the pair of you soldiers, you think you are better than the rest of us." I slammed my fist on the table, upsetting my uneaten meal. I was starving, but anger trumped that. I followed suit with my father and left the dining room, slamming the door as I went.

Anger raged within me, and I wanted nothing more than to go back to my room, shutting everyone out, but having not eaten all day, I had the perfect excuse to head to the kitchens. I would need food for the journey. While Nyre would be able to kill small animals and eat them raw, that wasn't an option for me, and I wasn't confident enough of my fire-making skills.

The kitchen was winding down, with the chefs leaving and the clean-up staff getting to work on their parts. Nobody paid me any mind as I ran into the larder and filled a cloth bag with food. Nyre was tiny, so I couldn't take much, nor could I take anything heavy. Having Vasuki or Emba to carry me on their backs would have been the better option, but I knew better than to ask them.

Back in my room, I emptied the bag of food onto the bed and sorted it into my backpack. Putting in the clothes I would need, I also pulled out my boots and a thick coat that would keep me warm on the nights I'd have to sleep outside. Then, all I had to do was wait. Nyre knew better than to come to me while it was still light, so I whiled away the hours staring out of the window, waiting for the sun to fall in the sky. At least, the snow was abating. It was beautiful to watch the large flakes falling, but the cold would be a killer if I wasn't prepared. My hope was that we'd find shelter on the nights we were venturing to and from Urbis. Sheds and barns would keep the snow from us, and we'd be able to snuggle down in the hay. At least, that was my plan. This would all have been easier in the summer months where we could have slept under the stars or even in a normal Draconian winter, which were usually very mild. The snow, however beautiful, reminded me that this was not normal weather and was brought about by the darkness caused by the witch. My hope was that if I found out where I came from, I could find out what had happened to my mother and wake her up. My father had not found her spindle, and I know he would have knocked on every single door in Draconis to search. Which meant that Derillen was no longer in the kingdom.

Before Nyre came, I went to see my mother. My father sat next to her. He barely looked up as I entered the room.

"I'm sorry about my outburst, Azia," he said, his voice cracking. "I thought that if I brought the best doctors here, they'd find out what was wrong with her. Not even the mage from Enchantia knew."

I walked over to him and cradled his head as he sobbed.

"I'll make this better, Father."

He nodded in my arms, but I could tell he didn't believe me. Why would he? If the best doctors in the land couldn't cure mother, why would he think I could.

"I think maybe you should go and talk to Caspian and Charlotte," I said. I couldn't tell him where I was going, he'd only stop me, but once he found out I'd gone, I wanted him to know the truth. I'd written him a letter to explain, which was back in my room, but talking to Charlotte about Morpheus would make it more real to him like it had to me. Charlotte really believed that

Morpheus was involved, and I had no reason not to believe her. Hopefully, my father would too. "They think they might know how to get her back."

"How?" He asked, his eyes bloodshot from crying.

"Go see them," I urged. I pulled back from him and bent over to kiss my mother's cheek. I'd bring her back or die trying.

I left the room and headed back to mine, only to find Nyre waiting for me on the bed. She hadn't shifted out of her dragon form, so I picked up my backpack, threw my coat on, and climbed up onto the little window sill.

Nyre's talons caught in the back of my coat, and with a tug, we were both flying. It took a moment to get used to the sensation and to get over my crippling fear of being dropped. Once again, I wondered if it would have been better to go to the dragons and ask for help from a bigger one. One I could sit on the back of, but I liked Nyre, and I trusted her. I would just have to trust her with not dropping me because this was going to be a long journey. We flew over the courtyard, and she circled around the side of the castle to head in a southeasterly direction. We were almost over the outer wall of the castle when something zipped past my ear. At first, I thought the snow had started again, but this came too quickly for snow, and it came from below us, not above. Nyre rocked to the side as another thing flew past. This time I saw what it was. It was an arrow. My father's men were shooting at us. Jacob stood at the front of them and sent another arrow our way.

"Go faster!" I screamed at Nyre, but it was too late. She was already plummeting to the ground, and I was falling along with her. This was it. We were both going to die. As the ground rushed up towards me with dizzying speed, I knew then that I wouldn't be able save my mother on this trip. I'd had one chance, and now thanks to Jacob, I never would. My mother would die, and as I slammed to the ground and everything went black, I knew I would beat her in death.

GODDESS OF FLAMES

22ND JANUARY

"What were you thinking?" My father asked as he paced back and forth at the bottom of my bed, his face knotted with worry and stress. Stress that once again, I'd caused, although I had good reason.

I'd woken up with a headache and having my father shouting at me for a good ten minutes straight before I'd even thought about coffee, was not doing much to help it. Pain throbbed in my temples and pounded my brain like a carriage rolling over a rocky road.

I blinked a few times waiting for my father to take a pause in his diatribe so I could explain myself. "I told you. Charlotte and Caspian think Mother is stuck in a dream world and can't get out. The only way to release her is to find Derillen or Morpheus. As I don't know where Derillen is, I was on my way to Urbis to track down Morpheus."

My father massaged his temples and stopped his pacing. "Yes, I heard what you said, but you were being carried by a dragon, Azia. A dragon! Haven't you seen the damage they've caused? No wonder Jacob shot you down. He thought you were being abducted. Now I know you have something weird going on with them, but I can't expect everyone to know that. Heck, I don't want anyone to know that. I've told you before to stay away from them. Whatever you think, they are wild creatures. I don't care that they are shifters. They are still animals."

"What about Nyre?" I asked. "Where is she?"

Six beds filled the castle hospital wing altogether. When occupied, green curtains separated them, but now, all the curtains were pulled back, showing me that I was the only patient in the room. Nyre wasn't in any of the beds.

"And what is this nonsense about Morpheus?" my father continued, ignoring my question. "I didn't bring you up to be religious. The gods are made up for people who don't know any better. As a princess, you shouldn't align yourself with any religion. We have to show impartiality in such matters. If we go to a place of worship for one religion, we'd have to go to all of them, and do you know how many gods there are? Hundreds, if not thousands. It seems that everyone has their own personal god these days."

I pulled myself up in the bed as he ranted. "Maybe we are the ones that don't know any better, Father... Where's Nyre?"

"And I don't know how many times I have to tell you that Derillen is dead. I sent my men out to look for spindles because I thought there may be a copycat, but that doesn't mean I believe she is still alive. I may not have seen her body all those years ago, but there is no other reason that the brambles had begun to lose their magic when I broke through to free your mother. If she was still alive, we'd know about it."

I gripped the edge of one of my pillows in frustration. My friend was hurt, and I didn't know where she was. "Father," I emphasized, raising my voice. "Where is Nyre?" She had fallen from the sky when I did. The fall had knocked me out when I hit the ground, but I remembered the flapping of her wings as she valiantly tried to keep us up in the air.

"Who is Nyre?" My father asked with agitation. He stopped pacing and looked at me with a quizzical expression. "The dragon? It flew off when you hit the ground."

She flew off. I sighed with relief. If she could fly away, it meant she wasn't too injured. My fear subsided a little, and the pain that had begun to build up in my chest eased off.

"Was she hurt?" I asked.

"Does it really matter?" My father snapped. "She was able to fly back up the mountain if that answers your question. Jacob tried to get her, but she flew away too quickly."

"Yes, it matters," I shouted at him, a little louder than my aching brain could handle. "It matters because she is my friend, and she was helping me out. She was helping you out too. You've said many times you'd do anything to help mother, and that's exactly what we were doing. No one else can help her. How many doctors have you paraded through here, and not one of them has been able to do so much as to make mother blink?

At least, Nyre was willing to help, and she's never even met Mother!"

My father's tone softened a little, but I could still hear the hard edge to it. "I don't want to argue with you, Azia. You have a busy week coming up what with the competition. I need you back to health before that starts. Dr. Augusto looked you over last night, and he said that you have no broken bones. A few bruises, but he said you can get up on your feet whenever you like..." Dr. Augusto and a nurse were the two members of staff that worked in the small hospital wing in the castle. Dr Augusto was one of the first people to check on my mother when she first fell asleep, though he didn't know what was wrong with her any more than any of the so-called experts had.

I made to get out of bed, but my father stopped me.

"...Once you've rested. I want you to stay here this morning, and then after lunch if you feel better, you may get up. I have business to attend to."

He turned on his heels.

"What's happening with the dragons?" I shouted as he walked away, but he left the hospital wing, closing the door behind him and leaving the question unanswered.

I needed to go up the mountain to warn the dragons. I'd thought this was all over, but I didn't trust my father not to go back on his word. Not with the mood he was in. I stood up, the floor cold beneath my bare feet, but a wave of nausea hit me, and my head began to spin.

"What are you doing, silly?"

The nurse, a young woman named Amelia, ran over and helped me back into bed. "I've got strict instructions from your father not to let you leave until you are well enough. You've bruised your right arm and leg, and you've probably got a concussion too. Why not lie back, and I'll bring you some breakfast. What do you fancy?"

"Coffee," I mumbled, needing to clear the wool from my brain.

She nodded, giving me a brief smile and headed to the small room where she made coffee.

An image of Milo hit me with such force, I had to lie back down. I needed him. However much I hated to admit I needed anyone, I needed him right now. I ached for him to pull me into his arms and kiss the pain away.

"Amelia," I shouted, sending an echo through my mind. She popped her head around the door.

"Everything okay?"

I nodded carefully. Even the slightest of movements sent shockwaves of pain rattling round my head.

"Has anyone been to visit me? Before I woke up, I mean?"

"No," she replied. "I'm sorry. I don't know why that chap of yours hasn't been in. He surely must know you've been hurt. The whole castle knows what happened."

"It's ok," I lied, though I knew exactly why he'd not been to see me. I'd not seen him since he'd thrown the Draconian Sentinel at me with the photo of Caspian and I kissing.

"I'm sure he'll be in later," Amelia mused, minutes later after handing me a cup of coffee. "Your father mentioned that he'd told him. I expect he's held up, that's all."

"My father told Milo?" I couldn't imagine my father speaking to Milo unless he had to. I guess having his daughter almost killed constituted as having to. I took a sip of the coffee, and slowly my brain became less fuzzy.

Amelia gave me a strange look, and then her face brightened. "Here's that chap of yours now. I told you he'd be here soon." She gave me a slight nudge on the arm and a wink before scurrying off to leave me alone with Milo.

My heart leapt until I turned and saw Caspian walking through the door with a huge bunch of flowers. That was who Amelia was talking about when she said my chap. She'd been talking about Caspian, not Milo.

"You are a fool," Caspian said, throwing the flowers down on a bedside cabinet next to me.

"I'm fine, thanks," I threw back in a snarl.

"At least, you've not ruined that pretty face of yours. I'd hate to be standing next to someone resembling a troll on my wedding day."

I glared at him, fury filling my every pore. Not even the threat of me almost dying was enough to elicit any kind of empathy in the jerk. "Please find somewhere else to exist, dirtball. I'm not in the mood."

He grinned at me in the same way he always did, flicking up the corners of his gorgeous mouth lazily, making me want to kiss those delicious lips of his and punch him in them in equal measures.

"I love it when you are angry," he said, pulling up a chair. "You've got that gorgeous death stare down to a tee. It's a sexy look on you."

The infuriating part about his last statement was that it forced me into his trap. I either did what I wanted and glared even harder, or I had to soften my features. I folded my arms, keeping my face as impassive as possible.

"What do you want, Caspian?"

"Actually, I've come to update you on the competition, now that your attempts to run away from it were thwarted."

"I wasn't running from the competition," I spat out.

He cocked his head to one side and considered me. "Do you really take me for a fool?"

"Yes," I replied. "Most of the time, but you know I wasn't running from the competition. I was heading to Urbis to find Morpheus."

"So you say," Caspian said, "but you could have waited until after the competition. Until after our wedding."

"The wedding," I emphasized. "Not our wedding. How many times do I have to tell you I'm not marrying you?"

"Roughly the same amount of times I have to assure you that you are, I expect," he replied with a laugh. "I brought you some flowers. Aren't you going to thank me?"

He picked them up and handed them over. One of the flower heads fell from the stem onto the bed. It reminded me of the poppy Milo had given me a while back. The one that must have cost him a week's wages. These flowers probably cost a month's wages, but money was not something Caspian had to bother about, judging by his flashy clothes. Plus, he was living here rent-free. That must be worth a bunch of flowers or two. I pushed them away, and he put them back on the nightstand.

"Nope," I said.

"Hmm, well then," he sighed. "I'll just tell you about the competition and be on my way. Four judges have been appointed, and a stadium of sorts is being erected on the grounds. At final count, there are nine hundred and eighty-three men competing. The first round will whittle them down to a hundred, the second to ten, and then the last round will choose the winner...me."

I rolled my eyes. At least with so many men competing, the chances of him winning were slim. Slimmer than he thought.

"As I'm a competitor," he carried on, "I will stay in a tent behind the arena. From Friday, I, along with the other competitors, will sleep and eat in there. The judges will not allow me to talk to you during the competition."

"At least something good has come of all this then," I quipped. "I might get a break from you." The morning was shaping up better than I expected. Caspian only had a one in nearly one thousand chance of winning the competition, and I wouldn't have to speak to him for three days. Marvelous.

"Quite," he said lazily. "Your father has chosen the judges, and before you get all pissy, no, I didn't have a hand in choosing any of them. I don't even know them. The head judge is one of your father's guards. Jacob Hawkins."

"What?" I sat up straighter, and the headache that I'd managed to make subside thanks to the coffee now threatened to come back with a vengeance. "He's the man that shot me down. He's an asshole! He wants my father to go and kill all the dragons. Dragon balls, the man is more of a creep than you are."

"Never the less," Caspian continued, obviously not bothered about the dragons, or my derogatory term for him. Not that Caspian was ever bothered by anything that didn't affect him directly. "He's taken over the administration of the competition and made himself head judge. Your father signed off on it, so there is nothing you can do. The second is a member of staff at the local newspaper, Harry Parkes, third, some woman named Gina who is the headmistress at a local school, and fourth is some actor guy who I'm assured is famous here, though I've never heard of him. They were picked because of their backgrounds and impartiality, so don't get your panties in a bunch over it."

I sipped at my coffee and tried to keep my composure. I didn't care about the three other judges, but I hated Jacob with a passion.

"Have you seen Milo at all?" I asked, changing the subject. Asking Caspian about Milo was another thing I hated, but who else could I ask? Amelia didn't even know him.

Caspian sat back in his chair and folded his arms, a sly grin creeping over his face. "So he's not been to visit you then? Well, I didn't think much to the guy. Why have burger when you can have steak? That's what I say."

"Don't you have somewhere to be?" I asked, suddenly tired. "What about Charlotte? Why not go and bother her?"

"I've just seen her. We dined together. Why do you want me to see Charlotte?"

How was the man so utterly blind? "You know you keep telling me how you can read bodies, that you can understand body language? Well, how can you be so good at that and so confoundingly stupid at the same time? The girl is completely besotted with you. She'd walk to the ends of the kingdom on glass in bare feet if you asked her to."

"She has a little crush on me," he said, waving his hand airily.

"A little crush?" I huffed. "She spent every penny she had getting the Urbis Express here just because you asked her to. She didn't come to see the Draconis castle, and she certainly didn't come to see me."

"Pft! Nothing that will stop our wedding. You don't need to worry about her."

I opened my mouth to tell him he had a better chance of a skunk wanting to marry him than me when the door behind him opened.

"I'm sorry, I shouldn't have come." My heart almost exploded with joy as I saw Milo over Caspian's shoulder.

"You should have come," I said, pulling the covers off myself. "Caspian was just leaving. Isn't that right?" I gave Caspian a pointed look.

He ignored it and sat further back in his chair. "Actually Mikey, Azia and I were just talking about our wedding. It's shaping up to be a marvelous affair. Maybe you can be my best man...oh no, you can't. I'm the best man here."

Milo nodded and then closed the door behind him as he left the small ward.

"I really hate you, you know that?" I said, climbing out of bed and accidentally on purpose, spilling what was left of my coffee over his groin. It served him right. I only wished it was hotter.

I was dressed in only my nightgown, but that didn't stop me from chasing Milo down the corridor.

"Stop."

He stopped and turned. "I'm sorry for interrupting you. I guess you and your boyfriend were enjoying some quality time together."

"Don't do this," I begged, grateful that there was no one else in the corridor. I didn't need anyone else witnessing the painful exchange.

"Do what?" he asked. His face showed no emotion, but I could see in his eyes how difficult this was for him. He was hurting as much as I was.

"You know. Caspian isn't my boyfriend. You know he only goads you to make himself feel important. What does that say about him?"

Milo sighed. "I don't know what that says about him, and I don't care. It doesn't matter. I only came to see if you were alright, and now that I can see you are, I'll be on my way."

"Please, don't," I whispered as he turned to walk away from me. I couldn't bear it. In a few days, I was going to be engaged, whether or not I liked it, and I wanted to spend my remaining time with Milo.

"You kissed him, Azia!" he shouted. "All this time, you've been telling me how much you despised the guy, and then you kissed him behind my back. How many times did it happen? Was it going on all that time we were together? I mean, you told me enough times that you didn't want to marry me. I guess I know why now, huh?"

"It wasn't like that," I said, tears streaming down my face. "He kissed me."

He breathed in deeply, his teeth gritted together. Only the slight tremble in his lip gave him away.

"I saw the photograph, Azia. The whole of Draconis saw it. Your eyes were closed. You were enjoying it."

I remembered the picture on the front cover of the Draconis Sentinel. He was right. I did appear to be blissfully happy with kissing Caspian. I was drunk. That was all. At least, that was the official line. The one I was sticking to.

"It doesn't matter anyway," he said. "I came in to say goodbye."

Suddenly, the kiss melted away into unimportance. "What do you mean goodbye? I thought you were going to enter the competition. You said you'd fight for me."

"I've nothing to fight for anymore. I've withdrawn my entry, and we both know that when you marry Caspian, I won't be needed in the castle anymore. He'll fire me the second your vows have been exchanged. I'm going before I get pushed."

“No one will push you!” I cried as he turned to walk away.

“You already have,” he replied, leaving me alone in the corridor with only my tears.

23RD JANUARY

The noise of people talking outside my bedroom window woke me from a fitful sleep. I'd been warned that tents were being erected for the competition today and would it no doubt be noisy, but nothing had quite prepared me for how deafening it was. Dragging myself out of bed, I opened my curtains, surprised to find hundreds of men in the courtyard. On closer inspection, these were my father's guards and not people coming to erect tents. Beyond the castle walls, the people putting up the tents for the competition were there, so why were my father's men in the courtyard? Pulling on a dress, I headed outside to see what was going on.

My father was easy to spot in the center of the men. Although when I say spot, I heard him first rather than saw him, his voice booming out over the general throng

"What's happening, Father?" I asked, after pushing my way through the men. The man he was arguing with turned out to be Jacob. As soon as I saw him, a general feeling of unease settled in my stomach.

"We're going up the mountain!" Jacob replied for him. "We are going to kill the dragons before they kill you."

I was pretty sure my dying didn't bother him a jot, but he'd been desperate to take the army up to kill the dragons for a while, and now it looked like my father was going to give him a chance.

I turned to my father. "Why?" I argued. "I told you they wouldn't attack!"

He shot a glance at Jacob. "Look, Azia. This has been a long time coming. You've been seen twice in the grip of a dragon."

"You were lucky I managed to shoot you down last time," Jacob interrupted. "Who knows what would have happened to you if I hadn't?"

My anger spiked. "Lucky? You could have killed me. I spent the night in the hospital wing. You hurt Nyre."

"Who's Nyre?" Jacob asked, suspiciously.

"It's a friend of hers," my father said quickly. He obviously didn't want anyone to know that I'd voluntarily been flying with a dragon. It was much easier to pretend I was being kidnapped. "Azia, please go inside. This doesn't concern you. Thousands of people are coming to the competition, and I don't want any repeat performances from the dragons like they did before when they burned some of my men to death. I have the safety of the people to consider, not just yours."

"But..."

"Azia! Don't question me," he shouted sternly. "I've

told you to go inside, and I expect you to do it."

Behind him, Jacob smiled smugly, and it took everything I had not to punch him.

I ran back into the castle, but I wasn't going to stay there. I'd made Vasuki a promise, and I intended to keep it. Once I was out of sight of my father, I dodged around the side of the castle and into the back garden, where I ran through the gate leading to the woods. At the other side of the woods, I shot a beam of light into the air.

This time, it wasn't Nyre that came to me, but Vasuki. His beautiful blue outstretched wings glided over me before he grabbed me in his talons and whisked me up the mountain. He dropped me in the same empty nest I'd come to when I first met him. This time there was only him there. He turned back into his almost human form.

"What is going on?" he snapped. "I thought that we had a deal. I did not expect Nyre to come home last night with an injury caused by your men."

I sucked in a breath, deciding how to handle it. He was usually so calm, but the way he looked at me left me in no doubt that his patience had worn a little too thin.

"You remember when I accused you of hurting the castle guard, and you told me it wasn't your doing? Well, those men hurting Nyre was none of my doing. How is she?"

He considered my words for a minute before replying. "The arrow caught her wingtip. It will heal, and she can still fly, but it hurt her." He emphasized the last words.

"I know it did," I said, clearing my throat. "I'm sorry. I didn't mean for any of this to happen. My father is being pushed into it by one of his men. The man has the backing of the people. Just like Darius with you, my father cannot control everyone."

Vasuki seemed to contemplate this. "I understand how difficult it is to run a kingdom. My kingdom is very small, just one colony, but I cannot sit back and let my people get hurt. I can't let my daughter get hurt."

"I understand," I said, wondering how he was going to take what I was about to say. "That's why I'm here. My father has ordered many of his men to come up the mountain. They are in the castle courtyard preparing for battle. You need to get all your dragons down into your village where the men cannot reach you."

Vasuki gave me a bitter smile then looked down to his feet. My chest felt weighed down as I awaited his response.

"I'm afraid we have moved beyond that," he said quietly before looking back up. "I cannot hide anymore. I've done what I can, but nothing will stop this. Now we have to fight, or they will keep on coming."

Fear gripped me. "No. Please don't. My brothers are in the army. They have to do what my father says. They are only fifteen and sixteen. I can't lose them, Vasuki. I've already lost my mother to a terrible curse."

"Nyre is only sixteen. They hurt her."

I nodded my head. "They did. I hate that they did, but they did. The man that shot her is the same man who is making my father send the army up here. He wants to kill you all, but my father doesn't. Not really. Jacob is putting him in an impossible situation."

"But your father is in charge," Vasuki pointed out. "He is the king, is he not? Who is this man who thinks he is above the king?"

I shook my head. Jacob was a nobody. "Before a few weeks ago, he was just one of my father's men. My father ordered him to build a wall at the base of the mountain to stop people coming up here. Jacob made it clear that he didn't like it. While my father was trying to find doctors and deal with a stupid competition, Jacob managed to persuade many people that you all need to die. My father's hands are tied. He doesn't want to hurt you. He knows you are shifters, but he has thousands of people coming for this competition, and he's been brainwashed into thinking that the dragons will hurt everyone."

"Then tell him we won't. I have no desire to send my dragons down the mountain to disrupt your human events."

I sighed. "I know that, but my father will no longer listen to me. When Nyre was seen carrying me, Jacob told everyone that I was being abducted. Now, more people are listening to him than my father, and my father is trying to do too much. He's not slept properly in weeks, and his own health is fading. Why can't you just send all your dragons to your village for a few days until this all blows over? It's not accessible by foot. You'll all be safe, and the worst that will happen to my father's men is that they will spend a day getting cold on the top of the mountain. They'll soon stop listening to Jacob after that."

Vasuki brought his hand to his mouth and chewed on his thumbnail. He paced around me, deep in thought.

"I cannot think of a way around this, Azia," he said. "I've told you that your magic draws us to you, and every fiber in my being wants to do what you say. I'm almost compelled to do your bidding, the magic is that strong, but I cannot take all the dragons down to the village. Dragon eggs are laid in nests like this one for a reason. The baby dragons need the high altitude to grow and to hatch. If we take the eggs down, many will not hatch. I cannot ask the mothers to leave their eggs, and I cannot ask them to bring them down to the village. In hiding, my people will be killed just the same as if we fight. I have no desire to fight, but I do not have a choice. Please don't force me to leave them."

Don't force him to. I knew my bond with them was strong, but I didn't understand how much until now. I could make them flee, but then the deaths of their babies would be all on me.

He pleaded with me with his eyes. This wasn't the same strong Vasuki I knew. This was a man in an impossible position...just like my father.

"I've made so many mistakes in the past few weeks," I said, thinking of Milo and the competition, which was ultimately the reason my father was sending his men up in the first place. "I'm not about to make another. I will not force you to move the eggs, and I will not force you to not fight."

The relief on his face was obvious. He breathed out a sigh.

"I cannot let you fight alone, though. Take me back down the mountain, please."

He regarded me suspiciously. "Why? What are you going to do?"

"I'm going to get dressed in something better than this," I said, indicating my dress. "It's freezing up here."

Vasuki transformed back into the magnificent beast he was, and this time, waited for me to climb up onto his back before he flew me down the mountain. In the distance, my father's men were already beginning the climb. After dropping me at the bottom, Vasuki opened his wings once more and took off into the sky, presumably, to round up the other dragons. I couldn't use my magic to stop him fighting now that I knew what was at stake, but there was a lot at stake on my side too. My father was going up there and no doubt Hollis and Ash too. At least Milo had left us. It was the only consolation in him leaving. I wouldn't have to worry about him being blasted by dragon fire.

I raced back into the castle and up to my room. Jack stood guard alone on the corridor. My heart skipped when I thought of how weird it was that Milo wasn't there helping, but I had more urgent things to deal with to be mooching over a broken heart. In my room, I pulled on some warm trousers and a tunic, which I covered in the leather armor that Milo had brought for me back when we'd both started practicing swordsmanship. Picking up the dragon sword, I raced back out of the room as quickly as I could so Jack wouldn't have time to stop me. The castle bustled with people caught up in last-minute problems associated with the competition. No one paid me any mind as I dashed through, my sword by my side.

I had no idea how the men had managed to get over the wall, but I needed help to get over it. A pair of ladders that had been left behind in the fall were still in the garden, so I took them and managed to get over the wall that way.

The men had a huge head start on me, but I'd climbed this mountain before, and I had something they didn't. I had the lives of the dragons to save. I didn't know how I could stop this. I was winging it in the worst possible way, but I couldn't sit in my room watching people I loved go out to fight with other people I loved. I knew I needed to be there, I just didn't know what to do when I got there.

To my left, I could just about see the men in the

distance. Their guard uniforms stood out against the white snow and gray stone. Once we were further up, the redness of the rock would camouflage them. I planned to be ahead of them by that point.

My lungs burned, and my muscles ached with the effort of climbing the mountain, but thoughts of what would happen if I didn't spurred me on. My half-assed idea was to wait until my father got to the top and position myself between him and his men, and the dragons. Would it stop either side? I didn't know. My father wouldn't attack if he knew I would get hurt, but Jacob would fell me himself if it meant killing dragons.

Minutes turned into hours and exhaustion began to kick in, but a quick glance to my left told me I was in the lead. Pushing past the fatigue was hard, but I was so close to the top, I could see it. The dragons were already there, lined up along the craggy top. All of them perched along the mountain, waiting for the onslaught. None of them took to the skies, but as I moved closer, I could see Darius itching to be off. If only I could pit Darius against Jacob and leave the pair of them to it, then I'd be fine. Unfortunately for everyone else involved, I had no say in the matter.

The snow-covered rocks made climbing hard as I edged around the mountain. One by one, the dragons glanced my way before settling their eyes back on my father's army of men.

At the very front, my father led the group, closely followed by Jacob, who was the only one of the men to hold his sword out, ready for attack. When they were within about fifty feet of the dragons, my father came to a stop and held his hand to the side to stop Jacob or any of the others from running past him.

I could see, even from the distance between us,

the indecision in his eyes. He didn't want to do this anymore than I wanted him to. He was doing it because, in the past few weeks, the kingdom had fallen through the cracks, and though he knew they wanted a strong leader, he was not able to be one. The man had barely slept, and I'd not seen him at any meals for days. It was a miracle he was still standing, let alone able to climb a mountain leading a hundred men into battle. He was doing it because this was what people like Jacob needed to see. But in doing so, it meant Jacob got his way, and Jacob's way meant the destruction of a whole colony of Dragon shifters. I don't know what he had against dragons. He had no family hurt when the dragons came down the mountain and killed some of my father's men. Perhaps some of his friends had died, and he wanted retaliation. Maybe he wanted to steal dragon eggs to make some money. Maybe he just wanted to fight for the sake of it because that's what people like Jacob liked to do. I didn't know. I saw what was about to happen with absolute clarity. Both sides lined up ready to attack. The men with their swords, the dragons with their hot fiery breath. Not even running between them would stop them. Not with the likes of Jacob involved. But then, I knew what I had to do. Vasuki had told me that I could command him with my magic. I could compel him to do anything like some sort of dragon tamer, and if I pushed my magic hard enough, he would have to do it whether or not he liked it. I didn't want to force him to do anything, and I hoped it wouldn't come to it as I reached out to him with my magic. Before, I'd been throwing it out willy-nilly, and the dragons had come to me, urged on by the bright lights my magic produced. This time, I concentrated my magic on Vasuki alone. He cocked his head to one side and looked at me questioningly. He understood what I wanted without me telling him. This wasn't telepathy. I wasn't speaking to him in my mind. It was almost as though I was a part of him, and he was a part of me. I'd finally gotten my magic to work the way it was supposed to. I nodded my head at him, giving the explicit yes he needed. He crouched lower then pushed hard, unfurling his magnificent wings and taking to the sky. The men watched as he circled then fell into a dive. My father didn't have a chance. He'd not even had the time to pull his sword from his sheath.

Vasuki had him gripped between his teeth rather than in his claws. I winced at the thought of how uncomfortable it must have been, and how sooty Vasuki's breath was, but my father was wearing leather armor and would survive. If I played this right, everyone would. Vasuki turned mid-air and dived for me. He whisked us both to a nest away from my father's men. Behind him, another dragon sat. This one was bright yellow with orange-tipped wings. Vasuki shifted into his human form.

My father knew he was a shifter, but it didn't stop the look of astonishment on his face when Vasuki held his hand out for my father to shake.

My father stood still, his hands firmly by his side, wary of the shifter before him.

"This is Vasuki, Father," I explained." He is the king of the dragons. You would never listen to me when I told you that they don't want to fight, but maybe you'll listen to him."

"The dragon behind me is Kuda," Vasuki said, indicating the dragon. It watched us with frightened eyes. "Kuda was very young, sitting on her first batch of eggs eighteen years ago when some men stole into her nest. Not only did they steal her eggs, they also killed the hatchlings. Her babies would be the same age as Azia now, give or take a few months. Kuda never dared lay eggs after that. The thought of men coming and killing her babies stopped her. This year, she finally found the courage to lay again. You can't see them, but under her are five dragon eggs. They may be priceless artifacts to you, but to a grieving mother, they are her whole life. Kuda isn't the only dragon nesting. There are more. I do not want to hurt you or your men. I never did, but you understand that I will do what I have to do to keep them safe."

My father stood stock still; indecision plastered all over his face. I felt sorry for him. There was no winning here. He wasn't a bad person, and he could no more take those eggs from Kuda than I could.

"You don't understand." He turned to me. "Azia, you don't know what's been going on. Jacob has been organizing an uprising. If I don't let him fight the dragons, he will bring an army of his own to help him. Why do you think he is on the panel of judges at your competition? I ignored what was happening for so long because I was worried about your mother, about you." He turned back to Vasuki again. "I want no bloodshed. My sons are down there as are men that are far braver than me. They are waiting for my order to attack. If I don't give it, Jacob will."

"Then I can't help you. I will fly you back down to your men. When you give the order, they will attack us. At that point, I cannot stop my dragons from defending themselves. You might have swords, but we have the advantage of fire and height. You cannot win this."

"I know," my father said despondently. "I'm sorry it has come to this. I tried. I really did. I built a wall."

“No!” I screamed. “Father, you are signing a death wish. What about Ash and Hollis. What about me?”

“Ash and Hollis knew what they were doing when they came up the mountain. You can stay here. You will be safe. Maybe Kuda and her eggs will be safe too.”

“You can’t do this!” I screamed. I’d lost my mother, I was about to lose my brothers, and I’d lost the man I looked up to. The man I respected.

I ran towards him, but I was too late. Vasuki had transformed quickly and grabbed him in his talons, leaving me in a nest, too high up to do anything other than watch on in terror from above.

I sat on the very edge of the nest. Another two inches more, and I would plummet to my death. Vasuki had chosen this nest on purpose. He didn’t want me in the line of fire any more than my father did. They both knew I’d run between them and, in doing so, would get myself killed.

Vasuki dropped my father to the ground about twenty feet above my father’s army and thirty feet or so below the line of dragons. No one had made a move yet, both sides waiting for their leader to come back.

I could stop this. I could use my magic and compel the dragons to retreat, but in doing so, I was leaving their eggs vulnerable. Kuda’s eggs would be safe, no matter what Vasuki said. The sheer cliffs around her nest protected her, but there were so many dragons that weren’t—the mother dragons who had roosted on lower outcrops and nests.

Vasuki would never forgive me. I would never forgive myself, but then would I be able to forgive myself if I let my father and brothers perish in dragon fire? The thought of it burned at my heart.

“I’m sorry,” I whispered as I began to pull my magic

in. Pulling the dragons back would mean the baby dragons would die. The hatchlings, the eggs, but by not pulling them back, everyone would die.

A hand on my shoulder ripped away my concentration, and my magic ceased. I turned to find Kuda in her near-human form. Her bright yellow hair was greying at the temples, and laughter lines gave away her age.

"Don't do it," she said. It wasn't a warning. She spoke with a soft voice. "Your father still has time."

I turned to look back over the edge. She was wrong. There was no time. Both sides were ready to fight. One word from my father and chaos would happen.

He held his hand up in the air at around the same time that Kuda gripped mine. She dangled her feet over the edge and sat next to me.

I held my breath, almost unable to watch the inevitable onslaught.

"I..." my father began but faltered. I could just about hear him even at the distance separating us.

He walked forward, climbing the incline towards the dragons. No one else moved.

"What is he doing?" I whispered. "He's going to get himself killed."

"He did sound like a man on the edge," Kuda said, taking my hand in hers. "Maybe he thinks this is his only way out."

So that was my father's plan. Suicide by dragon so he didn't have to deal with any repercussions about what he was about to do.

Just as I thought things couldn't get any worse, he pulled his sword from his sheath and charged at Vasuki. With just one strike, Vasuki crashed to the floor. I screamed as my father brought his sword down, again and again, raining blows upon Vasuki's body. Nobody else moved. The dragons and the humans watched on. Jacob yelled something in excitement, but I didn't hear it over my own scream.

"He is dead!" My father shouted. "The king of the dragons is no more."

Below him, the men cheered, but the dragons didn't attack. They took to the skies, flying away quickly.

"Without their king, they are cowards," Jacob roared, charging to my father to bring him into a hug. "We are the victors."

Tears streamed down my face as I took in the scene below. My brothers were safe, but Vasuki was dead.

"They will not attack again," My father shouted. "Tonight, we go back down the mountain and celebrate our victory."

The men cheered again, relieved in the fact that none of them had been broiled alive. Only Jacob didn't move.

"Now hang on," he huffed." You killed one dragon. What about the others?"

"I killed the king of dragons," my father countered. "You saw how quickly the others fled. They will not dare to come down and fight anymore. Not without their leader. Come and have a drink with me as a guest in the castle."

Bile filled my throat as I thought of the pair of them drinking over Vasuki's death.

"What about the eggs?" Jacob asked.

My father shook his head. "They are eggs. They will die without the warmth of their mothers. We do not need to worry about them now."

"But...but. They are worth a lot of money."

My father put his arm over Jacob's shoulder and began to lead him down the mountain. "Come now, Jacob, you wouldn't want the people to think we were only coming up here to steal eggs. Not a man in such a high position as yourself. We have nothing to worry about now. Let's leave it at that."

Jacob didn't look too happy, but there was nothing he could do.

I watched them walk down the mountain until they were mere dots.

"You are shivering lass," Kuda said. "I'd take you back down the mountain, but as your father himself said, my eggs will die if I leave them too long without warmth. I expect Vasuki will do it for you."

"Vasuki?" I murmured. "Vasuki is dead."

"Am I?"

I nearly fell over the side of the nest as Vasuki spoke. I turned quickly to find him in his human form next to me.

"I saw my father kill you!" I whispered. my heart beating a percussion in my chest.

Vasuki smiled. "You saw your father hitting a stone between my wing and my body. I'm glad to know I am such a good actor that I fooled you as well as your father's army. I really expected more from you.You are my queen, after all. If one of the dragons really died, you would feel it."

"But how?"

They hadn't planned this. There was no time when just the two of them were together in the nest.

Vasuki gave me a smile. "It was your father's idea. He told it to me as I flew him back to his army. I couldn't answer, of course, so he had to hope I'd heard and would play along. Did I really do that good a job of dying?"

"Er, yeah," I nodded. "What about the other dragons? Why didn't they attack?"

"You are not the only one who can compel the

dragons. You might be the queen of dragons, but I am the king." He gave me a wink. "Please tell your father I'd like to see him when he is ready. We might have tricked this Jacob character for now, but I doubt he will let this rest. I'd like to see if we can figure out a peaceful solution to all this."

I nodded my head, amazed at what had just transpired. My father was the leader I knew him to be, after all. He just needed to be put in a position where he could show his true colors. He needed a push. I laughed as Vasuki transformed and flew me back down to the woods.

24TH JANUARY

My father woke me up the next morning by knocking on my door.

"I came to apologize for not doing better," he said, shutting the door behind him so Jack couldn't eavesdrop. "I should have stood up to Jacob, but I was afraid of the repercussions. It was wrong of me."

I jumped out of bed and flung myself into his arms. "Are you kidding? You were amazing. No one was hurt."

"What about Vasuki? I assume it was he who flew you home."

"Yes. He'd like to speak to you," I replied. "He wants peace, and he'd like to make sure that nothing like yesterday ever happens again."

My father nodded and sat on the bed. "I want that too. I will go up and speak with him once the competition is over. I managed to get Jacob drunk last night, and he's forgotten about the eggs, but I'm sure once the competition is done with, he'll find a way to go back up. It's very clear that's all he's interested in. The danger of the fight and the monetary gain if he steals the eggs."

"Why not throw him off the judging panel?" I asked. I didn't like the thought of that man helping decide my own fate.

My father shrugged his shoulders." He was the one who instilled himself as a judge, but I think it's the best place he can be right now. It's keeping him occupied, and if he's busy with the competition, he won't have time to go back up the mountain. Besides, I saw your competition ideas. How much trouble can he cause when all he has to do is oversee the question of who is the queen of dragons?"

"You know who that is, right?" I grinned at him.

"I have my suspicions." He brought me into a hug. It was the first genuine father-daughter moment we'd had together in weeks, and I didn't want to let it go. "You know, when I saw your beautiful face for the first time, I never in my wildest dreams understood how amazing you'd turn out to be, nor all the gray hairs I'd get just watching you have your adventures. You were the type of child that would scrape her knee and then get right back up without flinching. I will never understand how you came to be the queen of the dragons, but I can't say that it surprises me."

Later on, once Father had left, Dahlia came to my room to wake me up and bring me coffee. In all the years I'd known her, she'd never brought me breakfast in bed. Not that a cup of coffee could be construed as breakfast, but it was close.

"I heard on the grapevine that Milo is leaving," she

said warily, placing the coffee on my nightstand.

The adventure yesterday had kept my mind away from the heartbreak, but now that she'd mentioned his name, the pain came back full force.

"I know," I replied, trying to keep my emotions out of my voice. "He was worried that Caspian would fire him."

Dahlia shook her head "Why would he worry about a thing like that? Caspian has no say in what goes on in this castle, no matter how much he likes to think he does. He could no more fire Milo than I could. Anyway, that's not what I mean. He came to the admin office this morning and asked for a reference. He says he's leaving Zhore."

I sat bolt upright in bed. "Leaving Zhore? Where is he going?"

Dahlia shrugged. "I don't know, Maureen, the head of admin didn't tell me, but she did get the feeling it wasn't only Zhore he was leaving. She thinks he might be leaving Draconis altogether."

Pulling back the covers, I jumped out of bed and ran to the door.

"Where do you think you're going?" Dahlia asked, rushing over to me and holding her hand to the door so I couldn't open it.

"Please, let me out," I cried, trying to get past her. "I need to find Milo before he leaves the castle."

"He already left the castle," Dahlia pointed out.

I shook in frustration. "Then I'll go to his house."

Dahlia looked me up and down. "In your pajamas?"

Damn! I pulled on some jeans and a t-shirt, and this time, Dahlia let me leave. I ran all the way to Zhore, muddying up the bottoms of my trousers in the process on the snow that was quickly melting and mixing with thawed mud underneath. The streets of Zhore were quiet, but the beginnings of the decorations for the wedding had already been erected in the main square. Even though my wedding was to take place in the castle, the people wanted to celebrate themselves. In the dim morning light and with the hint of fog that was drawing in, the whole thing looked as miserable as my own heart. I knocked loudly on Milo's door, willing it to open, but he wasn't in.

"Please, don't have already gone!" I whispered to myself. I couldn't bear it. The pain of him leaving without saying goodbye was indescribable, but no one answered, so I had to conclude he had already left. I began the walk home, pain filling my chest, and as I passed the Dragon Roost Inn, I decided to go in on the off chance he was having a very early morning drink.

The bar was as dim as it had been the first time I'd gone in, the day I'd told Milo about our fake relationship. Just thinking about it pierced my chest. The place was almost empty save for the barmaid, Lisa, and a couple of other customers.

"A beer please," I said, scrabbling in my pocket for some loose change. She slammed down a beer in front of me, sloshing it all over the counter, as I realized I'd come out without any money.

"I'm afraid I don't have any cash on me." I apologized, trying to explain. "I'll bring some down next time I come."

She pulled the beer out of my reach and moved her face closer to mine. "Then, I'll pour you more beer the next time you come."

Yeah, this girl might not have recognized me as the princess, but she sure as shit knew I was the girl Milo came in here with.

I almost apologized to her for existing when someone sidled up beside me and tapped my shoulder.

"I'll pay for it," the person said, throwing down a couple of coins. Lisa begrudgingly pushed the beer back to me, slashing more on the counter for good measure. I turned to find Gladys standing next to me. The last time I'd seen her, she'd been at Milo's house. I was beginning to get used to her sneaking up on me.

"Shall we get a booth?" she asked, nodding at my beer. I picked the glass up and followed her to one of the darker booths.

"You won't find him," she said before I even had a chance to speak. "He's a good lad, that one, but his heart is broken."

"I know," I said. "I'm the one who broke it."

"I think that goes without saying, Lovie. I did tell him not to go getting mixed up with a princess, but would he listen? I told him that you were better suited to that fae chap in the paper. He's a man of power by the looks of his photo, and you, well, I already told you that you have power. Milo was just a normal lad, and normal never mixes well with power and money. You and he were like oil and water."

"I was more like Milo than you think," I replied, thinking of all the snatched moments in the castle, and all the times we practiced sword fighting out in the woods. Maybe I was raised a princess, but inside I was a warrior, a protector, just like Milo. Or at least I wanted to be.

Gladys called me out. She waggled her finger in my face. "Just because you like someone doesn't mean you are like them, and just because you dislike someone doesn't mean that you aren't the same. Take this fae fellow. Milo said he was an arrogant trumped-up ass, but he also said he was strong and resourceful, and eager to show people that he was a capable leader. Now doesn't that sound like you?"

"Not really? I'm no leader." And I didn't want to think of myself as being like Caspian.

She raised her eyebrows. "That's not the impression I get from reading the papers. I don't see your father doing much these days, but you are in the paper every day, giving interviews, reassuring the people. I saw what you said about your future husband, that he'll never be king and never be above you. You are stronger than you think you are."

I sighed. "I don't feel very strong at the moment," I said, nursing my beer. I was yet to take a sip of it.

"That's your heart talking. Ignore it for a moment and listen to your brain. What do you want?"

"At the moment, I want Milo."

"No," she said, smiling kindly. "Look beyond Milo. What do you want for you? And don't tell me you want to save your mother and you want to not have to do this competition thing you've gotten yourself into. All of that is just circumstance you've found yourself in. What do you want for yourself?"

I thought about it. So many things had required my attention over the last few weeks, that I'd almost forgotten what it felt like to just be me. Three weeks ago, I'd just celebrated my eighteenth birthday. I remember wishing I had a horse. It seemed so silly now. "I want to run Draconis," I said firmly. "I want to be a good and fearless leader, and I want to be able to do it for myself, not with a husband because I've been told I have to. I don't want to be protected, I want to be the protector."

"Spoken like a true leader," she said, sitting back, a wide smile on her face. "Now, drink up that beer. I'd hate to see it go to waste."

I downed the beer, more because I was feeling sorry for myself than to feel less guilt that she had bought it for me. After her telling me not to think about Milo, my next question almost embarrassed me, but I had to find him.

"Do you know where Milo is?"

She shook her head. "That I cannot say. I've not seen much of him around here lately, but he is exactly where he is supposed to be. I feel it. You, on the other hand, are not. Why don't you go home and concentrate on doing what you need to do and leave Milo to nurse his wounds? If you are meant to see him again, you will."

I thanked her for the beer and left the pub after saying goodbye.

Back at the castle, I had nothing to do. Part of me wanted to go to my room and lock the door. A couple of weeks ago, I would have done that and spent the afternoon crying over Milo. I couldn't be that girl anymore. I'd told Gladys that I was going to be a fearless leader, and fearless leaders didn't sob in bedrooms over guys. To take my mind off Milo, I decided to go to the castle administration office, which had now been taken over as the center of operations for the competition.

The admin staff, which usually consisted of a lady called Maureen, her two assistants, and her cat, had grown to a team of twelve over the past week, and still, they were swamped with paperwork.

Stacks of it piled up high filled the room, and as I closed the door behind me, a stack almost toppled, saved at the last second by a harassed-looking assistant.

"Final count is just over a thousand men," Maureen said when I found her at her desk hiding behind a pile of paper. Her cat snoozed on another pile of what looked to be applications of entry. A thousand men! That was even higher than the figure Caspian had given me days prior.

“How are the details for the competition going?” I asked, figuring out I should at least have half a clue of what was going on. The castle was filled with people, and everyone seemed to know what was going on except me.

Maureen brought her hand up to her necklace and twisted it around her fingers. “There’s been a setback or two,” she admitted. “We’ve ordered tons of clay for the first round, but the supplier dumped it outside without letting us know, and it dried out. I’ve put in another order, but it will be touch and go if it gets here on time.”

“It was a stupid idea anyway!” someone piped up from the back of the room. I looked over the frantic workers’ heads to see Jacob sitting with his feet up, smoking a cigar. Plumes of smoke wafted up to the ceiling.

“What are you doing here?” I snapped, deliberately not keeping the annoyance out of my voice.

“I’m helping is what I’m doing,” he said. “This competition of yours has turned into a shit show, and someone has to run it.”

“Maureen was running it perfectly fine,” I said. “And please put the cigar out. It stinks.”

“The only thing that stinks,” he said, standing up and walking over, “is the organization of this competition. Who orders a ton of clay and then gets it delivered before the event starts?”

“Look, just do whatever you want!” I huffed. “Just get out of my sight.”

He gave Maureen and me a filthy look and stubbed his cigar out on a stack of paperwork before heading out the door.

"I'm sorry about him," Maureen apologized, picking up the cigar and stack of paper, which thankfully hadn't been set alight. She tipped the lot in the garbage.

"The tents have been going up all week," Maureen enthused, changing the subject. "We have a temporary stadium, a huge tent for the competitors to sleep and eat in, and another to get changed in. I've ordered costumes for all of the competitors, and the entertainment is booked, so it's not all doom and gloom."

"Entertainment?" I inquired.

"Yes," she said, ticking something from a sheet on her clipboard." We have thousands of people coming to watch, so I've had to organize entertainment for before each part of the competition. This thing will go on for three days, and I don't want anyone getting bored. I've also got the kitchen working triple time and organized caterers from Zhore to help with the rest."

Clay problems aside, she seemed to have the whole thing mostly in hand, and there was nothing I could do to help. This had started as my idea, and somewhere along the line, it had gotten out of control and run away without me. I'd started all of this as a way to get out of marrying Caspian and being able to marry Milo. He was right when I told him I wasn't ready for marriage. I'd told him over and over, not realizing how difficult it would be to hear. I had pushed him away.

"Do you have a list of all the contestants?" I asked Maureen.

A look of pure panic crossed her face before one of the other staff members passed a list to her.

"Oh, yes. I knew I had one somewhere. Here."

She passed it to me. The names were listed alphabetically by surname, although I noticed Caspian's name at the very top despite his last name being Montblanc. No doubt, he'd had a hand in it. I scanned down until I hit the k's. Milo's name was there, but with a thick black line through it. I'd hoped he would change his mind, but it was wishful thinking on my part. He'd gone. I'd lost him for good.

"Thank you, Maureen," I said despondently, passing her back the list.

"Don't you have a photoshoot later? "Maureen asked. "Maybe you should go and get ready for that."

"Do I?" I couldn't keep up with everything these days. There was so much going on, and what with dragons, competitions, and doctors, things like photoshoots were very low on my list of things to worry about. Still, just because I wasn't worried, didn't mean that Dahlia wouldn't be. I could imagine her running around the castle in an increasing state of panic looking for me.

"I should go," I sighed.

I found Dahlia in the state of panic I expected in the castle kitchens. She fit right in with the general air of stress in there. Food covered every surface, and the head chef barked orders at anyone who dared to come close to him.

"I thought you'd be down here trying to grab a sandwich, seeing as you missed breakfast," Dahlia said. "I managed to get you one. Here." She passed me a sandwich and bustled me out of the door. "They are making food for all the contestants, not to mention all the guests. The head chef has brought in a catering company to help, but now, they are taking over the kitchen, and he's not happy about it."

"What's the photoshoot for?" I asked, not really caring. "The Sentinel? Haven't they got enough photos."

"There can never be enough photos of you, but no.

Reporters from all the kingdom's main newspapers have come in. We need you looking pretty."

"Great!" I replied sarcastically. I expected a complete shit show. After all, the whole thing had been a disaster from start to finish, but when I walked into the main hall, dressed up to the nines with my hair styled and my makeup on point thanks to Dahlia, the photographers were seated in chairs in a perfectly civilized manner, waiting for my arrival.

My father introduced me as I walked in. It was such a difference from the week before when a thousand men had been invited to meet me. I could hear a pin drop as I walked across the floor to a small stage that had been erected with a painted backdrop for the photos.

The reporters clapped politely as I took my father's hand and stepped up onto the stage.

"You look beautiful," he whispered as he took his place next to me. "Your mother would be proud."

I gave him a shy smile. It was nice having my father back to his usual self.

Photographers from the Sentinel, the Atlantice Conch, the Floris Observer, the Badalah Beacon, and all the others stood up to take photos of my father and me as we posed. The prideful father and the almost-wedded daughter. The only kingdom not represented was Elder, which never seemed to care about what was going on in the other kingdoms. They didn't even have a newspaper as far as I was aware.

Once they'd finished photographing me posing with my father, who had also dressed up for the occasion, they wanted snaps of me on my own. I was painfully aware that my mother should have been standing by my side, but she was still upstairs wasting away in her bed.

After the photos, I readied myself for the onslaught of questions, but instead of the men and women reporters fighting over themselves, someone handed me a list and told me to choose which questions I wanted to answer. As far as photoshoots and press conferences went, it was one of the most pleasant I'd had to deal with.

"I told your father to warn them all to be civil," Dahlia confessed afterward as she took me back to my mother's dressing room. She would have had me dressed up in the beautiful dress all day, but she knew she'd have to listen to me complain about it. I pulled the dress off and stepped back into the jeans and t-shirt combo I'd left there before Dahlia went to work on removing my makeup. I hated wearing the stuff. It made my face itch.

She was taking the hairpins out when we both heard a crash next door. The room next to the dressing room was my parents' bedroom. I caught Dahlia's eyes in the mirror. My father was still downstairs talking to the reporters. There should be no one in my mother's room.

"Mother!" I shot up, almost knocking Dahlia over in the process. We both rushed to the room. My heart beat in triple time at the thought of my mother wakening up. She'd been asleep for so long. There was no other reason for the crash. Even if she'd fallen out of bed, it meant that she'd woken enough to move. I knew for a fact that the maid was not on duty at the moment.

Excitement filled me as we crashed through her door, but it was to be short-lived. She was still asleep in the same position we had left her in. Beside her, a photographer I recognized from the press conference was snapping away so intently he'd not even noticed when we came through the door. The crash we'd heard was a vase he'd knocked over which lay on the floor as water from it seeped into the carpet.

"What the hell are you doing?" Dahlia shouted, which made him finally take notice. Panic overcame his features as he tried to make a dash past us. I jumped in his way, blocking his path and grabbed his camera. There was no way in this kingdom. I was going to let him go with those pictures.

He was stronger than I anticipated, and the harder I pulled on the camera, the harder he pulled back. Beside me, Dahlia screamed and waved her hands around. The guy pushed me into the doorframe in an attempt to hurt me enough so I'd let go of the camera. My head smashed against the frame sending shockwaves through my body and causing me almost to black out. I cried out in pain as everything began to spin, but my grip on his camera only tightened. My mother had always prided herself on her appearance, and although she was as beautiful in sleep as she was awake, she would hate having those photos printed. And they wouldn't just be printed in the kingdom that this reporter creep was from. They would spread so that everyone would see them.

My head hit the frame again, and I felt the camera being tugged from my grasp. I wanted to hold on, but a surge of nausea overcame me.

I pulled in a deep breath to orient myself, but as my vision cleared, the reporter went flying past me, almost hitting me as he crashed into the wall next to me. Caspian ran towards him and punched him in the face, knocking him out cold. He waved his hand, and the camera gave a little sputter then erupted into a ball of flames that died as soon as they had appeared. What was left of the camera, Caspian threw at the unconscious reporter.

"Dahlia, please get a couple of guards to come and collect this garbage," Caspian said. "You'd better find out which kingdom he came from and get him on the first Airship home."

Dahlia nodded and ran off down the corridor.

I brought my hand to my head. Already a lump was forming somewhere under the hair and hairclips.

"Are you alright?" Caspian asked, bringing his hand up to my face. I'd never felt so vulnerable in his presence before. I nodded. I would be alright, but it had shocked me. What with everything else going on, I'd not thought I'd need to worry about protecting my mother from photographers.

"I'm sorry you had to deal with that," he said, caressing my face. "When we are married, I'll protect you. I promise."

I looked into his eyes and believed him, and for the first time, I didn't correct him.

25TH JANUARY

I could already hear the noise of the people gathering without having to open my curtains. I knew it was going to be crazy insane after seeing the lines of people and all the tents yesterday. Not that I was remotely ready for it. How could I be ready? I had a thousand men waiting to make a clay figurine of me and not enough clay to go around. I'd have to look beautiful and charming all day, and all I wanted to do was stay in bed, hiding under my covers. Any second, Dahlia would waltz through the door with yet another dress for me to wear and jabber excitedly about the upcoming event. As if she read my mind, there was a small knock at the door followed by Dahlia calling me lazy and threatening to pour ice water over me to get me out of bed.

"I'm getting up already," I croaked before she had

time to carry out her threat.

The dress she'd picked today was a pale powder blue. Not quite dark enough to match my mood, but blue enough to hint at it. I grabbed it from her and pulled it on before she tried wrestling me into the bath.

"This is so exciting," Dahlia enthused.

She clapped her hands together and pushed me into the chair by the window so she could work on my makeup and hair. I reached forward to open the curtains, but she batted them out of my hands.

"Don't spoil the surprise," she admonished. "You'll get to see it all later."

"Great!" I muttered, lacking any enthusiasm. The only good thing, as far as I could see, about the next three days was the fact that I wouldn't have to speak to Caspian. It meant that, at least, I could eat meals in peace without having to worry about his company. He was staying in one of the huge tents that had been arranged for the competitors. I didn't get the feeling that Caspian was one to stay in tents as a rule. Plus, it was freezing cold outside. I allowed myself a little smile at the thought of Caspian freezing his bits off in the tent. I couldn't see him being too happy about molding clay either. He just wasn't the artistic type, and he would hate getting his hands or clothes dirty.

I swallowed back a laugh as Dahlia pulled my hair into a high up ponytail.

Half an hour and one rushed breakfast later, and I was due to go outside.

A trumpet fanfare sounded out as my father took my hand in the entrance hall to the castle.

"Ready?" he asked, squeezing my hand.

I nodded, my stomach in knots. I wasn't ready, but I never would be. This was an echo of what my father thought was to come with my wedding next week. This was practically a trial run for him. He thought he would be escorting me out to adoring crowds then too.

Outside, a long walkway with high fences had been erected out to the pastures where the first leg of the competition would take place. It meant that the crowds hadn't seen us yet, and I could walk in quietness. The calm before the storm.

I gripped my father's hand as we rounded the corner into what I could only describe as a huge stadium. One of the palace staff greeted us and showed us the way to our seats up some stairs at the back. Still, no one had seen us. My father held me back before a pair of curtains in front of us opened.

"You ok?"

I nodded and faced forward. Faced toward my future, whatever that would be.

The trumpet fanfare started again, and my heart provided a handy percussion accompaniment.

The curtains parted, and the roar that happened afterward deafened me with its magnitude. The whole stand shook as thousands of people stood and clapped at our entrance. Two golden thrones had been placed for us high up in the middle of the stand, and a pang of sadness filled me when I realized one was not for my mother, but for me.

I walked silently to the throne and waved, plastering a fake smile to my face as the crowd went wild.

Next to me, sat Remy and beyond him, Hollis. To my left was my father's throne, and next to that, Ash gave me a thumbs up. When the noise finally died down, I sat and gazed around the arena. I'd known it was going to be big, but nothing could have prepared me for just how colossal the place was.

“How many people fit in here?” I whispered to my father as a man rode on horseback to the middle of the arena.

“Twenty thousand members of the public have been let in, but I’ve been told there are thousands more outside. A thousand men can fit in the center of the arena to fulfill the tasks.”

The crowd went silent as a man dressed in a ringmaster’s costume on a horse trotted into the arena. He did a lap as an excited buzz filled the stadium. The crowd went wild as he jumped up on the back of the horse, which continued to trot despite the man standing on its back.

“Ladies and Gentlemen,” he began as the horse obediently trotted around in a circle so he could address everyone, “Your Majesty, Your Royal Highnesses. Welcome to the show.”

Show? This wasn’t supposed to be a show. This was supposed to be an important event. Just as I was thinking that this was being lowered to nothing but entertainment, a group of jugglers dressed in Draconis national costume ran out of a tunnel.

“The Draconis National Circus, ladies and gentlemen,” the ringmaster said, before trotting back through the tunnel he’d come from.

My stomach fell as the performers gathered into the middle. They didn’t walk or run. They back-flipped and cart-wheeled and juggled their way to the center.

All around me, the crowd lapped it up while I sat further into my seat and pretended I was still in bed, and this was some horrific dream. It wasn’t that I didn’t like performers. I usually loved anything like this, but my plan of getting this madness over and done with was rapidly falling away from me.

The performers gathered into almost a ball before an explosion ripped through the stadium. My heart leapt into my throat, and a good many of the public screamed before a huge dragon made of fire erupted from the performers. It was all part of the show, but it amazed me how real it all looked. To the sound of drums, the fire dragon flew around the stadium, supported by the performers underneath to whoops and hollers coming from the delighted crowd. Even I, who had not wanted any of this sat on the edge of my seat, waiting to see what would happen next. Beside me, Remy stood up in his seat, shouting "dra'a" as the performers passed us.

The percussion increased in pace, building up the tension before the dragon erupted in flames, and the performers collectively danced, pirouetted, and backflipped into a line. They bowed down to my father... or to me. I stood and clapped, feeling that my day might go better than expected.

How bad could it be? It might be quite nice to watch a thousand men trying to recreate my likeness out of clay. The performers left as the ringmaster came back upon his horse.

"And now for the main event. The reason you are all here. The first competition for the Princess Azia's hand in marriage."

I offered up a shy smile as twenty thousand pairs of eyes swiveled my way.

"Please welcome our contestants."

Another cheer went up as the men began to pour out. I sat, literally on the edge of my seat, craning to see the competitors. Most of the men came out, their hands held aloft, fist-bumping the sky, and generally playing it up for the crowd that was loving it.

It took over fifteen minutes to get all of them in the

arena. The floor of the arena filled right to the edges leaving very little space for the clay. I watched as the ringmaster trotted back out through the tunnel, and a pair of doors closed behind him. They would open shortly with the huge amounts of clay needed for them to sculpt with. While I waited, I scanned the men again. I found Caspian quickly even though he was wearing the same red outfit as the rest of the men. He'd hate that. There was nothing Caspian liked more than to feel superior with his spiffy way of dressing. Nevertheless, he seemed happy enough as he waved to the crowd along with the others. A few seats in front of me, I saw the back of Charlotte's head as she stood and waved enthusiastically back. I'd not had a chance to speak with her this morning, but I knew she was more excited than I was about this competition.

The tunnel doors opened again, and I sat back into my seat, more excited than I thought I'd ever be. I reflected that making a sculpture of me would be a rather boring event after the earlier performers, and the crowd would be sorely disappointed with the lack of action in the first part of the competition I'd planned. Not that it really mattered. What mattered was whittling these men down to a hundred for the next part of the competition tomorrow.

If sculpting was the way to do it, then so be it.

I was just thinking with dismay that I wasn't going to see Milo's rendition of me now that he'd left when something orange appeared in the corner of my eye.

Somewhere someone screamed, but this was not the scream of excitement. This was fear.

I did a double-take as the screams became louder and not only from the audience. The men nearest the tunnel surged towards us as the orange thing became clear in my eyesight. It was about as far from a lump of clay as anything could get. With bared teeth and sharp claws, the tiger strolled out into the arena.

"What's this?" My father raged, standing up and thumping his fist on the arm of the throne. "I never agreed to this."

I gulped with fear when I realized I had. Inadvertently, but even so, I'd told Jacob to do what he wanted. I'd not expected him to add a tiger to the mix. It wasn't just one tiger. Behind the first walked a second and a third, and behind that, many more.

"The men are unarmed!" I whispered as my father stalked past me in a hurry.

I could only watch on in horror as the men ran screaming away from the giant cats. Fear gripped me to my chair as more of the hungry beasts walked out. I fearfully scanned the men again as the first tiger pounced. A scream of pain followed by the sound of a growling tiger ripping flesh came to my ears. I didn't count, but there must have been more than a hundred tigers brought into the arena. A hundred tigers looking for their next meal. I was going to murder Jacob myself if my father hadn't already done it.

I wanted to close my eyes, but the horror of what was happening before me left me unable to. People all around me were screaming, some were jeering, and some were actively enjoying the spectacle. Right at the front, the line of judges sat still, seemingly impassive to what was happening to the men in front of them. Jacob must have warned them in advance.

My whole body trembled as the tigers attacked. Chaos abounded below me, but some of the men were escaping through the original tunnel. Many more skirted the edge of the arena doing the best they could to get out before the tigers got them. A hundred tigers, a thousand men. They all had a good chance to escape if they were quick enough. Not even the hungriest tiger could eat ten men. Many of the men tried to pull themselves up over the barrier into the crowd. Some succeeded, but many failed simply because they were not tall enough to reach. Caspian was well over six feet four and could grab the edge and haul himself over, but no matter how hard I looked I couldn't see him in the melee. Andrew, Dahlia's son ran for the tunnel and disappeared down it without getting hurt. At least, Dahlia would be happy with that. Not all the men were so lucky. My eyes drifted to one of the tigers near the tunnel entrance. Its prey was in its sight, but the man chose not to run, not to escape the way Andrew had. My breath caught in my throat when I recognized the curls.

"Milo!" I screamed, my voice being lost to the noise of the crowd.

Hundreds of men ran past him down the tunnel, but he held his ground, watching the tiger intently.

My body trembled as I willed him to run as hundreds of others had. He was standing right next to the tunnel. Why didn't he go? Tears ran down my face as I realized he was doing this for me.

"Please run!" I whispered, barely able to get the words out. I wanted Milo to win, but not like this. I never expected him to put his life on the line for me.

As the men thinned out, I was able to see more clearly. The crowd had gotten over their shock, and now they jeered and booed with as much enthusiasm as they had before. Below me, I saw my father gesturing to Jacob to follow him. Jacob's face held a stern expression as he filed past the seated people to my father. I couldn't hear what my father was saying, but it was clear by his expression that Jacob was getting balled out. I took my eyes from them. What did I care what happened to Jacob? With any luck, my father would have his men throw him over the side so he could taste a little of his own medicine.

With every man that ran past Milo into the tunnel, and with every man that clamored over the side, the ratio of men to tigers lowered. Most of the tigers were now busy shredding their catches, chewing down to the flesh and bones of the men who had dared to enter this stupid competition. Nothing was worth losing one's life over and especially not some silly competition to marry a princess. A princess that never wanted to get married in the first place.

"Get out," I shouted, but Milo couldn't hear me. How could he with the screams and shouts of twenty thousand others all shouting at the same time?

I held my breath as the tiger walked closer to him. His eyes fixed on it, but he didn't move.

"Run, you beautiful idiot," I cried, wringing my hands together in terror. Men kept running past him, but the tiger paid them no mind. He was as fixated on Milo as Milo was on him.

"That tiger's a bit close to Milo, don't you think?" Ash said.

I didn't answer. I was afraid that if I opened my mouth, I'd either scream or throw up. My stomach churned as I itched to do something, but what could I do? Not even my father could stop this madness now. As though he'd known I was thinking about him, he passed me and sat down in his throne.

"I didn't know this was going to happen," he said gruffly to me.

“Can’t you stop it?” I cried. Jacob was already walking back to his seat.

My father shook his head. I can’t. The tigers are trained to leave the arena at the sound of a whistle. That whistle will only be used when there are about a hundred men left standing in the arena. Those hundred will go on to the next part of the competition.”

“But you’re the king!” I exclaimed. “Make them sound the whistle!”

He shook his head. “I’ve spoken to Jacob. He kept this from me, but he had good reason. He says that there has been news on the grapevine that the people are ready to revolt. They are upset with the way I’ve been running the kingdom over the past few weeks. They are upset that my men have been out searching for spindles, they are upset that I built a wall to keep people off the fire mountains but did nothing to keep the dragons from coming down the mountains.”

“They are dragons. They can fly. How are you supposed to keep them from coming down? Anyway, you already knew about this. Jacob is the one who planned the revolt.”

“ Jacob set up meetings with the ringleaders in the revolt. He promised them this in exchange for keeping their peace. There is nothing more I can do. It’s out of my hands. If we do what you wanted to do and have the men answer quiz questions and make statues, we will be overthrown. If that happens, Draconis will be without a royal family to lead it, and we will not have the money needed to keep bringing doctors up here.”

“We don’t need doctors!” I screamed at him. “She is under a curse. No doctor will be able to save her. Why are you letting Jacob blackmail you? Milo is out there... Your friend Caspian is out there. “

He looked me dead in the eye, sadness clouding his expression. "I know that, but they can keep her alive until we find someone who can break this curse. I can't lose her, Azia."

My heart broke at his words, but he was putting my mother's life up in exchange for everyone's out there, including Milo's and Caspian's.

"You are sacrificing other lives for her. She would never want you to do that."

"We'll never know, will we. Not unless she wakes up." He stood from his throne and walked back down the rows of people. This time when he walked down the stairs, he never came back.

My heart pounded wildly as I turned back to the arena. Milo was gone. I stood up to get a better view as tears poured down my face. I found him. He was still in the arena, but he'd moved. Unfortunately, the tiger had moved too. It stalked around him, moving from side to side, hemming Milo in against the fence separating him from the crowd.

"Jump over the fence," I murmured, but I knew he wouldn't. He kept his back to it as the tiger drew ever closer.

It reared itself, readying to pounce, and still, Milo didn't move. There was only one way for him to go, and that was up the fence behind him, but he didn't make to turn; he just stood there.

Bile rose in my throat as I saw the one person I could ever love inches from death. I cried out again, but my voice was lost in the shrill sounding out of a whistle.

I began to breathe again as the tigers, including the one ready to pounce at Milo, turned and prowled out of the tunnel, leaving those still standing to fight another day.

"Thank you," I mouthed to whatever god was listening. I'd never been religious, but as I was putting all my trust in the fact that Morpheus existed, it stood to reason I could do the same about the other gods too. I'd pray to anyone who would listen to keep Milo safe, and now he was. The first part of the competition was over, and Milo had escaped unscathed.

As I was getting my breath back, the doors to the tunnel opened again, and a number of people with stretchers came out to pick up the injured and the dead.

"I wonder if they are disqualified if they are injured," Ash said.

I turned to him. "For their sake, I really hope they are."

This was only day one. I couldn't keep to the hope that tomorrow would bring a day of figuring out a puzzle. If Jacob had anything to do with it, things were only going to get worse.

As though my mind was being read, the tunnel doors opened again, and the men with stretchers ran from the arena as the contestants who had exited ran back in. I 'd thought that was it, that the madness was over. I couldn't have been more wrong.

I almost fainted when I saw what came out next. Where the tigers had been, now, a hundred lions took their place. They looked no less hungry and mean than the tigers, but now, there were fewer men to each lion. To make matters worse, the doors through which the men had been able to escape earlier had now closed behind them.

The screams and cheers intensified as the world spun around me.

I pulled in a huge breath and steadied myself as dizziness raged within me. If my father wouldn't deal with this, I would.

"Where are you going?" Hollis asked as I edged past him and Remy.

"I'm going to put a stop to this," I replied through gritted teeth.

Running back through the curtain, I took three steps at a time and almost barrelled into Jacob, who stood up when he saw me coming.

"Stop this. Stop it now!" I screamed at him.

"I'm afraid I can't do that, but don't worry. The crowd is loving it. It's the event of the century. People will be talking about this for years."

"I don't give a shit about the crowd," I said, eliciting a gasp from one of the other judges, a young woman in her mid-twenties who probably was the head-teacher Caspian had mentioned.

"What?" I snapped at them. "You are happy to watch innocent men being torn apart, but you get offended when a princess says shit?"

She turned berry red and moved her eyes back to the nightmare in the arena.

"There's no use talking to the judges like that," Jacob grunted. "They aren't to blame. If I remember, this whole debacle was your idea in the first place."

"Not like this, though. I was going to have them make a sculpture, and you know it."

"Now look here," he said, pushing his ugly face into mine. "No one wants to come out and watch thousands of men make a sculpture of a narcissistic princess. They are here because of this." he swept his hand out behind him. "And if they are here watching this, it means they are not planning to overthrow your father. Now, if you'd prefer, I can call the lions off, but it would mean the people will leave early and get restless. Maybe they'll go home and organize a revolution. All twenty thousand of them."

He grinned at me, knowing he'd backed me into the same corner, he'd backed my father into. But there was one difference between me and my father. I wasn't scared about being overthrown. My only fear was for Milo, who was locked in an arena with lions who wanted nothing more than to feast on his body.

"Do it!" I commanded. "Call them off. I don't care about your threats. Just put an end to this."

The smug grin left his face, but I stood tall, my hands on my hips. I wasn't going to back down.

He stamped his feet on the ground, his fists clenched by his side, but he didn't move. I ripped the whistle from around his neck, breaking the chain holding it and putting it to my lips. Before I'd had the chance to blow, another whistle sounded. Someone else had finished the competition. I turned my head to see why. There were only a hundred men left standing. A hundred men and a hundred well-fed lions. The tunnel gates opened for the last time, and the lions trooped out. I scanned the men, terror filling my very soul that I'd not find Milo, but there he was, mercifully, unscathed. Seconds later, the second wave of people with stretchers came out to mop up the mess left behind. Blood splattered the sand-covered floor, making me feel sick to my stomach. I flung Jacob's necklace back at him and hurled myself over the fence, much to the excitement of the already over-excited crowd.

Milo was much easier to see now that the men had thinned out so much. I raced across the arena to him, not caring who was watching, but before I was halfway across, someone grabbed me. It didn't matter who it was, they were stopping me from getting to Milo, and I needed to speak to him. I needed to tell him that I was wrong. I needed to tell him that I loved him.

The man holding me back turned out to be one of my father's guards. As he was much bigger than me and armed with a sword, I had no choice but to watch as Milo and the others were ushered out of the arena.

"Milo!" I screamed in frustration. I thought he saw me and turned his head to me, but just like that, he was gone. He disappeared into the tunnel with the other ninety-nine men who would have to go through this nightmare again tomorrow. As the last of the men left the arena, I caught sight of the back of Caspian's head. So he'd made it through to the next round too. I knew he would. Still, I felt a moment of unexpended relief that he was alive. Despite everything, I'd actually grown fond of the jerk.

That night, I headed straight for bed. There was no point in going to see my father, nor was there any point going to the castle's admin office. I didn't even want to know what tomorrow would bring, because nothing I could say or do would stop it. Like everything else in my life recently, I was powerless to make any change. In my room, I looked out of the window to the pasture. To the right of the arena was the huge tent where Milo would be spending the night. I wondered what was going through his mind and whether he was as scared as I was at what tomorrow would bring.

26TH JANUARY

I was in no mood for company, but I'd not eaten anything since breakfast the previous day, and my stomach was threatening to implode if I didn't eat soon. I walked wearily down to the dining room to find only Charlotte there, eating her breakfast.

"You've just missed everyone," she exclaimed. "Well, your brothers. Your father didn't come for breakfast at all."

"I bet he didn't," I said, pulling a plate toward myself and heaping it with pastries and cold meats.

"I saw that Milo got through," she said. "Caspian, too," she added.

"Yes, but how many didn't get through? How many died just for the chance to marry me? The whole thing is a crock." I slammed the butter onto the bread, spreading it so violently it made a hole in the bread.

"They knew what they were getting into," Charlotte pointed out.

"No, they didn't," I argued, though I don't know why. Charlotte had nothing to do with this. I needed to take my frustration out on someone, and she was the only one there. I pulled the Sentinel towards me and held it up so she could see. A photo of one of the men staring down a tiger filled the front page. "They printed the competition I gave them. These men thought they were going to be making a small statue." I threw the paper back down on the table where it landed on the papers from the other kingdoms. I pulled out the paper below it. The Atlantice Conch. I was on the front cover of that one. Someone had taken a photo of me being held back by the guard when I'd jumped over the fence.

I sighed and threw that one down too. I didn't even want to go through the other kingdoms' papers. The whole thing was embarrassing enough as it was. I didn't need to read about it.

"I don't suppose you know what today's competition is going to be, do you?" I asked. There wasn't a chance that my fantastic puzzle was going to be used.

"I don't know," Charlotte said, shrugging her shoulders. "I only hope it's not as brutal as yesterday. I almost had a heart attack when one of the lions ran over to Caspian. He would have gotten him too if he'd not performed a spell."

I raised my eyebrows as Charlotte brought her hand up to her mouth.

"I wasn't supposed to say that. Please don't be mad."

So Caspian was using magic. It figured. I'd put a blanket ban on all magic, but since when did Caspian listen to a word I said and followed my rules? Precisely never, that's when, and I guessed I couldn't hope for him to start now.

"Don't worry about it," I reassured her. "I don't even care anymore. I just want Milo to come out of this alive, I don't care who wins now, not even if it's Caspian. I should have married him right at the start and avoided all this."

Charlotte nodded, but I could see in her eyes that she didn't agree with me. Of course, she didn't. She wanted to marry Caspian herself. I sighed and bit into my soggy bread.

After breakfast, I waited for my father to walk me outside to the arena, but he was nowhere to be seen.

"Dahlia, do you know where my father is?" I asked impatiently.

"Actually, I do. He's asked me to walk out with you. He says he's not feeling well and not up to watching more of what happened yesterday. Not that I can blame the man. It made me sick to my stomach too."

My heart leapt into my throat. "He's not well?"

Dahlia took my hand as the doors to the castle opened. "I think he doesn't want to watch his subjects being killed. I know his situation. He's letting the competition continue because he doesn't want the kingdom to go to wrack and ruin. The competitors are collateral damage in this whole thing."

She tsked and shook her head.

"I forgot to ask you yesterday. How is Andrew?" Andrew was Dahlia's son and the light of her life.

"He's fine. Nearly wet himself yesterday when the tigers came out, though. The kid couldn't get away fast enough. I told him not to enter, but would he listen to me? Oh, no. At least, he's out of harm's way from whatever monstrosity Jacob's planned for today's entertainment. He's at home licking his wounded pride and probably eating all my homemade pies. Come on. we can't put this off any longer."

The pair of us walked out to another trumpet fanfare. As long as I lived, I'd associate the sound of trumpets with the stench of death, and I had a feeling that today was only going to cement that connection.

We walked down the same covered pathway we had done before, ending at the same staircase. I knew where to go without help, but I couldn't let Dahlia's hand go. She was my emotional crutch, and without Milo by my side, she was all I had. After climbing the stairs, I stood behind the curtains waiting for them to open. As they had yesterday, they opened, but to my surprise, the other half of the stadium was no longer there. I'd not checked out of my window this morning and so I'd not seen the massive amount of work that must have happened throughout the night. Dahlia practically dragged me to my throne as the fanfare started again. The view of the Fire Mountains took my breath away, even through the soft snowflakes that had begun to fall. Looking left and right, I could see that the stadium had been extended outwards and was now a half-oval shape open at one side. My stomach turned as I wondered what exactly this meant. What could they possibly need more space for? They'd managed to fit a thousand or so men in the arena yesterday, along with numerous lions and tigers. Today, there were only a hundred men to fit in. There was no way they were going to spend the day doing a puzzle, no matter how tricky.

"Good morning, Your Highnesses, Ladies and Gentlemen," began the ringmaster, sending the audience into silence. Beside me, Remy and Hollis looked on intently, while at the other side of my father's empty throne sat Ash. Right behind me with her hand on my shoulder, sat Dahlia. The ringmaster was back on his horse, but now, he carried an umbrella to protect him from the snow. He trotted up and down, repeating his greeting for the benefit of the people furthest away.

My nerves tightened as he came back to us. Behind him, the men left were brought out, lining up. Picking Milo out was much easier today. He was about a third of the way along the line, and when the Ringmaster introduced the men, he bowed along with everyone else. It broke my heart that he didn't look my way once. Caspian, I noticed stood right in the middle, and unlike Milo, who looked anywhere but me, had his eyes trained on mine. He gave me a wave when he saw I was looking. The rest of the men had a variety of expressions ranging from out-and-out fear to excitement of the unknown. I wondered if they'd feel so excited once this part of the competition started because I doubted all these men would return home to their families after this day was done. The organizers had done a good job of covering up the blood spilled yesterday, but it was still visible in the darker shades of sand that covered the arena floor. I only wished it would snow harder so it would cover the dark patches completely. Every one of the men carried a sword.

The ringmaster waited for the noise from the crowd to die down before speaking again.

"Today, these fine men while be whittled down from a hundred to ten. Only ten men will be able to go through to the final round to compete for the princess's hand in marriage. The rest will go home tonight with the knowledge that they had done their best but ultimately were not good enough."

Would they, though? I wondered. Would they go

home tonight, or would they end their day, lifeless in a wooden box?

A woman in a beautiful dress walked out into the open arena. She carried something in her hands that she passed to the ringmaster. It looked suspiciously like...

"This," the ringmaster said, holding the object aloft, "is a wooden egg. Ten of them have been hidden up the Fire Mountains behind me. Each has a number etched into it. The number corresponds to the order in the man finding the egg will complete tomorrow's task. In one minute exactly, I will blow a whistle, and the men will race to find these eggs and bring them back. Remember, there are only ten. They have been hidden amongst the real dragon eggs up there. Are you ready?"

Fear filled me as the hundred men readied themselves for the race. Sending a hundred men up the mountain would spoil everything I'd worked toward. The peace between the dragons and the humans was tenuous at best. This would destroy everything.

"No!" I screamed as he blew the whistle, drowning out my voice.

The men dashed to the base of the mountain at roughly the same speed I ran downstairs to confront Jacob. Two burly guards stood at each side of the judges' table, anticipating my reaction. They both stood to attention as I approached.

"What are you playing at?" I screamed at Jacob. "You can't have a hundred men going up the mountain. They'll upset the dragons."

This was his revenge for the other day when he'd not been able to kill any of the dragons, He'd done this on purpose as an excuse. Dragonfire, I hated that man.

Jacob checked that his guards were nearby before

he spoke. "So? It wouldn't be much of a competition if we buried the eggs in the snow, would it? Besides, who cares if a few dragons get killed along the way?"

All around us, the audience had stopped watching the men, and now, all eyes were on me to see what my reaction would be. I'd caused enough of a stir yesterday by jumping over the fence separating the audience from the arena floor. No doubt, everyone was wondering if I'd do the same thing again today. Thoughts of Milo getting fried and my friends Nyre, Vasuki, and Emba being hurt, spurred me into action. I turned on my heel and ran for the exit to the arena. I didn't get very far before Jacob's guards grabbed hold of me, pulling me back to Jacob.

"Princess, princess, princess," he said smugly, rubbing his hands together. "You caused a scene yesterday. I don't think your father would be happy if you did the same again today, would he?"

I gritted my teeth. "You don't care what my father wants. He wouldn't want this." I held my hand out to the base of the mountains where the competitors were running.

He gave me a smug smile. "I don't like holding you against your will so publicly, but if I tell everyone you are planning on going up the mountain, they will understand why I had to stop you. No one wants the kingdom's favorite princess to get hurt, especially so close to her wedding day."

"I'm not going up the mountain, you imbecile. I'm going to speak to my father."

I hoped he'd believe my lie. My father was no use in this, and Jacob knew it.

"Fine," he said, nodding at the guards who let me go. "Good luck. You might want to be back before nightfall.

The action will start at twilight when the men get back."

Behind him, the men had already reached the wall my father had erected. Ladders stood against it at ten feet intervals. There were only twenty or so of them, so some of the men had to wait their turn, but it took less than two minutes for every man to jump over to the other side.

Leaving Jacob and the arena behind, I raced back to the castle. It was completely deserted, thanks to the event out front. Most of the staff had been given leave to go watch the competition, which meant it was extremely easy to slip through unnoticed and out through the back garden gate to the woods. Once I was through, I used my magic to call for Nyre. I was far enough away from the stadium that she could come down the mountain and not be seen. She was small enough to pass for a large bird of prey from a distance, even if she was seen. I only hoped she'd be able to get away from the other dragons. I'd left Vasuki on good terms, but she had been hurt, and he was her father. I knew how protective my own father could be.

I didn't need to worry because she soon appeared, a little purple dot flying through the snow.

"Nyre!" I cried out when she landed on the ground beside me. "Are you ok? I'm so sorry about what Jacob did to you."

She nodded and held out her wing. There was a nip out of the very edge of it. I brought her into a quick hug. She pulled back and positioned herself as though she was about to shift.

"No," I shouted. "Stop. I need you to take me up the mountain...now!"

She must have heard the urgency in my voice because she jumped quickly onto my shoulder and pulled me into the air. My breath was lost to the bitterly cold air, and goosebumps appeared on my arms as we flew upwards.

In the distance, the crowd in the stadium cheered the men along. The sound was soon drowned out to the silence of the snowfall. We flew through the clouds to the peaks, and Nyre dropped me in the same nest I'd first come to. Only then, did she change.

"What's up?"

"We're in trouble." I wheezed as a blast of cold air hit the back of my throat. I wrapped my arms around myself to keep warm. The dress I'd put on this morning was not nearly warm enough for standing on the top of a mountain in the middle of winter. "The competition... The castle admin staff...Jacob has had fake eggs planted up here. There are a hundred men on their way up here now to take them back."

Nyre's eyes widened. "They can't. Our eggs are up here. How did they even get them into our nests in the first place?"

"I don't know. They did it last night under the cover of darkness. I need to see your father. He needs to be made aware."

Nyre shook her head violently. "No. He'll freak out. He's been patient, but he won't like this. You promised him that no one would come up the mountain. You've promised him a few times, Azia."

"I know I did," I said, feeling sick to my stomach. "I didn't ask them to come up. I tried to stop it, but I can't. They are already on their way. Can't we just fly around the nests and collect the real dragon eggs and take them down to your village? Even if it's just for a few hours."

I already knew her answer. I'd asked Vasuki the

same thing, but I was clutching at straws.

She folded her arms and glared at me. I could understand her anger at me. I deserved it. ever since I'd first journeyed up the Fire Mountain, there'd been nothing but trouble.

"No. The eggs have to be up here. They are too fragile to move, and I can't risk it. Besides, the mothers of each egg will be roosting on them, keeping them warm. Do you want to explain to them that we need to endanger their children's lives for some stupid human competition?"

She stamped her foot in the snow. At any other time, the gesture would look adorable on her, but now, it broke my heart and sent me into a panic.

"I'm sorry."

"Look. No point saying sorry," she huffed. "We need to fix this, and we need to do it quickly before my father finds out."

I thought for a moment.

"We need to figure out how castle staff got the eggs up here. If you say that the mothers are protecting the nests, how, in all the kingdoms, would they have been able to get the fake eggs in there? Are there many other empty nests like this one?"

Nyre shook her head impatiently. "No. This is the only one. The rest are occupied. I guess they might have got the fake eggs in while the mothers were feeding?"

I took a deep breath and considered my options. I didn't really have any. Either we tell Vasuki and start a war or get those eggs before the hundred men climbed to the top of the mountain. Neither option sounded promising, especially seeing as I was already freezing cold from the weather.

"Ok," I said, coming up with a plan. "We have time

on our side. It's a five-hour climb to the mountain tops. These men will probably be faster than me, so we can lower it to four. The weather might slow them down, but I don't want to factor that in and be wrong. Let's aim to get those wooden eggs in the next four hours. We'll get each one while the mother is feeding. You can fly me down, and we can throw each one at the men, so hopefully, they'll see that they don't have to go up the mountain any further."

Nyre glared at me as though I was insane, and I probably was.

"You want to steal eggs from the dragon mother's nests? Do you know how insane that sounds? You might think Darius is an angry fellow, but let me tell you, he's nothing to a mother dragon. They are fierce!"

I nodded. "I'm aware of the insanity of the situation, but to sit back and watch everyone getting hurt would be much worse. I'm doing this, Nyre, with or without your help. I'd prefer with..."

I could have compelled her to do it, but I needed her to make the decision on her own.

I waited for her to decide. Finally, she wavered. "Okay, but we can't touch any of the real eggs. They might be dragons, but they are babies, and they are precious."

"Agreed, "I said, throwing her a smile. I'd never taken her to be the motherly type, and here she was, clucking over some eggs.

When I'd come up with the plan, I'd thought we'd easily be able to fly from nest to nest, grabbing each wooden egg and hurling it down the mountain. What I hadn't counted on was the fact that none of these dragon mamas were hungry. They paid us no mind as we flew over their heads. I was no threat to them, and neither was Nyre, or so they all thought. And yet, none of them moved.

"Can't we just ask them to move for some other reason?" I shouted up to Nyre when we were out of earshot of the dragons. Nyre couldn't speak to me in her dragon form, but she didn't need words to convey the message. She shook her head and glared at me again. So we waited....and waited...and waited. If I used my magic to force them to move, they would fly straight down to the village and tell Vasuki the second the spell broke. Just as I had let Nyre do things her own way, so I had to wait for the mama dragons.

"Why aren't they moving?" I whined a few hours later. I could no longer feel my toes; I was that cold, and flying around in the talons of a dragon was not making the situation any better. I'd just about given up on the whole thing when the first dragon took off into the air. She soared away majestically, her lemon yellow wings out fully as she skimmed the mountain tops, thankfully, in the opposite direction to the men coming up the mountain on the other side. This had been something else I'd thought about in the hours I'd been pointlessly flying around. What if one of the dragon mamas decided to go and find food at this side of the mountain? I didn't know what they ate, but judging by the bones left in the nests I'd seen, I was guessing they survived on a diet of mountain goat and the odd cow. Now while they'd have to fly further afield for a cow, there were plenty of mountain goats on the side of the mountain facing the castle. I tried putting the thought from my mind as Nyre swooped me lower towards the empty nest.

Finding the wooden egg was easy. Despite it being practically the same size as the other eggs, it was smooth in texture and not mottled like the others. Also, it was made out of wood and had the number seven engraved on it. As Nyre dangled me above it, I pulled it out slowly, careful not to disrupt any of the other eggs. It came out nicely, and Nyre was able to fly me down the mountain. The clouds were low in the sky, so the arena below us was hidden. I couldn't help but think that it must be very boring to watch from the ground when all anyone would be able to see was clouds. Not that Jacob cared. He spoke of spectacle and excitement, but he just wanted the dragons dead so he didn't have to send his men out to build any more wall, that and the fact that without the dragons around, he'd be able to come up later and steal the real dragon eggs without a fight.

It was both good and bad. The men were still below the cloud line, which meant that none of them could see what I was up to. This was good because they wouldn't head back down the mountain and tell Jacob, just for him to send more men up to fight. It was also bad because I couldn't see them and if I couldn't see them, it meant Nyre couldn't see them either. If we waited for the men to climb above the cloud, we'd run out of time. As it was, the hours of time I thought we had to collect the eggs were quickly decreasing, thanks to the mother dragons.

Nyre dipped into the clouds. Instantly, the coldness I felt worsened as dampness was added to the mix.

As she flew, I scanned the ground for any of the men. Finally, we saw one. I didn't recognize him, but he looked extremely fit. I whistled loudly, and as he looked up, I threw the egg at him. He caught it and gazed down at it as though he couldn't believe his luck. When he thought enough to look to see where it had come from, Nyre and I were already up through the clouds.

Over the course of two hours, we managed to collect seven more of the wooden eggs easily. Much more easily than I had first thought. Each time we grabbed one, it was thrown to one lucky man who could then turn around and march home. With each egg we threw, the men climbed higher and higher up the mountain, and with it, the fear that we might not make it. My plan was to tell all the men that there were no eggs left once they broke through, but as I threw the eighth egg, it was beginning to look like it wasn't true. The last two mothers were still sitting comfortably upon their nests and not looking like they planned to move any time soon. All I could do was watch impatiently, waiting for the first man to break through the clouds and get to him before the other dragons saw him. My nerves were frayed by the time the ninth dragon finally left her roost to feed. Nyre sprinted to the nest, but I could see we'd left it too late. The men were already appearing through the cloud just fifty meters or so below us.

I hurled the ninth egg down to them, hoping one would catch it, but once they saw what it was, they made a dash for it. I counted fifteen of them brawling for the egg on a precarious ledge.

"Do something!" I screamed to Nyre, but what could she do? She was tiny and had been working enough to haul me about all morning. If she flew down to them, the surprise would surely topple them from the edge.

And then, that wasn't my problem anymore.

As I'd been watching on with horror at the men fighting over the egg, I'd taken my eyes from the tenth dragon. She was way off in the distance, and so I'd paid her no mind, but it was hard to ignore the sharp blast of fire erupting from her mouth.

Nyre swerved around towards her before I had the

chance to ask her. When she flew, it was almost like we were one. She understood where I wanted to go instinctively, and I knew where she was going. It might have been something to do with the dragon magic I held. Not that it was going to be much help now. I could summon the dragons. If I summoned the mother dragon to me, she would be compelled to come. It would save the lives of the men I could see climbing up the mountain below her, but it wouldn't save anything else. She would report me to Vasuki, and I'd have all the dragons out on the mountain.

"Stop!" I demanded of the men below her. The ones that were still alive. The charred remains of two of the men smoked on the mountain, and the smell of burned flesh filled the air. My stomach churned as I tried to keep my composure.

Nyre dropped me to the ground roughly halfway between the dragon and the charred bodies. with my fingers crossed that the dragon wouldn't flame me, I addressed the men. I shouted loud enough so the men fighting over the ninth egg could hear too.

"There is only one egg left. I've been throwing them to the men who beat you up here. This dragon behind me holds the last one, but if any of you step closer, I will ask her to flame you all alive."

Behind me, I could hear the beat of Nyre's wings as she hovered between me and the mama dragon.

"Go back down the mountain. I will not have you harm this dragon or any other. This is a mother protecting her young. As the Princess of Draconis, I command it."

I stood tall, as the men wavered. Some turned to leave, but almost as soon as I thought I'd diffused the situation, some of the men charged me. All hell broke loose as the men that had joined a competition to marry me were now scrambling towards me with their swords out. I was above them. If I had my sword and it was one on one, I could have beaten them easily. As it was, I had no sword, was wearing a dress, and couldn't feel my own fingers. More than ten chased toward me. As the first one reached me, I kicked out, sending him reeling down the mountain. The scream he emitted as he fell through the clouds would haunt me, but I had no time to worry. Another one was rapidly approaching. I fumbled backward, climbing up the mountain to get away from him. But I was heading toward a much more deadly foe. The mother dragon had been watching with interest, but as I turned to her, I could see the nervousness in her eyes. She wasn't scared to kill. She was a dragon . It was in her nature. She was scared to kill me. The Queen of Dragons. I was the one getting between her and the men she thought wanted to steal her babies.

I had no choice. The men had made their decision and would have to suffer the consequences. I couldn't save them now.

"Go!" I pleaded with them one last time as I stepped aside to let the dragon breath flames down the mountain.

And then something happened that had me rooted to the spot. Milo appeared below them . If I moved now, Milo would be killed alongside these strangers. Milo, who was only in this competition for me despite the fact he thought I was dating Caspian.

My heart lurched as I watched him climb around the other men, but it was too late. He wouldn't be able to save any of us.

A flash of purple caught my eye as Nyre flew down the mountain and plucked him up in her talons. She dropped him beside me as the first man caught hold of my ankle.

"Don't you dare touch her," he screamed, bringing his foot down hard on the man's hand. The man screamed and let go, dropping his sword before falling ten feet or so below us. Milo drew his sword and faced the men.

"If one of you lays a finger on her or even thinks about harming this dragon or her eggs, I'll kill you all. With my bare hands if I have to."

But he didn't have to. He had his sword, and he was above them. He had every advantage. I watched on as he fought them one by one. A couple were picked off by Nyre, who dodged their swords and flung them down the mountain. Behind me, the dragon mother bellowed. I turned to see one of the men climbing into her nest. The fear in the eyes of the dragon was obvious. She wanted to kill this man, but indecision had her rooted to the spot.

"Kill him!" I shouted out. She didn't have to breathe fire. She could chew his head off or swipe him with her talons. But I could see that what was stopping her was her eggs. She didn't want to move for fear of trampling them. As I watched, another man pulled himself up into her nest, spurred on by the bravery of the first and the fact that the dragon was stock still, paralyzed with fear.

If she couldn't do anything, I could. I picked up the sword dropped by the man earlier and sprinted upwards while Nyre and Milo fought the men below.

They were coming thick and fast now, more of them emerging from the cloud, eager to fight it out over the remaining wooden egg.

"I'm here to help you," I said to the terrified dragon. She nodded with tears in her eyes. If only people understood that dragons were not the terrifying creatures they were made out to be as long as they were not provoked.

I patted her snout then turned towards the men. They'd both seen the wooden egg and were approaching it quickly. I ran towards them, my sword out ahead of me. I'd trained my whole life for this moment. The first went down quickly. He'd not expected the princess to fight him and so had not defended when 'd stabbed him right in his heart. He died with an expression of shock on his face. The second had a couple more seconds to ready himself, and so I had to be better. I had to be better than him because this was a fight to the death, and we both knew it. He didn't care that I was the princess, nor the prize in this stupid competition anymore. His focus was on winning, and that was all that mattered. I fought bravely, but he was good. I struggled to attack and could only defend. It wasn't helping that I couldn't feel my hands, and the cold weather combined with the ridiculous dress slowed me down. I moved backward with each thrust of his sword. He hesitated for a second, and I managed to get a swipe in, but he was quick to regain his momentum and attacked again. My back struck the edge of the nest. This was it. I kill him, or he would kill me. I defended each of his attacks, but with my hands being numb, I couldn't move as quickly as I would like. He reached back and swiped my sword right out of my hand, leaving me weaponless and hopeless.

I pressed my back into the edge of the nest and waited for death to come. This was it. I closed my eyes and waited, but then the sound of crunching bones had me opening them. I heaved as I saw the sight before me. A pair of bloody legs stood in front of me, the torso and head ripped from them. The legs fell over as I caught sight of the dragon having a fine feast of warrior torso for dinner. I heaved then threw up over the side.

Behind me, something grabbed me and hoisted me into the air. At first, I thought it was the dragon, but then I realized it was only Nyre. She plucked me from the nest and began the flight back to the castle. As we descended the mountain, I got a peek at the other dragons approaching the nest of the tenth dragon from the other side of the mountain. Hundreds of them. I recognized Vasuki at the front.

"Stop!" I murmured, but it was too late. She usually obeyed my wishes, but I was too tired and cold to shout louder. She was ignoring me anyway. My dragon magic was at an all-time low, and I had nothing left in me to give. She didn't drop me at the back of the woods, but in the castle garden, before flying off again.

"Stop!" I shouted again. "Milo is up there. The dragon mama!" She ignored me and disappeared into the clouds as the world began to spin. I fell to the ground only vaguely aware that some of the castle staff had run out to me.

I awoke hours later in my own bed. "As soon as my eyes fluttered open, Dahlia shouted to someone to bring me soup. One of the castle staff must have run to pass on the message because she closed the door and ran over to my bed."

"I've been so worried. You silly girl. What did you think you were doing?"

"Milo?" I croaked.

Just then there was a knock at the door. As Dahlia was busy fending off whoever was at my door, I used the opportunity to jump out of bed and check the scene from my bedroom window. From this distance, I couldn't see much, but the low level of light told me I'd been out for hours. Torches lit the arena in the dim twilight. Without looking back, I opened the window and standing on the ledge, compelled Nyre to come and get me. Behind me, I heard a commotion and the clattering of a bowl on the stone floor. A quick look back told me Dahlia had seen what I was up to. The clattering was my soup. She dashed toward me, followed quickly by a kitchen servant and Jack. As though everything was happening in slow motion, I leapt outward as Dahlia reached the window. Her fingers brushed my ankle, but it was too late. I was already falling toward the cobbles in the courtyard below.

Dahlia's scream filled the night. Inches above the courtyard, Nyre swooped in as I'd known she would and pulled me into the air.

I'd known she would catch me in time. We were so in tune with each other that leaping from my bedroom window was not the feat of insanity it must have appeared to be to anyone watching.

I'd expected Nyre. What I hadn't expected was a fleet of dragons following in her wake. We flew through the air, Nyre and I in the lead with a V-shape of dragons behind us. So much for Vasuki not finding out.

Nyre swooped into the arena.

The men that had already managed to get back scattered as we came to land amid a wave of screams and commotion.

As we landed, only three men ran in our direction. My father, Jacob, and Milo.

Milo ran straight for me, sweeping me off my feet and spinning me around much to the delight of the crowd.

As tears dripped down my face, Milo kissed me. The audience loved it, judging by the oohs and aahs that now took over from the screams of before. My whole world came to a standstill as a wave of happiness overcame me. Someone in the crowd began to clap, quickly followed by others until, like a peal of thunder, the sound engulfed us, surrounded us until, like the beating of my heart, that's all there was. Just Milo and I and the thunderous applause of twenty thousand people, telling me that I'd been right all along. I wanted Milo.

As he pulled away, the grin on his face made me laugh, and my tears turned to tears of happiness.

"Kill them!" Jacob screamed to his men, taking me out of my moment of euphoria. He raised his sword, aiming at the long row of dragons that lined the edge of the arena floor.

"No man and no dragon will die here tonight." My father said, stepping in front of him.

My father looked up and addressed the crowd. Now that they had seen my father, the crowd became silent, eager to see what would happen next.

I held my breath as Vasuki walked forward. As he walked, he shifted into his half-human form. The audience gave a collective gasp when they saw him change. He walked to my father and held out his hand. This time my father shook it.

"This is my friend, Vasuki," My father shouted out to the people. "He and his kind are welcome in Draconis, the kingdom named after them. There will be no more killing. From this moment on, The Fire Mountains are prohibited to all humans by decree of the king. Anyone caught up there without permission from Vasuki or anyone caught with a dragon egg will be punished to the highest degree of the law."

"You can't do that!" Jacob yelled, holding his sword up to Vasuki. "As the king, you can put forward a law, but it has to go through Urbis to get it passed. It could take months. Until then, I am legally allowed to do what I want regarding the dragons."

"That's true," my father answered, pulling his sword, "but you'll have to come through me."

He swiped at Jacob's sword, knocking it away from Vasuki. The crowd went wild, never having seen their king fight before. I held my breath as Jacob lunged at my father. Neither man was wearing armor, and one thrust to the abdomen would kill either one of them. Milo gripped my hand tightly to stop me from running between the fighting men. I guess he knew me too well because, despite the fact I had no sword and was wearing only my nightgown, that's exactly what I wanted to do.

My father was more skilled than I had anticipated. He blocked Jacob's thrusts, parrying and thrusting with his own sword. I could only watch on with bated breath as they danced around each other, fighting in a whirl of speed and flair.

The noise of the crowd increased, and over the deafening roar, I could just make out Remy's voice shouting, Dad!

My father seemed the stronger of the two, but he mistimed his step and fell, allowing Jacob to hold his sword to my father's neck. Milo's grip on my hand loosened as the crowd booed Jacob. I ran toward them, unsure of what to do. Jacob's face was contorted with rage, and he knew as well as I did that he would have to kill my father or lose face. A lifetime in prison awaited him if he carried out the murder of the king, but he was too far gone to stop now. He pulled his sword back, ready to strike, and at that moment, he flew into the air, carried by a dragon with yellow scales. Kuda flew up through the clouds as a cheer erupted through the crowd. I held out my hand and pulled my father up into a standing position.

"The men have been picked," my father addressed the audience. "I think today has been eventful enough. We will see you all back here tomorrow for the final round. Goodnight."

He waved with one hand , taking my hand in his other one. Milo raced over and took my free hand. What did any of us care anymore who knew that I loved Milo? I didn't care. We had only one night left to be together, and I was going to make the most of it.

27TH JANUARY

Milo's soft breathing beside me told me that yesterday hadn't just been a wonderful dream. No one had stopped us when we'd walked hand in hand to my room, and though the guard outside had tried, my father had told him to leave us alone.

A small knock on the door had Milo stir, but he didn't awaken. I had a curse on my lips for Dahlia for waking us up. She knew Milo was here. She must have. But when I opened the door, it was only Jack with the morning's breakfast on a tray.

"Dahlia asked me to give these to you," he said gruffly. "She said you might not want to come down for breakfast, so she had it brought up."

He eyed me suspiciously as he handed the tray over.

On it were two plates of cold meats and cheese, along with two croissants and a pot of jam. Two cups of coffee and the morning papers took up the rest of the tray. He tried looking over my shoulder to see who was with me, but I managed to close the door before he saw his precious work-mate in my bed. It would blow the poor man's mind, although if he'd had bothered to check the papers on the tray he'd have seen the pair of us kissing on the very front page. I stifled a grin as I thanked him and took the tray, closing the door firmly behind him.

I looked at the front covers of the Draconian Sentinel on the top as I placed the tray on my side of the bed. It was the second time in a week that they'd posted a photo of me kissing someone. I was becoming quite the scandal! Putting the Sentinel to one side, I checked out the covers of the other kingdoms' newspapers. Most had the same or a similar photo with the story of my competition. I was becoming famous in all the other kingdoms. The only cover not to feature me was the Atlantice Conch. It had a story about how things were beginning to change, about a shift in the energy in the water. It felt horribly familiar. I threw the papers down, not really caring. I had better things to think about.

Milo opened his eyes as I slid back into the warm bed beside him. Thankfully, I'd rested the tray beside me because he brought me toward him, catching me in a kiss. My heart beat in triple time as his lips lingered upon mine, and my body danced a whirl as he pulled me closer, our bodies touching.

Last night had been about new beginnings, new feelings, and new experiences. Experiences I desperately needed to feel again, feel for the last time with Milo, because in a few short hours, the last day of the competition would begin.

"I wish this could last forever," Milo said, threading his fingers through mine.

His words were bittersweet. It couldn't last forever. At worst, we had hours; at best, we might be able to sneak time before the wedding. We'd wasted so much time, and now my wedding was almost upon us. A wedding which Milo would definitely not be a part of. He was out of the competition. He'd not managed to bring back an egg. At least, Caspian hadn't managed it either, I'd not even seen him up on the mountain. Not that I cared anymore. I was going to have to marry someone and that someone wasn't Milo. It would be a stranger. Someone I didn't know and had likely only met briefly. It didn't bear thinking about.

"Don't think about it," Milo said as though he could read my mind. "We have some time together. I promise that I won't leave your side for any of it, and when the day comes for you to get married, I'll step back and let you get on with your life."

"What do you mean?"

"I'm going to The Forge and live with my mom."

Tears streamed down my face as I took in his words. I knew it had to happen even before he said it, but hearing it out loud made it all the more real. He was right to go. I wouldn't have been able to bear him being so close to me in the castle while I pretended to be happily married to someone else. It would be impossible for him too. Milo kissed away every tear, and as the tray fell to the floor with a crash, sending cold coffee all over the floor, he pulled me back to him.

The urgency in his touch was apparent. Where last night, he'd traced my skin, giving me goosebumps as we'd taken our sweet time getting to know each other's touch, now with the promise of the competition starting soon, time was a luxury we didn't have. Despite my hope that we might be able to snatch a few secret hours before the wedding next week, it was unlikely. I would need to concentrate on my new fiancée. I blocked it all out as Milo crushed his lips to mine, obliterating every thought. I pressed my body to his and surrendered myself to beautiful oblivion.

~

Light poured into the room filtering through the gauzy curtains, signaling the end of our time together. I kissed Milo softly on the forehead, tasting the salty taste of sweat from our exertions.

"I have to get up," I sighed, glancing at the brightening sky, just peeking through my curtains. "I have to go to the competition. " I'd put it off as long as I could, but the sound of the general hustle and bustle of the castle had been going on for a while, and I knew it wouldn't be long before Dahlia came to fetch me.

Milo didn't stop me climbing out of bed, though the pain in his eyes almost broke my heart. Today was the day I would finally meet my husband to be. I tried not to think about it as I pulled on a dress from my wardrobe. I didn't have Dahlia to help me today, so I picked a dress I thought she might choose and pulled my hair into a high ponytail. The dress I was willing to do, but I wasn't going to spend hours on hair and makeup. My husband to be would just have to take me as I was. He had the advantage of knowing who I was to begin with. I didn't even know that about him.

As I stepped to my door, Milo took hold of my hand.

"You can't come out into public with me," I reminded him. The whole kingdom would see us on the cover of the newspaper this morning, but I couldn't be seen with him again. It wouldn't be fair to the competition winner

"I know," he replied softly, "but I'll be with you every step of the way until then."

I gave him a sad smile as I squeezed his hand. Our time together had been so brief, and it had almost run out. So many regrets ran through my mind as I opened the bedroom door, but sleeping with Milo wasn't one of them. I only wished I'd done it earlier... wished I'd spent more time with him. Jack's face was a picture when he saw who was with me. I gave him a smile and was just about to say something when there was a tap on my window. I turned to see Nyre flapping her wings outside. Running to her, I opened the window. With a wink, she dropped something heavy at my feet before once again taking to the sky. I looked down to find a wooden egg. The same wooden egg I'd protected against the two men in the nest the day before.

"Of course! There was an egg left." I whispered as I picked it up and showed Milo.

"You're still in!" I squealed, jumping up and down.

Milo caught my excitement. "I'll win this thing, Azia. I'll win it for us." He brought his lips to mine, and for the first time since this infernal competition started, I thought I might actually begin to enjoy it.

"You'd better hurry up, lad," Jack said. "They competitors have already been called out."

Milo gave me a grin and took off down the corridor, the egg in his hands.

I found my father in the entrance hall waiting for me to go out with him.

"I'm so proud of you, Azia," he said, taking my hand. "Whatever happens today, I want you to know that."

My heart swelled as I stepped outside. It was too

late for my father to call this thing off now, but I knew in my gut that Milo would win. He was an amazing swordsman and the only member of my father's guard to have entered. He was taught by the best, and he'd practiced endlessly with me. Now that Caspian was out of the competition, I had every faith that Milo had it in the bag.

Happiness flowed through me as my father and I ascended the stairs. When the curtain was pulled back, we both headed to our thrones. My brothers were there exactly as they had been for the past two days, with Remy next to me and Ash next to my father. Hollis sat next to Remy, and beyond him, Dahlia sat, giving me a mischievous wink as I passed.

The crowd roared as the ten winners from yesterday were brought onto the field.

Milo came on first, waving at the crowd as though he didn't have a care in the world. In his hand, he carried the egg that Nyre had brought to us, not ten minutes before. A roar filled the arena as he held the wooden egg into the air. He'd gone from a nobody to the kingdom's favorite. The crowd wanted him to win as much as I did. Another nine men trooped out and took their place beside him. Not one of them got the same reaction from the crowd as Milo had. Each of them carried an egg. I scrutinized them one by one as they stood in line. Never had I seen a meaner bunch of men, each burlier than the last. It was only when I came to the last man in line that I let out a gasp of surprise.

"What's Caspian doing here?" I whispered to my father. I was sure he'd not gotten an egg the day before.

"He fought one of the men coming down the mountain with an egg," my father explained as the men took a bow.

Now that Caspian was back in the game, my excitement faded. He was a great swordsman. I'd never once beaten him. I consoled myself with the fact it wasn't me having to fight him. It was Milo, and Milo had beaten him that one time.

The ringmaster lined them up in the order of the numbers on the eggs.

"Today, a new prince will be picked. A man fit to marry the Princess Azia. These ten men have bravely fought tigers and lions and dragons for her hand in marriage. Today, they will only have to fight each other. Each man will be paired up with another. When we have a victor in each pair, the winner will move on to the next round, with the winner being the only man left standing. There are only two ways to win. If your partner dies or if your partner holds his hand up in submission, thus taking himself out of the competition. We will keep going until there is only one man left. Now that you've seen the men, we will have an intermission while they put on their armor. We don't want to make it too easy. While you wait, please welcome the Draconis Opera."

The men walked off as some singers came into the arena. The opera was amazing, but my mind was on other things. Namely Milo and Caspian. I didn't care about the others. I didn't think they would win, but in an ironic twist of fate, it had come down to the two men it had started with. Like it or not, this time next week, I was going to be married to one of them. I just didn't know which one.

Two men came onto the arena floor as the main singer finished her aria. They were covered head to toe in armor, so it was difficult to see who they were. The ringmaster stood them five feet apart and instructed them to draw their swords. My heart was in my mouth as he blew his whistle, and the men began to fight. I knew both Milo's and Caspian's style, which meant I thought that neither of these men was either of them. I wasn't a hundred percent confident, though, and as the first man was brought to the ground, I held my breath. He held his hand up, and the ringmaster blew his whistle. When the fallen man was unmasked, I saw I'd been right. He wasn't either of them. After being helped up by the ringmaster, he walked off, leaving the masked winner in the arena

Two more men came in, and once again, they began to fight. One of these I recognized. When the whistle had been blown, one of them jumped forward, thrusting mercilessly. I knew in my heart this was Caspian. His opponent was quick to raise his hand.

Two men down, and both Caspian and Milo were still in the game.

Caspian took his place next to the victor of the first round. Another two were brought out to fight. Both of them were useless, running around each other rather than attacking, so their round went on much longer than the two rounds before. There was no way either of them was Milo. Half an hour later, the crowd began to get restless, and the two men had barely touched swords. The booing started, spurring one into action. He thrust his sword forward, piercing the chainmail of the arm of his opponent. When he saw the blood seeping off his sword, he put his hand up in submission. The guy who was bleeding won the round by default. Once the first man had been unmasked, the second fell to the floor. A stretcher came to carry him off, and the ringmaster declared him out of the competition too. Which left four more men to come. I gripped the edge of my seat as the next two men walked on.

"Milo!" I whispered. I knew in my heart it was him. I recognized his sword.

His fight terrified me more than any other, but that was because it was him. His opponent was better than the last two, but in the end, he was no match for Milo. He raised his hand.

"We have only one more round to go before lunch," the ringmaster announced. "And I've just been informed that our opponent with the wound will make a full recovery. He's up at the castle getting stitches. He's said he wants to continue the competition, so he will be back this afternoon."

Some of the crowd booed. His fight had been boring, but he was up against different men now, and there was no way it was going to be dull.

The last two came on and fought well. They were also evenly matched, but they gave a much better performance than the two who barely hit each other. I watched them closely, noting their weaknesses and where Milo would be able to beat them. Eventually, one gave up, putting his hand up in the air.

When the fifth man was unmasked, the ringmaster turned to the audience.

"Ladies and gentlemen. I'm sure you are all enjoying the show, but we are giving everyone a break. The king has thoughtfully provided food for everyone outside the arena. we'll have half an hour break and be back for the thrilling conclusion!"

"Oh, ay?" Remy asked as we all trooped downstairs to where the food was being served.

"I'm fine, Remy," I said, giving him a hug. "I just wish I'd not started this competition. I only did it to get out of marrying Caspian."

"Ca-pia!" Remy grinned, holding out a pretend sword and waving his hand around.

"Has Caspian been teaching you sword fighting?" I asked. Remy nodded enthusiastically.

Maybe I'd misjudged Caspian. I'd seen him once play-sword-fighting with Remy, but I'd thought it was for the benefit of my mother. I hadn't realized that he'd kept it up since mother was asleep.

"I'm glad he's been nice to you, Remy. I still don't want to marry him, though."

Remy seemed to understand, well, as much as Remy could understand anything. Still, he was the only one who'd picked up on my frayed nerves.

I grabbed a sandwich and a cup of juice from the massive spread. The kitchen staff had outdone themselves with the massive spread. Even with help from an outside catering company, I don't know how they managed to fix so much food. I barely had time to take a bite before we were all told to head back into the stands.

I munched down on my sandwich in a very un-princess like manner as I took my seat and the ringmaster and the five competitors walked back in.

"Ladies and Gentlemen, Your Majesty and Your Highnesses," the ringmaster began, "welcome back to the final round in the princess competition. This afternoon will work a little differently to this morning. Now, we are going to have the remaining men fighting together. On my whistle, they will fight. The last one standing or to not raise his hand will win the hand of our princess. Good luck, everyone." He blew his whistle, and the men drew their swords. My eyes were only on Milo. I didn't care about any of the others. I watched as he started off strong, jumping right into the middle of the other four. Then everything was a blur. I knew Caspian was good, but the other three were strong competitors too. Two of them fought each other as the third, a very tall gentleman, thrust his sword at the pair of them. I turned my eyes back to Milo, watching him like a hawk as he fought Caspian, then one of the others. It seemed none of them was going to go down quickly. I'd underestimated how good the competition could be. One of the men eventually went down, brought down I thought by Caspian. He raised his hand, and the fighting was paused long enough to pull his helmet off and for him to walk out of the arena.

I kept my eyes on Milo as he once again fought Caspian. It was hard not to stand up and publicly root for Milo, but I was a princess and supposed to be impartial, despite that I'd spent the night with one of the contestants.

They were magnificent together, and although I couldn't shout for Milo, it didn't stop Charlotte screaming her lungs out for Caspian. She didn't want him to win. That would mean marriage to me, but she was caught up in the excitement of the moment, and I guess she didn't want him getting hurt. Neither did I if I was going to be honest. I'd kind of gotten used to his special brand of smugness, and though it wasn't to my taste, I didn't want to see him leave on a stretcher.

Milo was just that bit better than Caspian. I was practically bouncing in my seat as they fought. It was thrilling, and the crowd was eating it up. As Milo went for the final strike that would bring Caspian to his knees, one of the other competitors ran forward and barrelled Milo to the floor. Caspian turned to the fourth man, the tall one, as the one who'd pushed Milo down rained blow after blow down on him. The clang of metal upon metal thundered through my ears.

"Put your hand up, Milo!" I screamed. So much for being impartial. But my voice was lost in the noise of the crowd.

"Stop it!" I begged my father, but there was nothing he could do. Unless Milo raised his hand, he was still in the competition, and while he was still in, the competition would go on. The man stomped down upon Milo's leg and continued to kick and hit him. Without thinking, I stood up and raced out of the stand. If no one else was going to stop this, then I would. I raced past Hollis and down to the bottom of the stand. I knew where the men got ready. They had a separate tent. There was no one there to stop me.

I pulled on one of the suits of armor and a helmet quickly and selected one of the swords. I'd have preferred my own sword, but beggars couldn't be choosers, and I didn't have the time to run back to my room and pick it up.

The crowd roared as I raced onto the arena floor. No one could possibly know it was me, but they would know a new competitor had walked onto the field. Caspian was busy with the fourth competitor, so I raced to Milo. His armor was dented with the force of the blows from the other man. Blood blossomed on the weak spots in his armor, the places where chainmail covered the joints.

Anger surged through me as I charged the man, knocking him away from Milo. He soon got over his shock and began to thrust his own sword. I ducked quickly as he swung his sword at me, missing me by inches. The crowd gasped as I thrust again, catching the metal of his breastplate. The sound of the ringmaster rang through my ears as he began narrating the action.

"Ladies and gentlemen, we have a new fighter. I don't even know who it is, but they are good. They are amazing. Look at these two go."

I tried blocking him out as I concentrated on my opponent, matching his speed and skill. His sword caught my arm, sending reverberations through the suit of armor, but I wasn't going to go down that easily. I thrust back as the ringmaster spoke again.

"And we have one more out of the competition."

In my peripheral vision, I saw two men with stretchers come for Milo. His hand was raised in submission. He was out of the competition.

Seeing him lifted onto the stretcher only caused my anger to intensify. There was no way I was going to marry some lout who cheated by kicking and stomping on his opponent. I thrust forward, and he began to topple. When he hit the ground, I held my sword to an exposed piece of flesh of his neck.

He raised his hand, and the crowd went wild. The whistle blew, and the ringmaster came running over. The man's helmet was pulled off. I didn't know the man, but I recognized him as one of the men fighting over the eighth egg on the mountain the day before. Looking around, I saw that Caspian had defeated his foe too. Caspian's sword was still sticking out of his chest. It had pierced right through the metal. The ringmaster ran over as I pulled my helmet off. It was over. Caspian was the winner. the crowd went insane as I bounded over to Milo's stretcher that was still on the field.

"Oh my goodness," the ringmaster said, losing his shit entirely. "Ladies and gentlemen, the fighter was the princess herself. I've never seen anything like this before!"

I ignored everything else he said and the thundering

noise of the crowd as I spoke to Milo. I held his hand.

“I’m sorry,” I said.

“I’m not,” he replied, his face white as a sheet. “I would do this a hundred times for you. I only wish I could have won.”

“It doesn’t matter,” I whispered back to him, tears falling down my face.” I only care that you are ok.”

“I think he’s got a broken leg, at the very least,” one of the men with the stretcher informed me. “We need to get him urgent medical care.”

I nodded. A broken leg sucked, but it was survivable. Behind me, I barely registered the ringmaster announcing that Caspian’s opponent was dead. What I couldn’t miss was the wail from Caspian. The men with the stretcher began the walk back to the castle as I turned to Caspian. His face was a picture of utter misery. All around me, the crowd went silent, and a thrill of fear passed through me.

Almost in slow motion, I looked down to Caspian’s opponent. Looking sightlessly up to the sky was my baby brother. I screamed as I remembered the ringmaster’s words. Remy had sacrificed his life for me.

28TH JANUARY

"I didn't know it was him," Caspian cried, cradling Remy's head. Tears streamed down his face, falling into Remy's hair.

My first thought was how weird Caspian seemed without the smug expression he usually wore.

Somewhere behind me, a bell rang twelve. It was already midnight, but time stood still.

I was vaguely aware of the ringmaster telling everyone that the competition was over, and the results would be posted in the Draconian Sentinel tomorrow, but it was already tomorrow, so did he mean today or the day after?

None of my thoughts turned to Remy. They couldn't, because if what I was looking at was real, if I put any thought into it at all, then that would mean he was dead. Really dead, and he couldn't be. Not my beautiful, sweet, innocent brother.

As the world came crashing down around me, and all I could see was the anguish on Caspian's face, another voice permeated the fog.

"Why was he out here?" My father rushed over to Remy, beating the medics who were half a second behind him.

"He was out here for me." The last thing I'd said to him was that I didn't want to marry Caspian. Somehow Remy had decided to wade in and fight for me knowing that if he won, I wouldn't have to get married at all. He was dead because of me.

The crowd filed out of the stadium in silence as the medics removed Remy's armor and pulled the sword from his chest. They didn't need to confirm his death again. It was obvious to everyone that he wasn't coming back from his injury.

Caspian moved back to let my father in. I'd never seen him like this before, so raw, so utterly desolate. I don't know what hurt more. The fact that I'd never see Remy again or that Caspian was blaming himself.

"It wasn't your fault," I whispered, walking over to him, taking his hand in mine.

He didn't speak, but he didn't need to. I could see it in his eyes. He'd killed Remy, and this would kill him. He wrapped his arms around me and broke down completely, sobbing into my shoulder.

I closed my eyes and held him like that, our bodies trembling together. We were no longer enemies. We were just two people united in grief.

I wasn't aware of anything else going on around me. All I could feel was the weight of Caspian and the pain tearing my heart to shreds. Time fractured and splintered, and what felt like an eternity lasted probably no more than five or six minutes.

"Caspian!"

Caspian pulled back. I turned to see an ashen Charlotte looking at us.

"Guards were stopping people rushing out to the arena," she explained. "I had to tell them I was with you."

"I didn't know it was him," Caspian said again, this time for Charlotte's benefit. His voice was monotone and flat as though he was almost in a trance.

"I know you didn't, but that's not the point. Use magic on him before it's too late."

She grabbed his hand and pulled him away from me.

"Get out of the way," she commanded. She sounded so strong that even my father took a step back from Remy's body.

"I don't know what you mean," Caspian said. "He's dead. I killed him."

"No. You've healed people. I've seen you do it. Heal him."

Caspian shook his head. "He's dead, Char."

Charlotte almost pushed him to his knees. She wasn't the timid little thing I'd taken her for. I guess watching death changed everyone.

"Heal him!" she commanded again, pointing to my brother's body.

She ripped open Remy's tunic, exposing the wound.

Blood had already started to congeal around it, turning from bright red to deep brown. My stomach heaved at the sight of it.

Caspian put his hands on Remy's chest and closed his eyes. I'd seen him do this before when the dragons had attacked. I'd seen with my own eyes him close wounds and heal with magic.

"Can he bring him back to life with magic?" I asked, hardly daring to hope.

"No," snapped Caspian, but I could already feel the buzz of energy around him.

"I've seen it done once. Not by a fae, but by a mage," Charlotte said. "The man had only just died, and they caught him before his soul departed his body. It has to be quick before the brain completely stops functioning, but it's been less than ten minutes."

"I can't do it, Char!" Caspian hissed.

I placed my hand on his shoulder. "Remy wanted to be like you," I said to him. "He loved practicing with a pretend sword because you showed him how."

It wasn't quite the truth. Remy had often played at sword fighting before Caspian came along, but if it would make Caspian persevere, I'd say anything.

The energy around me thickened, and the weird buzzing that came along with it intensified to the point that it hurt my ears. None of the others seemed to be affected by it, but I could see that Caspian was struggling. His eyes were scrunched up in concentration, and heat radiated from him.

I took my eyes away from him for a second to see that Ash and Hollis had joined us on the field. Apart from the two medics, everyone else had gone. Milo had been taken to the castle for his own medical treatment. I'd not even said goodbye to him.

Charlotte rubbed Caspian's back as he worked his magic, but it was clear that the wound wasn't healing. How could it? Remy was dead.

"I ...can't...do..it!" Caspian said, sweat cascading from his brow.

"You can!" Charlotte encouraged, but no amount of encouragement was going to help him. He was weakening. The massive amount of energy he'd generated was beginning to wane.

I looked up. I'd never believed in gods, and even after my talks with Charlotte about the subject, I still wasn't sure I did, but I was willing to pray to anyone who would listen if it brought my Remy back. In the sky, something flashed overhead. It was no god. It was one of the dragons flying high up on the mountain. I'd seen its silhouette as it flew across the moon.

"The dragons!" My magic only worked when they were around. I could summon them, but I could also do other things when they were near. I'd splattered Caspian with magical paint right before they first came down from the sky. I held my hands up and pulled my own magical energy to me. A shot of pink light flew up into the sky. A beacon guiding the dragons. Almost instantly, the sky filled with dragons, circling down around the light, and as they did, the energy I'd felt before came back, and this time, it was magnified. It surged through me, filling me with power. As the dragons came into land around us, I placed my hand on Remy's chest. Caspian's magic merged with mine until it was one, surging through our bodies. The air around us blazed with pink and yellow light. As the last dragon landed, there was a massive flash, and then everything went dark. Only the torches that lit the arena for the benefit of the crowd remained.

"Wha...what just happened?" Ash stammered.

My body shook with both the cold and the effort, plus the remnants of the magic.

"Aza?"

"Remy!" I squealed. His chest had healed, and all that remained was the dried blood and a bruise where the sword had sliced through him. “Are you okay?” I pulled him into a hug, tears drenching his shoulder.

“Unsqua, Aza!”

I started to laugh through the enormous relief of having my brother back, and the shudders of sobs turned into tremors of joy.

“Remy win?”

He’d just been brought back from the dead, and all he cared about was that he’d won the tournament. I didn’t have the heart to tell him the truth. That Caspian had won.

“Yes, Remy. You won. You are a hero.” He beamed up at us, unaware of the reason we all had tears in our eyes.

The two medics rushed to pull him onto a stretcher, but my father had to tell them to take a step back when it became apparent we were scaring Remy. Instead, he walked with us back to the palace with my father’s arm around his waist and me on the other side, holding his hand.

My father took him to his bed to let him sleep, and once they were both in Remy’s room, I slipped into my own, glad that the day had finally come to a close.

Later after a long bath, I threw myself into bed and slept for what felt like hours. The magic had drained all my energy from me, rendering me exhausted. I slept the dreamless sleep of the dead.

Dahlia woke me early the next morning.

“Breakfast is being served,” she said, folding the clothes I’d thrown in a pile on my floor the night before. “It’s just after midday, but everyone else slept in too. It’s been an exhausting couple of days, hasn’t it?”

“Have you seen Remy? Is he ok?”

“Okay?” Dahlia laughed.” He refused to wait for

everyone to get up and has already eaten breakfast. He's now waiting for everyone else to get their lazy asses out of bed so he can have a second breakfast."

I smiled. That sounded like the Remy I knew and loved. I pulled myself out of bed and grabbed some jeans and a t-shirt out of my drawers before Dahlia could wrestle me into another dress. I'd be wearing a white dress in less than a week, whether I liked it or not, so I was going to wear what I wanted up until that point.

"What about Milo?" My mind had been so consumed with Remy that I'd put Milo to the back of my mind.

"You'll see," she said. "Now get up before Remy comes looking for you. He's been harping on about more bacon for the last half hour. I swear that lad eats like a horse."

Remy grinned at me when I entered the dining room. Apart from him, the other chairs were empty.

"I expect the others will be along shortly," Dahlia said. "I'll go and see what's keeping them."

I wanted to hug Remy again, but he wouldn't understand why there were tears in my eyes, and I didn't want to frighten him. He looked pointedly at one of the wait staff who ran off and returned a minute later with a huge plate full of bacon. While I waited for the others, I pulled the papers toward me. As expected, Remy's 'death' was on the front cover of all of them, eclipsing Caspian's win. I wondered how he'd react to playing second fiddle to the man he'd branded an idiot when they'd first met. I suspected he'd be okay with it. I'd seen a side to him I'd not seen before. I'd seen love. Real love. Without realizing it, Remy had become a brother to him. I pulled the first paper toward me. I'd have to get the admin team calling the papers as soon as possible to put the record straight on Remy's death. The only paper where Remy had been relegated to the second page was the Atlantice Conch. Problems in their own kingdom trumped ours, it seemed. With a sigh, I threw the papers back down. I waited impatiently for my father and brothers to come down. Now that I knew Remy was okay, I needed to see Milo. I missed him so much it hurt, and with my wedding less than a week away, our time left together had dwindled to almost nothing. Once the papers had been set straight about Remy not dying, they would run a feature on Caspian. He would be catapulted to the most famous person in the kingdom for a brief spell, even eclipsing my mother. Thoughts of my mother were interrupted by the arrival of Ash, Hollis, and my father, who all took a seat. Just behind them came Caspian, looking like he'd just rolled out of bed and Charlotte right behind him.

"Congratulations, my friend," My father said. "Welcome to the family!"

I stood up quickly before my father had time to say anything else. Luckily, the staff had just started bringing the breakfast out, so I was able to take Caspian's hand and whisk him out of the room.

"I wanted to thank you for saving Remy yesterday," I began.

"It was me that put him in that position," he reminded me. "I honestly didn't know it was him. I would never..."

I held my hand up to his lips. "I know. I know you would never have hurt him if you'd have known."

He nodded, relief flooding his eyes.

"I know I've made it clear that I don't want to marry you, but I want you to know I'll be honored to be your wife..." I hesitated a moment, knowing what I was about to tell him. If I was going to be Caspian's wife, he had to know everything. I couldn't start my marriage built on lies. "I should be honest and tell you I slept with Milo the other night."

He nodded again, but he didn't seem at all surprised by my confession.

"Actually, there was something I wanted to tell you too."

Just then Charlotte poked her head around the door. "Are you two alright? You need to get in quickly before Remy eats all the bacon. There's hardly any left."

On her left-hand ring finger, I noticed a ring inlaid with amethyst.

I turned back to Caspian and mouthed, "Charlotte?"

He nodded again, and I swear his cheeks turned a cherry red. "Why you sly old dog!" I said, grinning from ear to ear.

He was engaged to Charlotte. I didn't have to marry him. I could now marry the man in second place. The man who had never come second in my own heart. Technically, Milo had come third, but there was no way I was going to marry the man who had stomped down on Milo. Hopefully, after the excitement of the final round, no one would notice or care.

I couldn't wait to tell him. I kissed Caspian's cheek and began the run to the hospital wing.

Milo was sitting up in bed reading a paper when I walked in. His face lit up when he saw me.

I kissed him and sat by his side on the bed. "How are you?"

"I'm fine. I heard what happened to Remy. Is he ok?"

I grinned. "If you can call eating a huge pile of bacon okay, then I'd say he's doing fine. Listen, I have an important question."

Milo arched an eyebrow as I got to my knee at the side of his bed.

"I know it's customary for the man to ask the woman,

but it's also customary for a princess not to compete in a tournament to win her own hand in marriage, and since when have I listened to customs and traditions anyway? Milo...will you marry me."

He pulled me into a kiss that said it all, except it didn't.

"No," he replied in a whisper. "I want to marry you more than I've wanted anything my whole life. I would do anything for you, and that is why I'm saying no. I want you to go to Urbis and do what you have to do. I want you to go with Nyre and save your mother. I want the wedding you talked about a couple of weeks ago where your mother cries tears of joy as you walk down the aisle. Come back to me when you are truly ready for marriage and ask me again. I'll wait for as long as you need."

"But...I'll wait, and you can come with me to Urbis."

He shook his head. "I'm not part of your adventure. My leg will take six weeks to heal, and I don't think you'll be able to wait that long. I'll still be here. Then we'll have our own adventures. I've changed my mind about going to The Forge. My mother will have to visit us here." He kissed me again, and this time, I fell into him. Nothing else mattered.

We were interrupted mere moments later by my mother's maid calling for Dr. Augusto to come quickly. My mother was getting worse.

I ran to get my father from the dining room. He was busy tucking into his breakfast and reading the Atlantice Conch.

"Atlantice is having some dreadful times," he mused as I ran in. "It's almost as if the darkness is spreading there too."

The darkness. In all the excitement over the past

week, I'd forgotten that dark magic was coming back into the kingdom. Derillen was still out there somewhere, and we were no closer to finding her.

"Father..." I wheezed. "It's Mother... Dr. Augusto wants to speak to you."

"The queen's health is fading fast," Augusto said as we all crowded around my mother's bed five minutes later. My father and my brothers had all dropped their breakfast to follow me to my mother's room. "A curse it may be, but her body cannot sustain it much longer."

My father lowered his head into his hands at Augusto's words. I could feel his pain as acutely as my own. This was breaking him.

"How long does she have?" I asked through streaming tears.

Augusto shrugged. "I cannot say. A month. Maybe two."

Having just gotten over Remy dying and then being brought back to life, my heart wasn't ready for the loss of my mother too.

"Maybe Caspian can bring her out of this," I babbled. "He saved Remy from death."

"No," Caspian said. He'd been so quiet coming into the room that I'd not noticed him. "This is not like Remy. Remy's brain waves were still there. Your mother isn't sick, and she isn't dead. You know the only way to bring her back. Either find Derillen or find Morpheus."

"Derillen?" My father asked. "Not this again!"

"Alec, my dear friend. I think it's time we faced the truth. She is back. Azia is sure of it, and so am I. Charlotte thinks Briar Rose is trapped in Morpheus's dream world. We've invited Azia to stay with us in Urbis while she looks for him."

I noted the use of the word we. It seemed Caspian's

time here was finally coming to a close. And more surprisingly, he was going home with Charlotte.

A thought struck me. I ran from the room and up to my own. From under my bed, I pulled out a box. A box that held a magic necklace. I ran back with it and handed it to Caspian.

“Charlotte thinks this is a necklace from the gods. Will this save her?”

Caspian took the necklace from the box. I’d not thought to show it to him before now.

“This is very powerful. I’ve never seen anything like it.” The stones changed from diamonds to amethysts in his hands. I’d never seen anything like it either. “Where did you get this?”

“It doesn’t matter. Will it help her?”

Caspian laid it carefully around her neck, clasping it at the back.

Color came back to her cheeks, but she didn’t stir.

“This is miraculous,” Dr. Augusto said, feeling her pulse. He performed a couple of checks, but after a minute or two, his excitement waned. “I think you’ve bought some time with this necklace, but she is still cursed.”

“Father,” I began.

Without speaking, he stood up and walked over to me. Taking my hand, he pulled me outside of the room.

“I know what you are going to say to me. I’ve known this was coming for days. After the courage you showed at the competition, I have no reason to stop you now.”

“So, you mean...”

He nodded his head.

“I know when I have been wrong, and it seems I have been wrong about a lot of things lately. I’ve made mistake after mistake, and you’ve tried telling me over and over again. I'm sorry for everything I've done to you."

I brought him into a soggy hug.

"You didn't do anything, Father. Are you really allowing me to go to Urbis?"

"I think I've learned enough to know that you'll go with or without my permission, but you have it if that makes it easier for you. My permission and my blessing."

"Thank you."

"I'm counting on you, Azia. I can't let her die."

I nodded my head. "She won't. I have Nyre to take me there and Charlotte and Caspian to help me find Morpheus. I have everything I need."

"You cannot travel by dragon," My father replied. "It is a nice idea, but you'll be spotted way before you get to Urbis. I don't want anyone knowing you are there."

I furrowed my brow with frustration. "Then how? If I take the Urbis Express, people will surely recognize me."

"Take one of the castle horses. I think I owe you one for your birthday anyway, and you won't have to count on a tiny dragon hauling you all the way there. You can still take your friend. She's one feisty girl, and I rather like the idea of you being looked after...even if you can fend for yourself."

I grinned. "That would be great. Thank you, Father."

"Since we have time, I think we should go eat first. It's not every day I send my daughter out into the world by herself."

"Not by myself. I'll be going with Nyre, remember, and Charlotte promised to let me stay with her and Caspian in Urbis."

"You know. I always thought you were too good for

that chap," he said, draping his arm over my shoulder. "I'm rather glad he's engaged to that Urbis girl."

I shoved my father playfully in the side.

Later, I stood in the castle entranceway, waiting for my family to come and wave goodbye to me. My bag was packed, and I'd picked a horse for the journey, a black one aptly named Adventure. The kitchen had outdone themselves with so much food it would last me for days.

The morning papers were out on a side table. I sorted through them until I found the Atlantice Conch. Something about their story intrigued me.

Eventually, everyone came out to wish me goodbye. Father, Remy, Ash, and Hollis, as well as Caspian hand in hand with Charlotte. Dahlia shuffled out behind them, and lastly, on crutches, Milo joined us.

We all walked out into the courtyard where Adventure was waiting.

Nyre flew around up in the air waiting for me to leave.

"I still can't get over my big sister kicking ass!" Ash explained, thrusting an imaginary sword at Hollis the way Remy liked to do.

I felt for the dragon sword by my side. I'd not been able to use it in the tournament, but I knew it would keep me safe on my adventure. I'd never be without it again.

"I know, right?" agreed Hollis. "You should make her a knight, Dad."

"She's better than any knight!" My father replied, pulling me into a hug. "You stay safe in Urbis. I want my daughter home in one piece!"

I took a deep breath. "Actually, I'm not going to Urbis."

Everyone looked at me with surprise. I'd been

thinking about changing my plan for the last day or so. I only had Charlotte's word that Morpheus would be there, and even then, she wasn't so sure. He was a slippery character who only left the house of the gods when it suited him. No, I had more of a chance looking for Derillen. I was sure she'd left Draconis. None of my father's men had found her. But something was happening in Atlantice. Something awfully familiar. Whatever had shifted in the magical energy here, it seemed had happened there too.

"I'm going to Atlantice."

"Atlantice?" my father asked. "Whatever for?"

"I will go to Urbis," I explained, "but I know in my heart that whatever is happening in Draconis is spreading and think it's going to hit Atlantice first. I've been seeing strange news reports in the Atlantice Conch for a while, but it was only this morning that I put two and two together."

"Please keep in contact," my father said. "Send letters when you can so we know where you are. I know the Royals in Atlantice. Be sure to seek them out. They will help you."

"I will," I said, kissing his cheek. I'd already said goodbye to my mother, but this was somehow harder. My father was aware of how dangerous my journey could be.

I hugged Dahlia and my brothers before getting to Caspian. There was so much I wanted to say to him, but nothing would come to mind. I was sure I'd come up with a million things once I left. "I'm glad I didn't kill you," I said.

He grinned. "And I'm glad I didn't kill you." He brought me into a hug, and for the first time since we'd met, we came together as friends.

Then there was only one person left to say goodbye to, and this was going to be the hardest goodbye of all. I'd kept it together so far, but tears were already beginning to form as I took Milo's hand in mine. The others walked back to give Milo and me some space.

"I'm going to miss you," I said, my voice cracking with emotion. "You are the best fake, almost fiancé I ever had."

He snorted a laugh. "And you were the best princess I almost got to marry."

"Princess, you will marry someday!" I corrected him. He brought me into a kiss. Our last...for now.

Afterward, I jumped up on Adventure. He brayed a little when Nyre came to rest on my shoulder.

Tears streamed down my face as the horse began the first part of our journey. A journey that would take me first to Atlantice and then who knew where. I wanted to think that I'd find out what I needed in Atlantice, but something deep within me knew we'd end up eventually in Urbis. That was where my story had begun. That was where my story would come to an end...

Carry on the Adventure in Queen of Mermaids...

BLAISE

DAUGHTER OF LITTLE MERMAID

GRAB THE NEXT BOXSET IN THE KINGDOM OF FAIRYTALES SERIES

MEET THE TEAM

The Kingdom of Fairytales Series was a team effort. Below are the people that made it possible:

EQP Management: Rhi Parkes & J.A. Armitage

Our authors: J.A. Armitage, Audrey Rich, B. Kristin McMichael, Emma Savant, Jennifer Ellision, Scarlett Kol, Rose Castro, Margo Ryerkerk, Zara Quentin, Laura Greenwood and Anne Stryker.

Our Editor
Rose Lipscomb

Our Beta Team
Nadine Peterse-Vrijhof
Diane Major
Kalli Bunch
Stephanie Woodwood

Our Proof Reader
Tina Merritt

And to all the wonderful people who loved the world we created and reviewed our stories.
Thank you

READING ORDER

SEASON ONE
SLEEPING BEAUTY
Queen of Dragons
Heiress of Embers
Throne of Fury
Goddess of Flames

SEASON TWO
LITTLE MERMAID
Queen of Mermaids
Heiress of the Sea
Throne of Change
Goddess of Water

SEASON THREE
RED RIDING HOOD
King of Wolves
Heir of the Curse
Throne of Night
God of Shifters

SEASON FOUR
RAPUNZEL
King of Devotion
Heir of Thorns
Throne of Enchantment
God of Loyalty

SEASON FIVE
RUMPELSTILTSKIN
Queen of Unicorns
Heiress of Gold
Throne of Sacrifice
Goddess of Loss

SEASON SIX
BEAUTY AND THE BEAST
King of Beasts
Heir of Beauty
Throne of Betrayal
God of Illusion

SEASON SEVEN
ALADDIN
Queen of the Sun
Heiress of Shadows
Throne of the Phoenix
Goddess of Fire

SEASON EIGHT
CINDERELLA
Queen of Song
Heiress of Melody
Throne of Symphony
Goddess of Harmony

SEASON NINE
ALICE IN WONDERLAND
Queen of Clockwork
Heiress of Delusion
Throne of Cards
Goddess of Hearts

SEASON TEN
WIZARD OF OZ
King of Traitors
Heir of Fugitives
Throne of Emeralds
God of Storms

SEASON ELEVEN
SNOW WHITE
Queen of Reflections
Heiress of Mirrors
Throne of Wands
Goddess of Magic

SEASON TWELVE
PETER PAN
Queen of Skies
Heiress of Stars
Throne of Feathers
Goddess of Air

SEASON THIRTEEN
URBIS

Kingdom of Royalty
Kingdom of Power
Kingdom of Fairytales
Kingdom of Ever After

BOXSETS

AZIA
BLAISE
CASTIEL
DEON
ELIANA
FALLON
GAIA
HALIA
IVY
JAKON
KELIS
LYRIC

www.ingramcontent.com/pod-product-compliance
Lightning Source LLC
Chambersburg PA
CBHW020354310726
48979CB00015B/2585/J
* 9 7 8 1 9 8 9 9 9 7 2 3 9 *